T0013705

ONE

CURSED

ROSE

Also by Rebecca Zanetti

The Dark Protector series
Fated
Claimed
Tempted
Hunted
Consumed
Provoked
Twisted
Shadowed
Tamed
Marked
Talen
Vampire's Faith
Demon's Mercy
Alpha's Promise
Hero's Haven
Guardian's Grace
Rebel's Karma

Immortal's Honor
Garrett's Destiny
Warrior's Hope

The Realm Witch Enforcers series
Wicked Ride
Wicked Edge
Wicked Burn
Wicked Kiss
Wicked Bite

The Scorpius Syndrome series
Scorpius Rising
Mercury Striking
Shadow Falling
Justice Ascending

The Deep Ops series
Hidden
Taken (e-novella)
Fallen
Shaken (e-novella)
Broken
Driven
Unforgiven
Frostbitten

Laurel Snow Thrillers
You Can Run
You Can Hide
You Can Die

ONE CURSED ROSE

REBECCA ZANETTI

KENSINGTON
PUBLISHING CORP.

www.kensingtonbooks.com

Content warnings: Dark themes; Obsessive and morally gray hero; Spicy bedroom scenes for mature readers only; Light bondage; Nudity; Spanking; Swearing; Torture; Inappropriate use of bathrobe belts

KENSINGTON BOOKS are published by

Kensington Publishing Corp.
900 Third Avenue
New York, NY 10022

Copyright © 2024 by Rebecca Zanetti

All rights reserved. No part of this book may be reproduced in any form or by any means without the prior written consent of the Publisher, excepting brief quotes used in reviews.

All Kensington titles, imprints, and distributed lines are available at special quantity discounts for bulk purchases for sales promotion, premiums, fund-raising, educational, or institutional use.

This book is a work of fiction. Names, characters, businesses, organizations, places, events, and incidents either are the product of the author's imagination or are used fictitiously. Any resemblance to actual persons, living or dead, events, or locales is entirely coincidental.

To the extent that the image or images on the cover of this book depict a person or persons, such person or persons are merely models, and are not intended to portray any character or characters featured in the book.

Special book excerpts or customized printings can also be created to fit specific needs. For details, write or phone the office of the Kensington Sales Manager: Kensington Publishing Corp., 900 Third Avenue, New York, NY 10022, Attn. Sales Department. Phone: 1-800-221-2647.

Kensington and the K logo Reg. U.S. Pat. & TM Off.

ISBN: 978-1-4967-4836-2 (ebook)

ISBN: 978-1-4967-4835-5

First Kensington Trade Paperback Printing: July 2024

10 9 8 7 6 5 4 3 2 1

Printed in the United States of America

This new dark romance series wouldn't be the same without Alexandra Nicolajsen, Alicia Condon, and Lauren Jernigan, who not only inspired but also played a pivotal role in its development, even with an enchanting recommendation to "add a touch of magic, won't you?" Thank you for your support, great ideas, and faith that the story would come together.

I hope you like it.

PROLOGUE

❦

Thorn

The shadows shift uneasily in the chilly night as I prowl against the brick buildings, rainwater dripping from the eaves high above. Accustomed to swallowing interlopers, the dark mass slithers inches away from my flesh.

For now, I have better things to worry about, so I tolerate the shadows, and they know it.

The moon breaks through the clouds above, glittering on the wet asphalt and torn pieces of trash littering the sidewalks. Palo Alto is one of my least favorite places in the world, full of too much money and too little sense. The giggling crowds exiting the bars instinctively keep their leather loafers and spiked Prada heels away from the tendrils of shadows twisting against the worn bricks, and thus away from me.

All prey have survival instincts.

I've timed my arrival perfectly, yet my heart rate increases as I stalk between narrow alleys and finally turn, halting across the street from the Urban Elixir, the city's hottest new nightclub, my back to the building, my shoulders rock hard. The garish pink and green lights from the neon sign above the main door flicker in time to the pounding music from inside.

A drunk trips by, mumbling, and the taste of sodden tobacco fills my mouth. Fire lances through me and I growl in warning. The man scurries down the street and out of sight.

The taste slowly dissipates, leaving my tongue singed.

Then *she* emerges from the bar. Alana Rose Beaumont. The paparazzi rush forward, hampered by the velvet ropes and security guards that protect the glitterati from the commoners. It's a dance unchanged through the ages.

My body settles as much as possible considering time isn't on my side. Even now, my hands are degrees colder than they were a month ago. But she's all that matters. I hate when she's out of my sight.

Tonight she's wearing a sparkly yellow dress, if it can be called such. Thin spaghetti straps hold up a generous bodice that narrows impossibly to her tiny waist and barely reaches the tops of her golden thighs. For a petite woman, her legs are surprisingly long, with five-inch pink heels giving her added height.

I've dreamed of those legs wrapped around me.

As is her custom on a night like this, she allows one of her assistants to lead her to the side and a waiting camera crew. Well, a waiting woman, often seen with Alana, and her smart phone. The woman's name is Rosalie. She's twenty-five, was raised by her janitor grandfather, and has a cat named Bruiser. I know everything about her, as she is often in Alana's vicinity. She poses no threat to Alana, or she'd already be dead.

"What would you like to say to your followers?" Rosalie asks, holding her phone in front of her face. Rain dots her thick black hair but she ignores it, remaining in the best position to film.

Alana smiles. "That the Urban is the place to be."

I tap my earbuds to zero in on Alana's Aquarius Social media account, although I can hear above the flashing cameras and people jockeying into position to get closer to her. Aquarius is an emotional-intelligence platform that works on a combination of live video and popular sounds with a much simpler algorithm than my own social media company, but their AI capabilities are close to matching mine, which is a concern for tomorrow.

Tonight is about the woman.

She chuckles, and the throaty sound shoots right to my balls. More importantly, my mouth fills with the taste of honey. Pure, sweet honey. Then she continues speaking, and I nearly groan from the delicious words. "Make sure when you come by that you have an Urban gin martini because they're fabulous," she says as if speaking to a treasured friend. Millions of them, actually.

Her hair, a wild and teased mahogany that cascades down her back, flows in the slight breeze as if alive. But it's her eyes. Those deep, dark, impossibly beautiful eyes that only a moron would call mere hazel. There is no color, no description, no label that accurately describes the hue.

Except . . . haunting.

That's what she does. She haunts my days and my dreams, and she hasn't a clue.

The voices around her start to resonate through my EarPods, and with them different tastes prick my tongue. I swallow and push all sounds except her sweet voice away. It's the only taste I want.

A hint of danger rides the wind, and I look around, seeing nothing amiss. Is there somebody else watching her? Do they not sense me? I have no problem taking out not only threats but rivals.

She continues speaking to her nearly six million followers, and I can feel the power in those numbers. A power most people will never realize exists.

Rosalie lifts the phone higher. "I noticed that Stacia and

Corinda Rendale failed to attend this grand opening. The sisters are normally first to find the hottest parties."

Alana's eyes widen and she leans toward the phone as if about to tell a great secret. "I heard that the sisters"—she looks around as if to make sure nobody is listening, although, of course, millions are—"were possibly *not invited.*"

Rosalie properly gasps. A slight taste of strawberries slides across my tongue, but I push the tang aside to enjoy Alana's tartness at the moment.

Amusement ticks through me briefly and I breathe the sensation deep. The Rendale sisters are heirs to the second strongest social media company, and their rivalry with Alana is cute. Sniping from any of them earns millions of clicks and thus results in empowering energy that can't be bought. It's a transfer of sorts. The more subscribers use and like different posts, the more traffic generated on the sites, and the stronger the crystals running the companies become. With that vitality comes the ability to offer more benefits to subscribers, which leads to more power and more money.

As well as longevity and health for the family members physically connected to those crystals. We all want to live longer than we should.

Of course, if the enmity between the women ever becomes a danger to Alana, I will take care of the matter.

The skies finish their tentative light rainfall and open to deluge the hapless world with gleefully aimed liquid spikes.

Alana retreats against the building, and I wish I had stood there. To be so close to her and to refrain from touching her is slowly driving me mad. It wasn't a long journey to begin with.

She's beauty personified, and she knows how to work a camera. I want her in a way that isn't healthy . . . for either of us.

My fingers curl into fists, and I remain in the shadows, the flavor of her lingering on my tongue. Every molecule in my body wants to burst through the tempestuous storm and take her right now, but witnesses are a hindrance. No doubt I'm going to hell with my plan, but I'm past caring. Since my time is severely limited, I should leave her be.

The high road is no place for me, and that I can find a sense of honor is a lie I don't bother telling myself. Deep down inside me, the monster that devoured my soul years ago knows the truth.

For her? It is already too late.

She looks up, and our eyes lock. Hers widen. Her pupils contract.

Definitely too late.

ONE

❧✦❧

Alana

Dark eyes gleam from the darkness by the brick building across the street, and I shiver. Just eyes. Bodies, space, and pouring rain separate us, and all I can see are eyes and perhaps the shape of a man. A large one.

But that gaze.

His stare thrusts into my body with a sense of warning more foreboding than the thunder bellowing in the distance. Lightning flashes, too close, and I jump.

"I'm glad you enjoyed your evening," Rosalie purrs, carefully keeping her new phone out of the rain. "Is there anything else you would like to say to your friends?"

I turn, angling my face so the neon lights emphasize my good side. One of my cheekbones is two millimeters higher than the other. It's sad that I know that. Worse yet that I'll exploit it. "Oh yes. Please remember to either attend or pledge to support the runners in tomorrow's Dash for the Doggies." The stupid name rolls nicely off the tongue, but unfortunately this tidbit won't lead to half the clicks my insult to the Rendale sisters will. "Those little puppies at the pound need our help." I smile and lower my chin for my flirty look.

Rosalie giggles appropriately. "Will you be running, Miss Beaumont?"

I allow my cheeks to pinken. "In these shoes? Never." I lift a bare and now freezing shoulder in my best "aw, shucks" move. "I have to attend an Aquarius Social board meeting tomorrow, but I've pledged to support several of our joggers. I hope all my friends out there will do the same. Also, I'd so appreciate it if you'd explode-star and share this little emote-video of mine." I wink, giving our signal, perfectly masking my unease at having to attend a board meeting after all this time.

She ends the video. "Should we get a drink?"

"No." A hard body emerges from the crowd, flanking me as a near duplicate mashes to my other side. "Miss Beaumont is leaving now." They usher me through the bodies to a running Mercedes, assist me inside, and shut the door. Nameless bodyguards that I barely look at tonight.

My father rotates all security personnel after an unfortunate crush I developed on a bodyguard at the age of fifteen. The man was at least twenty-five, starkly handsome with blond hair and mellow blue eyes, and knew how to whistle war ballads. It was the whistle that intrigued me. He gave me my first kiss in the front seat of a Mercedes, and that moment was amazing.

It also sealed his death. A lesson I will never forget.

Tonight's driver maneuvers the vehicle through the crowd and I turn, seeking those eyes by the building, but only find shadows now. Shivering, I lean forward and turn up the seat warmers as well as the heat. The driver is quiet, his broad hands appearing loose on the steering wheel as he expertly maneuvers out of the commercial area to the residential, ultimately pulling to a stop in front of my unimposing building, where two bellmen hurry out into the rain to escort me inside.

God forbid I turn an ankle.

Of course, they're both packing, so I suppose I won't take a bullet, either.

I look up at the charming four-story brick-and-mortar building that my father hates. He likes chrome and glass, and while I enjoy items that sparkle, love them really, I wanted something homey when I moved out of the mansion after college. Since I was merely the spare and not an heir, and since I have a uterus and not balls, my father grudgingly gave in.

Things have changed.

I shiver and duck my head against the rain, my face cooling from the harsh drops. One of the guard dogs holds an umbrella over my head as he swivels around, scoping the trees and bushes as if waiting for the hydrangea to shoot poisonous darts. Unfortunately, the wind isn't cooperating and slashes the rain sideways and under the umbrella. The harsh wetness stings my face.

Relief fills me as I enter the comfortable entryway and clip-clop on the impossibly high heels to the elevator, not showing my discomfort. A blister burns on my left heel, and I bite my lip to keep from stepping out of the shoe.

Instead, I rise to the top floor, regretting the need, or rather demand, for me to live at the top.

A basement apartment would suit me just fine. Of course, it's easy to say that since I was raised in mansions or high-end hotels my entire life. I can be self-aware when necessary.

I enter my apartment, ditch the sparkling dress and offensive heels for torn yoga pants and a faded pink shirt older than I am before raiding the fridge for leftover Chinese. I use a fork. Nobody is here to see, so why dig for chopsticks?

My place is comfortable with cream-colored furniture, aquamarine accents, and hints of rose quartz. I finally relax.

After eating too many calories, I wash my face, brush out my impossibly wild hair, and lie in the bed until exactly three a.m.

My bed is soft and the pillows plush. Here I have more of the rose quartz decorating my lamps, sparkling in picture frames surrounding family and friends, and woven throughout a thick rug that covers my hardwood floors.

However, there is no sleeping tonight for me. My childhood nightmare, the one I thought I'd banished, is back after my brother's recent car accident and death. Finally, it's time to move. I can't hear the click of the security cameras being tricked onto a loop, if there is a click. Instead, the moment the clock ticks three in the morning, I stand, grab a flashlight, and silently make my way through the four-bedroom apartment to the landing outside. Then it's a simple matter of walking down the five flights of stairs in my socks to the basement.

I can probably use the flashlight, but just in case, I leave it off. It's for emergencies only.

Winding through the basement, I come to a heavy cement wall and click in a code on the barely there keypad. A hidden door opens.

Sprawling on a threadbare sofa, Rosalie looks up from a gallon of Chunky Monkey. She's changed from her overcoat to sweats and a shirt even more faded than my own, although her protective angelite pendant still hangs between her breasts. "You sounded properly ditzy tonight. You sure you aren't an asshole in disguise?"

I toss the flashlight onto the sofa, just missing her knee. "We're both assholes." I angle my head to see that she's eaten the entire carton. Definitely an asshole. "Why in the world did you ask me for a drink? We both need sleep." Does she know I'm having nightmares again? I try to retain some distance from my friends, hoping to keep them safe, but they know me too well.

"Please. The dark circles under your eyes beg for a triple vodka before bed."

The door at the far end opens and Ella peeks out from our

main computer hub, her citrine-encrusted glasses partly down her nose. She shoves them back up with her index finger. "Did either of you bring me anything to eat?"

I wince. "Rosalie ate all the ice cream." And I the entire carton of orange chicken.

"You're such buttheads," Ella says without much heat. Her blonde hair is up in a ponytail, and her blue eyes are wide behind the thick glasses.

"We just decided that as well." Rosalie shoves to her feet. "Where are we on the projects?"

A man clears his throat. Loudly. "Some of us are in here working, while others are stuffing their faces with enough dairy to cause flatulence for a year," Merlin snaps from the other room.

I snort. "Merlin is in a mood."

Rosalie coughs, her eyes red. Has she been crying again?

"I'm sorry Charlie dumped you, but he truly was a moron, and you're better off." I keep my tone gentle, but the truth is that Charlie ghosted Rosalie, which means he isn't worth the crap in the bottom of an old drain. My tough friend is a true romantic with terrible taste in men.

She stands and holds her stomach. Yeah. That much ice cream can't be good.

"Come on." I sling my arm through hers and drag her around the sofa to the main computer hub. Well, our only computer hub. Ella is already back in her corner with her three monitors, while Merlin sits in his corner opposite. "We should have brought you two dinner, and we're very sorry," I say, meaning it.

The three of them use a hidden entrance to the building from the back alley, and Ella makes sure to note the timing of the patrols my father has in place. So far, we've been both good and lucky in avoiding detection.

Merlin turns and lifts one bushy gray eyebrow. He is around

sixty with thick gray hair a few shades darker than his eyebrows, and he rents a room in the Victorian home Rosalie inherited from a distant aunt. As usual, he wears a suit with a bow tie; today it is a burgundy color. When I purse my lips, he looks down at the tie, apparently preparing to continue our usual argument. "You're wrong. Burgundy and maroon are colors."

"Are not," I return per the rules of our long-running game, pulling out a chair to sit at the dented wooden table in the center of the room. "Those are *'not colors.'*" While the table is old, the chairs are new and plush, and the computer banks top of the line. Most of them are not available for consumers yet.

We're not consumers.

He sadly shakes his head and waves a hand in the air to dismiss the topic. "Do we know why you've been called before the Aquarius board tomorrow?"

Claws slash inside my abdomen. "No. I'm sure it's a routine type of thing, the annual meeting." My voice emerges way too shaky.

Rosalie pales. "Do you think they want you to take Greg's place?"

At the mention of my dead brother, my only sibling, my heart aches. We weren't close, but I have good memories from childhood when he used to play with me at the beach. And I don't blame him for becoming harder as he grew up. Our father and our lives did not give Greg a choice. "I doubt it." My father has never seen beneath my surface, probably because I look just like my mother, who died young. From what I can tell from her diary, she was more concerned with the newest handbag or lipstick than real life.

Of course, most people say that about me these days.

Merlin straightens his already perfect posture. "That's a concern for another day, and we have work to do. It looks like the fun run for the animal shelters is on lots of donors' radar after your video tonight."

"Last night," Ella corrects, typing rapidly. "In addition, our

Backpack program has sent additional funds to the New York, Minneapolis, and Boise areas."

I love that program. Kids without enough to eat can take a backpack full of food home from school every Friday and return it Monday. We're in all fifty states now, and I'd like to be in every high and junior high school by the end of the year. "Good. Do we require more funding?" I need to arrange my next several videos carefully. It's time to hide more of my spending habits from my father. I take funds from my various trusts to supposedly party and buy high-end goods, but actually funnel the money into various charities.

"Yes," Ella says. "I'm tapped for the month, and so is Rosalie. You could probably buy a boat or something—or at least look like you're doing so. Your father hasn't checked your actual accounts in months."

That's because he doesn't care, which is a hurt for another day.

"I'll make it happen." Being involved in good deeds can only help my social media profile, but I have to be careful about how many charities I appear to support. More importantly, I can never reveal what I truly love. Revealing my soft underbelly, so my brother had once told me, will always be a mistake with our father. "Where are we with the women's shelters in Southern California?"

"Building three more safe houses within the next two months," Rosalie says, reaching for a binder and flipping over a page. "I know we want to operate on a large scale, but it was a win helping the California state senator's wife after she left the hospital."

"She's in a safe house in San Diego for now," Merlin adds.

Good. The sight of those bruises will haunt me forever. I am just fine helping one person at a time. "What about the senator?" I hold my breath.

Rosalie looks at Merlin. "We could take him out, but it'd make the news."

Merlin's head draws back, briefly giving him a double chin.

"We can't afford the scrutiny, and it isn't like we can go to your father for the name of a hitman."

I hate that he's right. "I could do it?"

Merlin's eyes widen, Ella stiffens, and Rosalie laughs outright. "I love you, Alana. I'm sure you have a gun, and I have no doubt you could go to his house. But you won't pull the trigger." Her voice softens, as do her blue eyes. "You're not a killer, and that's a good thing."

Right. Women like me have other people do the killing for them. I flash back to the funeral of the driver who kissed me, when his mother shrieked and threw herself on the coffin. My brother and I stood far away, watching.

"I did this?" I whispered, bile rising in my throat at the horror in my fifteen-year-old heart.

Greg shrugged. "Maybe, maybe not. He might've been killed even if he'd just looked at you. But I want you to see what happens when you step out of line. Don't go kissing any more employees. Next time, it *will* be your fault, Alana."

It is a lesson reinforced daily. I disappointed my father one other time, and my beloved collie disappeared. When I asked about Macbeth, nobody had an answer. It is still possible the dog just ran away, but there is no way to know.

Ella clicks her keyboard and flings a picture of two little girls up on the far screen. "Speaking of personalized rescue: Ana and Abbi Klostcky. Their mother and stepfather were just investigated for child abuse in Chicago, competing experts in the courtroom battled it out, and they have been returned to the pervert." The girls are about five and six years old with wiry black curls, tawny brown eyes, and pinched faces.

I can feel the pain in them. "Were they evaluated?" My breath stalls.

"Yes," Ella says. "The caseworker, doctor, and shrink all found abuse. The stepfather is a distant cousin to the judge, though that was not disclosed. I barely found it."

I swallow. "Try bribing the parents first." It still shocks me how often people give up loved ones for money.

"If that doesn't work?" Merlin asks.

"Take them," I say simply. We have a series of safe houses especially geared toward abused children. "I'll get the money."

Merlin swivels his chair, facing me and tugging on his bow tie. "Are we sure your funds will continue?"

I gulp. The subject is one we've avoided for months. While I do have trust funds left to me by my mother and other various relatives who have passed on, my father is the Trustee and most likely has the ability to slow the trickle of money to me should he choose.

Ella follows Merlin's move, turning to face me. "The new industry report came out earlier today. Aquarius Social is in last position of the four social media giants, which is not good. The further you fall, the lower your . . . power and reach."

Her concern is for us both. "I know."

Rosalie chews on her full bottom lip. "Maybe that's why you've been summoned to the board meeting. There might be a marketing plan in place."

"I can only hope," I whisper, feeling deep in my gut that it will not be that easy. For now, I have more people to save. "Where are we on the affordable housing initiatives in Georgia?" I'll worry about my future, if I have one, when I step into the board meeting.

For now, I still have freedom, and I'm going to use it.

TWO

Alana

As I enter the boardroom, I'm immediately drawn to the floor-to-ceiling windows in the far wall. The sun bounces off them, not strong enough to pierce the fortified glass, but it's the city stretching out in front of me, the vibrant Silicon Valley landscape, that catches my attention. I turn away to keep myself from walking right to the very edge and staring down the way I had as a child.

"Hello, Father," I say.

My father looks up from a stack of papers at the head of the table, at the helm and in control as usual. Flashes of gray tinge his thick black hair, especially by his ears, accentuating his fierce jawline and even fiercer brow. There are no laugh lines near his eyes or his mouth, but time has carved her path in his skin anyway. His eyes are a deep brown, much deeper than mine, and lack the flecks of green gifted me by my mother. "Alana, good. You're here. Sit." He gestures toward the seat to his right.

I pause. No doubt that had been Greg's seat. It hurts that my brother is not here. I falter and look across the table at my cousin. "Hey, Nico."

"Alana." He nods. While my father looks somewhat like our Italian ancestors, Nico is *all* Italian. Dark hair, dark eyes, muscled frame in a black suit. "You look lovely," he says, no inflection in his voice. He's Greg's age and they were the best of friends.

"Thank you." I reply in the same tone, my heartbeat thundering in my ears. I need to reach out to him, but our grief is too strong right now.

For this meeting, I'm wearing a navy blue suit with pink flowers embroidered on the skirt and understated jewelry comprised of aquamarine crystals and rose quartz stones. My talismans. As the face of the company, I know how to present myself.

"Now, Alana." My father narrows his focus to me. Aquamarine crystals decorate his thick watch, glowing at the nearness to his skin. His talismans, too.

Taking a deep breath, I roll the heavy blue leather chair away from the thick marble table and sit, crossing my legs. I have to get a grip.

"You're now a director," my father says without preamble.

I jolt. "Father, I—"

"It is done." He looks back down at a tablet he smacks on top of the papers. "I'm also considering bringing two of your distant cousins in but am still weighing the options."

Interesting. I've always owned shares, and it'll be nice to have some say in the direction of the platform now. I requested a position two years ago, but my father didn't want to change things at that time. It's good he's ready now. However, I hate that Greg is dead. I will need to rearrange my schedule, which is okay. Perhaps I can somehow leverage this new job position into funneling additional funds to the Backpack program. Or I could build several more houses for battered women in Southern California.

"*Alana,*" my father says harshly.

I jerk and heat spurts into my face. Once again, I am caught daydreaming.

My father shakes his head. "Nico, you were saying?"

"I'm saying it's a bad idea," Nico snarls.

The vitriol in his voice catches me and I press back into my chair.

"Shall we ask Alana's opinion?" Nico asks quietly. There's a tone in his voice I can't quite read, but I know I don't like it.

I clasp my shaking hands in my lap. My rose quartz necklace begins to heat against my skin and I absorb comfort from the stone, calming myself. "How about you both stop snapping at me?" I say serenely. "As usual, I'm happy to help."

"Good," my father says. "Because it is time for you to step up as the sole heir to Aquarius Social and the one with the strongest connection to aquamarines. There can only be one in every generation, and you're somehow it. As you know . . ."

A knock sounds on the door and I jump; the two men don't move.

My father sighs and reads his watch. "Let's get this part of the meeting finished. Come in," he calls out.

I turn and look over my shoulder to see two people enter. The first is Wesley Whisper, who is the chief product officer for Aquarius Social. The second is Val Vicconi, our chief legal officer.

Val pulls out a chair and sits next to me while hefting a large stack of file folders in front of her. Wesley moves toward the far end of the boardroom and grasps a remote control, then turns on a screen that takes up most of the west wall.

I find him intriguing. Wesley's about five foot nine with unruly blond hair, symmetrical features, and dark-rimmed glasses. There's no doubt he's the brains behind the current algorithms at Aquarius, and the stress lines cutting grooves into his fore-head attest to that fact. Yeah, I'm a little jealous of him as well. I've always wanted to learn how to code, but my boarding school taught us manners and how to influence people and not the humdrum ability to program computers. I still need to find the time to learn.

"All right, I'll be quick." He sounds as if his mind is already several years ahead of us. "We're in trouble."

My heart sinks. "Trouble?"

My father stares straight ahead at the screen. "Tell us."

Wesley nods. "We've lost five percent of market share to Malice Media in the last quarter alone."

"Damn it," my father says. "How?"

Wesley lifts a shoulder. "Their software is more complex than ours, and the crystals that run their computers are stronger. While our platform uses advanced AI technology to analyze our users' emotions in real time, Malice is doing the same while adding thoughts and experiences directly. They're getting more followers and, more importantly, users who share content." Several lights bloom on the screen.

"Whoa," Nico mutters. "That's some power they're amassing."

"I've been trying," I say, my mind reeling. "I have been appealing to deeper emotions lately." Our AI is an emotional-intelligence platform that uses advanced AI tech to analyze users' emotional states. The key is in the real time updates of connections.

Wesley sighs. Numbers and statistics scroll across the screen. "We're losing power. We need a good seven billion exploding stars a day just to keep us at current levels. We're not getting that."

I rapidly think through my options. To like an emote-post or share on our site, a user must click on an exploding-stars icon. One thing I'm not is a computer programmer. However, I am an influencer. "I'll create a new campaign that's centered around exploding stars and hints at more than emotion." I chew on my lip, knowing that my father is set in his ways. "I think we also should look at expanding user engagement."

"What do you mean by 'expanding'?" Nico asks.

I slowly inhale. "We all know that we receive energy and power from exploding stars. What if we share it with our users?"

"Share our energy?" my father asks incredulously. "We spend hours upon hours disseminating misinformation about crystal energy and its restorative power. It has taken the four families centuries to convince the public that magic does not exist."

Nico snorts. "Magic in the conventional sense does *not* exist."

I don't agree. No matter how many scientific principles are applied, our most brilliant scientists have never been able to completely explain how we derive energy from crystals and then use them to basically gain popularity that then enhances our health and longevity. It has something to do with story-telling from the time of the romantic poets to the dawn of the internet, where stories are now shared via social media posts. Who knows what the wide use of AI will lead to for us.

Even I do not know how the crystals work, and I have a stronger connection to aquamarine and rose quartz than anybody ever mentioned in the history books. "Crystal energy is a fact, and I think if we get people to understand the power they wield in creating that energy, they would take ownership and contribute, perhaps enhancing their own health and lifespans."

Nico shakes his head. "That's ridiculous. Most of the world has absolutely no idea that human energy can be harnessed via crystals, and we need to keep it that way. Such energy must be a zero sum game—there's only so much to go around. Keeping that secret is the only treaty among the four families that has stuck for eons."

That's true. From the dawn of time, different connections between humans and the Earth's crystals have created energy for the four ruling families, but the power of that was dying out until the advent of the internet, which then became enhanced via social media. Now the holy trinity is complete with Artificial Intelligence. Social media and AI are only strengthening the capture.

The more energy, the more glamour, the more subscribers—which leads to more money. All are important, but nothing comes close to the health and longer life benefits we glean.

However, Nico probably is correct. We've discovered that even by using computers and social media to connect people, there is only so much power to be gathered by the four families, which each set up a social media company at the birth of the new opportunity. At the moment, Aquarius Social is in fourth place. That means three other companies, or rather families, are leashing more power.

Social media is the new magic and it all runs on crystals.

"I still feel there's a way to turn the algorithms around," I say, looking at Wesley. "We gain so many interactions from the snide and bitter videos we push. What if we flip that around? I think there's an untapped market." There's a reason people stop to watch puppy videos.

"No," my father says. "Wesley, go work on the algorithm. I want to have something productive from you by the end of the week."

Wesley falters. "Yes, sir." His focus finally shifts to me. "I need you in the lab sometime later this week."

"Already?" Nico asks.

"Yes. I've integrated a thousand more aquamarine crystals into the hardware of our primary AI system, and I need them charged. Alana's mere presence ups the voltage from my devices." He grabs his backpack off the floor and saunters from the room.

Nico's frown darkens his face. He has never hidden his anger that I channel the aquamarine energy more effectively than he does. When my brother died, my connection to the stones strengthened even more. No doubt Nico had hoped for a different result.

My father looks at Val. "Do you have the documents?"

"I do." She smoothly hands a red file folder past me to my father.

I'm never sure what to make of Val Vicconi. She's much taller than I am and has an intimidating, statuesque grace. Black hair curls to her shoulders and a perfect peach color tinges her dusky skin above fiercely cut bone structure. Besides being wildly beautiful, her eyes shine with intelligence. She meets my gaze and quickly dismisses me.

To her, I am a bunch of fluff, yet I would bet my best pair of sparkly new Caovillas that she follows me on Aquarius Social and enjoys the sniping between me and the Rendale sisters.

My father flips through the file folder. "This looks good. Thank you, Val."

Val immediately stands, looking powerful in a red skirt suit with black patent heels. "Very well. Thank you." She turns and exits the room.

My heart beats faster though I don't know why. "Father?"

He clears his throat. "We don't have a choice here, Alana, so you'll do as you're told." He hands over the file folder.

"What is this?" I open it, the blood roaring through my ears, even though I have no idea what I'm about to read. Sometimes my instincts are excellent; other times, especially when dealing with men, not so much. My gaze catches on the heading of the first set of documents. It's a prenuptial agreement. I gulp. "You're getting married?"

My father chuckles, a sound as rare as a pink crocodile. "No, you are."

I rear away from the contract like it's a hungry tarantula that wants a bite of my flesh. "I am not getting married."

"You most certainly are."

Nico grunts. "I've been telling you that she's not a pawn."

"No," my father snaps. "You're not going to jump in and act like Greg. You're her distant cousin, not her brother."

I blink twice. Had Greg been protecting me all this time? "Nico?"

He looks away. I scan the documents. "Wait a minute. You want me to marry Cal Sokolov?" It is unthinkable. Cal is the youngest brother of the family that owns Hologrid, a 3D-holographic social media platform currently in third place. The guy is a notorious playboy—no way is he looking for a ball and chain. Could his family be shooting him down the aisle in a power play?

"I see you're getting it," my father says, already looking bored. "If we merge with Hologrid, we can kick Malice Media and TimeGem Moments down the ladder—maybe to the ground."

I have my doubts about that. Malice Media is owned by Thorn Beathach, whom nobody has seen for years. TimeGem Moments, in second place currently, is owned by Sylveria Rendale, who would like to see me in the ground after my fights with her daughters. I'd like to see her buried beneath a pile of concrete for her cruel treatment of Ella, her stepdaughter.

Staring at my father, I try to gather my thoughts. I barely know Cal. Sure, we've run across each other at various events, usually bar openings or society parties, and he might have flirted once or twice, but he flirts with everybody.

I glance at Nico, but he's transfixed by the screen still lit with blue dots as if the answer to every question in the universe is before him.

How could my father think he has any say in whom I marry? We live in the modern age, and it appears as if I have everything, but my only usefulness to him is as a bargaining tool. That reality shouldn't hurt me after all this time, yet my entire chest aches. "You have lost your mind." I snap the file folder shut and push it toward him.

"Are you sure we can rise above third place and gain energy for Aquarius with a . . . well, merger?" Nico avoids my gaze.

"I'm sure," my father says. "This is a done deal. Alana, sign everywhere you're supposed to sign. You and Cal will meet tonight and make arrangements that will suit you both. We'll announce the engagement at the Silicon Shadows and Secrets Ball next weekend."

The ball is held every year to benefit several local charities. We always attend. "Dad, I—"

He continues as if I haven't spoken. "The wedding will take place the following weekend. Cal's mother is making all the arrangements, so all you have to do is show up."

THREE

Thorn

The rain slaps my face and continues to beat against the city sidewalk, scattering used needles and smearing fresh feces. At least the deluge washes the blood off my neck and arms. It has been a rough night already, but I have another errand before we head to the nearest port to take control of a tech shipment that isn't mine.

Yet.

I maneuver silently down what was once a bustling avenue full of sparkle and light that now has turned to grim desolation. I pass street after street of scenes that belong in an apocalyptic movie, not in real life. Reaching the far end of the current block, I stop at a dirty orange tent, flap billowing in the storm. Before I can grasp the zipper, Justice is in front of me ripping it open, his garnet signet ring flashing in the night.

"I've got this," I mutter, crunching loudly on the burning mint in my mouth, hoping it deadens my taste buds long enough to navigate this night. I rarely let him accompany me, but my recent illness is making me slower, so I agreed. This time.

"So do I." He reaches in and yanks out two bodies. I would call them human, but it would not be an accurate description. They are two gaunt forms, bruised red and purple, covered in needle scars, open sores, and scabs. They're both male and could be anywhere from twenty to sixty years old.

One turns his head to the side and hacks wildly, shaking his skeleton-thin frame. Showing no mercy, Justice throws them up against the brick wall of a nearly vacant building. I hear a bone break. The first one somehow manages to shove back his greasy blond hair and glare. "Who the fuck are you, man?"

"I'm with him." Justice jerks his head toward me.

Both of the wraiths turn and then visibly shrink away upon seeing my face. Or maybe it's my eyes. I don't bother to conceal the hatred rippling through my bloodstream.

"You're Max and you're Joe. Right?" I ask, nothing but death in my tone.

Joe, his head shaved clean to show all of the mottled sores across his scalp, gulps and nods. "Yeah, man, that's us. Why? You need product?"

I lean in and regret it as the stench of their unwashed bodies envelops me. So far, the mint is working and I can't taste their words. "No."

Max tugs on his ear and blood flows down his arm. "We can get you girls, man. Is that what you want?" He sweeps a hand toward the many huddled tents across the street. "I can get you any age you want."

"That's what I've heard," I reply. Desolation pounds all around us. Every time I clean up a block, more human filth moves in. "I'm looking for your source."

"The kids are five tents over." Joe visibly relaxes and starts to twerk, even his eyelids twitching. The man's body needs a fix. "You got money?"

The mint continues to blister the back of my tongue. "I have a lot of money," I say, turning toward the tent. "How many kids do you have?"

"Right now, eight. Any age." Max sounds triumphant.

I smile and enjoy when he tries to step back. "I'm not asking you again. I want your source."

"Why?" He tries to sound tough but comes off as petulant. "I'll get you any age or sex you want."

I kick his knee and drop him to the pavement. Grabbing his greasy hair, I lean in while shoving my knife between his ribs. Low.

His eyes widen.

I pull out the blade and fresh blood covers my hand. "There's something you should know, Max," I say congenially.

"What?" He claps both hands over his rib cage as if to keep the warmth inside.

"I like killing people." I crouch so we're eye to eye. "A lot." I figure I should be honest with the guy since he's about to die. "You know why?"

Tears flow from his eyes and red snot drips from his nose. "Um, no?" He looks frantically around but Justice has his buddy against the building, and the smell of blood is thick in the air. "Why?" It's like he thinks he can appease me.

"I'm a sociopath. Maybe a psychopath. Or who knows? Just the fucked-up villain of the piece." I usually don't spend much time thinking about it.

He presses harder against his wound. "Please don't kill me."

"You're gonna die, Max. It's a fact." I study his breathing, which seems shallow. Maybe I nicked his lung. "But I can make it fast. Who's providing you with kids?"

"Why?" He coughs, his eyes wide in pain. "Why do you care?"

I stab him in the thigh, and he squeals like a pig. "Because I lead an organization, and if you're a member, you're protected.

In other words, you're *mine*. Somebody made the colossal mistake of kidnapping and killing a little girl of one of my men." Right off the street. It used to be that if you were protected, everyone knew it. Not now. The criminals aren't in tune with the . . . well, criminals. "So I owe it to him to draw blood. I can't have my men thinking I don't have their backs, right?"

"I didn't kill no little girl," Max whines.

"I know." She fell out of the van during the initial chase and died. It has taken me two weeks to track this guy down, and he's not the one I want. "Give me the name, or I'll start cutting off body parts." I slice off his ear. "Oops. Started early."

He shrieks and plants one hand over the hole, probably to keep his tiny brain inside. "His name is Nelson. That's all I know. I give him whatever money or drugs I can get, and he hands over the kids. Most are homeless or came alone across the border and nobody knows they're here. Nobody's looking for them. Your little girl must've been a mistake."

I stand and smoothly kick him in the neck, making sure to dig in with my heel. The crunch is satisfying as his larynx collapses. His eyes widen with a flicker of terror, and a gasp of air somehow makes its way out of his mouth. He claws at his throat, trying to reestablish an airway that has crumpled. Gravity wins, as she always does, and he drops to his knees to drown in his own blood.

He is forgotten within seconds.

The crack of a neck breaking echoes to my left, as Justice becomes bored with his knife and finally takes care of the other pimp.

The wind shrieks through the night, spinning the rain end over end with the stench of waste. God, I hate it here.

Justice stares down the many rows of tents and makeshift cardboard boxes before stepping gingerly over another pile of shit. I look up at the tall building with its seventy percent vacancy. The first several floors used to carry high-end designer stores, while the upper ones were luxurious apartments. The more homeless on the streets, the quicker anybody who can flee San Francisco does.

"Is the building in foreclosure yet?" I ask, not feeling the rain or the wind, dressed as I am in clothes I'd never wear in public. Contrary to popular opinion, I do not hide out in my fortress. People just don't know who I am. Or if they do, they either forget rapidly or stop talking altogether.

"Couple more weeks." Justice looks down at his boots and sighs. "All I got is a name. Nelson," he says, his gaze scanning the area for threats.

"Me, too." I look around. "Do we know who put these homeless on this street?"

Justice snorts. "As far as I can tell, Beaumont is spreading the drugs."

Mathias Beaumont is an asshole, but I have to admire his business acumen. He floods the streets with drugs, turning the homeless into walking zombies who force property owners out of the city. Then he bribes or coerces local government into creating laws that allow the disaster to continue down the spiral to hell. When all the property falls into foreclosure, he buys it up cheap. How he plans to rid the city of the homeless after he owns all the property, I don't know yet. I can't imagine his plan is a pretty one.

For now, I offer more cash for the buildings than Mathias can.

Justice taps his phone and scrolls down. "Huh?" The strong mint that I've had in my mouth dissipates and his tone slides over my taste buds like good coffee. It is one of the reasons he's sometimes allowed close to me. He reads the screen of his phone, having already forgotten about the two dead bodies on the syringe-covered sidewalk. "There has been a development with Alana."

Hearing her name sends the fleeting taste of honey across my tongue. "What kind of development?" My voice goes hoarse.

Justice looks up, no expression on his face, but concern in his eyes. "I don't know. According to my source, something is going down with her in an hour. Something dangerous."

Everything inside me tightens and goes deadly still. "Move. Now."

FOUR

Alana

My five-inch stilettos stick to the floor as Ella, Rosalie, and I converge in a back corner of Martini Money, which can only be described as one of the cheesiest bars in Palo Alto. The clientele is a combination of wealthy startup owners and underage girls. The music is thick and throbbing, the booth hard and bright, and the alcohol expensive.

"I cannot believe he wants to meet you here," Ella says, her eyes carefully hidden behind thick glasses and her figure under what could only be considered a potato sack. Sometimes I feel as if she's taking her need to stay under the radar a little too seriously, but then again, considering my family is trying to force me into marriage with somebody I don't know, perhaps she has the right idea.

Rosalie snorts. "What are you worried about? Why don't you just go give the youngest Sokolov brother a good ride? Aren't you tired of not getting any?"

I roll my eyes. It's an old argument and one I don't have the patience for right now. "Why would I do that?"

"Yeah," Ella chimes in. "Alana wants true love, not a ride on a dick of a . . . dick." She chuckles.

Rosalie sighs. "It's so much fun to talk about sex with the two of you."

Ella gulps her martini, her eyes wide. "I still think this is a bad idea," she says. "We can get you out of the country within an hour."

"I honestly don't think there is a place on earth my father can't find me. I have a better idea than running away." I stir the olive in my gin martini glass.

Rosalie tips back the rest of her drink. "You think you're going to talk Cal Sokolov out of marrying you?"

I have no plans to marry him, yet we can help each other. "Yes. He likes his single life." The guy has more escapades on social media than do I. "If we combine forces, we can strengthen both platforms. Our families will just have to stand down on this."

"What?" Rosalie asks. "Stand down? Have either of your families ever stood down?"

I don't know the answer to that question, so why respond?

Rosalie looks over her shoulder at the VIP area, where red velvet couches and faceted mirrors decorate the area. "We have to figure out a way you don't have to marry that himbo."

"Himbo?" Ella laughs. She takes out her phone and scrolls through Cal's account on Hologrid Hub. She's the best hacker around, probably because she's traveled all over the world to train with legendary geniuses while staying under the radar of her stepmother and stepsisters. No doubt they tracked her, but hurting her would be too visible, so they haven't made a move yet. "All Cal really posts about is working out, getting laid, and driving cars." She winces. "He's definitely not the brains behind the business."

"No. That would be his older brother Hendrix." Rosalie exhales. "I've heard that guy is as evil as they come."

"Aren't there three brothers?" Ella motions for another drink.

I motion as well, wanting a nice buzz before I head into the VIP area. "I remember there being another brother."

"What's his name?" Ella taps her chin.

Rosalie smiles as the waiter places three more drinks in front of us. "Alexei."

"That's right. I'd nearly forgotten. Alexei is in prison." Ella looks up, her eyes cloudy behind the glasses. "He brutally murdered the husband of his lover. Remember? The story dominated the news for weeks."

I shiver. "I do remember." Every news outlet had shown his hard and furious face. The last thing I need is to end up in a family that thinks adultery excuses murder. Not that I'd commit either, to be honest. "I'm surprised his family didn't make it all go away."

"There were too many witnesses," Rosalie murmurs. "Money doesn't always buy everyone off."

I pat her hand. My friend has the kindest heart in the world, even when she's encouraging me to ride men like horses. She's an attorney who's as ambitious they come. "Sometimes the right things actually happen in life."

"I know," Rosalie says, staring at me. "You aren't really going to marry this guy, are you?"

I bite my lip. "No. I'm not. At least I don't think I am."

Ella shakes her head. "You're pale, Alana. Did you get any sleep last night?"

"No." I'm a terrible liar, so I don't bother with my friends.

"Nightmares?" Rosalie asks, losing the teasing glint in her eye.

I try to banish the images from my mind. "Yes."

Ella sighs. "Maybe we should try hypnotism again. You need to access those memories to get over this."

"They might not be memories. I could've just seen a scary

movie too young," I whisper, even though I have tried to banish the images several times.

Rosalie glances at Ella and then looks at me. "The key is in your phobia."

I lift a hand. "I don't have a phobia." At least not one recognized by any medical establishment.

"Yes, you do," Ella says gently. "It's called a specific phobia, and you know it."

What I know is that I don't want to endure "exposure therapy" again, even if that is one way to deal with a phobia. Mine is weird. It's an aversion to the argyle pattern, especially in windows. "Listen. This only happens during times of extreme stress, and I'm still grieving for my brother."

"Hi, ladies." Nico suddenly comes into view and reaches our table before I can continue my denial.

I lean back, grateful he's saving me from another discussion about my nightmares. "Nico, it's nice to see you. What are you doing in this place?" The corny tavern with the bright lights and beer-crusted floor is the last place I'd expect to find my elegant cousin.

He sneers at the sticky floor and then nods to both Rosalie and Ella. "I feel bad about how the board meeting went." He stares into my eyes. "I promised Greg a long time ago if anything happened to him that I would protect you."

At the mention of my brother's name, my body goes cold. Then hope unfurls in my chest like a freshly watered flower. My brother was ten years older than me, but there were times we played together like kids. He was my sounding board for most of my life, and even after he turned all serious with the business, he was still easier to approach than our father. "He asked you that?"

"Yes," Nico says. "I know that he turned hard, but Greg always cared about you and wanted you to have a good life. He was more than willing to take over the company so you wouldn't have to be anywhere near it. Not that you haven't helped and done an excellent job as an influencer," he hastens to add.

"Thank you, Nico," I say, warming again. Somehow it helps to know that Greg cared. "I'm all right with whatever I have to do for the family." But marrying a man I don't know? How does that make sense for me?

Ella shifts to the side. "Have a seat, Nico."

He pats her shoulder, and she beams. "Thanks, El."

El? Interesting. They make a lovely couple, actually. "Sit with us, Nico," I urge. "We can figure this out. I'm sure of it."

Nico sighs. "You've grown up nicely, Alana, and you definitely have a brain. A good one. I understand your commitment and agree if you and I work together, we can convince your father there's another way. I just don't know what it is."

"I'll figure something out," I say, noting both of my friends watching my handsome cousin, who's still standing close to Ella. "Would you like to have a drink with us?"

He glances at the aquamarine-studded watch that matches the ring on his index finger. "No. I'm wanted back at headquarters. We're trying to hack into Malice Media this week."

My ears heat. "Seriously, you think you can hack Malice?"

"We're trying." Nico reads the screen of his phone and tucks it away in his jacket. "If we can just get our hands on their AI interface technology, we could finally take that bastard down."

"Have you ever met him?" Ella asks, leaning forward.

Nico turns to her, his gaze appraising. "I don't know anybody who has met Thorn Beathach. Sometimes we wonder if he exists."

"Oh, he exists," Ella says. "I've tracked him enough through the web to know that he's a real person, a deadly one."

Nico shifts his weight, and emotion darkens his handsome face. "Don't track Beathach on the web. He'll know, and he'll kill you. Ella, be smart."

Ella's chin lifts. "I can cover my tracks."

Yeah. You go, girl. Even so, unease tempers my pride in her. "Why do you say he's deadly?"

She shrugs. "Any time there's a mention of him, it's either retracted, deleted, or the person posting it disappears. Accidents, you know?"

Right. Accidents that are anything but. Perhaps I *should* combine Aquarius's resources with Hologrid Hub's, if for no other reason than to counter the evil obvious in Malice Media. Seriously. The name itself shows Thorn isn't trying to hide his agenda. For me, it's like a red flag waved in front of a bull. *Come and get me,* he whispers.

Ella swallows. "I don't think any of us want to make an enemy out of Thorn Beathach."

Nico appraises her, his gaze warm. "I agree, although I'm sure we're all on his radar already." He looks over his shoulder as if afraid somebody is listening.

"What is it?" My instincts start to hum.

"I just want you to be careful. All right? We have two guys on you here in the bar, and I'm sure Sokolov will have protection as well."

"I'm not in danger," I say. Sure, I often get the odd fan from Aquarius Social who thinks they're in love with me, but they're normally dissuaded easily.

"That's not what I mean." Nico's dark eyes flash. "Greg is already dead and you're the heir."

That might be true, but there's always another heir. "If something happens to me, then you can be the heir. You're probably next in line," I say gently.

He shakes his head. "No, I'm not. I don't have the power or the connection with the crystals that you do. If anything happens to you, your father would be left without an heir—I mean for now."

Ella cocks her head. "What do you mean 'for now'?"

Crimson spreads across Nico's handsome face. "Nothing. Forget it."

I set my martini glass down on the chipped table. "Forget it? What do you mean? Is my dad trying to make new heirs?" He is ancient. Would he really do that? My stomach sinks as I realize that he would.

Nico steps back from the table. "I've said too much, but be careful. I don't want what happened to Greg to happen to you." His shoulders go back. "There were cameras along the route he took that night before crashing off Vulture's Perch, and they're all burned out. Destroyed. It's too suspicious."

Rosalie looks at me and then looks over at Nico. "Greg was in a car accident."

Nico visibly gulps. "Bullshit. He was an excellent driver, and he was sober that night. Just watch your back." He glances again at Ella. "All of you. Be careful." With that, he shoves his hands in his pockets and storms through the crowded bodies to the door.

FIVE

❧❧❧

Alana

I watch my cousin go, unease rippling through me. What does he know about Greg's death that I do not?

"That was weird," Ella says.

"I think he has the hots for you, Alana," Rosalie murmurs.

The idea turns my stomach. "Nico is just worried about the company and has turned all big brother on me."

"He's definitely big and is just a distant relative. Turn that overprotectiveness into something hot. Why don't you take him for a spin?" Rosalie asks.

Ella leans back farther from us and drops her gaze to her drink.

I look at Rosalie. "You are the worst sometimes. How are we friends?"

"How are we *not* friends? You need me," she says.

"Yeah, I need you like I do a fall down a black diamond ski hill," I retort.

She snorts. "That wasn't my fault."

"Yes, it was. You ran into me because you were ogling that hot guy from Sweden." Sometimes my left arm still aches—especially when the weather turns cold like it is right now.

"He had an ass I could bounce a quarter off," Rosalie says defensively. "You were ogling him too."

Actually, I had been trying not to fall on my face, which had turned out to be an unrealistic expectation. But every adventure we've had is worth it. The three of us met at boarding school. My father dropped me there because he couldn't deal with a daughter and his grief; Ella's stepmother sent her away because she couldn't kill her as a kid; and Rosalie's grandpa had worked as a janitor at the school. We somehow found each other and have been best friends ever since.

Rosalie checks out her bright pink nail polish. "All I'm saying is that you might as well have some fun if you do end up marrying Cal Sokolov. What kind of name is that anyway? Who names their kids Hendrix, Cal, and . . . what was the other one?"

"Alexei," Ella supplies.

Rosalie grins. "Yeah, Alexei."

"Alexei is half brother to the other two, and I wouldn't mess with Cal's mama, if I were you," I drawl. Lillian Sokolov is a fierce woman with sharp nails.

Rosalie leans forward and I hope the pounding music will prevent anybody from hearing what she says. "Listen, Alana, we both know if it's to save Aquarius Social, you'll marry whichever of the Sokolov brothers your father puts in front of you at the altar. So don't you think you should have some fun first? Take Nico for a spin. Heck, even take all three of the Sokolov brothers for a spin. Maybe the killer one gets conjugal visits. Once you're married, I know you. You won't break that vow, no matter what."

No, I'm not a woman who breaks promises. As usual, Rosalie is right, but jumping on Cousin Nico isn't how I want to spend my last days as a free woman—especially since Ella blushes every time his name is mentioned. I glance at my watch. "All right, I'm going in."

"We'll be here," Ella says loyally. "If you need us, just yell. Loudly."

I have no idea what she thinks she can do if Cal and I don't hit it off, but I pat her shoulder anyway. "You're a good friend." I cut Rosalie a hard look. "You're just okay."

"I'm fabulous," she says, winking.

I shake my head because she's right, at least about our friendship. I stand and find my balance. For this meeting, I'm wearing my signature yellow in a low-cut halter top with an aquamarine skirt and fuck-me five-inch heels with encrusted diamonds decorating the top. My hair is teased wildly and my makeup is flirty.

I'm too nervous to post on Aquarius Social, and my emotions are too volatile for me to want to share the moment with our emotion-catching-and-dispersing interface as I wind through the crowd to the VIP area flanked by two bulging bouncers. I don't know if they've been waiting for me, or if they recognize me, but they both step aside and allow me to pass. I make my way through private booths to reach a cordoned-off section. Someone smoothly releases the rope so I don't even have to break stride.

Cal Sokolov sits on a red velvet sofa flanked by a blonde who has already fallen out of her top and a brunette who has one leg over his. Both women are giggling.

"Hello, honey," I murmur.

He looks up, his gaze lazy. I have to admit that Cal is a good-looking guy who could star in any movie as the lead. His hair is a shade of blond that reminds me of better times at the ocean playing volleyball. It's unruly and yet somehow expertly styled. His eyes are a piercing blue and his bone structure classic and symmetrical.

For our meeting tonight, or rather for whatever the heck he

is doing here, he's wearing tan slacks and a black button-down shirt that reveals his bronze neck and part of his torso. His smile is both mischievous and sharp. "Alana, hello." He snaps his fingers and men appear out of nowhere to assist the two women off him. The blonde protests but isn't given a choice, and soon they're standing on the other side of the rope. "I apologize. I didn't know you would be here as of yet."

"Are you apologizing that I caught you with the bimbos or that you were *with* the bimbos?" I ask.

He does not stand. "Let's not pretend this is anything other than what it is." He gestures toward the seat next to him, the one vacated by the dark-haired girl.

I angle my head to make sure she's left behind no wet spots since she was obviously well into him. It looks dry enough. I sit.

"What would you like to drink?" he asks.

I look over at a hovering waitress who appears to be about to have a panic attack. She bounces like an exuberant puppy as if waiting for a command, her gaze longingly on Cal.

"Dirty gin martini, three olives," I say, hoping she doesn't soil herself.

She waits until Cal nods. I roll my eyes. As she scampers off, he reaches out and trails his fingers down my arm. It shocks me how badly I want to punch his perfect face. His nose is a little too straight but I can fix that.

"So we get married in a couple of weeks, huh?" He winks.

I blink. "I thought maybe you and I could work together to avoid that." I say the words slowly, trying to read him.

"Why would I want to avoid our union?" His gaze rakes me from head to toe and then warms. "You're a hot little thing, Alana Beaumont. Everybody I know has been trying to get in your pants for a good ten years. I'm looking forward to being the one who finally does it."

My stomach revolts, but I smile. "I don't think you know what you're getting into."

He shrugs. "Doesn't really matter. We're both going to do

what our families tell us to do, and then you're going to do what I tell you to do."

"That isn't how it works," I say dryly. "Believe me, I'm more trouble than you want." It is only fair to be honest with the guy.

He sighs as if bored. "I don't believe that to be true. You'll be a good little girl and a good wife and probably a good mother to how many little hounds you shove out. You can have all the freedom you want in this marriage, but stay under the radar and don't embarrass me."

I look over my shoulder to where the two women who'd been hanging over him press against the rope, trying to get back in. "What about the vows?"

"Oh, please," he says. "I'm a man."

"Are you?" I look him over. "I'm not so sure. You seem like a castrated dog to me." If I mean to insult him, it doesn't work.

He laughs. "I'm exactly what I want to be. I'm about to marry the princess everybody lusts after and win more responsibility at Hologrid Hub. When we combine your algorithms with ours, we'll be able to take down Malice and TimeGem. This is a good thing, Alana. Toe the line."

A waiter strides toward us and hands me a martini. He's tall with lighter blond hair and sparkling brown eyes. "You didn't specify the gin, Miss, so I chose the Botanist. It's my favorite."

I accept the drink. "Thank you."

His grin flashes two dimples. What is he? About twenty? For some reason, he makes me feel old. "Can I get you anything else?"

"Thanks, but no." I return his smile, noting how well he fills out the dark T-shirt.

Cal clears his throat. "About our engagement, darling . . ."

The waiter's grin fails as he looks from Cal back to me, as if asking what in the world I'm thinking.

My smile widens. Perhaps I should introduce this guy to Rosalie. Oh, she'd eat him for breakfast, but he's adorable.

Cal coughs. "Plan the wedding, Alana. Now."

So much for us combining forces and preventing this ridiculous union. "I have to tell you, Cal, you don't want to marry me." I focus back on him.

"Oh, but I do." His gaze drops to my breasts. "I actually can't wait for the wedding night." He looks at his watch. "You have a doctor's appointment tomorrow, and as soon as we receive those results, I'll sign the papers."

What is he talking about? "I have a doctor's appointment?"

He laughs. "Didn't you read the papers your father gave you?"

Right now they're stuffed in my purse. I have neither read nor signed them. "No."

"You have a doctor's appointment tomorrow to make sure that you're healthy, can bear children, and . . . well, you know . . ." His voice drops into a slur.

I lean toward him. "I don't know."

"Sure you do. We have to make sure that little hymen is intact, don't we?"

My jaw drops. It's rare that I am taken aback, considering I spend most of my life in front of a camera. "Are you serious?"

"Of course I'm serious. How am I going to brag about being the only one to bang the princess if somebody's been there before me?"

My ears heat until I'm sure they're beet red, absurdly pleased the cute waiter has moved down the line in the VIP area and can't hear this crap. "Oh, you're a dick." I stand. "This wedding is not happening."

He stands, towering over me, and I take a step back. I didn't realize he's at least six feet tall. "There's no getting out of it, Alana. If you try, it means war." All of a sudden, Cal drops his ever-present charm.

For the first time, an actual chill sweeps through me at the thought of marrying him. Just beneath the charm and the good nature is something else, something I don't want to see. Someone brushes by my elbow, and I turn to see his older brother.

"Hendrix. What a surprise," I say. The man doesn't belong in this dive in his gray designer suit.

He looks me over, surprise flashing and then cooling in his blue eyes. "Alana. You're stunning." He sounds shocked.

"Thanks?" I'm on social media constantly. Maybe the guy running the show at Hologrid doesn't have time to follow accounts. "I'm not planning on joining your family."

His gaze locks on my lips. "Perhaps we should renegotiate. You're much more my type than Cal's. He likes blondes. I adore brunettes. You've grown up nicely."

Cal elbows closer. "You bang blondes and marry brunettes. The contract is with me, brother."

"We'll see." Hendrix gives a little bow, turns, and strides confidently out of the VIP area.

Cal rolls his eyes. "Forget him. I'm sure you're accustomed to that response from any hot-blooded male who meets you in person."

Multiple marriage proposals? Um, no.

Suddenly, a shot rings out and the mirrored wall to my right bursts into pieces, sending shards flying. I yelp. Cal screams and ducks down, with his hands over his ears. I turn, trying to find the shooter. Three men, all masked, rush through the crowd toward us. I search for an exit as Cal huddles on the sofa yelling for his guards.

Another shot is fired and I duck, scrambling toward what appears to be a door to a back room. The cute waiter yanks it open. "Go, go, go," he urges, trying to wrap his big body over me.

I run inside with him on my heels as more shots ring out.

"God, run. We have to get out of here," he huffs, slamming the door shut.

Strong arms yank me into the dark. I catch sight of eyes. I know those eyes. I've seen those eyes before.

It's the man from the darkness. I push against him, trying to find a path to safety when danger lies in every direction.

The waiter tries to nudge me aside and tackle the man, but a knife flashes, and blood instantly spurts from the waiter's throat, washing over my front. His eyes bug out, and he grabs his bleeding neck, dropping to his knees.

I scream and try to help him, reaching for the convulsing kid.

But his killer grabs my hips and tosses me over his shoulder, and my stomach lands against what feels like solid rock. The air bursts out of my chest and my entire torso protests in pain.

Then, we're running toward the storm.

SIX

Alana

Panic stifles the scream in my throat. This impossibly strong man has an arm around my legs as he jogs through what appears to be a storage area and kicks open a door. How could he murder the sweet waiter like that? The guy was just trying to help me.

Terror clogs my throat, but I keep my lips shut. The waiter's blood is on them and I don't want to taste the fresh liquid. Then we're barreling through the abusive rain. I'm tossed into the backseat of an SUV and I roll over, my shoulders hitting the far door. The murderer jumps inside. "Go," he snaps.

The driver punches the gas, and we speed down the alleyway. I scramble to sit up, trying to focus my eyes in the darkened interior. I futilely try to wipe the blood off my face. "Who are you?"

The man turns toward me. Everything inside me goes quiet before exploding tumultuously alive with raw terror. A jagged scar slashes from his forehead, through his left eyebrow, and across the bridge of his nose to the other cheekbone, and blood also dots his lower jaw. From the poor waiter.

The killer's mere presence is a warning as he takes up more than his fair share of the backseat. In contrast with the men in the bar I just left, he wears a rough black leather jacket, ripped and faded jeans, and battered but high-end combat boots. Rain dots his thick black hair, curling the mass beneath his ears. The breadth of his shoulders alone intimidates me, and that's before I notice more blood on his neck and the bruises on his knuckles.

So I turn, facing him, pulling one leg up on the seat in case I need to pivot on my knee and attack him. The difference in our sizes makes that idea stupid. But I know letting any kidnapper take me away from a public space is a death sentence.

"Who are you?" My voice trembles this time. His eyes are black with, I swear, flecks of silver. Not gold, not brown, not amber, but silver. I have never seen the color before, but I know those eyes. "You've been watching me." I flash back to the other night.

"You're very watchable," he says, his voice deep and rich like a Macallan Sherry Oak 18 Year Old scotch.

A chill snakes through me and I shiver. "Why did you kill that poor kid?" I whisper. This guy is big enough he could've just knocked out the waiter.

"He was in my way."

My stomach revolts and I wipe frantically at my lips.

"Stop it."

I stop. Hopefully the blood is off my mouth, at least. I can feel the stickiness on my shirt, soaking through to my bra. I don't want to die. "You don't know my father, but he won't pay a ransom." It's the truth and a fact that has been drummed into me since I was a little girl.

My kidnapper's eyes twinkle for a second as if I've amused

him. If he doesn't want money, what does he want? Panic has me pushing away from him. "Just let me go." I reach behind my back for a door handle.

"That door doesn't open," the driver says, sounding bored, even though he's driving so fast the buildings on either side of the rainy night meld together.

I look again at the man who carried me so easily away from the building. "Did you plan this whole night? How many people just died?"

"You'd do better worrying about yourself than others right now," he says, losing the amusement.

I search for any sort of escape.

He settles his massive shoulders against his seat. "You should relax because we have a bit of a drive in front of us."

I focus on the scruff covering his jaw—his very angled, cut, and masculine jaw—with the waiter's blood down his neck. Surprising tears prick the back of my eyes.

All of a sudden, the driver yanks a phone to his ear and starts barking orders in Irish Gaelic. Something about three ports of entry and taking control of shipments. I taught myself Gaelic in order to read several histories about crystals . . . as well as poems. I enjoy Gaelic poems.

I love languages and I love to read, and many books aren't in English, so I set myself to learning several languages on my own years ago. For now, I try to comprehend.

My captor lifts his own phone to his ear, his voice a low rumble that licks across my skin with both fear and something else I can't identify. I tremble. What the heck is wrong with me? Did I hit my head? Am I suffering from some sort of nervous system malfunction from nearly being split in two by a bullet?

Why do my feet feel like they're falling asleep? Does fear do that?

Snapping out a bloodcurdling series of orders dealing with movement, timing, and sanctioned bloodshed, the dark-haired brute next to me ends his call and slaps his phone against his muscular thigh.

Yep. Short-circuited. "Listen," I say softly, scrambling again for a lever to open my door. Based on what I decipher from the calls, my captor is orchestrating strategic hits against the shipments of his rivals. There isn't a doubt in my mind that he's in the Irish mafia, which does not bode well for me. At all. The one good thing is that they have no idea I comprehend Gaelic. Most of the scary words, anyway. "It's obvious you two are busy, so how about I take off now?"

He turns toward me, lifting his head slightly with his nostrils flaring, as if catching some sort of scent.

There's nowhere for me to hide.

"Say something else," he orders. No man has ever looked at me like he's starving and I'm the perfect meal. Until now.

Air catches in my throat. I clear it. "Why?"

"Something sweet."

If he's trying to terrorize me, he's doing a good job. I try to firm my jaw and face him directly, but my lips tremble. I lick them and then wince at the taste of copper.

"Damn it." The driver swerves, one hand still on the phone at his ear. "Thorn? We should be at the port." He spits the words in English.

Thorn? As in Thorn Beathach? I gulp. "Um . . ."

"This is more important," Thorn growls. "The boys can handle the job."

My fear of the Irish mafia pales as reality slaps me upside the head. Hard. "You're Thorn Beathach?" I whisper, my heart clanging against my rib cage so fast my chest compresses. I hope I'm too young for a heart attack.

His lips part slightly. "Say my name again."

There is a reason Beathach has stayed out of the public eye: he's nuts—as well as being a cold-blooded killer. I can't find the door handle and start to babble, as is my defense mechanism when terrorized. "I seriously doubt your boys will succeed without you at the port, so how about you drop me off and go get your work done?" No doubt the job is illegal and I don't want to know anything more than what I just heard.

He breathes in as if he's breathing *me*.

His phone buzzes and he lifts it to his ear, instantly launching into a spate of Gaelic.

I have to get out of this vehicle before he wraps those humongous hands around my neck. If my door is locked, perhaps his is not. The guy is twice my size, if not more, and looks like solid head-to-toe muscle. But I know better than to let them take me to the woods or wherever they plan to kill me. So it's now or never.

When he turns to look out the window and issues even more orders, I find my chance. Taking a deep breath, I launch my body across the seat, elbow him hard in the throat and yank on his door handle. The door starts to open and my heart leaps into my throat at how fast the wet asphalt flies by. Doesn't matter. I have to jump.

Without seeming to move, Thorn manacles an arm across my waist, dumps me onto his hard-assed lap, and slams the door shut.

I jerk and look up, meeting the driver's gaze in the rearview mirror. "Fuck," he says, the tone almost admiring.

Sitting perfectly still, I try to calm my breathing, hunching in on myself to protect my face in case Thorn starts punching. My skirt has ridden up to my thighs, and the material is trapped beneath my rear, so I can't pull it down. Not only are Thorn's thighs hard, his entire body is warm. Hot, even. The heat seeps toward me, circling me hotter than any hellfire threat.

He finishes his call and places his phone on the armrest. "Look at me, princess."

I feverishly push against him, trying to retake my seat. His abs are rock hard and ripple beneath the T-shirt. His arm doesn't tighten but I'm held immobile. The arm is solid steel. Where is that knife of his? I almost whimper, reliving the murder of the waiter. So I turn, my breath catching at the raw heat in Thorn's eyes. Instinctively, I know that begging won't work with a monster like him. "Let me go."

"No." His gaze drops to my lips, and they swell. Or at least, they feel like they swell. None of this makes sense. He continues in that raw and now dominant tone. "I hadn't planned on establishing your rules until we arrive, but apparently I need to do so now."

Rules? My head jerks and my legs shake. "Rules? Before you kill me?"

He licks his bottom lip and lets out a soft hum. "I'm not going to kill you."

Oh, God. My insides feel hollow, but I can't ask the question—the one careening through my head. What are his plans? Instead, I focus on anything else. "Where are we going?" I ask, my butt feeling soft against his legs.

"My place."

"You're going to kill me at your *house*?" I lean in, studying his eyes. Clear pupils, no sign of being on drugs. Then I lose it, so much fear in my head all I can do is babble. "You know that's a mistake, right?"

One of his dark eyebrows rises. "Do tell."

My brain finally just explodes and my mouth takes over for my mind. "You know, DNA evidence—blood, saliva, tears, and all of that. If you're going to murder somebody, you want to do it far away from your house. Also, leave the murder weapon." Though, looking at him, I know he *is* the murder weapon.

He cocks his head and a glint of what I hope is humor flashes briefly in his eyes.

I take that as encouragement, my ears ringing. "Now that you know those facts, you should plan better. How about you let me off here, and I'll meet you near the Golden Gate Bridge next Saturday night? That way, there's nothing to connect us." I know it's stupid to hope he's *that* crazy, but it's all I have going for me right now.

"You promise you'll be there?" he asks.

I brighten, a sliver of hope cutting through my fear. "Absolutely."

His free hand settles across my throat, his long fingers wrapping all the way around to my nape. His massive paw is heavy and heated, and there is no doubt he can snap my neck in a second if he chooses.

I jolt, swallowing and then finding relief that I *can* swallow. But my breathing turns rapid and shallow, and I can't draw in enough oxygen to relieve my lungs.

He leans in and slightly squeezes, and my palms start to sweat, even through the chills attacking me. "That makes two rules of mine you've broken within ten minutes, Alana Beaumont. You break another one before we get home, and I'm going to flip you over and spank that perfect ass until you're screaming and the taste of honey is the only thing in my head."

The threat, from another man, would infuriate me. But this one? His hard and possessive tone paralyzes me. More tears fill my eyes. I can't move. He won't let me. "What do you want from me?"

"At the moment? Obedience." He glances at his buzzing phone.

"Bummer," I blather.

His gaze returns to me. "Excuse me?"

"There's a gene that creates a tendency to obey," I say, my head spinning. He's holding me too tightly for me to grasp the door handle again; I need to loosen his grip. "Researchers have identified it on the Y chromosome, which I do not have." I try to push away from him . . . but don't move an inch. His strength petrifies me. "But the good news is that learning to live with disappointment builds character. So with more disappointments like this, you should be a decent guy in about a millennium. I'm grateful to have started you on this journey."

His stare deepens and I want to blink but can't look away. "You have a sense of humor. I had not expected that."

I tremble. Somehow, I tear my gaze from his, looking down at his broad chest. "You have enough going on, Thorn. You don't want to start a war with my father." Is there a way to reason with him before he kills me? Or worse?

"I'm already in a war. Having another adversary doesn't change the chess board much," he counters.

I gulp. "Um, I don't understand the honey reference. How would, um, well, spanking me fill you with honey?" My butt clenches as I say the words and for a second it's a relief to concentrate on anything but that knife he must still have close. Perhaps if I understand his insanity, I can work with it.

"I have a form of Lexical-Gustatory Synesthesia," he murmurs.

What in the world? I've read about synesthesia but have never met anyone who has it.

He clears his throat. "It's a rare form of synesthesia where people's voices trigger certain tastes in my mouth. You're all honey, baby." He describes the condition as if I'm not smart or educated enough to know what it is. Oh, I get it. He thinks he knows me.

I look up. "You follow me on Aquarius Social."

He nods.

"And in real life." I know I've seen his eyes in the darkness before.

"Yes. You're an obsession."

Adrenaline shoots through my veins. "That's awfully honest." In fact, telling me about the synesthesia shows a level of trust that doesn't make sense.

"One of my rules," he says quietly. "Number one, actually. There will be no lies between us. Ever."

Between us? Just how long does he plan to keep me? So I violated his rule when I said I'd meet him at the bridge to die. "What other rule did I break?" I have to believe there will be a chance to escape if he lets me live long enough to do so.

He loosens his hold on my neck and swipes a callused thumb along my jawline. "We're traveling at a hundred miles an hour, and you tried to jump out of the vehicle. Rule number two is to stay out of danger. Period."

"You're all danger," I say without thinking.

His grin is quick and so fleeting I'd wonder if I saw it if my chest didn't heat quickly. "Smart girl."

Obviously he doesn't think that, which is good for me. Being underestimated can only help. "Are you going to kill me?"

"No."

I narrow my gaze, trying to read him, but it's like staring at a wall of slate. "I'm going to fight you."

"Good."

My vision tunnels in, darkening the interior of the shadow-filled vehicle. Then I waver, my head turning heavy. Shouldn't terror shoot adrenaline through my system? Why is my body shutting down? Is it a defense mechanism? "Why are you taking me?"

"I want you."

Simple words. Terrifying ones. I need to get my hands on that knife. "That's too bad."

"Is it?" He leans in, his lips brushing my neck.

My body performs a tremble head to toe. Confusion blankets me.

His hand rests on my bare thigh and heat flashes up to my core. "I'm thinking you like danger." His hot breath singes my throat, and my nipples harden against my flimsy tanktop. His chuckle, right against my skin, rumbles through my body. "Want me to prove it to you?" That heated palm slides up my leg, his fingers curling around my thigh.

"No," I squeak, partly because the driver is right there, and partly because I'm not sure what Thorn will find. My body is rioting.

He inhales deeply, his voice a dark whisper in my ear. "You're wet. We both know it." But his fingers don't move.

I look down at his bruised and cut knuckles. He didn't get those in the brief scuffle with the waiter. "Why are you bleeding?"

"Fought on the streets earlier."

Thorn Beathach fights on the streets? An odd hobby for a billionaire. "How many people have you killed tonight?" I ask, my voice hoarse.

"Tonight? Just five."

Oh. God.

Then his damaged hand slides up, and one finger flicks across my clit. Shock spirals through me along with electricity. A dark need. Heat bursts into the apples of my cheeks, and I duck my head, hating my body as much as him.

His chuckle moves his muscled abs against my flank.

I clench my bare thighs together and barely bite back a moan. "I would like to get off your lap now," I say primly. How is this possibly intriguing? What's wrong with me?

Thorn studies me. "Pity." Then he releases his hold, lifts me, and settles me safely back in my seat.

Shock catches me for a minute. Is he trying to keep me off-balance? My eyelids become heavy. Shockingly so. Coldness sweeps along me and I miss his heat as I yank my flimsy skirt down as far as possible, which isn't very damn far. There's only one reason he's kidnapped me. He doesn't need money, and he's already at war. "My family will come after you with everything we have."

His eyes actually burn through the darkness. "Let them come, as I love a good fight." He lowers his chin. "Besides. Your family has absolutely no idea where you are. Nobody does."

SEVEN

❧❀❧

Thorn

Astonishingly, she falls asleep on the drive out to the coast, leaving the softest hint of honey on my tongue. Reaching into the front seat next to Justice, I secure a worn sweatshirt and cover her with it.

She cuddles into the material, her fingers wrapped around the collar, and shifts closer to me. What the hell? Murmuring something, she nudges my shoulder with her head. Frowning, I lift my arm and let her head fall onto my thigh, where she snuggles in with a soft sigh, turning on her side and curling her legs up on the seat. Her smooth, bare, soft-looking legs. Jesus. She might actually kill me and not know it.

Just how much alcohol did she drink? She shouldn't be asleep.

My gaze rises to meet Justice's in the mirror, and he quickly banishes the amusement he let lurk in his brown eyes for a moment.

I look back down as streetlights and then shadows take turns dancing on her smooth profile. Her mountainous hair flows across my thigh and her back, and even a saint couldn't refrain from sliding his fingers through those curly tresses.

I'm no fuckin' saint.

At the first touch, I learn that silk isn't the softest material in the world. Her hair . . . is. The playful strands wrap around my hand. This close, with the lights coming and going to torture me, I can see different colors in the thick mass. It's a deep sable with red, blonde, and even a darker tone in it. I bite back a groan, and my zipper cuts into the flesh of my cock.

Why does she feel safe with me?

Oh, there's no doubt she's sheltered and possibly innocent. Funny and truly stunning, and she obviously knows how to influence the masses. While she might not be a rocket scientist, she surely has to be smarter than this. Yet I look closer and see dark circles beneath her eyes, the ones that makeup camouflages.

When was the last time she slept? Has her impending wedding to Cal Sokolov kept her up? Her brows draw down as if she's reading my mind, and it takes every ounce of my self-control to refrain from rubbing the small wrinkle away. My hand in her hair is the only allowance I'll take with her asleep. She's safe for now.

She is a foreign creature to me. The women in my life are tough and live their own lives, expecting nothing from me but a rough night of sex that leaves us both panting. Satisfied physically. Not once have I felt this overwhelming sense of ownership. Yet knowing myself as I do, I easily recognize the edge beneath that feeling. It's darker and deadlier than anything she will ever want. She's too pure for me, but that won't last long. She's meant to be mine, and someday she'll crave the darkness.

No question.

"Are you sure about this?" Justice asks quietly.

I look up and give him my death stare—the one that makes

anybody in my organization piss their pants and then offer to stab themselves in the heart.

He looks back at the road, but not before I see the genuine concern in his eyes. Maybe it's for me. Or perhaps for her. He does know me, after all. "She's too good for an asswipe like Cal," I retort. A moot point considering she's mine.

"Agreed." He snorts. "She did surprise me when she tried to jump from the car."

My lips twitch and it takes me a second to recognize the feeling of a smile. "Her elbow made a decent impact on my throat." I like that she thought through her options and decided to escape the vehicle without screaming, crying, or threatening. She calmly and quietly tried to destroy my larynx and run.

"I expected more of a hysterical shriek or two." His gaze now turns appraising.

Not me. I've watched her for over a year, in person and on social media. The woman is calm and collected under pressure. "She was startled by the night's events and apparently exhausted." In sleep, she looks even more fragile, and warning passes through me. I'm not a bull in a china shop. No. Instead, I'm the silent whisper of death right before the pain starts. I can admit to myself that if anybody deserves the sickness imposed upon me, *the curse* as Justice calls it, it is me. Poetic justice. "I have no doubt she'll come at me again tomorrow." Truth be told, my neck is a little sore. I grin and then quickly frown.

What is wrong with me? Thank God Justice didn't just see that. What nonsense. I take my phone and speed-dial Wynd to make sure he hasn't killed everyone.

"Wynd."

"Status." I keep my voice low so as not to awaken Alana, and yank a harsh mint out of my pocket to eat and burn my taste buds temporarily. Wynd's words taste like pine needles, which isn't necessarily bad but is sometimes annoying.

"I left several breathing." My enforcer sounds calm but

slightly defensive. If he wants to succeed in our world, he needs to mask his emotions better.

I nod to Justice, whose jaw tightens. He'll take care of the matter. "Good. What did we get?" Hopefully a shit ton of pyrope garnets. I need them. Now. My phones are the most secure in the world, so he may speak safely.

"I checked with all three teams, and we secured a boatload of regular quartz data crystals and four odd pyramid-shaped crystals."

Damn it. No garnets. "Tell me about the odd ones."

"They're green if I look at them one way and kind of red in a different light."

Fuck. "Those sound like alexandrite crystals." I had expected the data crystals because Alana's daddy and thus Aquarius Social need a stronger storage device, and we've discovered that a blend of quartz crystals captures more data than any other element, but they burn out faster. So having more on hand is necessary for anybody with servers like the four competing social media companies.

The possible alexandrite crystals, so rare, are a surprise. I despise surprises. "Can you determine where the alexandrite came from?"

"No. At least, not yet."

That means he has left enough of the pickup crew alive to question. There is a good chance these are just couriers, but I will find out. I absently stroke Alana's hair and she sighs, scooting closer to me. My balls light on fire. "Pack those carefully and send them to my main headquarters along with the quartz."

"Of course," Wynd says.

The alexandrite, with its ability to change colors, has the propensity to speed up transfer and then store more data much faster than currently imaginable—and possibly a way to save my damn life. Apparently I'm not the only one with an eye on the tech. To think that Mathias Beaumont had almost gotten his blood-soaked hands on alexandrite is infuriating. I need to find out who else is this far ahead with the technology. If it isn't one of the three other social media companies, then we have a new player on the board who sold the alexandrite to him.

Wynd clears his throat. "Do you want to meet at the boat-house?"

I look down at the sleeping woman as darkness flows through my blood. The boathouse near the ocean is where I interrogate and play. "Yes. I want answers. There were supposed to be red garnets in those containers."

Wynd chuckles. "Yes, sir. Man, Beaumont is going to be pissed he's lost some of his shipments."

That isn't all he lost tonight. "Don't call again until you have relevant information." I click off.

Justice makes another turn. "No red garnets?"

"No." Like the other three families, one member has always been tied to certain crystals. In the stone ages, the ability looked like magic because the connection led to such great health and charisma, which helped gain power. In the computer ages, the bond put our families ahead of all other technological users. And now, in the social media era? We've become gods.

Unfortunately, an enemy figured out how to infect my main garnet, the one that runs all of our servers, with a freezing type of deadly virus that also transferred to me. I need healthy garnets to keep Malice Media running . . . and hopefully save my life. If I can just transfer my connection from the diseased main garnet to a healthy one, a large fucking one that I've been unable to find, hopefully I'll also be saved.

"We'll find a large garnet," I say, dialing my chief operating officer, the smartest computer programmer in the world.

"Kazstone," he answers as the sound of a keyboard clacking comes across the line.

"Search social media for Alana Beaumont." When I say her name, she shifts slightly, her nose scrunching. I tangle my fingers in her hair and knead her nape. The soft sound of pleasure she purrs nearly has me waking her up to better use that sweet mouth.

"Alana last posted before dinnertime tonight." More keys. "There's nothing more about her."

Good. Then he won't have to scrub the web this evening. "What about a shooting at Martini Money?"

Kaz is quiet for a moment. "Did you just say Martini Money?"

I let my silence speak for itself.

Keys clack again. "Nothing from the news outlets, but there are a few social media posts from private citizens. Scratch that. Nothing from Aquarius Social . . . or Hologrid Hub."

So Mathias is handling it from his end, as is Cal Sokolov. Or rather, his older brother is taking down any videos or statements regarding the night, and one of them got to the legacy news outlets, at least.

"Scrub anything from Malice Media, and full hack on Time-Gem Moments if you can do it." That takes care of all four of the big social media companies, where most of the world now gets their news. "I want no record of the shooting or of Alana after she posted."

"Not a problem." He sounds assured, just like I require him to be. "Anything else?"

I try to shift my weight but I'm still throbbing and fighting the urge to wake her up to force that sound of pleasure from her when she's conscious. Justice drives onto my property and the vehicle jostles us as he maneuvers over the bridge. "Yes. What is Mathias Beaumont up to right now?"

Kaz finds the info faster than I expect. "He's at home but his men are fanning out over the city looking for . . . Alana." The tempo speeds up. "Do you need me to find her?"

"No. Just keep an eye on Mathias as well as the Sokolov brothers. Check in hourly. If you have time on your hands, search the world to find anybody researching uses for alexandrite. Look for somebody new." I end the call. Now that we're on my property, my body finally relaxes. I look up to see the turrets glowing, maybe not with a welcome light but a familiar one. "Call Mrs. Pendrake and have her send clothes for Alana," I say to Justice.

"Got it." Justice stops the vehicle at the front door.

I open my door and slide out, carrying the woman with me. She feels light and defenseless in my arms, and beast that I am, I want her even more. Two days ago, I would have bet my entire fortune that such a thing was not possible. I was wrong. I curve my body to protect her from the rain and stalk inside, nodding at the guards and striding up the curved staircase to what I suppose is the guest bedroom. It has never been used.

Flicking on the light, I take in the king-sized bed with ivory bedspread. The room is decidedly feminine. Apparently my decorator expected a woman or two to visit. I pull back the heavy coverlet and gently lay her down, waiting for her to awaken.

She does not.

Instead, she mumbles and curls onto her side, facing me. Her skirt rides up and her blood-soaked halter rides down. The tops of her breasts are full and flawless. I blink and then catch sight of her ridiculous heels.

It's a miracle she was able to get to the storage room.

I don't want to leave her in those, and I need to touch her. Silently, I drop to my haunches and reach for one strap, releasing it and sliding the shoe away. My fingers brush the smooth skin of her ankle, and we both groan.

Jerking, I look up to see her eyes still shut and her mouth partly open.

I'm quicker with the second shoe, and then I stand, pulling

the bedcovers tight to her neck. I take a deep breath, inhaling the scent of honeysuckle. Is it her perfume or shampoo? Or is it just her? Whatever it is, the scent is made for me. Just for me.

So I turn and walk out of the room, glancing at my watch with its garnet crystals. It's time to go draw blood to gain answers. The woman may sleep peacefully tonight.

Tomorrow will come soon enough.

EIGHT

❦

Alana

I stretch awake, cocooned in luxurious silk and cotton. Yawning, I sit bolt upright in the bed. My nerves jangle and I suck in air. How could I have possibly fallen asleep the night before? I've been kidnapped by Thorn freakin' Beathach.

Had he somehow drugged me?

The sound of the ocean beating mercilessly against rocks filters through the room. I grind the heel of my hand into my left eye. Those three drinks were stronger than I thought, and coupled with the adrenaline of being shot at, my system must have shut down. But even so, where the heck am I?

The room is dark, so I fumble to the side and discover a bedside table and a lamp. It takes me a few seconds, but I find the knob and twist it to illuminate the room.

Panicking, I hurriedly look at the other side of the bed. It is empty. Good. Relief flows through me and I take in the fact that I'm still wearing my uncomfortable tanktop and skirt. Glancing down, I see dried blood all over my top and even my bare chest. My skin crawls, and I push my hair back over my shoulder.

The room is full of plush textures and opulent materials. I'm in an expensive four-poster bed with a gold-gilded frame up against cream-colored walls. Heavy velvet curtains cover what appear to be massive windows. They must have blackout materials, because no light is really coming in. The bedspread is a golden cream and the pillow's a light peach. The room is decidedly feminine, yet in looking around, I can see no personal touches.

There is no doubt that garnets are the room's highlight, as they are woven into the decor. I see the deep red gems in the drawer handles of the bedside tables and the matching armoire. Two overlarge garnet candleholders decorate the mantelpiece, and when I look closer, I discern delicate garnet accents woven into the throw pillows shoved to the side of the bed. Even if I hadn't noticed these, there is no question the sparkling garnet-and-crystal chandelier in the center of the ceiling displays its owner's talisman.

My gaze catches on stacked boxes near what I assume to be the main door, and I climb out of the bed, walk over, and open a couple. Clothes, from skirts to dresses to undergarments, overflow the containers.

How long does he plan to keep me here? I shiver.

I gingerly test the doorknob and am shocked to find it unlocked. But first, the bathroom beckons. I hurriedly grab a skirt, a sweater, panties, and cute black tennis shoes before running in and using the facilities, including an ultrafast shower to clean off the blood.

I'm a little too thrilled to find a toothbrush, and I clean my teeth before attempting to smooth some of the curls out of my hair. As usual, I fail, so I scramble through one of the many drawers and find a clip to pull part of the mass away from my face.

Dressing in the clothing, I pull on the tennis shoes, and then for some reason tiptoe toward the window. At the very least, I need to see where I am.

I start to open the shades and then stop instantly as I see the argyle pattern of multiple *X*s, created by hammered metal within the glass. The one that rules my nightmares. My stomach drops and I gag.

Reacting as if I've been burned, I backpedal hurriedly toward the main door. I don't have time for a full-blown panic attack. I open it as quietly as possible and peer into a vacant hallway. Its length stretches past multiple doors to a staircase at the end.

Huh? Well, this is just weird, but if I have a chance for freedom, I have to grab it with both hands. I slip outside and walk down the hallway to see a circular staircase leading down to what appears to be a foyer. The chandelier at least three stories above it is a good five times the size of the one in my temporary bedroom. The garnets gleam, beautifully polished, glinting cold fire.

I gulp. He brought me to his lair, and yet, there's nobody around. Does he truly think I'm that harmless? If so, I might as well push my luck a little bit more. I walk silently down the stairs to the polished tiles of the entryway. They're black and red and white, and the pattern is intriguing. I look around and see not a soul, so I cross to the front door and open it, walking quickly outside to a cobblestone driveway.

The world stretches out in front of me. A wide, perfectly manicured lawn all around the structure is surrounded by . . . Holy crap. Is that a moat? Yep. It's an actual moat.

Figures move at the far tree line, obviously on patrol, and I fight the urge to duck. At the moment, I have no idea what Thorn's orders are to his people, so I might as well test my boundaries. Trying to calm my nerves, I look up at the sky and note dark clouds gathering again, but at least the rain has ebbed. However, there's no doubt the earth has already been saturated.

Crossing the cobblestone walk as if I have every right to explore, I soon reach the large expanse of drenched grass. The individual blades cling to my tennis shoes and soak them as I keep walking, wishing I had searched for a jacket, but it's too late to turn back now.

Halfway across the expansive lawn, I pivot and glance back at the home. What I see makes me stumble, and then I straighten my legs. On all that is holy. The guy has a castle fortress. The structure is very modern-day, with stone in varying shades of gray and blue that match the tumultuous ocean on its far side. Craning my neck, I can see down the coastline. We're atop a huge cliff, and the ocean, angry and stormy, rolls out before me.

Rosebushes, red and white, line the entire drive, their thorns evident from where I stand.

Shivering, I turn and continue on my trek across this wide—way too wide—lawn. Oh, I understand the defensive strategy that anybody crossing the clearing remains in clear sight. I get that. What I don't understand is why nobody has stopped me.

As I near the moat, I see the raised metal and wood bridge with garnets inlaid in its intricate railing. The guy actually has a drawbridge. I shake my head. This place would be mystical and magical if it wasn't owned by my enemy. I look closer at the moat. The water curves in a half circle from one end of the property around to the other, ending on either side at the cliffs. I wonder how often he has to fill it, or if the rain does that for him.

On the other side of the moat is another clear space of manicured lawn before the trees take over. The narrow driveway continues on until it disappears out of sight. All right. I learned how to swim when I was just a child, so I can escape right now. Perhaps Thorn didn't expect me to have the courage to run away.

Insult and hope mingle inside me.

Just as I'm about to gather my courage and dive into what no doubt is freezing cold water, several men emerge from the forest on the other side, all with guns pointed at me. I cock my head. If they have orders to shoot, they would have already done so. Even so, I wring my hands together.

A shot fires behind me, and I jump a good foot before turning and swallowing wildly.

Thorn Beathach is already halfway across the lawn, today dressed in black slacks and a white button-down shirt that looks much more at home on him than the casual clothing he wore the night before. He smoothly tucks his gun at the back of his waist, and I can see that there's something else in his other hand, an object wrapped in white paper.

He cuts a sharp figure against his moody castle as he strides calmly over the meticulously manicured lawn. His sleeves are rolled up, revealing tautly muscled forearms, and the top of that crisp shirt is unbuttoned, offering a glimpse of bronze skin with ink. I hadn't noticed his tattoo the night before.

The breeze picks up and ruffles his hair as if she can't resist his pull.

It shocks me then. He's good-looking. Not just handsome but brutally so. A stirring tugs deep in my abdomen that doesn't make sense.

Isn't there a saying about predators holding beauty? All natural hunters are striking. Heat flushes into my face and I have to force myself to remain still. I want to take a step back, but falling into the water would dampen my defiant glare. So instead, I set my stance and watch him walk closer.

He's even more devastating in the gloomy morning light than he was the night before. The scar across his face gives him a look of danger. No, scratch that. He *is* danger. The scar merely confirms the fact. I'd forgotten already how big he is, six foot six at least. The silver in his eyes looks mellow this morning, and I try to gather my thoughts. How is he not angry that I'm attempting an escape?

Or is he about to strike?

"Did you have a nice walk?" he asks calmly as he nears me. While his body is relaxed, those eyes burn with threat and promise. A deadly combination but one that almost has me turning to run away. But I don't stand a chance fleeing him. With him comes that inevitable heat he gives off, as well as the scent of . . . What is that? Testosterone and cedar? I truly don't know.

"I thought I'd head home," I say lamely. "Have you seen my phone?"

"I threw it out of the window last night," he says in the same conversational tone.

My legs feel weak. "I need a phone."

He isn't fazed. "You haven't earned one. *Yet.*"

I clench my fingers. If I decide to fight him, a surprise attack is my only chance. "I'm not staying long enough for you to acquire a phone for me."

"You're staying as long as I want you." He hands over the white-wrapped package.

The paper crinkles in my hand and my throat goes bone dry. "What's this?"

"Open it."

My hands tremble slightly as I unwrap a raw steak. "I don't eat raw food."

"It's a steak."

"I know it's a steak," I burst out. "Why are you handing it to me?"

He chuckles, the sound rough. "Throw it into the water."

My lungs seize, and I slowly pivot to stare at the quiet water. Oh, this is so not good. Nevertheless, curiosity rides me, so I gingerly grasp the side of the bloody meat and toss it into the moat.

An instant frenzy explodes as whatever is in there fights for pieces. Water sprays, and bubbles blow in every direction. A high-pitched shriek splits the surface. I take an unwilling step back.

He smiles. "I wouldn't swim in the pond if I were you, beauty."

"What is in there?" I ask, my voice hushed.

"Everything you don't want to encounter. There's even quicksand at the bottom, though what's in there won't let you sink that low before consuming you."

I shiver and look around. Apparently, the drawbridge is the only way across that killing field. This at least explains why nobody seemed too concerned when I walked out of the castle. I look furtively toward the ocean.

"It's a sheer rock cliff," he says. "There's no way down— except via gravity and the certainty of painful death."

I don't believe him. There is no question in my mind that he has escape routes from this fortress. However, I have no idea where they are. "You know this is kidnapping?"

"I'm well aware. It's the least of my sins." He gestures back toward the house. "I don't think trying to sneak out of my house is being very obedient. I'm giving you this one because you didn't know you have the run of the property if you want. There's nowhere for you to go."

We'll just see about that. He'd never trap himself in a situation like this. I know it. There have to be tunnels out of here. "I'll see you in prison for this."

He blinks. Just once as if I'm boring him. "You have to be hungry. Come back inside."

I set my stance. "I'm not agreeing to stay here."

"I don't need your agreement." His brief smile lightens his whole face, and I can only stare. He's no more approachable than before, but the flash of white teeth and tilt of his eyes contrasts so starkly with the cruel scar that he is masculine beauty personified. The rawest and most primitive incarnation of maleness is right in front of me. My knees weaken. Oh, I don't like this side of myself, but curiosity has always plagued me. Even when I know I'm going to get burned.

Something boils red hot inside me. I should be angry and I should be kicking him. "You don't want me for an enemy." I'm deadly serious but have no idea how I'm going to back that up.

"Call yourself whatever you want." He takes my arm, his touch electric and firm. "I'm calling you *mine*."

NINE

Thorn

When we arrive in my palatial kitchen, I indulge myself and grasp her waist, lifting her onto the sprawling marble counter.

Her small gasp is tinged with honey. "I can sit in a chair."

"I prefer you here," I say, noting the breakfast spread on the island. Mrs. Pendrake must've gone to the grocery store before cooking eggs and bacon.

Alana looks over at the wide windows revealing the churning ocean, and her shoulders relax. I ponder her reaction. Is there something about the ocean that calms her? Interesting.

I spear a piece of juicy cantaloupe from the platter and press it against her lush lips. "Eat. It's your favorite." Mine as well, which is why we keep the fruit on hand.

Her eyes widen and she stubbornly presses her lips together. She's cute. Adorable, even. I clamp one hand on her thigh and she startles, opening her mouth so I can push in the delectable treat.

She glares but chews and swallows. "What makes you think I like cantaloupe?"

"It's your favorite. I know everything about you."

Her chin lowers. "I'm not eating out of your hand."

"Don't throw out challenges you can't meet," I retort. "Would you like coffee?"

Need sparks in her eyes.

My balls respond in kind.

Without making her ask, I pluck a mug off the top shelf and pour her a good portion. I know from my research that she likes oat milk and honey with her coffee. "As I wasn't planning on taking you quite yet, I don't have anything with which to lighten this except regular milk."

She accepts the mug, wrapping both of her small hands around it. A lovely pink color filters over her skin, and I can't help but wonder what she'll look like in the throes of orgasm. Pleasure belongs on her face. "Why the unplanned kidnapping?" She takes a deep drink and her delighted hum nearly knocks me to my knees.

I frown. "You always take yours with sugar."

More challenge tilts those unreal eyes, sharpening the green. "Don't believe everything you see."

Fair enough. I move into her, pushing her legs apart and settling where I want to be, standing while she's balancing on the counter. "I like that about you."

More color fills her face. That statement pleases her, and she doesn't want it to. Oh, I can sense the sweet lightness in her, and she's a perfect blend for the darkness in me. Soon she'll admit the truth. "Back away," she snaps.

"You don't want me to." I lean in, noting her quick intake of breath. "Why do you hide the way you take your coffee?"

"Because I can."

Now that, I understand. How intriguing. Just how much do I actually know about her?

She clears her throat. "Again, why the unplanned kidnapping?"

"Sources informed me about the raid on the club, which was focused on you. To kill or take, I don't know. So I decided to take you first."

Her nostrils flare. "You're a killer and I don't like you."

"Yes I am, and I don't care."

Her jaw tightens. "I need to contact my friends."

"No." I lean to the side and scoop up a spoonful of scrambled eggs to press against her mouth.

Glaring, she accepts the treat and swallows. "Please."

Please. Said as a soft entreaty. I would've instantly shut down yelling or demands, or even worse, crying. But the gentle request hits me hard in the chest. Why, I don't know, since there's nothing in there. Is she playing me?

She tilts her head, studying me right back. Most people can't maintain eye contact with me for long. Oh, she struggles, but her shoulders tighten and she meets my gaze, her blush deepening.

I admire that. Hell. I knew I wanted her—not in a million years did I expect to like her. "Why?" I ask.

She blinks. Finally. "They'll be worried about me."

I find it interesting that she wants to reassure her friends, not her family. "I'm sure your merry band of do-gooders can survive without you for a short time."

Surprise darkens her eyes. "What do you mean?"

"Don't play dumb," I warn her. "I know all about Rosalie, Ella, and once in a while Merlin, who lives at Rosalie's boardinghouse for the ancient. Getting the state senator's wife to safety was a risky proposition. Good job on that." I feed her another bite before focusing on her again. "I understand you don't have a way to dispose of the senator. I would be happy to do so for you."

She sips her coffee again, obviously thinking through my offer.

Fuck. I like her even more.

Regret turns down her plush lips. "Thank you, but I don't want that on either of our souls."

Her answer surprises me. "My soul is black as tar. Don't worry about it."

Her chin lifts. "It's never too late to reform, Thorn. I won't be responsible for adding to your burdens."

That makes zero sense. I've kidnapped her, for crap's sake. I reach for a wooden spoon with garnets decorating its handle and stir the eggs on the platter.

Mrs. Pendrake hustles in from the nearby laundry room with another carafe of coffee. "I didn't know if you wanted decaf." She places it on the counter.

Alana stiffens.

I frown and turn, looking at Mrs. Pendrake as an outsider would. She's around sixty with spiky white hair and burn marks down one side of her face into her clothing from a fire she barely survived in her thirties. Before I hired her to manage my homes. Tattoos line her neck and arms, and she has more piercings in her face than ten rebellious teenagers put together. She's box-shaped and wearing old jeans and a bright blue sweatshirt that makes her look even boxier. "Alana, this is Mrs. Pendrake. She'll get you anything you want."

Mrs. Pendrake nods, her expression blank. "There's a notepad in the drawer by the fridge. Leave me a list, and I'll go shopping immediately." She glances at me. "Two cameras caught you in downtown San Francisco last night. I'm having them wiped but will need more discretionary cash."

"Of course." I fight a grin as Alana tries to press her knees together and force me out from between her legs. Nobody will ever force me out of this place, and she might as well learn that now. So I grasp her thighs and spread them further apart, digging in my thumbs, the countertop cold against my legs.

The little squeak she makes sends a dark thrill through me.

Mrs. Pendrake turns and leaves, no doubt hiding her disapproval. I don't care.

Alana looks at her half-full coffee mug.

"I wouldn't," I warn.

"You have no sense of decorum," she snaps, smartly deciding not to toss the liquid at my face. "What were you doing in San Francisco last night that you don't want on camera?"

"Killing five people." I had promised her no lies.

She pales, but unmistakable interest shows in her expression. "Why?"

"Because I wanted to." Sometimes the simplest explanation is best.

A knock on the side door has her jumping. "Come in," I call out.

She struggles again and I press in, lifting her thighs and forcing her to either wrap them around my waist or fall back on the counter. Grunting, she puts down the coffee mug and grabs my shirt for balance. "You're such an ass."

Maybe, but her thighs are wrapped around me and unwilling desire is darkening her eyes.

The side door opens and Justice walks in, his intense gaze taking in the scene. "*While this is cozy, even with the news blacked out, you need to know that the entire fucking city is on high alert because of her disappearance.*" He speaks in Gaelic, which might be considered rude.

Alana just looks at him. Is she accustomed to being dismissed in such a way? I find I don't like that. At all.

"Stop being a prick and speak in English, Justice," I say in English, partially turning my head so I can see them both.

One of his dark eyebrows rises.

She watches him. "You know, I didn't see it last night, but there is a resemblance between the two of you."

The entire world thinks I'm the last standing recluse in my entire family. Her keen eye is yet another intriguing aspect to her. "You're right," I say. "We're brothers."

Shock sizzles in Justice's eyes for a second. "You're going to kill her?" He speaks in English this time.

She pales.

"No," I growl. "I promised her no lies last night. Remember?" Justice looks like he's about to fall over a cliff.

I give her a glare. "She'll keep our confidence." My voice is heavy with threat.

She looks from me to him, paling. "Thorn and Justice? Seriously?"

Justice shuffles his massive boot. He's dressed in dark jeans and a black shirt, and no doubt he's been prowling the city all morning. "Our father didn't exactly like us."

She bites her bottom lip. "I'm sorry, Justice. I know how that feels."

Justice draws back.

I save him before he can propose to her or do something equally ridiculous like try to save her from me. It is one thing to know she's beautiful and creative and quite another to realize her heart is truly as sweet and pure as advertised. Plus, she's courageous. I hadn't expected that. "Justice? What have you found?"

He focuses. "The three gang members who infiltrated the club to take Alana last night are dead."

"Killed by Sokolov's men?" I ask.

He nods. "The guards fired almost instantly, and my sources relate that Hendrix took out at least one of them. I've tracked down two more members of their gang, Twenty-One Purple out of Oakland, and we can speak with them tonight after we leave them on ice all day."

Good. I'd like to know who has orders regarding Alana sooner rather than later, and I'm well acquainted with that gang. They run drugs and women, and like most gangs, are incredibly territorial. I don't like that they have her in their sights.

As if reading my mind, she narrows her gaze. "Why are you trying to help me?"

It's a good question. "I told you. I'm obsessed with you."

The words should terrify her. Instead, she purses her lips. "You don't know me."

I am learning that to be true.

"So you're just a superficial bastard who likes what he sees."

I grab her ass and pull her tighter against me, my cock against her pretty blue panties that look like one of the thongs I'd purchased for her. "I fucking love what I see. Do you have a problem with that?"

The pulse beats wildly in her neck. I can see it. "Yes." She spits out the word, but adorable confusion lingers in her angry eyes.

I don't blame her. She doesn't understand the raw connection I'm forging between us yet. She will. She'll learn to crave it. "You're in danger, and nobody threatens what's mine." It's as close as I can come to explaining to her, and I don't explain to anybody.

She sweeps a hand toward the back doors. "Your own brother knocks on your door. You obviously aren't close to anybody."

I remain distant from Justice so I can keep him alive. "You and I are going to be so close you won't know where you end and I begin. Even more importantly, you won't fucking care."

Justice keeps his expression carefully blank. "Do you want me to plant a trail for her? It's not unthinkable to believe she might run away after being thrown to the Sokolov man-child."

Panic lights her eyes. "Just how long is this kidnapping going to last? I have work to do."

The longer she's away from Aquarius Social, the easier it is to take them down. I don't like the idea of hurting her, and leaving her with nothing is not my intention. "You're with me so long as I'm alive."

One of her eyebrows arches. "Why?"

There are many answers I can give to her, but I go with the

simplest truth. "You're my reason for breathing, and you were meant to be mine."

That intrigue enters her eyes again and she shoves it away. Poor confused girl. "You're nuts."

"Quite possibly," I agree. "Are we any closer on the other matter?" I ask Justice.

"Yes." Justice runs a hand through his thick hair. "Kaz says the alexandrite crystals we stole are faster than anything he's ever seen and thus may be able to solve your problem in time." He wisely keeps from revealing that I'm dying.

I switch to Gaelic like the unrepentant asshole I am. *"How close is he?"*

"He's talking to himself, which is a good sign," Justice returns in our native language. *"He might even be able to trace the virus back to the source. At least we'll have a starting point."*

Humans break easier than technology.

Vengeance fills my body with heat. Good. Whoever is trying to kill me needs to bleed. Now it is just a matter of having enough time to dig out the leads. Since I'm being an ass and speaking in a language foreign to her, I figure I'll get it all out now. *"I want Wynd on the op tonight when we speak with the two gang members you've secured to question about the hit on Alana in that stupid bar. He needs to see more blood."*

"Agreed," Justice says. *"Sorry we didn't acquire more garnets in the other raid."*

Sometimes rumors are false. If Malice Media is going to continue to operate successfully, we need a new garnet for the servers. One that will hopefully connect to Justice. *"It wasn't false intel. There are garnets out there we don't have."* It makes sense one of the other families is collecting garnets. It isn't like I don't have plenty of stores of their crystals on hand.

He glances at Alana. *"We're being jerks and she's just watching us curiously and enjoying that coffee way too much. Did you put honey in it?"*

"I'm out of honey," I retort. *"She's surprisingly adaptable."*

He shrugs. *"You need a calm and submissive woman. Why don't you keep her?"*

"I said adaptable. Submission is something a man earns." The idea of her on her knees before me tightens every muscle in my body. *"Where does her father think she is?"*

"He has no idea," Justice says smugly. *"Your name is being bandied around, along with the names of his other enemies. There's also a thread suggesting she has run away."*

That's what I figure. *"Any problems?"*

"Yes. Her pal Rosalie has gone to the press three times, and that little hacker Ella is busy planting seeds online trying to find her. They're both a pain in the ass."

I look to where she's calmly watching us speak. *"The three of them seem surprisingly close."* On the surface, anyway. I've watched Alana try to keep her distance, some distance, from those she cares about. She's smart. Those you love are liabilities, and unless you're strong enough to take out any enemy, not worth the risk. She's worth it. I'll demolish anybody who tries to hurt her.

"Do you want me to take them out?" Justice asks.

"No. We'll take the two men requiring interrogation to the boathouse. Has the place been cleared?" The crystal couriers of the night before had known more than I thought but didn't resist my persuasion very long. One seemed truly opposed to pain. In fact, he'd had an appointment to fetch an underage girl from the tent city as soon as he had finished work. Their bodies are now feeding the fish in the ocean.

"Yes. I'll take care of it." With a nod to Alana, he strides out of the kitchen.

I turn back to my woman. "Sorry about that."

"No, you're not."

No, I'm not. Her scent envelops me and I want to toss her onto her stomach and explore her stunning backside. Instead, I figure she's done challenging me for the moment so I set her back on the counter.

Her thighs immediately drop and she pulls down the skirt, trying to shimmy away to the other side.

"Stop moving." I reach into my back pocket and drag out a secure satellite phone that even Kaz can't hack. "Call your friends and lie."

She accepts the device, calculation in her gaze. "Isn't rule number one no lying?"

I lean in, making sure I have her attention. "No lying to *me*."

"Ah." A small dimple twinkles in her right cheek. "I see." She cocks her head. "What do you want me to say?"

"Up to you. But if you don't convince them that you're fine and to stop looking for you, I'm going to kill them." I let her see the killer inside me. It's time I stop hiding from her, anyway.

She pales and her hand trembles as she dials. Then her face brightens as her friend answers, and if I didn't know better, she'd convince *me* that she's decided to take a stand and disappear for a while. When she retells the part about Cal asking about her hymen, I can hear the ring of truth. Finally, after her friends promise to stop being nuisances, she ends the call and throws the phone at me.

I snag it out of the air and deposit it safely in my back pocket. "Are you a virgin?" I ask bluntly.

Her chin lifts and her eyes glitter. "Yes. Rumor has it that breaching my hymen leads to certain death unless said use is sanctioned by my father." Her tone is pissed.

Good. It should be. Her father is an ass.

She continues speaking. "Apparently that's a requirement for marrying Cal. Bragging rights and all of that."

"That's not going to be a problem for long."

She opens her mouth to argue, no doubt, and I take it. She tastes like cantaloupe, coffee, and honey, and I dive in, taking every ounce of her in a brutal kiss. For a heartbeat, she struggles, and then opens beneath my assault, meeting my tongue with hers.

I slide my hand beneath her sweater and move up to cup her breast before pinching her nipple.

She stiffens and then moans, leaning into my touch.

I release her, knowing if this goes any further we won't be leaving the house all day, and I have too much work to do. Mainly to survive.

She stares at me, eyes wide, cheeks rosy, lungs panting.

"Remember your rules today, Alana." With that, I walk out of the room while I still can.

TEN

Alana

I eat half of the massive breakfast and then clean the kitchen, my mind burning. What is wrong with me? I was aroused in seconds by a cold-blooded killer. He doesn't hide who he is from me, so that's no excuse.

That kiss nearly blew off my head, and if he'd tried to take it further, I would've let him. I've never felt like that admirable of a person, but needing his touch is sick.

It's pathetic, but I mean, the man looks like a god. That's no excuse, but still. My girly parts would have to go dead for me not to notice, and frankly, one look at him and they'd probably come right back to life. Sure, I shouldn't have challenged him. That much I know. But the moment was too perfect, and I have a feeling nobody challenges him. He's too scary.

I want to be different from everybody else to him. Why, I am choosing not to examine because nobody wants to see the darkness inside themselves. Well, nobody but Thorn. He embraces it.

The talk about a virus was intriguing. Is Malice Media having a computer problem?

There has to be a way out of this place, and I'm nearly panicked enough to risk the monster in the moat. I have to get away from this man.

The simple skirt and sweater won't work, so I wander back up to the guest room to find all of my new clothing unpacked in the opulent closet. Humming, I run my fingers across the many fabrics, deciding upon a mint-green minidress with an aquamarine belt.

The thoughtfulness of the belt startles me.

Gulping, I change into it as well as bright red stilettos, then enter the bathroom and discover a trove of new makeup in a side drawer. Soon my lips are as red as the shoes and my hair teased wildly into what appears to be sex hair. Well, so I've been told.

Giving myself a silent pep talk, I gather my discarded clothing from the night before and return to the vestibule, trying to drum up tears. Darn it. I'm not a crier. Even for effect. Sighing, I hustle through the sprawling castle to the kitchen and dig an onion out of the fridge, sniffing until my eyes properly swell. I do need to learn how to cry on demand.

My eyes burning, I sling the offensive vegetable back into the drawer and hurry to the front door, yanking it open and stumbling across the cobblestones. The clouds have opened, causing more rain to drum down. Good. I'll look even more pathetic soaking wet.

The guards allow me to make it onto the wet grass before one intercepts me. Thank goodness. I thought for sure I'd have to walk to that terrifying moat, and these heels are not made for a lawn.

"Miss?" The guy is young with dark hair and concerned green eyes. A thick accent colors his words. Fully Irish. "Ya need to get yerself back inside. A storm's a'comin."

I look at him, the fake tears mingling with the rain on my face. "I can't," I hiccup. "I mean, he kidnapped me. I must get home to my family." I flutter my eyelashes and look properly sad. "Nobody will feed my cat. Sir Hissalot."

His eyebrows rise. "I'm sure somebody will feed the animal." He gently takes my arm. "Please let me escort yer back inside."

I turn and stumble in the mile-high heels, catching his jacket as I go.

"Whoa." He helps me up.

"Thank you," I sniff, straightening. With a shudder, I allow him to walk me to the front door and deposit me safely inside. When the door shuts, I grin and kick off the heels before drawing his phone from my left hand. He'd secured it inside his breast pocket and hopefully won't discover it missing too soon. Looking around, I run through the castle to the kitchen and then outside the back into the storm. If Thorn has listening or tracking devices in the structure, I'm safer outside.

I walk out onto a covered deck with a barbecue toward the cliff and peer over. With the rain and crashing waves, any listening devices won't catch everything. Studying the phone, I determine it's probably protected, anyway.

The thing is locked. Damn it. I try several codes, trying for anything related to garnets or the Irish mob, but I need the young soldier's face.

All right. There's only one solution. Every phone, even locked, can dial an SOS emergency call. I press the buttons and wait. I have to escape Thorn before I get all twisted up and want to stay. It's unthinkable. I push the buttons again.

Nothing. Not a thing.

Biting my lip, I do it again.

Shoot. Thorn somehow disengaged the emergency function on his people's phones. There's no way to get help.

I give up and walk over the wet cement to the kitchen, wondering where to look for the secret passages. Beyond the kitchen is an extravagant dining room with a man's study next. The windows have the offensive argyle inlays and I instantly feel sick. Gulping, I close the heavy velvet drapes and examine Thorn's desk. It isn't made of wood. Instead, it's all obsidian, heavy and solid. A plasma television, wide and long, is mounted across from the desk, along with filing cabinets and a bar, complete with much older Scotch than I've ever seen.

The place smells like him. Like testosterone and danger with a hint of the wild forest. My thighs clench. This hold he somehow seems to have on me has to be ignored. I have a job to do.

I sit in his tall leather chair and meticulously go through his drawers. There's nothing of interest anywhere. In fact, I don't see any bit of personalization in the room—or the parts of his home that I've searched so far. It's as if he lives here but not really. Several large garnets in raw form are placed strategically around the room.

Going to the walls, I tap along them, trying to find a hidden door. There is nothing.

I blow out air. This is actually getting boring.

So I exit the room and wander through several sitting rooms until I open a door and nearly orgasm on sight.

It's a library. No. Not just a library—but the library of all libraries. A cluster of tables sits in the middle of a three-story room beneath the largest chandelier I've ever seen. Beyond the desks are reading areas, several including sofas. But it's the books. Obsidian bookshelves line three full walls of the room from the floor to the high ceiling. Each wall has a ladder that moves along the marvelous tomes.

The final wall is a wide window overlooking the angry Pacific. These windows are clear without the argyle crisscross shape, and my entire body sings. I pause at the sight of a glass-topped table near the door and then hurry over to peer inside. The books are all about crystals and appear ancient. Holding my breath, I lift the lid and pull out a book inlaid with rose quartz. It warms in my hand. My heart heating, I open the front flap to read in Gaelic about the ancient stone. There's even a fairy tale I've never heard about lost love.

Smiling, I place it carefully back in its place and run my fingers over the other volumes.

I turn and look for a place to hide my ill-gotten phone and decide upon a lower bookshelf between original volumes of an ancient and mostly unknown Gaelic philosopher that look well read. I spend the following hours poring over first editions, discovering new philosophers that even I haven't discovered yet. I break for lunch and then a dinner of more eggs, happy to be alone with all the books and trying to concentrate and not relive that kiss in the kitchen. Or how he'd forced my thighs apart and pinched my nipple.

I don't like pain.

But I did. I'm very much afraid I wanted more of it. I have to get out of here.

Finally, I take an edition of the early works of Seneca the Younger and a newer edition of *Catcher in the Rye* off the top shelf and sit on a sofa to read, allowing the pouring rain and the silent house to lull me to sleep.

"That's quite a choice you have there." Thorn's voice pulls me from a dream about misty moors and lost loves.

I jerk and sit up, letting the books fall to my lap. "I, ah, like the cover of this one, but it's in Latin." Which I read, by the way. "So I read a little bit of *Catcher in the Rye*. It's funny." Actually, it's poignant, but I'm feeling out of my element.

He drapes his black blazer over a chair and rolls up one white shirt sleeve. Something is off. His gaze doesn't leave me. "Where's the phone?"

I push myself to my feet, feeling too vulnerable on the sofa. I'm not quite awake yet. "What phone? I looked but couldn't find one in your office."

His chin lifts.

It occurs to me that I just broke rule number one.

"Bring him in," Thorn says with absolutely no inflection in his voice.

I turn as Justice pushes in the guard whose phone I stole. The younger man is pale but his jaw is set.

Thorn's eyes are cold. No humanity lurks in them, and I startle into being instantly awake, unable to swallow. He studies me. "I see you took his phone. Never play poker." He doesn't look at his brother. "Kill him."

"No." I burst forward and stop, my bare feet sliding on the chilly floor. "Don't kill him. It's my fault."

Thorn barely cocks his head. "Dermot lost his phone. You say you don't have it. That's unforgivable."

I gulp. Completely outmatched. "The phone is between the third and fourth volumes of Francesco Millentonic's *Philosophies*," I whisper, trying not to wring my hands together.

Justice silently moves to the bookshelf and finds the phone. Perhaps he spends a lot of time in here—most of the world has never heard of Millentonie.

My chest finally fills with air.

"Good. Now toss his useless ass off the cliff," Thorn says, still pinning me with his glacial gaze. Whatever warmth I thought I'd seen in those silver flecks is gone. Had I imagined that?

"No," I say, my voice hoarse, looking up a good foot to meet those eyes. "You can't kill him. I took the phone. It's my fault."

Thorn finishes rolling up his other sleeve, revealing more tattoos of what look like garnets, rosebuds, skulls, and barbed wire along with a Gaelic saying or two . . . dealing with blood oaths. "It was his phone and he lost it."

Anger flushes through me so quickly I sway. "Yet it's my fault. Jesus. You're as bad as my father."

That catches his attention. "Excuse me?"

"With the emotional blackmail. I did something you didn't like, and you're going to put this poor man's death on my head so I don't do it again. That's not only pathetic, it's fucking evil." Wires of fury snap through me, and I look for a weapon. "It's not just unfair but fundamentally wrong for a man, a real man, to use a woman's emotions against her." My ears heat so fast, I'm surprised they don't burn right off my head. "Act as to treat humanity . . . in every case as an end withal, never as means only," I spit at him.

He pauses. "Did you just quote Kant?"

"It fits," I hiss, so angry my throat hurts.

He crosses his arms, looking even more threatening. I can handle the danger, but the coldness in his eyes is something else.

Justice clears his throat. "Thorn—" He instantly stops as Thorn levels him with a look.

"Please don't kill him." My anger morphs into fear. "I'm begging you."

He turns back to me, tall and broad, pissed and dangerous. "No, you're not."

Oh. Dread slithers through my gut. Fine. I drop to my knees, my head bowed. If it saves the soldier, it's worth the pride. "Please don't kill him, Thorn." The tile floor is freezing on my knees.

"Look at me," he orders.

I look up, surprised to feel tears in my eyes.

The silver flecks in his disappear. "Take him outside and beat the shit out of him. I'll let you know later if she's convinced me to spare his life."

I catch a flash of relief in Justice's eyes and a bit of dread in Dermot's. But at least he'll be alive for the time being.

I stand, my legs wobbling. "I'll be going now."

"You broke rule number one, Alana. I gave you fair warning of the consequences."

My head jerks and my heart rate skyrockets into the unhealthy zone. He isn't joking.

Like all prey, I let instinct take over and run.

ELEVEN

❦

Alana

He catches me at the doorway, one arm banded around my waist lifting me off the ground. I was so close. His low chuckle rumbles through the silent library and I realize he let me get that far. Temper streaks through me and I struggle in his hold, turning to punch him in the neck and following with several kicks to whatever part of him I can find.

Every blow glances off his hard body, hurting my hand but not hampering his stride. Panic rushes through me like a live electrical wire in water.

He sits on the vacated sofa and smoothly flips me over, face-down. My abdomen impacts his hard thighs and the air whooshes out of my lungs while my hair falls to the floor. This is not happening. He tosses my skirt up and cool air brushes my nearly bare ass. Why did I wear a thong?

The first jolt of his displeasure lands hard, smack in the middle of my butt.

Pain blows through me—along with more humiliation. I rear

up, shrieking, reduced to raw fury. Coughing, I struggle wildly, more animal than human. He plants a hard palm in the center of my back, eliminating any hope of freedom.

Then he hits me again.

I hear the slap before heated pain spreads out from his hand, down my thighs and up my back. Never in my life have I been treated like this. "You fucking son of—"

The next slap is even harder, and I suck in breath, the words sticking in my throat. I exercise and I know how to fight. Yet I'm helpless against his strength, and that, more than anything, infuriates me even more.

Until he rains down a series of blows that has my ass on fire. "You're gonna want to submit sooner rather than later, baby," he rumbles. He hits every spot with his over-fucking-large hand, top, bottom, and both sides, more than once, no doubt coloring my rear brighter than the garnets inlaid in the floor. I hadn't noticed them before.

Tears blur my vision.

Warmth rushes through my skin, pricking every nerve on the way. Somehow, the pain turns to something else—something with a bite I don't recognize. But I need. This makes no sense. I stiffen, fighting us both. A flash of fire burns right to my clit, making me throb. Wetness dampens my thighs and it takes every ounce of my self-control to keep from rubbing against him. My nipples sharpen so fast and hard they hurt in a way I've never experienced, and every inch of my skin feels electrified. And needy.

His hand moves from my lower back to tangle in my hair and he wrenches my head back, forcing me to meet his gaze. Those silver streaks are back, giving him a primitive look. A dominant, firm, unyielding look that I'll remember to my grave. "Submit." He says the word slowly, fully enunciating each syllable of the harsh order. His other palm flattens over my punished butt, pressing in the heat.

I moan. "I already did. I begged for the guard's life."

"No. You and me. Right here and right now. You submit." His eyes flare and for a second, I see the primal being at his core. His face is sharp angles and rough hollows, with his scar darkening as his nostrils flare.

I swallow, tears sliding down my face. "No."

He blinks. Just once. Then I'm facedown again and he's fully unleashed, spanking me with absolutely no mercy. The heated feelings inside me intensify, sparking my blood and nerves alive. The pain turns to pleasure then to need, raw and devastating. My muscles give, and I relax against him, my body taking over from my mind.

When I soften, he pauses, once again palming my butt. I moan again and move restlessly against his hand. "Good girl," he murmurs, pressing down.

I arch, trying to get my clit anywhere near his hard thigh.

"No, sweetheart. Submission is more than physical. Now you count out ten."

Tears leak from my eyes, the words far away. What did he say? My head is filled with cotton and my body is a strung electrical wire.

He smacks me hard, dead center. "Count."

"One," I hiss, wanting to issue a death threat but not having the guts. Not right now, anyway. I count them out, and he doesn't go any easier. Finally, we reach ten, and I sob the word. Finally, he stops. My breath is panting out, and tears are still sliding down my face, but my mind has gone blank.

His hand curves over my butt to my very wet pussy, and he pinches me.

I shriek and buck against him, nerves short-circuiting throughout me.

"We're not done." He slides one finger inside me and then presses on my clit with his thumb.

It's too much. I gyrate against him, desperate for relief. Even his chuckle is sexy.

"Admit you like this," he orders darkly.

"No," I protest instantly, my mind overriding my body.

He flicks me and then circles my clit, his other hand pressing down on my abused butt.

"Thorn," I whisper shakily, trying to ride his hand. I don't care about humility or even breathing right now. The need is too great.

He tugs on my clit and I bite my lip hard enough to taste blood. Then he rubs my sex, lightly, teasing me. "Say it."

"I like this." My body takes over for my mouth and shoots my brain to hell.

"You like me spanking you."

I blink and a tear falls to the garnet-encrusted floor. "Yes."

He smacks my ass. Hard. "Say it."

"I like you spanking me." I hate him. Really hate him.

"I know." He plunges two fingers inside me, slaps my butt again, and scrapes my clit.

I explode from within, blowing out into shards of ecstasy. Maybe agony. Both. The climax rips through me as he fucks me with his fingers, my body riding him as the sharp-edged pleasure rips through me. Finally, sobbing, I come down, my ears ringing.

He turns me over and plants me on his lap. I wince as my bruised butt hits his thighs. Gently, his callused thumbs wipe off my cheeks. "You did a good job, beautiful."

The praise is confusing. Part of me wants to snuggle into his chest and let him hold me. The other wants to find a gun. "I hate you," I say on a choked sob.

"Hate and love are but two sides of the same coin, forged in the same mixing of metals. Like pain and pleasure." One of his dark eyebrows rises as he runs his thumb across my jaw.

I shiver—and not from fear. I try to push away and he pulls me closer, tucking my head into the masculine hollow between his neck and shoulder, holding me. A sense of being protected washes over me and I crumble. His arms are solid, his chest wide, and for the first time in longer than I can remember, I feel safe.

And fucking confused.

So I curl into him and let the tears fall. Snuggling closer, I calm and listen to the steady beat of his heart against my ear. I don't know how long we sit there in the quiet library with the rain splattering against the windows, but finally, I come back to reality. He's warm around me and definitely aroused. Swallowing, I shift my weight.

Is that a groan?

I look up at his implacable face. The need there steals my breath. "Oh."

"Did you eat dinner?"

The question catches me by surprise. It's far past dinnertime. "Um, yes?"

"Good." He stands, easily holding me against his chest.

I clutch his dress shirt. "What are you doing?"

"You'll need lotion." He carries me through the darkened home and up the stairs, bypassing my room and heading to the far end where he nudges open one of a set of double doors.

Lotion?

Then we're inside his bedroom. I know it's his because his scent washes over me, tantalizing and male. The furnishings are black and the chandelier all garnets, no diamonds or crystals. Like the rest of the home, the furniture is masculine and solidly beautiful, and completely lacking in personal touches.

His bed is huge. Much bigger than a king-sized bed, it stretches out from the far wall, covered in a heavy black coverlet with white pillowcases.

I jolt.

"Relax. I'm not going to bite you."

I suck in a breath at the image.

He looks down. "Right now, anyway."

The words spark interest inside me. Which makes no sense.

So I fall back on my sparkling personality. "Guys like you can't kiss. The smooch in the kitchen was a fluke."

One dark eyebrow rises, and he halts in the center of the room. "Do tell."

"You're rich, beautiful, and sexy in a demon-from-hell kind of way. Women probably throw their panties at you when you walk by in a bar. You don't have to try."

Amusement filters through the lust still glittering in his eyes. "You think I'm beautiful? Have you hit your head?"

Oh, he's definitely beautiful. My body is taut like a vibrating guitar string, and I know I should want to kill him. But the expression on his rough face somehow gives me courage. Or a hint of insanity. Could be either. I reach up and run my fingers through his thick hair. It's softer than I expected. "Prove me wrong."

He stills. We're not moving, but his body just stops. His gaze drops. Then his mouth is on mine.

I expect finesse or brutality . . . and receive neither.

Instead, raw fire pours into me as his lips form over mine, taking me under. My eyelids flutter shut and I open for him, not that he's giving me a choice. He drinks from me and I want to give him everything. My hand against his chest, I can feel the growl that rumbles up before it rolls into my mouth and down through my entire body, sparking nerves into exposed tendrils of sheer need.

There is no feeling in the entire world like this. There can't be. The universe would burn down.

His hold tightens and I feel the bed at my back. When did we move? He deepens the kiss and I become lost again, his mouth taking me over as his body presses into mine. He's hard everywhere I'm soft. His hands rip into my hair and he clenches, holding me in place with an erotic pain, taking everything he could ever want.

We're both panting when he lifts his head and lets me breathe.

My mouth feels swollen. Bemused, I stare up into his glittering eyes. His erection is pressed against me, right where I need him, and a stirring starts deep inside me.

"You are going to be mine, and it's not to save your hymen from Cal."

I want this. Oh, I shouldn't, I know it's wrong. He's wrong, I'm confused, and this is too dark for anybody. But it's something I want once before I go home. There's no way I'm staying. "One night," I whisper.

He rolls over to sit, grasping my hip and bringing me with him. Then I'm straddling him, my bare thighs on either side of his hard ones. "Your virginity is mine, but you will give it freely. Lie to yourself if you want and say you're making a brief choice before marrying that moron. But it's a lie, and deep down, you know it. I'm going to fuck you so hard nobody else will ever get deep enough again. It's only you and me. But take your time, because the yes is coming from you."

The erotic image bursts into my head, igniting even more lust. Wings flutter inside me, striking my abdomen and flashing down to my sex. I clench. My hair is all around us, and he grips a mass of it again, those dangerous fingers caressing my nape at the same time. His voice is so low it's beyond guttural. "This is what's going to happen. I'm heading into that bathroom to find lotion for your sore ass. Then I have to go take care of something. When I return, you can be waiting in this bed for tonight to be the night, or if you want more time to lie to yourself, go to your own bed, and tonight I'll leave you alone. That choice is yours."

The words riot through my brain. Then, against all rational thought, I press against him. Shock cascades from my clit to my breasts and I gasp.

He bites his lip hard enough I see blood. Even that is a turn-on.

With impressive control, considering the rod of steel I can feel in his pants, he lifts me off him and strides into the bathroom. I hear shuffling through drawers. Trying not to moan, I clench my thighs together and pull down the short skirt. The aquamarine band around my waist flashes blue light and I try to take comfort from it, but even those small crystals are burning.

He returns with a small bottle of lotion. "Found some."

Jealousy, green and sharp, cuts through me. He has somebody else's lotion in his bathroom?

He pauses, his gaze sweeping mine. "It was in a kit. I never have women here. Ever."

How does he read me so well? And what the hell is a kit? I scramble to stand, hoping my legs hold me up.

"Turn around."

I lift my chin, needing to find some courage. "No."

He grasps my arm and twists me around, smacking me hard on my already punished butt. I cry out. "Rule Three. I'm done with the defiance." He plants a hand between my shoulder blades and shoves my head to the bed. "Hold still." Without giving me a chance to argue, he's spreading lotion over my rear. I have to admit, it feels good. The cool calming of whatever is in there eases a bit of the pain. "This will keep you from bruising. Too much." Then he tugs me around, sits me on the bed, and crouches in front of me.

My hair flips around and I push it out of the way. I feel like a lost rabbit in front of a mountain lion. Or a panther. Or something deadlier than either. Drawn by what can only be danger, I reach out and trace the hard contours of his face.

He draws in a breath. "The end result is absolute. But in this, and probably this only, you can determine the timing. Clear your brain because I won't ever accept the lie that I forced you into this. Into us. Even if it takes an eternity for you to be honest with both of us."

He's right. My head is a ball of fuzz and my body a bastion of need. I hate that he's being honorable for once.

He stands. "If you're here when I return tonight, it's for good—as long as either of us live, and if you're here, it's my way. Period."

Since I don't have a way, I can't argue with that. But I do need to clear my head.

With one last, hard look at me, he turns and strides right out the door. A small part of me, one I should embrace, hopes that hard-on kills him. The other part, the one I won't admit to anybody, hopes he brings it right back to me.

For now, I need a bath. Perhaps he has some healing salts in that kit.

TWELVE

Thorn

The boathouse is a shack cut into the jagged cliffs along the northern coastline of the Pacific, near a national recreation area that I have fully surveyed. My cameras are everywhere, but they can't be seen. Accessing the boathouse isn't easy. Even though we've cut in a decent trail, more than one of my men have fallen off the trail and into the abyss. I can hear the Pacific far below as I stride down the curved rock; it's dark tonight, and I know how jagged those rocks are below.

My balls are still on fire, and that has my chest heating. I'd forgotten the feeling.

My hands are steady but my gut aches like usual. It fleetingly occurs to me that I might have to let Alana go soon—before my body gives up the fight with this illness. Or curse. Or whatever the fuck it is.

If I can't protect her, I'll make sure she's around somebody who can.

I glance out at the vast dark sea. People looking from the

ocean as they travel by in their luxury yachts only see a raw and weathered cliffside, because that's what I want them to see. Camouflaging the trail was a simple task. There's no way to get close to the land in this area because of the horrific rocks jutting out all over the coastline. There already were some when I purchased the land and built my home several miles down the coastline, but I have discreetly added more through the years.

The wind whips against me, and I take it, unwilling to show any weakness to the men behind me. Most don't know I'm succumbing to the freezing pain. And that's what it is. I'm freezing from the inside out as the ancient garnet that powers Malice Media does the same.

It's infuriating, and I reach deep into my anger to keep myself warm.

I finally arrive at the cavern I had carved into the cliff. It is but a wide room, surrounded on all sides with natural rock that is chilling in its hardness. There aren't any garnets that occur naturally in this rock, but I placed many in the floor, ceiling, and even the four walls.

Even though we're inside, I can hear the ocean thundering in a frenzy outside. The two men Justice secured are sitting on metal chairs, arms bound behind their backs. I tug a burning mint, my own concoction, from my pocket, unwrap and shove it into my mouth.

Bags cover my captives' heads, which hang down. Their shirts have been sliced open, and blood already flows from cuts in their torsos.

Justice takes point at the doorway, as usual. Two of my men flank us, both with bloodied knuckles. I hadn't ordered them not to play.

I rip the hood off the first guy, who looks to be in his late twenties, and jerk his head back at the same time. He sniffs bloody snot up his nose and glares at me for a second before really looking at me. Whatever he sees has his eyes widening and his bronze face paling. He gulps and fights his restraints, his body square and muscled on the metal chair bolted into the rock. His lip is split, and his brown eyes look blurry, as if he's sustained a brain concussion.

At least one.

He stares at me.

"Do you know who I am?" I ask softly.

He swallows and looks wildly around, his gaze landing on Justice and then returning to me. "I think I heard one of your people call you by name. Are you Thorn Beathach?" There's a hint of hope in his voice as if he could be wrong.

"Right."

His shoulders slump and his chin lowers. "What do you want?"

"Shut the fuck up," his buddy hisses from next to him, his voice muffled by the hood.

I punch him square in the face and his head jerks back, not once but twice, and he flops forward as much as the ties allow. Out cold.

The guy in front of me sucks in a breath and tries to lean back.

"There's nowhere to go," I say congenially. Coldness ran through me before this illness and now, even my blood cells feel like ice. Except when Alana is near with her greenish-brown eyes and untamable hair. At the thought of her, I taste honey through the mint. "Who hired you to shoot anywhere near Alana Beaumont?"

His brows draw down quickly before he smooths them out. "Why would *you* want to know that?"

I fluidly draw my knife from the sheath at my calf, my reflexes faster than he's ever seen, and plunge the blade into the center of his thigh.

He screeches and then catches himself, sucking air rapidly into his lungs. Blood pours around the shiny metal, matching the garnet in the hilt.

None of my men move, and if I know Justice, he looks like he is about to take a nap.

Then I wait.

The guy sniffs again.

"What's your name?" I ask.

"Renaldo," he rushes to say.

It's a nice name. Much better than Thorn. "Who's the lead in this little campaign?"

He looks to the side. "Um, not me. Ratchet is higher ranked than me."

Great. I've knocked out the wrong asshole. "I suppose you're probably the lead now," I say.

He blinks several times as he catches my meaning. "Oh."

I'm thinking he's not the mastermind behind anything. "Alana Beaumont," I say, making sure the mint is properly burning my taste buds. No way do I want to taste this guy's words.

He squints as if desperately trying to remember. "We weren't supposed to kill her. Just scare everyone and kidnap her."

Irritation claws through me. "Then your people shouldn't have fired at her." Although, to be fair, nobody had hit her.

"Sorry. Really." Renaldo sags, lines of pain cutting into the sides of his mouth.

"Where were you supposed to take her?" I ask.

His chest heaves. "I don't know." The words are a low and mournful sound. "I was the driver."

Apparently he'd taken off when his friends had lost the firefight. Not very sporting of him. "Tell me everything you do know."

He straightens like an eager puppy. "Our group was paid a million dollars up front with a promised five million if we secured her." He glances at his still unmoving buddy. "The transaction was in cash and all communications via written notes that we burned."

Shit. Most folks aren't smart enough to stay away from the convenience of technology. "Who received the note?"

"Tarantula did. He's dead," Renaldo says.

Anybody named Tarantula deserves to be dead. I cock my head at Justice, who's now scrolling through his phone.

"*High up*," he murmurs in Gaelic as he no doubt reads the dossiers we've compiled on criminal organizations. "*We've never done business with him, but he's close to the top. Rather, he was.*"

Makes sense. "Do you know who killed your three fellow gang members?"

Renaldo looks away from the knife protruding from his leg. "Rumor has it the Sokolov family guards returned fire and Alana Beaumont escaped out the back." He focuses on me, the pain in his eyes evident. "If you're looking for her, I can tell you that nobody knows where she is. The Beaumonts have reached out to Twenty-One Purple, and there's a five hundred thousand dollar retrieval fee."

"Alive?" I ask.

He gulps again. "Yeah. Yeah, man. Definitely alive. They don't want her back dead. The rules are clear."

I do like clear rules. "What about the Sokolov family?"

"Nothing that I've heard." He looks around and then shows a fair amount of backbone by asking another question. "Are you going to kill me?"

"Should I?" I cock my head.

He coughs. "No?"

"Where's his phone?" I ask.

One of my men tosses it to Justice. He snatches it out of the air and walks over, holding the screen up to Renaldo's face. It unlocks easily. Justice scrolls through, no expression on his hard face. Finally, he shakes his head. Nothing illegal or offensive on the phone.

"Do you run kids?" I ask.

Renaldo grimaces. "Gross. No." He sighs. "The higher-ups run girls, and I hate it." His voice has the ring of truth.

"Drugs?" I ask.

"Yeah." He glances again at his unconscious buddy. I may have hit him hard enough to drive his nose into his brain. "I take orders and deliver, but I don't have access to the sources. I'm not very high up. Yet."

I reach over and yank the hood off the other man, noting his wide-open blank eyes. Yep. I did kill him. Blood covers the lower half of his face from his smashed nose. He appears to be around forty. "What about him?"

Renaldo shifts on the chair and hisses, his face turning the color of Italian marble. "He was higher up." A certain note in his voice catches my attention. Slightly elevated. I nod to Wynd, who's been quiet in the back of the little cave, and he goes to the body and removes a phone. It takes three tries to hold it in front of the dead guy's face before it opens. He scrolls through and his jaw hardens.

"Kids?" I ask.

He nods.

Fuck, I hate pedophiles. Guess I killed the right guy.

Renaldo sags as if knowing he's about to die. "I didn't know that but it doesn't surprise me. Ratchet was a jerk." He sighs. "I shouldn't say that, but why not tell the truth at the time of death?"

Because the truth is often both irrelevant and way too late coming. "What do you have to live for?" I ask, reaching into my back pocket for a piece of chocolate.

"A baby," he says softly. "I'm in the life and not leaving, but my girlfriend is pregnant with my first kid."

"Do you think that will keep me from killing you?" I ask, eating the chocolate to cleanse the mint from my palate.

He looks beyond me to the stone wall separating us from the sea. "No. I've heard about you. Everyone has. You're a killer."

"That I am," I agree as the chocolate takes effect. "I'm also a businessman."

He tries to hide it, but hope appears in his eyes. All humans, probably excluding me, feel hope whether they like it or not. I figure it somehow lurks in our DNA. I flash back to Alana telling me that the obedience gene is located on the Y chromosome. A tingling warmth slides through my frozen veins.

Renaldo waits, his instincts whispering not to speak.

I cock my head. "I have people on the inside of your little gang." Sure, those gang members are notoriously dangerous in today's world, but my people? The families who actually run this world? We're the ones to fear. "I wouldn't mind another mole."

His eyes narrow, proving he's not a complete moron. "You're going to let me go?"

The taste of parsley slides across my tongue. Not enjoyable, but nowhere near evil. "Yes. Wynd will get you sutured up and then give you a schedule for check-ins." I smile and enjoy how he draws back again. Not stupid at all. "You'll be chipped, and if you cross me, you'll wish I had tortured you for the rest of tonight before feeding the remaining pieces of your body to the sharks." I lean in, making sure he understands. "And it won't just be you. Everyone you've ever smiled at will join you in death. Get me?"

He nods so quickly I can almost hear his brain rattling against his skull.

"Good. The first thing you're going to do is get me information on who hired your gang to kidnap Alana." I keep his gaze. "I don't care what you have to do to find me information. No limits. Got it?"

His nod is slower this time, but like a trapped rat in a bucket, he knows there's only one way out if he wants to live. "I'll find out."

Good. False promises. That will lead to desperation and answers for me.

Justice drops Renaldo's phone and crushes it beneath his heavy boot. My brother's eyes burn, and I wonder at his headache. While my synesthesia localizes a certain way, his is far different.

"We'll get you a new phone, Renaldo," I say. It will clone the data on any phone he gets close to and then transmit all information to my computer hub. "You'll also be watched, and if you get out of line . . . well, you know."

He nods.

I need to get back to my woman. She's had plenty of time for her body to stop burning and her mind to take over. She wanted me after the spanking, but that was physical as well as emotional. As her desire cooled, what has her temper done?

I tear my knife free of Renaldo's leg and he cries out.

Wynd moves in to save his life, and I'm already outside in the night, climbing toward the stars.

Will she be waiting for me?

THIRTEEN

Alana

I stretch in the big bed—my bed—as drowsiness tries to over-whelm me. After a very nice bath, my brain returned, and I decided I'm not ready for a night with Thorn.

True, I'm not sure any woman could be ready. But I'm still confused, and frankly, I don't want to encourage his bad behavior.

Even if it did almost lead to the unicorn of all orgasms.

I tilt my head on the pillow and then fight the urge to punch myself in the face. Submitting to him, the absolute dark pleasure in doing so, feels like a drug in my system. One I have to purge before I get even deeper into this, before I drown in every sensation he evokes.

I'm not stupid. The only way to fight both of us is to escape him and his pull. But right now? I'm actually listening for him.

He's been gone for hours.

I'm an intelligent woman, usually, but I can't wrap my head around the badass enigma. There's no doubt he enjoyed spanking me, but then he held me safe while I cried, finally walking away when I would've definitely torn off his clothes. He's dangerous, and I'm not entirely sure which way his moral compass points. Or if he even has one.

Then there's the burn of his eyes. A sadness lives there—one that calls to me.

That is a good enough reason to avoid him for the night and then figure out a way to escape his sprawling fortress tomorrow.

I fall asleep finally, thinking of that kiss and wanting more.

My dreams are a kaleidoscope of ocean storms and lightning strikes, until I go deeper into dreamland, where I'm both vulnerable and too young to handle the world I was born into.

I'm six years old again, clutching my stuffed blue teddy bear with its sparkling blue eyes. My fingers curl over the bear's rose quartz necklace; the one that makes me feel better. There's yelling.

I shut my eyes and huddle on the cold floor, my feet bare and one cut.

What is happening?

I don't understand. Tears slide down my face and I rock, my shoulders hitting the wall. Then I stop. Mama told me to be quiet.

Quiet is my friend.

I don't know where I am, and it's so cold. Freezing, really. What is happening? A screech of tires comes from nowhere.

Somebody is screaming.

"*Alana. Wake up. Now.*" The voice is a low command that must be obeyed.

I jerk awake, sitting up and gasping. My ears ring. Furiously, I wipe tears off my cheeks. I'd screamed.

"What the hell?" Thorn strides to the velvet curtains and tears them open.

"*No!*" I shriek. "Shut them."

He instantly does so, partially turning.

I fumble for the bed table light. Then I wish I hadn't.

He stands against the cream-colored velvet drapes in form-fitting black boxers. The good cotton kind. His hair is mussed and his eyes sharp. But that body. I try to swallow but every ounce of liquid in my throat has headed south. His tatted chest is a scarred masterpiece with slashes, burns, whip marks, and bullet holes.

The evidence of past pain somehow—and I'll never explain to anybody how—promises strength. Muscles play beneath his skin, not lazy and natural, but sharp and deadly. Life is terrifying, and he's strong enough to beat it down. Every time. Ink covers the right side of his body and flows down his arm. Garnets, roses, knives . . . and skulls. The intricate design isn't meant to be beautiful.

It's a warning.

I make sure to breathe in through my nose, not wanting to pass out. The echoes of the nightmare weigh down my limbs.

"You a vampire now?" he asks, still watching me. Missing nothing.

I blink. "Huh?"

He gestures with his head back at the curtain. "No light. It's barely after dawn. Explain."

I don't want to talk about it. Instead, I memorize his chest and muscled arms before noting how his body tapers to a slim waist and masculine hips. Who knew that hips could be masculine?

"I'm not going to ask again. You were screaming bloody murder."

Embarrassed at the screaming, I curl my fingers into the bedclothes, having found a new T-shirt to wear to bed. "I don't want to talk about it."

"What makes you think you have a choice?" He moves then. Right at me.

I scramble back but the headboard keeps me from going through the wall. As if I could.

He twists off the light, lifts the covers, and shoves his inferno-hot body into me.

I sit there. "Wait a minute." My lungs feel like I've been buried under the ocean.

With an exaggerated sigh, he clasps my bare thigh and pulls me beneath the covers. "I swear, you're more contrary than a country cow." His warmth seeps right beneath my skin, yet his fingers are freezing.

Left with no choice, I snuggle into him, my back to his front. "Did you just call me a cow?"

"Of course not. Why did you scream?"

In the darkness, bracketed by his brutalized body, I feel safe. Somewhat. Kind of? "You said you'd leave me alone."

"I meant in the sexual way." His breath brushes my hair. "Not in the cuddling-after-nightmares kind of way."

Against my will, a smile tugs at my lips. "Do you have a lot of nightmares?"

"More than I can count."

The words sadden me. I want to lighten the mood, and I really don't want to talk about the nightmare or the window. "Did you kill anybody tonight?" I hold my breath.

"One out of two," he says easily.

Oh. "Did the one deserve it?" Not that Thorn's moral compass of justice points north, anyway.

"He surely did." An iron-hard arm wraps around my waist and he pulls me even closer, his mouth nuzzling my ear.

Wings flutter inside me. A warning. "You said no sex."

"If you think this is sex, you need better streaming services." But he stops. "Were you even tempted to wait in my bed?"

I don't like being overwhelmed, and there's no other way to describe what he's doing holding me so close. Yet I do like this.

My brain and my body have dramatically different ideas about how to handle Thorn Beathach. As if a wild animal such as he can be handled. "Stop fishing for compliments."

"I'm not. I just want the truth."

Yeah, he has a thing for the truth, doesn't he? "Yes. I was tempted."

He kisses the top of my head. "Good girl."

For telling the truth? Or for being smart enough to stay out of his bed? I'm not sure. "Do you really taste honey when I speak?"

"Yeah, though it's fleeting. Not too thick or sweet. Perfect, really."

Heat plunges into my face along with pleasure. I have no control over how my words taste to him, but I like that I can bring him comfort. How this makes sense, considering he killed a man earlier this night, I have no clue. But he did say the guy deserved it. My eyelids start to droop.

"You've stalled long enough. Tell me about the nightmare and why you're afraid of the dawn."

Part of me wants to confide in him this sleepy morning. The other part wants to tell him to get bent. Yet I figure that statement would count as defiance, and my butt is not up to another round with an irritated Thorn.

Sealing my decision, he runs one gentle palm up my arm and tugs on my ear, his body powerful as it covers me. "Trust me. Let it out."

"There isn't much to say. I have a recurring nightmare. I'm small and scared. It's raining and I hear . . . voices? Angry ones." I shiver and his arm flexes low on my pelvis. I can feel his erection probing my rear, and for the tiniest of seconds, I marvel at his control.

"What do you smell?"

"Vanilla candles," I say instantly. "And no, I don't see them. But I smell them."

He shifts his weight and groans. "Do vanilla candles mean anything to you?"

I shake my head.

He coughs out what is no doubt a healthy dose of my hair. "Have you ever been kidnapped? I mean, besides now?"

The reminder of my precarious position cools my interest in his heat and hard body. "Not that I know of." But I don't remember. "I've tried different shrinks and hypnotists, and nothing."

"What does your father say?"

"He's at a loss. According to him, I've never been kidnapped or put in danger. He has no idea where the dreams come from." I hate it when he looks at me as if there's something wrong with me. "I learned a long time ago to hide the nightmares but still sought help."

Thorn's lips brush the back of my head again, and electricity jolts through me. "Hear me when I tell you that if you need anything, I am at your disposal. I'll buy you any shrink, and when we discover the source of your fears, I'll slice off every inch until there's nothing left."

His vow rings true.

"Why?" I whisper. "We're enemies."

He rolls us over and settles his long form above me, holding the mass of his weight on his elbows. "We're not enemies."

I arch an eyebrow and try to ignore the hard-on against my core. It's impossible. My blood heats and speeds up through my veins, roaring loudly in my ears. I am so screwed up. "I'm the heir to Aquarius Social. You're the owner of Malice Media." I speak slowly because he needs to hear every word. "From the dawn of civilization, or probably before that, there have been four families." The four who have always ruled, regardless of country or even god.

"A history lesson? How intriguing." His dark gaze drops to my mouth. "From that dawn of time, men have consolidated power by creating unions."

I can't focus. "You want to create a union with me?" Should that idea terrify me?

"We're already connected, and you know it. Even though it's complicated," he murmurs, a hint of anger in his tone. "Why are you afraid of the dawn? Does it have something to do with the sun coming up?"

Complicated? Um, yeah. "No." I hate admitting this because it makes zero sense. My fear is as absurd as a porcupine in a balloon factory. "It's the windows. More specifically, the pattern in them."

He allows more of his weight to shift onto my body, and I feel every solid inch of him pressing me deep into the mattress. In addition, I learn I'm only human. My hands, I swear on their own, travel along the defined topography of hard muscle of his arms up to his shoulders. "The X pattern?"

"Yes. And before you ask, any good answer got lost in the mail somehow. The second I see that pattern, I want to scream, run, and hide. It's nauseating. It's a phobia but one that isn't common and hasn't been traced back to the source." I know the shrink talk because I've seen several established professionals. "If you want to truly drive me crazy, stick me in a room with those windows and toss in a couple of life-sized nutcrackers."

His upper lip curves. "Nutcrackers?"

"Yeah." I'm fascinated by his mouth and want to trace it, but instead run my finger along his brutal scar.

His chest rumbles in a sound I'll never be able to recreate. A cross between a purr and a growl. The lazy lion is satisfied for now. "Nutcrackers are harmless."

"Ha. Until they snap your neck in their jaws." I shiver. "Creepy. How can anybody see them as spreading holiday cheer?"

His gaze bores into mine while his heat pierces my skin and goes deeper, warming me. "I'll keep that in mind."

"You should. Those little buggers probably love big bad

beasts. With their wooden bodies and fake smiles, you're lucky you haven't already turned into their Christmas dinner. I bet your overabundance of muscle would make a good roast."

"Overabundance?" He looks slightly miffed.

I chuckle. "Okay. You have the optimal blend of brawn and sinew."

"That's better." He licks his lip as if tasting the best brew of his life. "The gang members I interrogated tonight wanted you kidnapped, not killed."

Should that be a relief? I guess it is. "Kidnapping me makes more sense now that I'm on the board of Aquarius. I guess I'm glad nobody wants me dead." Does that mean he's going to release me? I wonder if he'll let me borrow a couple of the books from his library. "Since we're talking so, um, closely . . . where did you get the scar?" I run my finger across the bridge of his nose.

"Justice, his mom, and I were kidnapped when I was a child." Thorn banishes all expression from his face. "I was tortured on a live feed to gain my father's cooperation. The attempt failed, but he did rescue Justice and me. Charity was killed."

My jaw drops. "I'm so sorry."

"He at least destroyed the people who took us. They were an up-and-coming internet company that he blew up." Thorn's eyes glitter. "However, my father and I were never close, and I knew he planned to kill me at some point—even heard him talking about it to his second in command once."

I gulp. "Why would your father want you dead?"

"I'm more powerful than most, and my connection to the garnet stone is a crucial part of the way we've learned to harness the energy of social media. He was threatened by me, figured he had plenty of longevity, and had started making plans." There isn't an ounce of hurt in his voice. "All threats require eradication, but he pushed me too far one day, and I guess I won that battle."

"What happened?" My heart hurts for him.

Thorn exhales, pressing his chest against my aching nipples. I gasp and try to cover the sound with a cough. The slight amusement filtering into his hard-flint eyes shows I fail. "I killed him. I was fifteen and Justice thirteen, and our father was beating Justice almost to death for some silly infraction. I chose my brother, and I guess, myself." Thorn shrugs. "I always blamed my father for Charity's death, anyway. She was Justice's mom. Almost my mom, too." His grinds his back teeth together.

I dig into the sides of his jaw with my thumbs, forcing him to relax. "Why? Your kidnappers killed her."

He presses a kiss to my nose as if he can't help himself. "She was taken from both of us, Justice and me. Charity was good and kind, and her words tasted like blueberry jam."

My heart aches for him. "Why blame him if he didn't kill her?"

"She was his," Thorn says simply. "He took her as his wife, and it was his job to keep her safe. His woman, his responsibility. Anything that happened to her was on him."

Whoa. Old-fashioned thinking, there. "Welcome to the current century, caveman. The game has new rules." I lessen the pressure on his jaw hinge. "We women can take care of ourselves."

"You might want to look where you are right now." His face is immovable, but his tone remains indulgent.

He isn't wrong. Worse yet, there's a strange allure to his worldview. With his unyielding strength and primal attraction, I can't help but feel safe. And confused. Worse yet, a veil lifts inside me. We're both damaged by who we are and by our families in the same way. That lost desperation inside me, that dark void I won't admit to anybody, has found an answering one in him.

Together, we click.

No. That's crazy. I am not clicking with a sociopath. Panicking, I start to babble. "I have a scar, too, on my lower rib cage. From the car accident when my mother died." We're both survivors.

He rolls to his side and lifts my shirt, palming my stomach and caressing until he finds the long scar. "That had to have hurt."

"I don't remember, really." His touch is killing me. If he just goes a little lower . . .

A knock sounds on the door. "Car's ready," Justice calls out, his footsteps quickly receding.

"I have to go." Thorn rolls over and gracefully stands. "Get some sleep. We'll talk later."

My body chills as I watch his graceful movements toward the door. "When am I going home, Thorn?"

He doesn't look back. "You *are* home." With that, he opens the door and prowls into the hall.

I rear up. "Wait a minute." My heart thunders. He's pulling me into his world way too fast, and I can't think clearly being in his space. "You can't keep me here!" I yell.

"Watch me." Then he's gone.

FOURTEEN

※

Thorn

My lab is nearly three thousand meters underground. There's no question the garnet crystals placed in the rock and metal help sustain this facility, much as I do. Whenever I'm underground, my ears pop. It's quite annoying.

At the moment, only Justice, Kazstone, and I stand in the digital jungle. In fact, the three of us are the only ones with clearance to be down this far. Anybody with a different biometric marker will set off multiple ear-shattering alarms.

Kazstone is seated at his customary desk in the center, more than a little annoyed that he had to call me in earlier than usual. I've learned one thing about him during our time together, and that is he likes his routine.

"Hey, Kazi." Justice smiles.

I'll never understand why, but Justice loves throwing Kaz off his game. I don't mind Kazstone knowing who's in charge, but I've also found that it's a good idea not to piss off the smartest person on the planet. Plus, right now, the baiting is fucking annoying. A waste of time. I shoot Justice a look that makes him lose the grin.

He keeps trying to get closer to me, and I keep shoving him back. For some reason, the kidnapping of Alana, my Alana, has brought us closer. He would've never questioned me about killing the guard even a week ago. What is it about that woman?

Kaz types on two different keyboards at once, somehow using the full range of his hands on both. He's thirty years old with dark blond hair, strikingly intelligent green eyes, and a strong chin. I noticed his chin the first time we met, when we were just teens. It juts out and has a dimple in the middle, like Cary Grant's.

"Did you find more of the alexandrite?" I ask.

He nods. "Yes. I just made a deal with the Kayrs family out of Idaho for two large stones."

"Really?" I say. That gives us six—far more than anybody else on the planet. At least for crystals that size. As far as I have known, the Kayrs family refuses to give up jack squat.

"Yes. They're also sending over a trove of red garnets but they don't have one big enough to be close to what we need."

The Kayrs family has been around as long as my own, but they aren't involved in the influence gathering or power acclimating of the four families. I keep them at a respectful distance and know that they'll be neutral in any war. They have their own agenda and keep it locked up tight. This is a very rare moment of overlap. "What do they want?"

"A favor in the future."

Shit. I don't like that, but I'll take it. "Fine." Sometimes I wonder if I should get out of the power game, but it's not to be.

My enemies would have me killed, and plus, I need to make a safe haven for Justice and possibly Alana. I don't want to let her go. Knowing she's protected at my fortress is giving me more peace than I've had in years. Unfortunately, right now, my feet are freezing from the virus, and I'm sure it won't be long before the ice encases my heart.

Kazstone looks me over. "I can tell, you're colder."

"I am."

Kazstone opens one of the many drawers of his desk and pulls out a bowling ball-large hunk of raw red garnet—my main garnet.

"Is that ice?" I ask, moving toward it.

"It is," he says grimly.

I touch the crystal and my blood hums. It is freezing from the inside out, just like me.

"You took it out of the mainframe?" Justice growls.

"I did last week," I say. The thing is freezing at the same rate as me. Even my fingers are pricking with cold. I'm not happy that somebody is successfully killing me, but still, the ingenuity of the person is impressive. I'll kill whoever it is once I find them, but I do appreciate a good curse.

"Can you explain this to me?" Justice rubs his right eyebrow like a headache is trying to kill him.

"Sure," Kazstone says. "As far as I can tell, a private user introduced a computer virus into our system—through a social media post. I've tracked down several possible entry points, and honestly, it is eluding me so far. Once the bug invaded our system, it lurked in the garnets, especially the main one." He nods to the now-icing-over stone. "The second you connected to charge it, the virus was transferred to you."

I charge the garnets by an exchange of energy, the same as the owners of the other three social media companies do with their crystals. The transfer occurs by touch and meditation. It's quite simple, really. I gain strength and longevity afterward. Usually. Now, not so much.

Justice shakes his head. "Magic and computer science."

"And quantum physics," Kazstone says cheerfully. "I've

deciphered part of the algorithm that created the digital curse. If I can unravel the entire thing, maybe we can find a cure."

This era of the internet, revitalized energy, social media companies, and the sheer volume of subscribers flinging more energy at us is a new world for everyone. None of us saw the danger coming.

"Who has the ability to create a computer or crystal virus like this?" I ask.

Kazstone glances at his monitor. "I have it. You have it. I would assume each social media family has somebody who could create it. There's no digital footprint yet. I don't know who it is." Frustration darkens his face.

His loyalty is absolute, and I hope he's as good as I believe. "Before I charge the servers, what have you discovered with the four new alexandrite pyramids?" I won't receive the ones from the Kayrs family for at least another day.

Kazstone nods toward the other two open computer hubs. "They transfer data faster than anything I've ever seen, and I'm just digging in to what they can do. I want to trace that virus that's killing you back to its source, and they're giving me the best chance."

The blood starts to thrum through my body—hopefully warming me. It has taken me a decade to find alexandrite that size, and the fact that I did it by robbing Mathias Beaumont makes the moment all the sweeter.

Justice vibrates in place. "Do you think we can stop the freezing?"

"I hope so," Kazstone says.

"We'll find an answer," I say grimly. For now, I can feel the servers weakening. It's odd I'm so in tune with the garnet crystals running our system. I walk past the center computer hub, having placed a leather thong bearing a heavy garnet around my neck, which pulses against my bare skin. The stone has been imbued with the raw energy of the earth. Most people don't know that they're standing on the biggest electromagnetic field in the solar system. But my people do. We've learned how to harness it, and the garnets are how I do it.

Justice watches me key in the code to the main hub. He doesn't know it yet, and hopefully he won't ever need it. "I can come with you."

"No." The door slides open and I move inside, waiting until it shuts behind me. He can't completely charge the main garnet until I'm dead and buried.

I walk to the heart of the server and see the three garnets now taking the place of the main one, which is icing over too quickly. I kneel and place a series of garnets from my pocket around the mainframe, creating a Celtic pattern that starts to sing and hum on its own.

Closing my eyes, I place a hand on the central three rocks and let the silence of them fill me. They begin to glow and their crimson light reflects off every surface.

Power flows through my arms, down to the floor, and then back up to the garnets, charging them. A pleasant hum fills the room and electricity arcs through the space as I spend fifteen minutes charging.

I step back and look at the silicon brains and cable arteries. For a moment, I stagger. I've given the servers all the energy I have available right now. Ignoring the pain, I walk out of the little room, back into the main hub where Kazstone and Justice wait for me.

"All good?" Justice asks, his gaze shuttered.

"Yeah," I mutter.

Kazstone looks at his screen. "Agreed. We're charged at least for the next week, but that took you longer than it should have, and I can tell the exchange abnormally exhausted you. We have to find a cure for this virus."

"Viruses don't have cures," I say, trying not to be glum, but we all know the truth.

"Yeah, but this is a virus caused by a curse." Kazstone throws his hands up.

I need a cure, not an explanation. "I'm being frozen from the inside out, or rather from the outside in," I mutter. "I already know what it is."

"It's called the fatal freeze," he says, shifting on his chair. "I found references to it back in an old code. Basically the target's body gradually lowers in temperature until, well, your heart freezes to death."

"I'm well aware." My heart was never all that warm to begin with. "Come on, I don't have all day." I move to the computer bank to the right as Justice heads to the other one. I'd like to get back to Alana.

"Okay, here you go," Kazstone says. "The alexandrite crystals are already plugged into each of the computer hubs, and I'm hoping they act as a turbo and speed up my algorithms."

I sit at the keyboard and start to type, my mind on Alana. I actually love the computer. I'm a better fighter than programmer, but in another lifetime, this could have made me happy. Hunting data in real time is a gift. That is the lesson of this century and what we've discovered by using the internet. Before, it was rumors and gossip and songs. Now it's raw, hard, sharp data that we can read.

Soon there's nothing but the sound of the three of us typing as we write algorithms to fix our servers.

Finally, I'm typing faster than the other two men as I take the lead. Hours go by. At some point, Kazstone puts coffee by my hand and I think I drink it. Finally, I reassemble all of the data. "I have it."

Kazstone and Justice stand and walk over to stand behind me. "What did you find?" Justice asks, his voice low.

I click a button and data starts scrolling across the screen.

"Is that a video?" Kazstone asks, leaning forward.

"It is." I click on it and a video comes up of Alana being interviewed on Malice Media by some influencer named Jackie. I recoil and then settle. "Alana infected our servers with the curse that's killing me?"

Kaz scrolls through his phone. "The influencer is a Jackie Lamberts, twenty years old, who died last week of an overdose."

Right. So either Alana, somebody at Aquarius Social, or an unknown actor uploaded the virus with this video. "Alana lacks the skill to create code," I murmur.

"If she didn't create the virus, then we have a problem," Justice says. "The only reason to use her like this is because . . ."

Somebody knows of my obsession with her.

Either way, this is fucked.

FIFTEEN

Alana

Today I dress in a longer blue skirt with strappy sandals and a pink quartz belt beneath a white tank top and pink cardigan. I'm surprised by the sheer amount of jewelry available to me, but even so, I choose a simple earring and necklace set of aquamarine. It matches the one I wear all the time, and I feel more grounded almost instantly.

It's a feeling I need. Desperately. I spend my morning wandering around the castle trying to find passageways, but once again come up empty. It's quite frustrating, really, since I know there have to be some around here. For some reason, I also can't find Mrs. Pendrake. While I doubt she'll become my ally, I'm going to give it a shot. If I can just find her.

I can't believe Thorn is planning on a forever kidnapping. My shiver runs through my entire body.

I haven't looked at a screen or posted on Aquarius in too long. I wander through the kitchen and glare at the counter. There's no phone in sight. I'm not receiving notifications, and I long for my phone. Sure, I'm probably addicted to social media, like most people, but it's my freaking job. How many users have we lost since my abduction?

Finally, around lunchtime, I dig into the crisper and make myself a sandwich and eat it like a jonesing rabbit before looking out at the rainy day to see Dermot emerge from the moat dressed in full scuba gear with several chunks taken out of his suit.

My heart leaps. Thorn let him live. Then I wince. The poor guy. It looks freezing out there.

For a second, gratitude flings through me. Then fury at the memory of me on my knees begging. I might be afraid of Thorn because I'm not an idiot, but I'm still independent.

So I scramble through the cupboards and find a thermos that I fill to the brim with fresh coffee. Tugging my cardigan closer around my chest, I hurry outside and all but run across the grass to reach the soldier.

"What are you doing out here?" he asks, blood flowing from his earlobe. A myriad of bruises show across his face and neck, and he's moving as if his ribs hurt.

My stomach revolts. "Oh my gosh, did you get bitten?"

"Yeah, I got bitten," he says, shaking his head. "I donna think yer supposed to be out here."

The rain mats my hair to my head. "I know. I just want to say I'm really sorry about the other day." I hand him the thermos.

"What's this?" He looks young and slightly confused.

"It's just coffee. I didn't mean to get you in trouble."

He opens the top of the thermos and takes a big drink. Red infuses his face. "That's okay. I guess it was a smart move to go for the phone, and ya did save my life."

"I thought I could find a way to call for help," I say, "but I almost got you killed."

He gulps and looks toward the cliffs and then back at the

pond. "It's okay. All of us need ta be faster to survive in this world, even underwater. And believe me, I'll be faster by the time I'm done with this assignment."

I turn my head to the side and sneeze.

He gestures toward the castle. "You need ta get back inside. I don't want either of us gettin' in trouble."

I agree. I pat his arm. "Thank you for being my friend."

Confusion crosses his face, and I chuckle. Even so, the wind picks up and I have to duck my head as I run back inside and note two men with sledgehammers in their hands. I skid across the marble floor. "What's going on?"

One burly man looks at the other. "We have orders to take out a few of the windows." Without waiting for a response, they turn and walk upstairs to the guest bedroom.

"Why are you taking out windows?" I ask, my heart stuttering. They don't answer, and soon I hear the sound of shattering glass. I can't believe it. Thorn is actually replacing the windows for me? I turn and hustle across the sprawling living room to his study and see that the windows have already been changed to clear glass that look out over the ocean. No more argyle pattern. Why is he being so kind to me?

Which makes me think. I've never reacted to any male the way I do to Thorn, and I also fully understand that we have no future.

But we could have one night. It's my decision, and I'm making it for good reasons. One, to defy my father. He doesn't own me or my choices. Also, just in case I need to marry Cal to save the company, I want one night of passion first. With Thorn. So long as he agrees to let me go afterward.

Not only will that night be memorable, but it will be my choice. Not my father's. I'll never forget the smug look on Cal's face about my virginity.

I'm choosing my first time. Period. And frankly, I deserve one good night of raw, unbelievable, rare passion.

I gulp, wondering if I'm lying to myself. Am I just giving in to the powerful current running between Thorn and me? Do I crave that darkness he promises?

No. Absolutely not. This self-doubt has to go, so I turn and head back into the library. My skin is tingling today, and I know it's because I haven't been online for two days. It's rare that I take any sort of vacation. In fact, when I do travel, I post about the entire experience. Aquarius Social's algorithm requires emotion. We are emotion-based. And without my emotions, I'm sure we're losing subscribers and energy. I have to get my hands on a phone soon. Tomorrow doesn't seem soon enough, but I also don't want to put any more of Thorn's men in peril. I have a sinking feeling that if I steal another phone, that person will die.

Thorn Beathach isn't a man to show mercy twice.

I start reading through books I know we don't have in our own library. There are so many, and I make a small pile of the ones I would like to take with me. Most have to do with different gemstones and crystals, and I'm delighted to find an obscure collection of philosophies from Gaius the Sage, an obscure and uncelebrated genius who lived 2,000 years ago. I only have one volume in my library and hadn't a clue there are more.

Darkness starts to fall and I'm getting bored. Pushing the books to the side, I make my way back to Thorn's office and the beautifully clear windows there. The idea that he did that for me is both confusing and enticing.

I sit at his desk and reach for the remote control to turn on the plasma television. It isn't a phone and I can't post, but at least it's a screen. I scroll through channels until I reach the local news. Not much is going on. More homeless, more drugs, and more people fleeing California.

Sighing, I scroll through channels to a local gossip show that I love. Oh, I shouldn't, but the host is delightful. Emmaline is around eighteen with bright blue lipstick, several nose piercings, and a penchant for hyperbole. I long for popcorn as I sit back and listen to her talk about the several up-and-coming breweries in town that didn't up or come. Several are leaving.

Where in the world is Thorn? I'm tired of my own company. I want his. If I proposition him, will he say yes? No strings, just one night? My thighs warm at the thought.

Emmaline's voice lowers on the screen and I jerk my attention back to her. Her cherub-sweet face falls and she clears her throat. "I do have a report in from the Palo Alto authorities that a body has been found in an alleyway behind the Crux Bar. The face has been beaten beyond recognition, but the victim is a woman in her midtwenties with long curly brown hair. She's dressed in yellow with high-heeled sandals while accessorizing with an aquamarine pendant, and she was raped before being beaten to death."

That's terrible. Nausea filters through me.

Emmaline leans forward. "Now, I know many people dress like Alana Beaumont because she's quite the fashion icon, and I understand that this might be a terrible coincidence. But I have to ask: Has anybody seen Alana since the night of the hushed-up shooting at Martini Money?"

I sit back, my ears heating. Emmaline has good sources, and I'm not surprised she was able to get info on the shooting, even if the main media isn't touching it.

She shakes her head. "I'm just saying. Alana never fails to post at least once a day, and we haven't heard a word. I've reached out to my contacts and nobody is talking." The screen flashes to a picture of me. "Have you seen her?" she asks.

I turn off the television. I'm not dead, but a woman with my characteristics is? I need to get back onto social media. I eat a salad for dinner, wondering where Mrs. Pendrake is hiding. Thorn's employees are invisible, they're that good. Still, it'd be nice to have somebody to chat with as I'm slowly going out of my mind.

So of course, I relive that orgasm from the other night. Sure, I've read about such climaxes in romance novels, but until that moment, I'd thought them exaggerated. Not real.

Thorn is all too real.

Finally, I return to the library to read some more, still wondering what I should do tonight. Besides Thorn. Dancing with the devil has never been my goal, and yet, here I am considering it.

Around nine that evening, I hear heavy footsteps. Both Thorn and Justice walk into the library. There's something off. I can feel it, but I can't see it. "What's going on?" I ask.

"Nothing," Thorn says, his expression inscrutable. He's once again dressed in black slacks, a white button-down shirt, and black suit jacket. All Armani. "Did you have a nice day?"

I look from Justice to Thorn and back. "I did, but I really do need to post something, unless you want Aquarius Social to go under." He doesn't move and my heart sinks. He does want Aquarius Social to fail. I can't let that happen.

He sighs. "Other people can post and explode all of the stars."

Oh. He has no idea I'm the one who charges the crystals. I lift my chin. Why is he continuously underestimating me? It'll be his downfall, I'm sure.

Justice looks at his brother. "*Are you going to tell her?*" he asks in Gaelic. I try to look curious and not like I know what he said.

"*Yes,*" Thorn replies in the same language. "*I'll question her later. You're excused.*"

Justice pauses and reads the screen of his phone. "*A couple of news outlets are reporting her death. Something about a killer in town murdering brunettes.*"

That didn't take long.

Thorn cocks his head. "That might come in handy. You're excused, Justice." He speaks in English this time.

Justice turns and storms out.

Come in handy? Does he plan to hide me from the entire world? "Why did you just hurt his feelings?" I ask.

Thorn stares at me. "What?"

How can he not see that? "Justice is your brother. He wants in on your life, but you treat him like an employee. It hurts him." I stand.

Thorn looks toward the now vacant doorway before glancing at his watch. "Don't worry about my brother. For now, answer one question. Do you know how to code?"

"No." Heat rises into my face. It's embarrassing that I don't code. Yet another subject I still need to teach myself. "Why?"

He studies me with that intense gaze I can feel beyond this second. "You know that if you try to kill me, I'll retaliate, right?"

My heartrate picks up. "Are you threatening me with death?"

"No. I won't kill you, but you won't be happy. For a long time."

"What in the hell are you talking about?" Sure, I want to kick him in the balls much of the time, but I won't murder him or attempt to do so. That's not me. Plus, I kind of want to get him naked now that I've decided to take my own destiny into hand. "Thorn?" I prod.

"Doesn't matter. Right now, you and I both need sleep. Move. Now."

I tilt my head, too unsettled to sleep. "I need to post something, Thorn. Let me borrow your phone."

His eyes blaze. "Why? Do you think I want to help you feed Aquarius Social? Let me disabuse you of that notion."

I take a step back. "I know we're rivals. But isn't there a sense of balance among the four families?"

"Balance? Who gives a shit about balance?" He scrubs a large hand through his thick hair. "Your father called three times today."

The change in subject throws me. My father was fishing, but at least he's looking for me. "What did he say?"

Thorn's smile holds a hint of cruelty. "Nothing. I didn't answer."

I roll my eyes.

One of Thorn's eyebrows rises. "I saw a post where an influencer named Jackie interviewed you."

I'm getting a headache from the fast switches in topic. "I get interviewed a lot."

"For Malice Media."

"Oh." I think back. "Yeah, I remember. I agreed because I pimped Aquarius Social the whole time." Is this why he's pissed? "That's not out of the ordinary, Thorn."

He's studying me as if he wants to dig right into my head. "Did you have anything to do with the upload of that interview onto my system?"

"Of course not. It wasn't my feed." Duh.

Yeah, he's irritating me, and it's obvious he's in a grumpy mood, but the man oozes sex appeal. I wonder if there's a way to bottle his pheromones and sell them. I'd make a fortune. Even better, what if I could somehow tie them to Aquarius and our user experience?

"Alana?" Thorn's smooth as bourbon voice pulls me from my thoughts.

I jerk. "Sorry. Lost in my own brain." Which always pisses off my father.

"What's twisting around in there?" Thorn asks.

I startle. He's asking about my thoughts? Not angry that I'm daydreaming when he's trying to talk to me? "About a way to bottle your sex appeal and sell it to lonely women." Heck. Happy women would want it, too.

He falls silent, his head cocking slightly. "Sex appeal?"

"Yes." I study him. He's so tall and broad—so strong. Add in the obvious intelligence and whole pissed-off, wounded male vibe, and every female cell in my body explodes. This is beyond wrong, but I don't care. I want the feelings from this night. The experience before I sacrifice myself for the company and my family. This is for me. "Speaking of which, I'm wondering if you'd like to pick up where we left off the night before."

He stills. Not in an obvious way, but more like a shift in the energy that surrounds him. "Are you messing with me?"

"No." I might be reckless sometimes, but I'm not stupid. Or suicidal. "If my father called three times, he has a good indication that I'm here. So I won't be here much longer. I thought that perhaps we could make one good memory." When he just stares at me, those dark eyes burning, I start to babble. "I want my first time to be my choice. You're a good kisser, and I figure you're good at everything else this entails. I'm tired of being a virgin." True story.

He makes a sound like a trapped alley cat.

I continue, afraid he's going to think I've lost my mind. Maybe I have. "You're not afraid of my family, and they can't come after you. You're safe, Thorn."

"Baby, I'm nowhere near safe," he says, clenching his fingers into fists.

Power thrills through me. Feminine power, because I can tell I'm getting to him. Being wanted by a man like Thorn is intoxicating. Even so, I have a functioning brain. "But we do need to discuss the whole obsession thing you admit to having."

"You afraid I'll have you once and become more obsessed?"

"How should I know?" But if his obsession with me feels anything like the demanding urge I feel to get back on social media, or the memory of his mouth on mine going through a loop in my brain, the matter needs to be addressed. "I can't have you trying to kidnap me every time I'm in a bar." My traitorous clit pounds in disagreement.

His nostrils flare and my body braces for attack. "You're misreading me, Alana. I have no plans to take you back."

"I'm a sure thing, Thorn. I just propositioned you. No need to go alpha male on me."

"Just thought you deserve the truth first."

I want to retreat but a sofa bars my way. "Even you can't control the entire world."

"No. Just you." His breath looks frosty.

I frown. "It must be freezing outside. Did you get chilled?"

He nods. Once.

"How about I warm you up?"

Then he's on me.

SIXTEEN

Thorn

Never in my life have I been offered something so sweet. I tunnel both hands through her luxurious hair and tip back her head, taking her mouth. She still tastes like the purest of honey, and this time there's a hint of my imported coffee with it. But beneath both is the taste of the woman herself, something so savory and uniquely Alana that I drink to fill myself as much as possible.

God, her mouth is delicious.

She presses against me, her lush tits flattening against my much harder frame.

I deepen the kiss, and her body melts until I hold her weight. Her response is unbelievably honest, and it could be her innocence, but instinct whispers that it's just the woman herself.

I believe her about not posting on Malice Media. I'd taste a lie in her words, and she's innocent this time. The thought that somebody used her to get at me is pushed aside for now.

She fits perfectly against my frame, and I give her more of

my tongue, one hand sliding down her fragile back to settle at her narrow waist.

Dreams featuring her have tormented me this last year, but not one comes close to the perfection of her in this moment.

Hell. It's worth dying if I can take this memory to hell with me.

Her fingers dig into the front of my shirt and then she's deftly unbuttoning it, her hands spreading across my torso. The soft hum of pleasure that emanates from deep inside her spectacular body slides into my mouth and surges through me like a live wire.

I fucking love how she's soft everywhere I'm hard. Oh, it's too late to save me, and my soul is doomed. But for the briefest of seconds, I can see heaven. Taste it, anyway.

Sweeping her up against my chest, I nearly stumble when she laughs, the sound free. Young and open.

Warning ticks in the back of my mind, but it's way too late for that.

Regaining my footing, I stride through my home and up the stairs to my bedroom. I've never had another woman in here, and it feels right that she's the one. No way am I going to examine that feeling.

I kick the door shut behind me and she smiles, leaning in and nipping my neck.

My girl likes to explore.

Then she sinks her teeth into the skin beneath my ear.

Fire roars down my spine to my balls, and I fight the desperate urge to push her down and fuck her until she's screaming my name. Instead, I place her gently on the bed and crouch before her, taking in the desire and curiosity in her eyes. "You're sure." My voice sounds as if I've chewed on rusty nails all night.

"I am." She hesitates only a second before reaching for my belt buckle.

Letting her play, I shrug out of my heavy jacket and then my shirt.

Her eyes widen and she reaches up to press her finger on a healed bullet wound. "There are three."

They landed across my rib cage but weren't a concern. The knife wound near my heart had almost ended things a week later, however.

She licks her lips. "So much pain." Frowning, she looks up at me, her hands pulling my belt free. "How many fights have you been in?"

"Too many to count," I say honestly, wondering if she's trying to kill me with the belt. I yank it free and toss it over my shoulder.

Her eyes widen and she looks vulnerable for the first time.

"I won't hurt you," I say, meaning it. I won't allow anybody to harm her while I'm still breathing. It shocks me that she can't see that in my eyes, but it's a good thing. If she knew her power over me, it would be disastrous. My hands shake briefly as I remove her small cardigan.

Her hard nipples press against her tank top. I owe Mrs. Pendrake a raise for buying it. Gently, with one finger, I trace a path from Alana's clavicle to one breast, pressing in at the nipple.

She gasps and her mouth opens. I drop to my knees and tear the tank over her head. Her voluminous hair falls down and she blinks, reaching behind her to release her bra, her shoulders twisting. The scar from her childhood car accident is beneath her rib cage on the right, reminding me of her fragility.

"I've got it." I brush her hand away and deftly release the clasp. There isn't another human being on the planet I'd willingly get on my knees for, but I doubt she knows that. I need to see her. So I pull the bra away and drop it to the floor. Her breasts are perfection. Perfectly round and smooth, on the smaller side, with light pink nipples.

I lean in and take one into my mouth. She grabs my hair and

digs her nails in, shooting erotic pain into my skull. I test her by nipping her.

Her moan is of pleasure. Good.

I lay her back and tear off her skirt, shredding her panties. If she were mine, she wouldn't be allowed panties.

I must've said the thought out loud because she cuffs me on the ear.

Releasing her, I lift my head. "What the hell?"

"I'm not yours, will never be yours," she says through gritted teeth, her color high and her eyes glittering with lust. "But if I were, I'd wear any damn thing I wanted."

I like this flash of temper and independence. Oh, I'll lay waste to both, but it's good to see where she is. "I see." Planting a hand on her stomach, I toss her back on the bed.

She struggles to sit up, but I force her legs apart and then indulge myself. Her clit is already red and swollen, and her thighs are damp. When I suck her clit into my mouth, she jolts and then relaxes as her thighs tremble against my shoulders.

Fucking heaven. I'm right there. But I lift up to see her face flushed and her eyes dazed. "Remember rule number one." I rest my chin on her cleft.

She tries to focus, and it's adorable. And sexy as hell. "Rule?"

"Yes." Unable to help myself, I turn and bite into her upper thigh.

Her moan slips from her mouth before more liquid spills from her core.

"Tell me," I order.

She frowns. "Rule number one. No lying?"

"Yes. That means honesty at all times. If you don't like something I'm doing, you tell me. If anything scares you, you tell me. If you're unsure, you—"

"Tell you?" Her mouth curves. "Fine. I don't like that you just stopped."

My heart turns right over and heats. For her. "Fair enough." I release her gaze and go at her again, taking every ounce of her that I can. Using my fingers, teeth, and tongue, I force her up to the edge, where she hovers, gyrating against me, desperate.

For a heartbeat, I hold us both on that precipice. Then I scrape her clit, and she arches, shrieking out as the orgasm takes her.

Turns out my girl is a screamer.

Alana

I'm pretty sure he's killed me. Death by orgasm isn't a bad way to go. But then he stands and his hands go to the snap of his slacks. A fluttering starts inside me, and I'm shocked to learn I'm not done. Not even close.

He kicks the slacks aside and then everything inside me stills. The guy is endowed. I mean, he has the ego for it, but who knew? Not that I have anything to compare him to, but there's no way that thing's fitting inside me.

I lever myself up on my elbows. "This isn't going to work."

His smile makes him look years younger. "You were made for me." Then he's on top of me, his dick against my still-thrumming sex, his mouth on mine.

He likes to be on top. I can tell.

The feeling of his hard body pinning me to the mattress, making it give, shoots desire right through my bloodstream again. I shift restlessly against him, but he's not done kissing me.

With a growl, he captures my jaw and then kisses me harder, going deep. I close my eyes to just feel. Then he leans back and slides both hands from my abdomen up my breasts, squeezing slightly.

I like the bite. Yet one more surprise that I'm learning about myself.

Then he lowers his head and encloses one nipple in his inferno-hot mouth. Are all mouths this hot? I don't think so.

Then he drives me crazy. There's no other way to describe the sensation. With his mouth and wicked fingers, he takes his time on my tits, leaving bites and light bruises that will be there for weeks.

As if he wants to mark me.

I whimper at the thought.

His chuckle is dark. Knowing. "You're garna give me everything, Alana Beaumont."

I like the way his brogue comes out at times like this. Normally I can't tell he's even Irish. "Maybe," I breathe, sounding like I've run a 10k. "I guess this is okay."

He rolls onto one elbow, tosses me onto my stomach, and slaps my ass. Hard. Before I can get out a protest, I'm on my back with him covering me again. "Doesn't matter where we are or what we're doing, break rule number one and I'll retaliate." He leans in, his mouth above mine. "And you might want to remember that your butt isn't the only part of you I can spank."

My pussy trembles. Hand to God, didn't know it could do that.

His eyes darken as if he can read every thought I've ever had. Slowly, he grasps my wrists and draws my hands above my head. "Keep them here."

But I want to touch. "That's not fair."

"I'm not fair," he says, sinking his teeth into the vulnerable flesh between my neck and shoulder. Marking me again.

"Please," I whisper, surprising myself. No matter what he says, we have to be temporary. This might be our only night.

He leans back and studies me. "Such a pretty please. All right. This time."

I thrill at the thought of this lasting more than one night.

He kisses me again almost as a reward and I realize it's a good thing we're temporary. If he gave it half an effort, he'd own me. As this stands, I think I'll remember this night until my dying day. My clit aches and I feel empty inside. He sucks on a nipple, and I nearly orgasm again but hold back.

He caresses my entire body as if memorizing each inch. "You're giving yourself to me. Understand?"

"Yes." I'd say anything right now. I feel like I'm drowning but have no desire to rise to the surface. But I frantically trace his body, trying to learn each hollow and sharp muscle, each wound and scar. There are so many. His back is shredded, and within the whip scars, I feel more pointed wounds from weapons. All sorts of weapons.

I push against him. Needing all of him. "Thorn?" I hiss raggedly.

He lifts up from my breasts, his nostrils flaring, looking like a predator in danger of losing its treat.

"I ache," I whisper, gyrating against him. A big, gaping emptiness is inside me, and I need him. Need him to feel this. Need to understand I'm not alone.

Something in my gaze catches his attention and he nods, pressing against my entrance. "You're on birth control and I'm clean."

I pause. "How do you know that?"

"I know everything about you."

He pushes the tip inside me, stretching me. "You're sure."

The fact that he asks again burrows deep into my heart and takes hold. "I'm sure." This is my decision and never should've been anybody else's.

Then Thorn is pushing inside me.

God, it hurts. I curl my nails into his taut arms and try to relax my body. I want this. Kind of. Maybe. Wait a minute—

He kisses me. Going deep, taking every thought out of my mind. Before too long, I'm kissing him back, my body on edge, my hands caressing up and down his arms to then tangle in his hair.

All the while, he continues pushing inside me. He reaches the barrier and we both hold our breath.

Truth be told, I wondered if it was still there. I had played sports as a kid, and hymens aren't all that reliable. Unfortunately, I know it's there, and he plunges right through it.

Pain shrieks through me and I arch, scratching into his skull.

"*There you go*," he murmurs in Gaelic, kissing me again, unleashed fully this time.

Sparks fly and nerves flare, even with the pain. Pleasure and pain mingle and become one, much as they had when he spanked me. Finally, he's inside me, all of him, and I feel way too full.

He lifts up, his eyes unfathomable as he watches me closer than anybody in the world ever has. Then he moves. Slowly at first, gauging my reaction, he pulls out and then pushes back in.

I hold my breath as more pleasure than pain ripples through me. Then he does it again, and when I widen my thighs for him, he growls. Low.

Releasing his hair, I scratch down his back and sink my nails into his tight butt.

It's as if I've let him off a leash. He pulls out and shoves back in, setting up a hard rhythm that bounces the headboard against the wall. Thunder rolls outside and lightning strikes before the rain beats at the windows. We're alone in this world, and there's nothing except the two of us and this moment. I feel myself climbing the cliffs again as lights spark behind my eyes.

The roaring comes in from somewhere, taking over my senses. Then I explode, fragmenting into a million shards. I cry out his name, loudly, and hold on, trusting him to get us through the storm.

Whatever I'm feeling is more than pleasure. There's no name. I whimper and soften just as he stiffens and hardens, his body jerking inside me. I can feel each ripple through his muscles, and I hold him, wanting to tether him to the world.

He pauses, still inside me, and kisses me.

This one is gentle and soft. Sweet and promising.

I blink. While I'd meant to give up that stupid barrier in my body, I'm very much afraid I've given up more than that.

Forget my heart. Does he have my soul?

SEVENTEEN

❦

Thorn

I run my hand down Alana's arm as she cuddles against me, her back to my front. With a soft patter of rain dropping against the windowpane, the sense of tranquility and peace wafts through me. Although I know it won't last, I take a moment to enjoy the sensation.

The dark possessiveness taking root deep inside me cuts a harsh path. She gave herself willingly to me, and I'm holding her to that promise.

Forever.

Stretching languidly, she yawns, the sound cute. Her hair is a wild mass that I spread over the pillow and up the headboard. I still can't believe how silky it is. I buried my face in its fragrant curls more than once during the long night. Even now, I run my fingers through it, captured by the feeling of the soft strands over my roughened skin. Yet another difference between us that seems right.

"How are you?" I ask, my voice deep in the calm morning.

"Good," she replies, her voice drowsy. I didn't let her get much sleep, but I can't find it in me to regret the night. She trails her fingers along my forearm in a soft touch, every word she speaks a small taste of honey on my tongue. "You have so many scars—who whipped you?"

I'm surprised by the question, figuring she would've already figured out the answer. Growing up within the violent world of the four families, there isn't time or space for naiveté. "My father."

She jolts and I realize that she doesn't belong in our dangerous world. She should be protected and secured far away from the violence and pain around us every day. Frustration bites at me that I won't be able to keep her safe if there's a war coming.

Everything inside me knows war is on the wind.

"I shouldn't have told you that." I roll her honey taste around on my tongue. Maybe I should record her voice to keep with me forever. It's much better than the bitter mints I use to protect myself.

"Why not? It's the truth. That's a thing with you, right?" There's amusement in her voice now and I wonder if I'd really heard the sorrow. Maybe not. "Why would your father beat you?" She sounds young and innocent again, tempting the beast down inside me that I've subdued.

I rub my thumb over a bite mark I left on her arm. "It was after Justice, his mom, and I were taken. Father was angry I let it happen." The memory bursts through me, and I hate him even more for interrupting our blissful morning.

She's quiet for a moment and I can almost hear the gears turning in her head. "Wait a minute. You were kidnapped, tortured, and scarred, and when he rescued you, he beat you?" Now outrage fills her voice.

I calm her by sliding my fingers through hers, being careful not to break her fragile bones. "Yes, I was ten years old and Justice only eight, Charity was murdered, and I shouldn't have let it happen."

"You were just kids," she bursts out, pushing against me.

"It was a long time ago, Alana," I say, trying to ease her. Is she outraged on my behalf? It was as it was and there is no changing it. The scar on my face makes that fact all too clear.

She scoots her sweet butt closer to my groin, and I fight the urge to take her again. Three times in one night, her first night, was probably too much. Perhaps there is time for her to take a bath before breakfast. "I'm glad you had time with Justice's mother, since it feels like she was kind to you."

I want to give Alana something of me, even though admitting my childhood foolishness seems silly. "The week she died? I had big plans to ask her to be my mother."

Alana curls her fingers tighter around mine and I realize she's trying to offer comfort. My heart thumps once. Hard. "Tell me your plan. Please say you weren't going to order her around." Now she's teasing me, and something inside me unfurls. A solid block around my heart cracks, letting in light for the first time I can remember.

"No, I was going to ask." I hold Alana closer. "I was going to pick flowers from the garden, yellow roses because those were her favorite, and I was going to ask her if I could call her Mom." I shrug, reliving the memory. "I had accidentally called her Mom several times and she'd responded just as she would to Justice. My own mother died when I was still a baby," I say. "I figured it would be nice to have one, and she treated me like she cared." She looked like Justice with her dark hair and pretty brown eyes.

"I'm sorry she died," Alana says softly.

My phone buzzes and I glance at the screen. "I have to take this." I press a quick kiss to Alana's head. "You need sleep. I'll awaken you in a few hours." Without waiting for a response, I slide from the bed and pull on my slacks before padding barefoot out of the room and down to my study.

After shutting the door and sitting at my cold desk, I settle into work. "What is it, Kaz?" He mumbles something as if he's talking to himself. "Kaz," I say, with more force.

"Oh, sorry. I'm on the mainframe and the charge isn't lasting as long as usual. Do you have the main garnet anywhere around?"

"Yeah." I stare at the chunk of rock I'd brought home and then left on my desk as Kaz's taste of red licorice fills my mouth. It's fleeting, as usual. More of the garnet has frozen. Ice encrusts the entire left quarter as if trying to bore inside. I shiver as I realize my feet and legs are doing the same. During my night with Alana, I hadn't noticed. Here in the light of day, it's all too obvious. "The rock doesn't look good."

Kaz types loudly, punching keys. "I'm doing deep dives on all quantum magical possibilities while trying to hack into the servers of the three other families, but their security is almost as good as ours. Having these alexandrite crystals will help."

The alexandrite, if there is magic on earth, is as close as we're going to get. "I'll be in later today to help with the search. I have to run an errand first." My skills are as good as Kaz's. Between the two of us, perhaps we can find some clue about where this illness came from.

"Are you feeling any better?" he asks.

"No."

He sighs. "I did trace the video featuring Alana to Jackie, who was paid fifty thousand dollars before posting. She knew what she was doing."

"Now she's dead."

"Yeah. I'm trying to track the source of the payment."

I've always had enemies, so this isn't a surprise. But when I find them, they'll pay for involving Alana. I keep my temper at bay because Kaz hasn't slept in a week and is doing his best. "Anything else?"

"Yeah. The dead body of the woman found outside a downtown bar has been determined not to be Alana Beaumont. But it took DNA testing to find out because her face is smashed. She's the third one in the last couple of years."

I consider the matter. "Third one? As in related kills?"

"Not sure. Young women, downtown San Francisco, killed. The city is a cesspool of crime, so who knows. I'll look into it."

Either way, Alana's days of frequenting bars have now ended. "I'll be down to the office shortly." I click off.

Without preamble, my phone buzzes again. I catch sight of the caller and then flick on a video screen. Mathias Beaumont's face comes into view and I shove all emotion into the void where it belongs. It took him longer than I expected to find my more public phone number. Well, as public as I get. "Mathias," I say calmly.

His face turns red. "Where the hell's my daughter, you miscreant?"

My mouth fills with the taste of burned chicken, and I swear. Where are my mints? "Don't tell me you were careless enough to lose such a precious jewel." I put enough of an insult in my voice that he prickles instantly.

He stands up, looking close to having a heart attack. "I know you have her. In the quick escape from the bar, your people missed several traffic cams in the area."

That's probably the truth. "She's staying here, Mathias."

"You sure about that?" He leans in, his nostrils flaring. "This isn't my first kidnapping or ransom."

I smile, knowing the sight is chilling. "I have what I want."

His gaze turns calculating. "Actually, I have what you want." He reaches to the side and uses both hands to lift a raw uncut garnet in front of the screen. It's at least ten pounds—even bigger than the one connected to me. "Rumor has it you're looking for this." Mathias plops the stone on a surface out of sight and fury claws through my chest. "I'm proposing a trade."

I've sent so many feelers out for a garnet that size, it's a waste of time asking where he gleaned his information. I let coldness glimmer in my eyes. "You seem to be forgetting that I have your daughter." Am fully planning on keeping her. But that stone. I can feel its power. Can it cure me? Save Malice Media?

He scoffs. "This is a onetime offer—my daughter for this crystal. An exchange like in the old days. If you say no, I'll cut this thing up and grind every molecule to dust." His gaze narrows. "It's bigger than the one you have, but not by much. Why are you searching so hard for it?"

I can't tell if he's playing me or not. If he knows why, then he had a hand in creating the virus to destroy my garnet and my life. If he doesn't, then he's probably in danger since I'm sure he's the person who charges the stones for Aquarius Social. "The why of it is none of your business." I rapidly think through my options and don't like any of them. "Your daughter is safe here. You failed to keep her so."

"No, I didn't. I had guards in the bar and they helped take out the would-be kidnappers."

So he has the truth as well. "Who was behind the attack?" At the very least, I'll put them in the ground.

"Don't know yet," Mathias says. "We've traced the squad to the Twenty-One Purple gang, but so far, nobody knows who hired them."

Fury pounds through me. Alana is mine and nobody can take her, especially her asshole father. "I have someone on the inside of the gang and will find out. Alana stays here."

"Absolutely not."

Heat slashes through my chest. She's mine and she's fucking safer with me. "Still need a sacrificial lamb, do you?"

He doesn't like my sneer and his cheeks puff out. "My family matters are not your concern. Watching this stone be ground down might be."

Damn it. I need that garnet, but Alana has slid right beneath my skin, and the idea of letting her go is unthinkable. Still, I'm no good to her if I'm dead—I'll do whatever I must to secure a future with her. The memory of her sighing my name last night calms me. Slightly. "I'll trade you an alexandrite in a natural pyramid shape for the garnet."

"No. I want my daughter back."

I'm surprised. Maybe he does give a shit about her. "If you fail to keep her safe, I'll hunt you down and rip off layers of your skin, piece by piece."

His eyes cloud and then clear. Obviously confused. "She's engaged to another man, Beathach. Let's just get this over with."

I might kill him anyway. I can't tell her why I need the garnet. She'll tell her old man, and he can't have that knowledge over me. "All right, but I want your entire cache of garnets in addition to the large one. I'll send you coordinates half an hour before the meet in two hours." That way my snipers will be in place long before his.

"If you've touched her, I'll kill you," Mathias threatens.

I've done a hell of a lot more than touch her, but that's none of Mathias's business. What happens between Alana and me is ours. I'm not sharing any of it with this asshole. "Don't be a moron."

"I want the quartz crystals and the four alexandrite pyramids you stole from me as well," he blurts out.

My smile feels cruel. "Sorry. Your garnets for one beauty. I'm keeping the crystals." I'm also keeping the beauty, as this is a temporary swap.

"Listen, you bastard." He leans closer into the frame. "If you want a war, I'll give you one. You won't win."

Considering I'm nowhere near done with his daughter, I might have to kill him if he doesn't retreat. That'll probably anger her. "Stop threatening me, little man. One more word and I'll forget my good intentions about returning your daughter. Piss me off, and I promise you'll never see her again." I glance out the window and see Dermot and another one of my men feeding the creatures in the moat.

Mathias snarls. "I want to see my daughter and I want to see her right now."

I glance at the darkened sky. "It's four in the morning. Your daughter is peacefully asleep. I'm not waking her up."

"I want to make sure she's okay."

I can't tell if he's being truthful or not. So far, in my opinion, he hasn't been a very good father. Does he miss his daughter or does he just need his best influencer for Aquarius Social? "Get used to disappointment," I mutter. "I'll send you the coordinates of the location fifteen minutes before the meet."

"You said half an hour," he sputters.

"I changed my mind." I click off. Appearing contradictory to one's enemies is a good thing. I don't want him having any idea what I'm capable of. I look again at the icy garnet on my desk. If he had anything to do with giving me this virus, I'll make sure he precedes me to meet the devil.

EIGHTEEN

Alana

Fury sparks like live wires in my bloodstream, and it's a feeling I hold on to with both hands. So much better than pain.

Thorn woke me with a rough order to get ready to go. No explanation, no hint of regret. I hurriedly dressed before meeting him down in the vestibule.

A blush of dawn begins to tinge the sky pink and peach as we drive through the outskirts of the Port of Redwood City. Tension fills the SUV, and I try to remain calm in the backseat but it's difficult to refrain from reacting. My entire body is satisfied and sore, and even the long bath I took earlier hasn't erased the evidence of Thorn's lovemaking. I mean, sex. Man. Now I'm seeing little hearts in my eyes, and he's trying to get rid of me. Seriously.

I have small nips, scratches, and bites in the most intimate of places. I feel like I have been completely and truly fucked—in a very good way.

Thorn may have ruined me for all other men.

I so want to question him right now but can't with the two men in the front seat of the vehicle. It's too embarrassing.

I truly hate him with the depths of hellfire. He got what he wanted. My stupid virginity? It's like Cal said: Everyone wanted in my pants, and whoever got there first could declare themselves the big winner. Thorn got there, and I let him. I said yes.

He won. The bastard.

He sits next to me in his customary black slacks and white shirt, but today he has a weapon in a shoulder holster as well as one at his hip. I believe they're both Glocks, but to be frank, I've never paid much attention to guns. His body is all tight muscle, and he feels more distant than the few inches between us. Whatever happened last night is over. He has moved on.

I feel like a painting that he brushed with vibrant colors of passion and need last night. Now with his sudden coldness, all of the hues are blotted out. I'm gray and lifeless. Listless.

And I'm getting maudlin. For Pete's sake. I propositioned him and said I was leaving.

But he said he wanted me to stay. As a liar, he's a master.

Justice looks back at us. "We have intel, long-range surveillance, that Mathias packed a chest of garnets to trade."

I want to puke. They're trading me for crystals? I'm being ransomed? Justice drives, and there's another guard in the passenger seat who was introduced as Sean when we started the journey. He's a barrel of a man with a crew cut and thick neck who looks as if he could run through a metal door without breaking stride. In front of us, two SUVs take the lead while two follow behind.

For stupid garnets? He's trading me for stones? "Isn't this a bit of overkill?" I ask. "We're meeting my father, right?"

"Exactly," Thorn says grimly, focusing his gaze out the window as if he's expecting an attack. He fills out his shirt with those cut muscles I memorized the night before.

I don't like the idea of anybody getting shot. If my father's men feel the same level of tension as these guys, lead will be flying in every direction. With my current luck, I'll probably take a bullet to the throat. "Can I have a gun?" Might as well protect myself.

"No." Thorn doesn't turn my way.

"Why not?" I push for any emotion from him.

He turns to me. "Because you're in no danger when I'm near you."

Finally, we pull to a stop in front of a row of rusty, battered, and dented warehouses. Thorn glances at his watch. "Sean, scout," he says.

Sean instantly slips from the vehicle and out into the rain. Dawn isn't making much headway through the clouds. But at the moment, I figure that might be a good thing.

"Snipers?" Thorn asks.

Justice nods, his hands loose on the steering wheel. "Yes. We've got the entire area covered." He glances in the rearview mirror and then launches into Gaelic. "*Why are you letting her go?*"

Yeah. Good question, Justice. I hold my breath and hope Thorn answers.

Thorn doesn't look at me and replies, "*I need the garnet and you know it. There's no other way to get it.*"

Justice's hands tighten on the wheel. "*You know Mathias has been collecting garnets, and he wants to bring you down. Let's take him out now. Weaken Aquarius Social. It's a good move.*"

Dread pools in my abdomen and I concentrate on the back of the headrest in front of me, trying to level my breathing.

"*I'm not ready to declare war,*" Thorn returns. He lifts his shoulder, and I can tell his thoughts are following a dark path. It's amazing how much I feel I know him after last night. He was rough, sexy, possessive, and then sweet. Oh, how he'd hate for anybody to know he could be sweet for a few minutes. But as he calmly plots murder, I wonder if it was just an act. If so, he was very good at it. *"I'd want to question Mathias before killing him, anyway."*

I gulp and try not to gag. They are actually talking about brutally torturing my father. I can barely breathe. Thorn is sitting next to me after the night we shared, and he's considering killing my father? I know he can be cold, but this is a shock. "I think I just heard my father's name. Why are you speaking in Gaelic?" Just how far will he take the lie?

"Because we're rude bastards," he says easily.

So. He tells the truth. There is absolutely no doubt or regret in his deep voice. Just who is this man? I want to punch him in the throat, but if I do that, I won't be able to warn my father. I guess last night was just a blip outside of reality.

Lightning zaps near the closest warehouse and I jump.

Justice straightens in the seat. *"Last chance. I could go rogue and just shoot him, covering you,"* he says, his voice monotone as if they're talking about the weather.

How can he ask such a thing with me in the vehicle? I look out the window as if bored because I can't understand Gaelic.

"Not here. Not in front of her," Thorn retorts quickly, his Gaelic fast.

Well, I guess there's that. Even so, if Thorn's going to declare war within the families, why care what I think? I swallow, and my throat feels parched. If we are enemies, why has he trusted me so? My gaze is drawn to him again. A thought occurs to me. Just how badly does he want to win? "Are there cameras in your bedroom?" What if this is all a game and I'm going to star in Malice Media accounts having sex for the first time?

"Of course not." His eyes burn with emotion, and I take a moment to gather my wits. He feels like an animal barely leashed, and the tension in the vehicle starts to choke me. "I don't share. Never forget that."

Both men go on full alert as another caravan drives into

place. I recognize my father's car in the middle. Thorn has positioned himself between me and my family. "Stay here and don't come out until I tell you," he orders.

"Wait." I grab his arm even though I don't know why. "Don't." I guess I don't want him to get shot. No matter how I look at it, last night is one I'll never forget.

"Stay here." He opens the door and steps out as Justice does the same. Unable to help myself, I scoot over to their side and look through the window. My father and Nico step out of his car as his men jump out of the vehicles on either side. All of a sudden, everybody has guns pointed at everybody else.

I can't let this happen. I shove open the door and hit Thorn in the back of his thighs. Without looking, he reaches in and grabs my arm to pull me out. Rain instantly smashes into me and I blink, trying to see.

"Are you all right?" my father asks.

I stand tall in dark jeans, wedges, and a yellow sweater. "I'm perfectly all right," I say. Hopefully I look calm and in control of myself. I'm not. My emotions are all over the map. "Nobody needs to get shot today."

"No," my father says. "That will come another day." He stares directly at Thorn as he speaks.

"I look forward to it," Thorn drawls. "Where are my garnets?"

The question slices through me sharper than a knife.

My dad points to the last truck in his caravan, where men are unloading a large metal trunk. Thorn lifts a finger, and two of his men take possession of the container, looking quickly inside, nodding, and then running it over to their SUV.

Seriously? He really did barter me for garnets. That ass! "How many garnets am I worth?" I ask, looking way up at Thorn's implacable face.

One of his eyebrows rises. "Many more than I'll ever get. I promise."

"Whatever." I turn and let out an exaggerated sigh. "Are we

about done with the posturing, boys? I really do have to get to work."

Nobody moves, and similarly, nobody seems all that impressed with my bravado.

"All right," Thorn says, releasing my arm. "Get in that car and away from the guns."

I take this last moment and partially turn to whisper. "Are you going to forget all about me?" Yep. I'm a glutton.

"No." There's no warmth in his tone as he says the word. "I promise you, Alana Beaumont, we are nowhere near done."

"This doesn't make sense."

"That's irrelevant," he says grimly. "I'm coming for you and soon. Don't for a second forget who you belong to."

I reach back into the car and haul out two backpacks before walking across the several yards of mudpuddle-riddled dirt road to reach my father.

He looks at me. "Did he hurt you?"

"No," I say honestly. Well, not in the way my father means.

"What the hell is in the backpacks?"

I swallow and try to keep from dumping them on the ground. They're so heavy. "Books." I already had a pile together when Thorn decided to kick me to the curb.

My father looks at me as if I'm insane but still opens the back door. I slide inside before he jumps into the front. Nico walks around and gets in beside me. The air is cooler here than in Thorn's vehicle. Did he keep the heat on for me? Man, I'm a moron. Of course not. I'm about to be in Thorn Beathach's rearview mirror for good.

Nico hands over a phone. "You need to post something and now. We're losing verified paying accounts by the second."

I accept the phone. Slowly, I roll down my window. "Hey, Thorn. It was real," I say.

He just looks at me as if he wants nothing more than to tear across the distance between us.

I swallow, heat filling my lungs. "You taught me a lot last night. Maybe I can teach you something as well." I smile, and it's forced, but I'm a woman who knows how to play for the cameras, after all. "Here it is. *You should never assume anything.*" I deliver the last in perfect Gaelic.

His eyes shift to a whole new color.

We drive away, and it takes every ounce of willpower I have not to look back. It doesn't matter. I can feel that stare boring into me.

Take that, Malice Media.

NINETEEN

❧

Thorn

The two garnets perch at the end of my desk, one diseased, one whole. Unfortunately, at the moment, I'm only drawn to the broken one. The other one is rich with red and black tones. While garnets are more beautiful after being cut and polished, they're more powerful in raw form.

Like me.

Angry ants march just beneath my skin, making my entire body feel too tight. Alana is out there, away from me. In danger, or at the very least, hurt. I blame Mathias for that.

I blame myself, as well.

The primal urge to track her down nearly has me rising, but first I need to determine her location. I hadn't figured on letting her go, so I currently lack the supplies to chip her. I won't make that mistake again and have already ordered Mrs. P to obtain the materials for me. Alana has only posted once, right after her father drove her away, and it was to smile and wink at the camera.

I turn and gaze out at the angry Pacific. Rain slashes the water hard enough that whitecaps spurt up as if ready to fight. Thunder claps with a harshness that rumbles through the stones of my dark castle, and the wind gusts a ghostly wail around my property.

Even the heavens are pissed I let her go.

Oh, she was mad.

I couldn't tell her about my illness. It's too early to expect full loyalty from her, and I'm sure she would've told her father. I can't have him learning of my weakness if he doesn't already know.

Justice strides in and plunks a mug of coffee at my elbow. "Feel anything with the new garnet?"

"Not yet." I'll take it to the servers later.

Justice turns to the full-screen plasma on the wall, where I have Alana's Aquarius Social account up. "Dude."

Did he just call me dude?

He leans against the doorframe, wearing his customary jeans and thick T-shirt. If he ever takes over this business, he'll have to step up and wear a suit. The thought cheers me. He drinks deep from his mug. "We'll find her and bring her home. Don't worry."

"What are you doing?" I ask.

He lowers the mug. "Supporting you. Being here for you. Being your fucking brother."

"I don't need support," I return.

He shrugs. "You do need a brother. Somebody who has your back no matter what." Leaning against the wall, he still appears deadly. "Alana is right. Your own brother shouldn't knock on your door."

Rumors had gotten around the boys about Alana saving Dermot's life by begging, and Kaz had reported in that several of them have started following her on Aquarius Social. We have their phones tapped just in case.

A couple of days here, just a couple, and she's leaving her mark. What will she do with decades? I grasp my mug and take a drink. Even that doesn't taste as good with her gone. It's like the light has deserted the entire property.

Justice cracks his neck. "Should we have put a hood on her head when we drove away from here? She was unconscious when we arrived."

"Yeah. Right. She knows she stayed in a castle by the ocean. Any helicopter can find us, Justice."

A frown darkens his face. "I'll up the security detail."

A new video loads on Alana's page and I stiffen, my heart speeding up as I turn to my laptop and prepare a tracing algorithm that I'll insert as a comment.

She smiles, now wearing a light yellow summer dress with sparkling aquamarine jewelry. Her hair is a free-flowing mane around her shoulders, and my fingers itch for a touch. "Hello, friends." Her throaty voice goes right to my dick. "I do apologize for being missing in action the last couple of days. I'm sure you heard rumors about a kidnapping at Martini Money's the other night, and they're true." Her eyes widen, and the green flecks stand out. "But I was rescued." She places a hand over her heart.

Justice straightens. "No. She won't—"

I can't determine much from her background and wait for the video to stop before loading my program.

She leans closer. "And guess who rescued me?" Her eyelashes flutter, and she looks every inch the ingenue. The damsel in distress with a sense of humor and more intelligence than most realize.

It's her joke. Her inside joke with her followers. They know it. They see it. They realize she's having fun and playing a part.

Yet I didn't. Oh, I saw her beauty and courage, and even her sense of humor. But not the obvious glint of genius in those eyes. No. I'd missed it, blinded by the absolute perfection of her form. And the taste of honey.

"Thorn Beathach, the reclusive owner of our rival, Malice Media, ripped me away from the flying bullets," she says with a flourish, her chin lifting in what my body takes as challenge.

My cock goes harder than any rock.

"She didn't," Justice breathes.

I sit back, my body humming. Misplaced amusement tickles through me along with awe. In one video, she's telling me, her father, and the Sokolov family to go fuck ourselves. While looking adorable and gaining energy like a tornado. Her feed is blowing up with exploding stars as her followers ignite.

She tilts her head. "I was with the reclusive billionaire for two full days, and boy, do I have a lot to dish." She winks. "Please explode-star this video so I know you want to hear more, and I'll return later today."

So many stars explode that they become a mass of sparks on the screen.

Justice yanks on his ear and chuckles. "She's using you to gain followers."

"And energy," I drawl, suddenly galvanized. The fact that she speaks Gaelic still stuns me. When did she learn? It's not in her school records. But she loves my library. Did she teach herself different languages just so she could read more books? It's possible.

"Let's get out ahead of this." He starts to pace. "You're an enigma to the world. A fantasy figure hidden away with your money and brilliance. Now you're a hero. We post about you now. On Malice Media, and take the moment away from Aquarius."

I like being obscure. "You want to put this ugly mug on our platform?" My scar alone makes me hideous to most people. Since I don't like most people, I'm fine with that fact. "We want more followers, not fewer, Justice."

He shakes his head. "Come on. Wounded badass in a suit? They write novels about guys like you."

Yeah. "It's called horror fiction." I dismiss the idea immediately. "No matter what she says, she didn't get any pictures." Nobody knows who I am, and I like my life that way. It occurs to me that when I take Alana again, for good this time, she'll need to acquiesce on that score. "She'll gain followers and interactions, but I have no doubt we'll earn interest as well." I explode one of her stars and plant my program, which quickly starts running on my laptop.

Oh, most people, even the US government, can't track her through the platform.

I'm not most people, and I channel the energy in Malice Media through our currently working garnets to give the algorithm an edge. Aquarius's programmers are good, and they'll spot it after it succeeds, then quickly close the door so I can't try again. I just need once. "How about you start an account and post *your* pretty mug for all to see?"

"No," Justice says. "I can't do my job if people know my face."

True enough. Justice is the best assassin in any of the organizations. I nod. "Very well, but we need to counter Alana's videos." She has the upper hand because of Aquarius's emotional-intelligence platform and her ability to project emotions. And now she's using me. However, we still have a better system because our neural interface allows users to share thoughts and emotions directly in real time. "She'd be unstoppable on our platform," I note.

He nods. "How about we pay the Rendale sisters a shit ton of money to debunk her claims about you rescuing her on our platform? We can say that she's lying to gain attention, and the Rendale sisters can look innocent and say they're posting on our social media system to set the record straight just because it's the right thing to do?"

The only threat to Alana is me. Nobody else. Period. "No, that would also help them out, and TimeGem is on our tail, and they're a bigger threat than Aquarius, by far."

Plus, if I am to demand her loyalty, she deserves the same.

The computers ding and I integrate a series of commands and locate Alana at Aquarius Social headquarters. Interesting. I would've bet she'd seek out her friends rather than dealing with business. Her father must not be giving her a choice. "She's at Aquarius. Send two details to cover her the second she leaves."

He lifts a hand. "Whoa. You sure you want to pursue war?"

"I'm just going to watch and protect from afar. I'm not giving the order to take her." If I know she's safe, I can focus on fixing this fucking garnet problem and the curse. My feet have frozen over, and I curl my toes to force blood into the tips. "Do you have plans tonight?"

"There's nothing on my calendar until we cure you," he says grimly.

A rare moment, a thump of emotion, shocks my heart. He's a good brother. "Then let's take the new garnet to headquarters and see what we can do." Nobody is as good with the interface as am I, but he's getting there, and just in case, I need to bring him up to speed. "I've already changed the language of the charter and the ownership percentages."

His shoulders go back. "I'm fine with my twenty percent."

"Too bad. Now you own thirty." If he has to take over with the garnet, I'll give him all of it. If not, it's still time to award him his due. "You're my only brother, and the only person in this world I trust, even if you do knock on my door before entering my home."

My computer dings again as the Aquarius techs no doubt find my plant. My connection shuts off abruptly. "I still have to head the Irish mafia, but you should take more of a role just in case the garnet kills me. I want you firmly in place so there's no challenge." The mafias make good foot soldiers for the four families. For mine, anyway. "Be ready to go in an hour."

"Copy that." He strides out of the room, his phone already at his ear as he barks orders.

I look at the frozen image on my screen and Alana's soft eyes before bringing up a feed from the video cameras in my library this week. She spent a lot of time in there. More than I realized. She's adorable when she reads. I zoom in and note that during her time with me, she read books in English, Gaelic, Latin, Chinese, Russian, French, and Spanish. And I'd thought her not a rocket scientist. She's smarter than all of the rocket scientists on my payroll right now. The woman must've taught herself multiple languages just so she could read more books.

The urge to jerk off takes me, and I shove it away. The only hand I want on my dick is hers.

I lift my phone to my ear and order it to place a call.

"Hey, Grumpy." Alana surprises me by answering, her voice a light sugary treat that zips through the phone line and into my mouth.

My blood heats. "Nice romantic swill you posted online earlier. Stop it, now." It's only fair to give her warning.

She snickers, and swear to the saints, my balls draw up tight. "Why? Which of your precious commandments have I broken?"

"All three of them." I settle back in my chair, my temper simmering. "You lied, because I'm no hero, and while here, you hid the fact that you speak and comprehend Gaelic." Which is both impressive and irritating as hell. "With your current video teases going on, you're obviously playing the rebel and thus defying me."

She sighs, and honey fills my mouth. "So that would be rules number one and three. Guess I missed the second one, huh?"

"Oh no, beautiful. Number two is to keep yourself out of danger. Pissing me off and challenging me is waltzing right into the cyclone's path. You're in danger, now."

I don't expect her to heed my warning.

She doesn't. "I suppose I'll be safe enough soon. Considering we're such good friends now that you're helping Aquarius Social by being the focus of my swoon-worthy emotional videos, I guess you should be included in my social events. Where would you like me to send your invitation to my upcoming nuptials?"

TWENTY

❦

Alana

I end the phone call more than happy with my performance and quite pleased to have poked the beast with all that marriage talk. He deserves it. I have a big heart, and he tossed it out the door. A little voice in the back of my head bellows that I'd go right back to him if he called.

No, I wouldn't.

My phone dings and my heart leaps into my throat. "Hello?"

"Hi! Are you okay?" Rosalie yells.

Wincing, I hold the phone away from my ear. "I texted you already." Unfortunately, the aquamarines required charging at the Aquarius Social servers, so that took up most of my morning. "I promise I'm fine and we'll catch up tonight after the board meeting."

"Oh no, you don't!" she shouts. "I want details right now about Thorn!"

Just the mention of his name makes my nipples sharpen. Damn it. "I'll give you full details when I see you." I maintain a calm tone of voice. While my phone has excellent security, no tech is absolute, and caution is my friend. "But you might want to get online. I'm about to dish publicly." I end the call as she's still sputtering.

Then I sit on the sofa in the lovely ladies' lounge at Aquarius Social, move aside Thorn's books on crystals that I've been devouring, double-check the lighting, and hold the phone up to my face. "I'm back. Thank you so much for all of the exploding stars. I guess you want to hear more." I look around and lower my voice to a whisper as if nosy ears are everywhere. "All right. So these three guys charged me with guns and I ran. Out of the shadows, Thorn Beathach scoops me up like a heroine in a romance novel and rushes through the rain to his SUV." I fan myself as if the memory is combustible. "He saved me. I have so much to tell you about him, but I have an Aquarius Board meeting on my agenda. Detonate all of the stars if you're craving more details." I end the video.

Guilt trips through me about that dead waiter. I need to find out his name and at least send my condolences to his family. It's my fault he's dead.

Yeah, I know Thorn will be pissed about my videos and I'm just getting started. When I stand, my knees wobble. Not that I'm frightened of him, because I'm not. I remind myself twice that I'm not. Shoving the phone in my pink, sparkly purse, I walk out of the ladies' lounge and stride through the top floor of the skyscraper, pausing outside the boardroom.

Margery Lips, my father's personal secretary, looks up from her desk. "These came for you."

My gaze is already caught. From a shockingly wide crystal vase, at least fifty red roses bloom with one white rose unfurling in the middle. I reach for the card and read: *To the one perfect rose. We're nowhere near done. ~Thorn.*

I can't breathe.

"They're waiting," Margery hisses. She's around ninety and looks like a crone, but she's right.

I leave the flowers and stride to the boardroom. When I walk inside, I stop and look at the people gathered around the table. "This is interesting," I murmur.

My father sits at the head with Nico to his left; to his right is the empty seat that I have come to consider mine. My distant cousins, Quinlan and Scarlett Winter, are seated by Nico. "Hello." I look at my father.

"Have a seat, Alana," he says, kicking out my chair.

My instincts hum. I gracefully walk inside and sit, wanting more than ever to get back to those books I borrowed from Thorn. Well, probably stole since I have no intention of returning them. Unless he wants to set up an exchange agreement, because there are many more books I want to get my hands on from his library.

"Hi, Alana," Quinlan says, his eyes widening. A stamp from a bar is on his left hand—something with a C. He'd partied with my brother a lot, so it's not a surprise. He works as a computer programmer for Aquarius and was good friends with Greg. I last saw him at the funeral. "I'm so pleased that you were found safely."

Found and exchanged for a bunch of rocks like in the Stone Age. I make a mental note to find out exactly what those garnets are worth. A girl does like to know her value. I swallow the bitterness I feel at Thorn's actions and force a smile. "Hi, Quinlan. This looks more of a family gathering than a board meeting," I say, nodding at his sister, Scarlett. She's a few years older than I am and has black hair and even darker eyes, having inherited her Chinese mother's exquisite bone structure, while her brother looks more like his Italian father. Their parents died young, and if I remember right, they've been raised by their grandmother, a distant relative. I believe Scarlett works in Human Resources for the corporation and travels quite a bit.

"Close enough," my father says. "After your kidnapping, I realized we need more family members involved in the business, especially those who have an affinity with aquamarines." He straightens his tie. "Just in case we need to replace you."

My mouth almost gapes open. Everybody thinks I'm expendable, apparently.

He leans back, catching himself. "Worst-case scenario, of course."

I study my distant cousins. So they make the grade, huh? While Nico is only twice removed, the Winters are far, far removed. "I take it you've been vetted?"

"Of course," Nico says. "Connection to the crystals lives in the blood. None of us are as charged as you, Alana."

"All right," I say. "I'm absolutely fine with the possibility of more family members sharing the load here. In fact, I like the idea of others charging the aquamarines."

Of course, my father dashes my idea of more free time. "Nobody has your affinity to the aquamarine crystals, but in a pinch, we could all combine to charge or protect the servers if necessary." He straightens his tie. "The more the better, right?"

As I have no intention of being kidnapped ever again, I see no reason to worry. Nonetheless, I flash a smile at all of my cousins. As far as I know, they're nice enough, but my father has always kept a tight rein on Aquarius Social.

Nico looks at me, his eyes burning. "I just found out about the changes that might be coming," he says shortly.

"Yes, I can see that." I narrow my gaze and then look at Father. "What's the new breakdown of ownership?" Apparently, Nico doesn't like it.

My father clears his voice. "I have the documents for you all to sign. After this transfer, I'll own sixty percent, and the four of you will have ten percent each."

A deep crimson creeps into Nico's face. "I absolutely do not agree with this plan."

My father shoots him a look that could ice over the Sahara. "I am not asking your opinion."

The phone buzzes in my purse, and I freaking know it's Thorn calling back. Somehow, the buzz holds a demanding weight. It has to be him. I swallow and stiffen my spine. "I'm with Nico," I say, crossing my legs.

My father slaps a hand on a file folder, and the sound echoes around the room. "Excuse me?"

With Nico watching me as if he's caught a lightning bug in a jar, I partially turn to face my father. "I'm with Nico," I say slowly and clearly. "We've dedicated our entire lives to Aquarius since before either of us could even type, and decreasing our shares to ten percent is an insult. It isn't fair, and I'm not signing anything that reduces our interests."

"I don't recall requesting your approval," my father says, his voice low with a thread of anger darkening the tone.

I cast a quick glance at my cousins. "You never do. I'm sure I don't have to remind you that I have the crucial connection to the aquamarine stones. That alone gives me a say." Not to mention that I'd have to sign the documents to give up part of my interest, and I'm more likely to run headlong back to Thorn than I am to do so. I wink at Nico. "Give us your take on this."

He blinks twice as if he's been slapped upside the head and can't believe the words flowing from my mouth.

Frankly, neither can I, but in the last week I have been kidnapped, devirginized, enlightened, and heartbroken. Right now, I'm just pure and simply ticked off.

Nico visibly relaxes. "It appears as if Alana and I are united here."

I look at my father. "I agree you have every right to retain a controlling interest in Aquarius. However, you may accomplish that by keeping fifty-one percent interest in the stock." I look at Nico. "Nico and I will remain at an ownership level of twenty percent each. We've done nothing to lose that. Period."

My father sits back and it appears as if his chest widens. "You're not going to dictate the future of this company to me."

I shrug. "I'm not trying to dictate, but I won't agree to any proposal that isn't fair."

Scarlett leans forward. "I didn't crawl out of the basement to take a measly four and a half percent."

I'm impressed she did the math so quickly. "Even a minority stake will make you millions of dollars a year. Feel free to return to your basement." I focus on my father. "Not only that, you still have a controlling interest, so even if we all decide to gang up on you, you'll still win."

Nico flattens both hands on the table. "I'm in agreement."

Yes, I bet he is.

My father exhales loudly, and he sounds like a furious bear. "I'll take this under advisement. Everyone please excuse my daughter and me."

The Winter siblings file out, while Nico remains in place. My father looks at him.

Nico shrugs. "Whatever you're going to discuss, I want to take part." Look at Nico growing a pair.

"I agree," I say. It doesn't hurt to have him in my corner.

My father looks from one to the other of us. "I don't like where either of you are taking this."

I try to keep my knees from knocking together. "That's not my concern."

My father glowers. "Nico, you will excuse us now."

Nico winks at me and then stands, smoothing down his perfectly tailored suit. "Very well. Alana, if you require me for anything, call." With that, he turns and strides from the room, shutting the door quietly.

My father pushes away from the table. "What is wrong with you?"

"Nothing. I'm just tired of being pushed around. What you were about to do wasn't fair, and you know it," I say, meeting his gaze directly. As usual, he looks away. I throw my hands up. "Why can't you even look at me?" He swallows, and it hits me. All of a sudden I know. "It's because I look like her, isn't it?"

He still has a picture of my mother above the mantelpiece. Even though I'm not allowed in his room, a while back, I needed something, I can't remember what, and I tiptoed in there to find her side of the bed just as it had been when I was young. Even her lotion is still in place.

"Yes," he says, the sound tortured. "Don't ever fall in love like I did, Alana. The pain isn't worth it."

I barely keep myself from laughing, because it's probably too late for that. "Did you court for a long time?" Please say yes. For years. It took years to fall in love.

"No. It was love at first sight."

Wonderful. As if things could get more brilliant. I'm fairly certain three orgasms shouldn't lead automatically to love, yet why does my chest feel like somebody is trying to open it with a crowbar?

Finally, my father looks at me. "What happened to you when you were kidnapped?"

"Nothing I didn't want," I say honestly, meeting his gaze.

He pales. "You and that monster?"

"He wasn't a monster. At least not completely." That waiter's face flashes through my mind and I push it away.

My father smacks his palm against his forehead. "How am I going to explain this to the Sokolov family?"

I want to punch him, so I fold my hands in my lap. "I don't know, tell them to join the current century? My sex life is none of anybody's business, and I'm tired of you acting otherwise."

He looks as if his tie is choking him. I try to have sympathy, because it can't be easy for any man to hear his daughter talk about sex, but seriously, enough is enough. My father presses his index fingers against his closed eyelids as if trying to banish a headache. "Will you at least consider a merger with them?"

I sit back, surprised that he's actually asking. "I will," I say. There's no future with Thorn because he tossed me on my ass for a bunch of stones. No woman would forgive that. Plus, I'd like to chart my own path in life, and there's no question that Thorn dictates to everyone in his world. "What's the value of the garnets you gave up earlier?"

Father shrugs. "Who cares?"

I do. "I just figure that Thorn has plenty of garnets." Had he just needed an excuse to get rid of me—maybe force a wedge between my father and me? I think of the sweet nothings in Gaelic he whispered while inside me. Romantic talk he didn't realize I understood.

"He does, but word on the street is that he's looking for the mother lode, and I had it. The thing is the size of a bowling ball and incredibly rare."

I frown. "Okay. I get why he'd want that, but their servers are faster and tighter than ours. He doesn't need another monumental garnet."

"That's what he wanted," my father says, turning back to the file folders on the table.

Yeah. All right. I feel sympathy for Rosalie that I never had before. I didn't understand being thrown out like a used napkin. My chin lifts on its own. "How much trouble is Aquarius in right now?"

My father shakes his head. "The last few days have been disastrous. We're gaining more subscribers now that you're back, but I'm afraid the hit we took may be too much." He looks at me, appearing much older than he did when I walked into the room. "You're needed. Badly."

"I know," I say softly.

His gaze drops. "I have to know. Did Beathach . . . hurt you? I'll kill him for the insult."

The insult? To me? Or to my father? "No," I say. "Thorn didn't hurt me." Well, yeah he did, but not like my father means.

"Good. I'm relieved about that." He taps the papers. "The future of the entire company is on you, Alana. You must do the right thing."

TWENTY-ONE

Thorn

Tension rides me hard as I type rapidly, watching code crawl across my screen. Justice and Kaz also work in silence, both wearing earphones. Not me. I'll never be caught unaware.

Except when it comes to Alana speaking several languages.

Honey drifts across my tongue. I hate that I can't see her. Oh, I have ten men on her reporting her every movement, and each one of them will take a bullet for her if necessary. But I can't see her myself.

It's just after supper, and she's having dinner with family members at the Ballroom on Sixth, an expensive restaurant with a high-end bar. So far, I don't have a line on Cal Sokolov, but my sources are good. If he ends up anywhere near her, I'll know about it.

For now, I lower my head and craft a tunnel through code, hunting the source of the virus that's slowly killing me. Closing my eyes, I type faster than I can think, allowing instinct to take over.

Tunneling through the internet with the powerful alexandrite crystals is like mining for gold. Or rather, garnets.

The challenge heightens my awareness. I catch a wisp of a trail, and I'm off and running.

Around me, the servers hum at a frequency I feel to my bones. It's mine.

My phone buzzes and I pause, pulling up Alana's social media account.

She's in the bar and her eyes are slightly drowsy. Has she been drinking? She leans in, and her emotions waft from the device, lingering over my skin. I don't like that anybody watching can feel the same.

Damn the Aquarius Social emotion-based userface.

I lift my chin and stare, letting honey take over my senses.

"So, thanks for hanging in there with me and for all the love." She hiccups and holds up a martini glass containing blue liquid. "I'm with my cousins tonight, having a drink and celebrating my freedom." Her smile is all siren and smart-ass. "So, you all know Thorn, and let me tell you, the stories about him are true. The man can seriously kiss." She leans in, letting her emotions coat the world. "And yes, we kissed. I mean, wouldn't you kiss the guy who saved you from raining bullets?" She winks. "Give me more love, and I'll be back later tonight with more deets. You're gonna want to hear this." The screen explodes with pressed stars.

I'm going to fucking beat her ass, and this time, she's going to remember the lesson. Apparently I went too easy on her before. The one saving grace, and I mean the only one, is that she didn't reveal her location to millions of strangers.

Returning to my program, I pound the keys until the *M* slides out of sight. Doesn't matter. I know all the keys by heart.

Kaz stops typing and tugs his phone off the counter to answer. "What?"

He's more likable every day.

Then he turns to me just as Justice removes his EarPods. "Sylveria Rendale is here to see you."

My fingers stop mid-stroke.

Kaz places the phone near his keyboard. "She could be guessing you're here."

Somehow, I doubt Lady Rendale would waste her time or an ounce of effort if she didn't know my exact location. "Both of you, find out who she's speaking with in my organization and cut the traitor's throat."

A vein pulses visibly in Justice's temple. "Kaz, double-check all surrounding cameras for a hack and the satellite for any signals we don't own. Then we'll go through phones and devices." He stands. "I take it you want to meet with her?"

"Yes." I stand and stride toward the elevator to palm the control so it opens. "I can handle it. You work with Kaz."

Justice steps inside with me. "If you're meeting with the enemy, I'm at your two o'clock." This whole new determination to outwardly be brothers as well as inwardly is becoming irritating, especially since he's putting himself in the crosshairs. I don't like it.

The door rolls shut and the craft climbs out of the earth and ascends high into the sky. My ears pop. Then I unwrap a mint from my pocket and shove it in my mouth, chewing quickly until my taste buds go dead. The doors roll open, and we stride into the waiting area of the top floor with its calm and peaceful peach-colored furniture.

Of course, garnets are hardwired into every wall and used as decorations.

Silveria Rendale has three men with her—all on the ground bleeding out.

I glance at my men, who are currently holding new weapons. "You were foolish to come into my building armed." I speak to her but make sure her men are well aware I'm weighing whether or not to kill them, if they aren't already choking on their own blood. I'm fairly certain the guy by the potted plant is in his last convulsions.

She straightens to her full height of about six feet, dressed in a silver-colored suit with tight skirt and bright red four-inch heels that match her silky blouse. Her hair is a thick dark brown and her eyes a deadly blue. Her aristocratic features are set in bored lines. She meets my stare directly. "Please. If I wanted to shoot you, I wouldn't have advertised the weapons." Her chin lowers. "We need to talk."

I gesture her ahead of me toward the door beyond where my receptionist would be if these were business hours.

She pushes open the door and sweeps inside as if she owns the place.

I follow her down the long hallway and beyond the many closed doors, noting several of my people still hard at work. Finally, we reach the corner office at the end and she walks inside, looking around. "I take it this is you?"

It is the biggest office and in the corner, so I just nod. "Please have a seat." I can't remember who decorated my office. A wide onyx desk that matches the one at home takes up most of the room by the window with a leather chair behind it. The credenzas and a small sitting area are all done up in light brown leather. Garnets and obsidian stones embellish the knickknacks in the place. "Can I get you a drink?" I offer politely.

"Yes. Scotch," she says.

I walk to the bar on the far wall and pour her a scotch neat that I deliver before pouring myself one. I look at Justice and he shakes his head, leaning against the doorjamb. I walk around to sit at my desk. "Mrs. Rendale, next time, make an appointment."

She takes a sip of the twenty-year-old double barrel. "Why would I do that?"

"I don't know. Manners?"

She smiles. "We don't have time to waste with manners, Thorn."

"What can I help you with?" The idea that Alana has been out of my reach for nearly eight hours is about to make me come undone, but I force a smile.

Rendale looks me over, every bit the stately owner of TimeGem Moments. The platform is in second place of the four families and definitely on my heels. In contrast to my neural link platform, TimeGem uses advanced temporal technology to record, save, and replay memories in real time. Their time-capsule posts and multimedia collections are impressive, and their user interactions complex.

"I thought we might consider a merger," she says smoothly, the twenty-karat diamond pendant hanging between her breasts scattering light in every direction.

Whereas my servers run on garnets, hers mainly use diamonds. One would think since it's the strongest stone that her servers are the fastest. They're not. I wonder if it's because she married into the family, and the family's true stone used to be citrine. Do any of her deceased husband's relatives have a stronger affinity with either citrines or diamonds? Perhaps little Ella has a gift. I know Mrs. Rendale has talent with diamonds, which is why Brooks had married her. These things are rarely kept secret.

"I am not interested in a merger. My business is fine," I say, swirling the liquid in my glass.

She smiles. "Come now. I know all about the plans to merge Aquarius and Hologrid. We should do the same. I have two daughters. Choose one."

My interest is piqued. "You don't know anything about me."

"I know plenty about you."

The woman has no clue. "Most people think I'm a real bastard."

"As do I," she says. "You know all about my daughters, I'm sure. You know what they look like. Blonde or brunette, Thorn?"

I study her, anger heating my throat. "What about the third option?"

She lifts her graceful neck. "I only have two daughters."

I incline my head. "There's really only one true Rendale woman. Ella. Brooks's daughter. I find it interesting your daughters changed their name to Rendale after Brooks passed on. What was their former surname?" Of course, I know their surname had been Diddle. I can't blame them for changing it.

She rolls her eyes. "Ella has been disinherited and never showed an affinity with a crystal, anyway. If you want this merger, forget her."

I already have. "You're not worried about throwing one of your daughters to me?"

She shrugs. "You kidnapped Alana Beaumont for days and apparently she's still intact. So no, I'm not worried. Alana is tripe, to say the very least. No doubt you were more than happy to dump her on her father's doorstep."

The words ring so false, heat flashes through my body. Justice straightens from his post as if catching the tension.

I cock my head. "What's your plan?"

She looks around as if hoping to find state secrets. "Your marriage to one of my daughters. We merge our two families. I am willing to share our interaction algorithms with you, if you do the same with us. In addition, both of my daughters have enormous influencer followings on TimeGem Moments. Whichever one you marry will take that with her to Malice Media."

"And post on both?" I ask, curious.

"Yes, she would post for both—making sure we both stay strong," Sylveria says.

I study her, looking for any hint that she knows Malice Media is in trouble. "I don't need help with Malice Media."

Her eyelids half lower, and her smile is cagey. "Don't you?"

"Spill it, Sylveria." I glance at the only exit in the room.

She swallows. "Just rumors and I can't verify them. Yet."

"What rumors?" Justice asks quietly, effectively blocking any way to freedom.

She purses her lips. The woman is about fifteen years older than I am and has the irritated look most mothers can manage. "The rumor on the street is that you're having server issues. We've been tracking Malice Media in real time and have yet to discern a problem." She places her glass on the nearby table. "However, when you kidnapped Alana Beaumont, I did have to wonder."

"Stop wondering." That was all about Alana, but I'm not telling this woman anything. If she sees Alana as a threat, then my woman is in danger. Considering she's not under my roof or control right now, the least I can do is keep a target off her back. "I need a mate who has an affinity with the garnets, as I do." Throughout the ages, families have sought mates with connections to the crystals, and it's logical I might want the same thing.

Sylveria's chest fills as if she's found an opening. "Both of my girls can charge diamonds. Think about combining them with garnets."

"Don't your servers also run on citrines?" Justice asks quietly. It's true, and we all know it. I need to do a deeper dive on Ella, considering she's Alana's friend. Perhaps she can charge citrines.

"Yes, but the diamonds are what have propelled us to number two. I want to be number one. I'm not going to lie to you." Sylveria's smile shows teeth, hungry ones. "But with Cal Sokolov and Alana marrying within the month, we need to shore up our defenses against a hostile takeover. You are prepared, are you not?"

I smile, and her eyes widen slightly before she covers her reaction. "I'm more than prepared. What do your daughters say about this offer of yours?"

"They're both on board." She lifts one toned shoulder. "They've always been a bit competitive, so whoever loses out will be quite ticked." She hums softly as if considering her next words carefully. "Mathias Beaumont will need a new heir, so I may take my next offer to him."

I grind my back teeth together, grateful the mint is still working. "Mathias is in his late fifties."

"So? My husband was two decades older than me." She stands and, for the first time, true emotion splashes across her face, leaving her perfect skin scarlet from anger. "Stop playing around here. You don't want to turn me down."

"I'll think about it," I say, not meaning a word.

Triumph glitters in her eyes. "How about you come over for dinner tomorrow night and meet the girls in person? You never know when Cupid might strike."

I'd like to get to her servers. She's difficult to read, and I suspect she'd have no problem infecting a server or garnet if she found a way. But I can't tell if she's the one who cursed me, and interrogating a woman holds little appeal.

Not that I wouldn't do it. But right now, kidnapping and torturing the head of TimeGem Moments, even if she's arrogant enough to walk right into my web, would be a mistake I don't have time to handle. My thoughts burn with the woman who's too far away right now. "Sounds lovely." I nod for Justice to escort Sylveria out.

The fire burns too hot inside me, and I'm done being rational. I have to find Alana.

TWENTY-TWO

Alana

I settle in with my third martini in the slinky bar and face my cousins, curious about them. Nico appears relaxed for once after having taken off his jacket, and he seems to be enjoying his Skrewball whiskey. The choice both surprises and amuses me.

He's the one who insisted we all go for drinks.

Scarlett is busy fending off free drinks from tech guys while sipping on a cosmopolitan, and Quinlan is drinking a bourbon, with his jacket hanging off his chair and his sleeves rolled up. He's handsome in a classic Italian way, and his gaze scans the area, as if looking for threats. "We weren't expecting the call to join Aquarius today," he says.

"How do you feel about that?" I ask. He was close with my brother, but I don't know this guy.

"I don't know or really trust you or your father," he admits. "I like my job at Aquarius as a computer programmer, and taking more responsibility for tech is a challenge I might welcome."

I appreciate his honesty. "Nico and I don't know you, either. However, it would be great if all of you could combine to help charge the crystals once in a while."

He looks at me, his gaze appraising. "I bet you do get tired."

Scarlett taps the table with a red nail. "I never really thought about it."

"Most people don't." Yet another thing Thorn and I have in common, and he doesn't even know it. Yeah, I feel a little vindicated that he assumed there isn't more to know about me than what everyone sees onscreen.

Scarlett snorts. "I've tried to charge crystals before and it's exhausting."

"Me too," Nico adds, motioning to the waitress to bring another round. She has to be in her midforties, and he's flirting with her with all he's worth. She's batting her eyes right back. "Alana, I've never seen you stand up to your father like that before. I was impressed."

"As was I," Quinlan says.

Scarlett shrugs, apparently bored. "Why don't you stand up to your father?"

I smile. "This is my first week on the board of directors. Before that, my job was charging the crystals and posting continually." I do like being the face of Aquarius and directing its focus.

"You have almost six million followers," she says, the sound slightly unwilling. Does she want me to be a bonehead, or is she seeing more to me and isn't sure what to make of it? Not that I care what my cousins think.

"It's necessary," I admit. "We're in trouble because of my absence the last few days, but I'm building on viewer curiosity fast."

Quinlan downs the rest of his glass. "I saw. You're obviously not afraid of Thorn Beathach."

My stomach clenches because that is not a true statement. I'd be an idiot not to fear Thorn.

Scarlett rears up. "Anybody who resorts to kidnapping deserves all the angst we can bring him."

Girl power, huh?

"I agree," I say, my face heating. I wonder where he is right now. I know that he's seen my posts and I can't imagine he appreciated them. Although, every time I send my emotions out into the masses about Malice Media, not only do I gain interest, so does he. So yeah, he probably owes me. I settle back in my seat and warm myself with that fact. The last person in the world I want to assist right now is Thorn, however.

Quinlan smiles as the waitress delivers additional drinks. "Thank you." He pays and gives her a good tip. "Do you know what my new board position means in terms of my daily activities? Your father was rather obscure."

"I have absolutely no idea," I admit.

Nico clears his voice. "I do. You'll be given an office up on the top floor next to Alana's. As will you, Scarlett."

Perhaps we can become friends. "If we really settle you in, you'll have to move back home to California. What do you think?"

"Oh, I'm ready," she says. "I mean, I've enjoyed traveling and working with our employees in other countries, but I wouldn't mind consolidating, having a home."

I make a mental note to help her find a good place to live. It'd be nice to get to know this cousin of mine. She's the closest one to my age but we've just never really had a chance to get to know each other. Much of my childhood was spent in boarding schools, as was hers. Different ones. I barely even remember her parents. I look at Quinlan. "You seemed surprised when I walked in today. Did you not know I was on the board?"

"Oh no," he snorts. "I know you're on the board. I watch you on Aquarius all the time. I just hadn't seen you in person in quite a while—the funeral doesn't count—and you startled me. You look so much like your mother. She was beautiful with all of that curly brunette hair."

I warm. "You knew my mom?"

"Of course," Nico answers for him. "We all did. The extended families were all much closer when your mom was alive. I think after her death, your father pushed everybody away and focused entirely on the business."

I swallow. "I barely remember my mother."

"She was a kind person," Quinlan says instantly, leaning forward. "She made the best peanut butter cookies."

"Oh my God," Nico says, sitting back with a fond smile on his face. "She did. I'd forgotten about that. She would put these pieces of . . . what was that . . . ?"

"Brownie," Quinlan says.

Scarlett laughs. "That sounds like heaven." She sobers. "I wish I could remember her."

As do I. She's merely a wisp of sound or scent of vanilla to me.

"Lanetta was instrumental in keeping the families close." Nico sobers. "When she died, it's like, I don't know, the light went out of everybody, especially Mathias. At least that horrible car wreck didn't take you from us, too."

Impulsively, I lean over and pat Nico's hand. "Thank you for sticking close to Dad and Greg." Nico and Greg were the best of friends. I was so caught up in my grief that I really hadn't checked in with him during the last two months with Greg gone. "How are you doing?"

"I don't know," Nico says. He looks down at his phone. "I hired a private detective to look into his death, and it's suspicious. I'd be better if I could figure out whether somebody killed him."

Quinlan jerks. "Killed him? I thought he was in a car accident over Vulture's Perch."

"An accident just doesn't make sense to me, especially in light of the attack on Alana the other night. It's like the family is on somebody's hit list." Nico scrolls through photographs. "I've been putting together a timeline." He shows a picture.

I sit back. "Is that your apartment?" On one wall is an entire murder board with facts, data, and a big timeline.

"It is," Nico says.

I look at him more closely. There are dark circles under his eyes as if he hasn't slept. "Nico, what makes you think that somebody killed Greg?" I can't breathe. The mere idea is unthinkable. "My father doesn't believe that."

"I don't know what your father believes," Nico says, looking at me bleakly. "He may be conducting his own investigation. I've tried to talk to him several times, but I can't get anything from him. If he has facts, I need to know them."

"So do I," I say, rearing up, my stomach clenching. "If you truly believe this, then I'm going to help you, but you have to tell me why."

He rubs the back of his neck. "We were together that night, partying over at the Green Train Tavern. Quinlan was there."

Quinlan nods. "Yeah. We had a lot to drink that night, and I left before you two."

Nico rolls his neck. "Greg was meeting some girl, I don't know. He had more women than I could count, and we had too much to drink. He drove me home, but he had sobered up by then. He seemed calm. We had a good discussion. Then all of a sudden he drives off a cliff on the way home from my place? Come on. You know what a good driver Greg was."

It's true. My brother had actually competed on the semipro racing circuit. "The police report says it was an accident," I murmur.

"But the police report can be faked," Quinlan says grimly. "Who would want to kill Greg?"

"Nobody," I burst out. "I mean, nobody I know. I guess it's possible one of the other families took him out. But why?"

A muscle ticks in Nico's jaw. "If something happened to one of us, Greg would've been the first one asking questions and demanding answers. I'm telling you, this stinks."

I sigh. "Okay, if we're really going to do this, let's meet to-

morrow morning at your place, Nico, where you've set up headquarters." A chill ripples down my spine, and I look around to
see familiar guards in several directions. "How many do you
have on us tonight?"

"Three teams. Keep in mind that somebody out there still
wants to kidnap you," Nico says. He looks at Scarlett. "Get
used to having a bodyguard because one will escort you home."

She blows out air, and I totally get it. Suddenly, I need a moment. "I'm hitting the restroom."

Nico gestures with his chin at two of the men not so subtly
hanging out at the bar.

"Seriously? Do they have to look like mafia men with full
suits?" I walk sedately through the crowd past the wildly thumping dance floor to the far hallway, making sure the guards can
easily follow without having to knock anybody out. I've seen
them do so before. Then, because I'm in a good mood, I stand
back while the first guy, a massive blond named Edward, kicks
through the women's restroom looking for threats. When he
returns, I even smile and thank him.

For goodness' sake.

I make use of the facilities and wash my hands, checking my
makeup. My gaze catches on a barely there bite from Thorn
over the pulse point in my neck. Fire lashes through me.

That reminds me. I should upload a new emotional connection with Scarlett as I give more details of my time with Thorn.
We can play back and forth. I hope she's all in with her new
job. I don't need to trust her to work with her.

The door crashes open and Edward flies toward me.

I yelp and leap out of the way. He lands face-first on the tile
floor, quickly followed by the other guy, who lands on him
with a solid thunk. They don't move. Almost in slow motion, I
look down at them and then back up to the doorway.

Which is filled by Thorn. "I've been waiting for two hours
for you to use the restroom."

My ears ring and my breath heats my lungs until they hurt.

He's angry I didn't need to pee? Asshole. "We have the entire bar covered." I can't believe my voice is steady.

"I'm aware." He steps inside and locks the door, looking around at the three open red stalls and a closed closet door. His intense gaze on me, he back-kicks the door and it flies open.

I jump. "What are you doing?"

Instead of answering, he ducks and yanks the dark-haired guy off Edward before tossing him in what appears to be a supply closet. Seconds later, Edward joins him.

Thorn shuts the door. "They're gonna be out for a while."

I look frantically around. At least there's no window, so no easy avenue for him to take me. "Have you lost your damn mind?" Now my voice shakes, but it's with anger.

"Yes," he says in a low growl. "I most certainly lost my mind the first second we met. How dare you hide your intelligence from me?"

My chin lowers and I search for a weapon. "How dare you assume I'm not smart." This is freaking surreal. Music pounds from the dance floor, and loud laughter trails beneath the door.

He leans back against it and crosses his arms, looking powerful and pissed.

I gulp, shocked at how hard my heart is beating. My nipples peak. He's dressed in his usual black slacks and white dress shirt with the sleeves rolled up, revealing his sinewed arms. There isn't a spot of blood or a wrinkle even though he just incapacitated two of my best bodyguards. From the silence in the supply closet, they're not coming to anytime soon.

The silver flecks in his eyes appear darker than usual, and his thick black hair is ruffled. He's so handsome, so starkly beautiful, I wish I could paint. Or even draw. Then he ruins it by opening his mouth. "That's three rules of mine, baby."

Anger billows through me so quickly, I'm shocked my head doesn't fly right off my neck. "You can shove your rules up your ass. We're done, remember?"

One of his dark eyebrows rises, the action making him look beyond arrogant. "I told you we weren't done."

"You traded me for rocks," I spit out. There's no way to get past him to the door, so I'll have to go right through the cocky asshole. I'm sure nobody has ever kicked him square in the balls before. It's time.

"I'm fairly certain I don't like where your mind has gone," he says. "The trade was necessary. Your anger isn't."

The words send my temper full-on nuclear, and I kick up, hard as I can, toward his dick.

TWENTY-THREE

❧

Thorn

She's shockingly fast, and I barely have time to swipe her ankle before she connects with my jewels. My temper matches hers and I charge her, lifting her up and planting her ass against the door. That flimsy dress lifts to her thighs and I press in, right where I need to be.

"You fuckhead." She slams both elbows down on my shoulders.

"Be nice with that mouth or I'll make sure it's too busy to talk." I tangle my fingers in her thick hair and jerk her head back, pinning her to the wall with my body. "Knock it off." Her scent surrounds me while the taste of honey floods my mouth. "Let's get a couple of things straight right now." My cock aches with desperation, but we need to talk.

She glares, her eyes sparkling spitfires. "There's nothing to discuss."

"Wrong." I lower my voice into pure domination, and her pupils dilate. "First things first. The man who dared touch what's mine. How far did he go?"

She frowns and struggles, not moving an inch. "I have no idea what you're talking about, moron."

"Call me one more name, and I'm beating your ass, and *then* we'll talk." I tighten my grip and force her head up more, enjoying the startled cry she issues. "In the bar," I bite out. "Minutes ago."

Her lips press together. "My life is none of your business." She swallows. "What's your problem with Quinlan?"

Quinlan. Good to know a name. I could only see him from behind when he put his arm around her shoulders. "He touched you, which means I cut off his fingers and feed them to him before I kill him. Learn that lesson right now. Unless he did more. Did he?"

The confusion in her pretty eyes calms the beast raging inside me.

She licks her lips. "Were you dropped on your head a lot as a child?"

That's it. I step back, drop a knee, and plant her stomach over it. Five hard smacks to her perfect ass later, I put her right back where I want her, my weeping cock against her light pink panties, her dress up to her waist. Those pretty eyes are startled and her mouth is open. "I asked you a question."

She snaps her pink lips closed.

I tilt my head in clear warning.

She rolls her eyes. "Fine. No. Quinlan didn't do anything. He's my cousin and was offering comfort because we were talking about my dead brother."

Cousin? "Quinlan Winter?" I know every person in her family but didn't recognize him from behind.

"Yes."

Good. I thought perhaps she was on a double date with Nico and Scarlett, who is also a distant cousin to her. "Are Nico and Scarlett dating?" It never hurts to know what's up in the enemy camp.

Female giggling echoes and then somebody pushes against the door.

"Closed for maintenance," I snap loudly. "Use the men's room."

Alana opens her mouth as if to scream and I press in, my mouth taking hers. Honey explodes across my taste buds and I kiss her under, taking her to submission. She gives a little moan, right into my mouth, and kisses me back.

God, the little smartass is perfect.

It has been hell being without her, so I drink deep from her sweet mouth, showing her exactly whom she belongs to. Finally, I lean back to let her breathe.

Her eyes blur with a lust that matches the urgency in my groin.

I draw in air, keeping control. "I'm not telling you again. Stop emoting about me. No more videos."

She trembles and looks down at my mouth with such sweet need that I almost give in. Then her head snaps back. "Why? You going to take your big, bad knife to me like you would've to my poor cousin?"

My fingers flex on her hip, no doubt leaving marks. Good. She'll wear my marks as long as I breathe. It's too late for her now. "If I take my knife to you, baby, it won't be to cut."

Her frown is adorable, and so are her pink cheeks and panting breath. Her lush tits are sharp diamonds against my chest, and her thighs are clamped to my hips as if her body is light-years ahead of her sharp brain about how this is going to play out. Then she makes the mistake of challenging me. "Come on. We both know that even though you're a psycho killer with rivals, you wouldn't dare use a knife on me."

Not much stuns me in this life.

She does.

Her absolute naiveté and innocence . . . not to mention lack of self-preservation. I release her hip and have my knife, one of them, in my hand before she can blink. "I understand that my *temporarily* trading you back to your father might have given you the impression that you're not mine. That I won't enforce every rule I have with you."

Her gaze slides to the knife, and she's not looking anywhere near frightened enough.

I flick open the blade, which is sharpened to a dangerous edge.

Her gaze lifts to mine. "Seriously?"

I shift my weight and put the blade to the top of her dress and press in.

She sucks in air, looking down. "What are you—"

In one swift motion, I slice through the sparkling material, making sure she feels the tip but it doesn't scratch her skin. Sequins bounce all over the tile floor, and those spectacular breasts spring free. Her nipples are a pink delight, and I want my bite marks on them. Soon.

Her mouth gapes open. "My dress."

"I'm not done." I reach those pretty pink panties.

Panic finally has her stiffening, but it's way too late. "I wouldn't move if I were you." Making sure to tuck the blade inside the material, I tear through the flimsy and very wet silk until she's bare to me.

She tries to shift away from the knife, but I don't let her. Her chest lifts as she holds her breath, desperately trying not to move.

I smile, lean in, and kiss her.

Alana

Tears fill my eyes from the force of his kiss. Not because I don't like it, but because I do. How does this make sense?

My mind tries to work out reality but my body is gone. I grab onto his shoulders and dig in, reveling in the feeling of his tongue taking mine. He's hard and dangerous, and something inside me softens, even as I'm on the edge.

I'm careful not to move. That knife is way too close to my tender parts, and I realize that I don't know him. At all. One night of passion and a mellow morning of him feeding me breakfast was a mere slice of time. My lungs shudder and I try to pull away.

He lets me and then bites my bottom lip.

Shock cascades down my body to my aching clit and more tears fill my eyes. Gingerly, I probe with my tongue and don't taste blood. Even so, my lip pulses with pain, and my body with fire.

I can feel wetness spill from me onto my thighs, and embarrassment heats through me.

He sinks his teeth into my upper breast. Pain and pleasure rocket together from the bite to ignite every nerve in my body. That one is going to last a while. Pleasure curves his full bottom lip and then he ducks his head again.

I suck in air, prepared for pain, but his heated mouth encloses my nipple. His tongue lashes me, and I'm unable to stop myself from pressing against him.

Metal probes my folds. The knife is at my sex.

I jerk and stop cold, my eyes widening.

He moves to the other breast, licking, sucking, and lightly biting the nipple until if feels like I'm going to detonate. But I try to remain still, because that blade is way too close.

Slowly, he penetrates me with the weapon. I jerk against him before realizing it's the shaft of the knife and not the blade. The metal is cold and hard inside me, and I open my mouth to protest when he flicks my clit with his callused thumb.

I tremble and lean against him. What is he doing?

He releases my breast with a loud pop and leans back, satisfied sliver streaks taking dominance in his eyes.

Somebody pounds on the door and I jerk, heat slashing into my face.

"Go the fuck away," he growls.

We could get caught any moment. My excitement heightens at the thought, and I move against the knife. His eyes flare and he pulls out the shaft, shoving it back in, slowly fucking me with the metal. "Stop," I whisper as I gyrate against it.

"You sure?" He speeds up and sparks flash behind my eyes.

I make a sound between a whimper and a moan that will haunt me later. He presses on my clit and wires uncoil inside me. I stiffen. And he slows down and then drives it much farther in. How close is the blade? The tip scrapes my thigh and I gasp. Will he really cut me?

"Don't." I'm so close to the edge, needing relief. God, this is too much.

"I'll do what I want to you," he whispers, pulling it out and fucking me with it. "You like it, and you know it."

I don't have an answer. The emptiness inside me is a vast and aching pain. One I don't understand. My brain fuzzes and my body screams for relief, even though I'm on the edge of being cut. Of being hurt.

He jerks my head to the side with his fingers caught in my hair, and pain crashes along my scalp. He leans in, his eyes nearly black, his nostrils flared. "Are you done fucking around with me?"

I can't move but try to nod, feeling like a trapped animal. An aroused one.

"Who is the only man who'll ever take this body?"

The words don't penetrate my overwhelmed brain.

He bites my lip and then licks the wound with his tongue. My pussy feels it as if he's in two places at once. "I own you. Say it."

My thighs tremble against his hips. He twists the knife handle. "You do," I say in a panicked rush, not caring that I'm lying my ass off. "You own me." Except, exactly who am I lying to? No other man will ever make me feel like this.

The look that comes over his face will terrify me later. For now, I can only stare. His eyes darken even more and his chin lowers, a dark flush highlighting his cut cheekbones and making that scar more prominent. "That's right. Don't you ever forget it." He shoves the knife in his pocket and yanks open the snap of his slacks before ripping down his zipper. He tightens his hold on me and then drives inside me with enough force that my shoulders bang against the wall.

Then he's moving.

Pain shocks through me followed by an excruciating pleasure that has me wrapping my legs around his hips and scratching my nails down his torso. Frantic, I tear open his buttons to claw his chest, leaving my marks on his taut skin.

He fucks me hard without a hint of the gentleness he showed my first time.

I throw back my head, feeling the gates start to open. Mini bombs detonate inside me, shooting out, and fire cascades as the orgasm takes me with a violence I wouldn't have thought possible. I cry out, and his mouth overwhelms mine, sucking all sound into his body. His powerful shoulders jerk several times with his own release.

Then everything stills. The entire world. We remain locked together, both panting, our heartbeats thumping hard against each other.

He looms over me, his gaze dark. "This was me being gentle with you, beautiful. Don't piss me off again."

I blink, still unable to capture an entire thought.

He steps back and allows my legs to slide to the floor.

A chill skates through me and I shiver, feeling vulnerable and alone.

One of his knuckles lifts my chin, forcing me to look at him. "You're the fucking reason for everything in my entire universe. I'll worship you until I die, and most probably after that as well."

I swallow. "That wasn't worship," I croak out, my throat bone dry.

His smile is an intriguing flash of teeth. "No. That was a lesson. But don't for a second think I wasn't worshiping you the entire time."

There's no question I'm way out of my element. Even so, my body feels satiated and well used. With a side of aching pain. I frown.

He rubs between my eyes before slipping out of his jacket and settling it around my shoulders.

I balk. "I'm not leaving with you."

He plants his hand over my left breast, above my heart. "Don't think I'm not considering it. But your people have three teams on you and the Sokolovs have three inside. Outside, additional teams roam the block and four snipers are perched high above the street. The only reason—and I mean the *only* reason—I'm not shooting my way out with you over my shoulder is that I won't risk your life. Plus, we've come to an understanding now, haven't we?"

I nod because there's really nothing else I can do.

"Good girl." He kisses me again and then looks at me, his eyes hard. "Post about me again, and I'm going to spank your bare pussy to orgasm and make you beg for it first."

My legs freeze. "Um, no. Not my thing." Seriously.

"We'll see. So long as you understand me. Enjoy your freedom while you have it." Turning, he unlocks the door and walks out, disappearing into the crowd.

I scramble to pick up my dress and panties, fastening the button of his jacket, which reaches to my thighs. Shame heats my cheeks until my face hurts.

Did that just happen?

TWENTY-FOUR

Alana

It's after three in the morning, and I sit in my underground safety office, with my friends staring at me, their eyes wide open. I dive back into a gallon of strawberry ice cream. It might be boring but it's my favorite. I wait until my entire story filters through their brains, my head still spinning and my body sore. The books about crystals are near me in my pack, and I'm halfway through a fascinating one on how emeralds and moonstones can be combined to create a love spell.

It's probably bunk, but I might return to reading if my friends stay silent forever.

Rosalie, unsurprisingly, is the first to speak.

"Holy fuck," she says.

"Yep." I lick off my spoon but am careful not to slurp, since mouth sounds bug Rosalie so much. She's explained the condition before, but it didn't make much sense to me. However, I don't want to make her uncomfortable. It's a good thing Merlin decided to take the night off, considering we're discussing wild sex.

Ella shakes her head. "Wait a minute, this is insane. What are we going to do?"

At the moment, I have absolutely no idea what I'm going to do. Even now, his flowers are up in my apartment, making the whole place smell like roses.

"It doesn't make any sense," Rosalie says, frowning.

Wait a second. Is she talking about Thorn declaring I'm the center of his universe? "What do you mean it doesn't make sense?" I'm not quite sure if I should be insulted or not.

"The logic of it, unless"—she casts a worried look at Ella—"he really is insane. I mean, we know he has issues."

I pause in the midst of scooping up another bite because she's absolutely right. If Thorn is so obsessed with me and still wants me in his life, then why did he trade me for a bunch of rocks? I cock my head and look at Ella. "I assume you've been doing a deep dive on the guy."

"Oh yeah." She pushes her glasses back up her nose. "The second you survived your kidnapping and returned home, I sent every search program I've written into every aspect of his life." She dives into her gallon of cookie dough ice cream. "I'm telling you, he has some amazing programmers."

"I think it's him," I say softly. "The man needs to control his entire environment."

"Well, he's beyond good," she says. "It is incredibly difficult to find anything on him other than what Malice Media wants out there."

That just figures. "Did you discover that he has a brother?"

She slaps her hand on her jeans-clad thigh, her mouth turning down. "No. That's not even part of the record."

I smash the heel of my palm into my left eye to try to ward off the headache I feel barreling my way.

Ella claps both hands against her face. "How did you get out of the bar last night?"

I haven't reached that part of the story because I figure they need a moment to digest what happened in the bathroom.

"With my head up high," I say, and then wince. "His jacket covered me, so I walked out, and oh man, I thought Nico was going to lose his mind." They immediately ordered three teams to go after Thorn, but he was gone. I don't want to be impressed by that, but I am. "What could be so valuable about a box of garnets that he would trade me for them?" I hold up a hand. "Assuming that he's telling the truth and he wants some kind of future."

"Do you want a future?" Rosalie asks, her entire face wrinkling with incredulousness.

"No," I say, too quickly. "Believe me, we are not on the same page."

"Yet, you haven't posted about him again," Ella points out.

Yeah, his last threat is ringing in my head. "Mainly because I was busy getting out of a bar, partially dressed, reaching home safely, and then hiding out in my room until three o'clock."

It took every ounce of my considerable charm to talk my cousin into keeping all guards on the exterior of my apartment building. There is no way an ant could get inside this brick structure without being shot, and the last thing I want is a bunch of guards in my hallway, or worse yet, in my home. At least the building is small so our forces can easily cover it.

Ella reaches for her laptop. "I did find a couple of hints that there was a problem with the Beathach family years ago."

"That could be when Justice's mother was killed and the boys were kidnapped," I say. "What did you find?"

She winces. "An obscure reference in a police report. The officer is named Tom Jack, and he's long dead. There's nothing else in any database anywhere, trust me."

"Didn't police officers used to keep their own handwritten notes?" I ask.

"Yeah." Ella flicks her finger across the screen. "This officer didn't have any heirs, but I can keep looking. It's doubtful I'll find anything."

I pause, my spoon in the carton, and wonder if I really want to travel down this path. "Aren't you supposed to know every-thing you can about your enemies?" I ask.

Rosalie snorts. "Are you sure he's your enemy?"

"He's definitely not my friend." I absently rub the bite mark on the top of my breast. "I'd like to know more about him and why he traded me for those garnets. You have nothing on the stones?"

Ella partially lifts one shoulder. "There are rumblings, some talk on the internet, about Malice being in some sort of trouble, but I can't get anything concrete. I've even been checking our fake TimeGem Moments account."

We've had some fun with that account, posting kitten and puppy pictures as well as fashion advice by using an AI-created profile and picture, and to date we have 50,000 followers.

"There doesn't seem to be anything concrete about Malice's problems, but the rumors start with the Rendale sisters." Ella keys in commands and the monitor on the far wall springs to life. "I can't believe these assholes took my last name. Here is Stacia's latest memory."

Stacia comes into view. She's a pretty woman with short black hair, bright blue eyes, and a rather long nose. TimeGem Moments uses advanced temporal technology to record, save and replay recollections. It's all about time capsules, and so, when they engage, it's already called a memory. Her newest memory comes up as she looks directly at the camera with some sort of tree in the background.

"Hello, friends," she says. "I don't know about you, but I've been hearing these absurd rumors about Thorn Beathach, the owner of Malice Media, kidnapping Alana Beaumont, the low-est-ranking person at Aquarius Social. I mean, come on. We all know Thorn is a sexy billionaire who could get any woman he wants; any man as well. You're telling me that he went out of his way to kidnap insipid Alana Beaumont? Please. This is a fantasy of hers, which I guess we can all understand, but to go public with it?"

She rolls her eyes. "I called the police station and there is absolutely no report of a kidnapping, so come on, let's cancel her silliness. We have better things to do, right?" She leans closer to the camera. "Besides, I caught wind that Malice might be in a bit of a bind. Have you heard anything? If so, post your memories right away so we can share them. I can assure you, we're offering our assistance to him." She clicks off.

"That's interesting," I say.

"What a bitch," Rosalie snaps.

That's Stacia's default setting, so I don't get too upset by it. "Yeah, but it's interesting. Have you checked the other platforms?"

Ella swallows more ice cream before answering. "There's nothing on Aquarius, which you would probably already know about, but on Hologrid Hub, there are a few low-level influencers who have picked up the question about Malice. To be honest, I can't tell who originated it, whether it was one of the Rendale sisters or somebody in the Sokolov family, but the rumors are out there."

Rosalie kicks back. She's wearing dark jeans and a red sweater, and she crosses her ankles on the card table. "Sometimes a rumor is all it takes for stock to tank. This could be a move."

I fidget with my spoon. "So somebody's trying to take Thorn down via rumor? What does that have to do with the garnets?"

"Hell if I know," Ella says. "You're right, though. The only thing that makes sense, if we believe he's telling the truth—and that's a big old if—is that for some reason the garnets he traded for you are more important than what he has planned for you."

Rosalie sighs and reaches for her discarded carton of Chunky Monkey, which is still half full. "Do you think we're going to have to kill him?"

I blink. "I thought we already dealt with that. None of us are killers."

"Yeah, but we may have to change that to protect you from him."

Deep down a voice I won't acknowledge promises that there is no protection from Thorn. My body is sore in places that still thrum, and every time I shift my weight, my clit aches. Damn him.

Ella drops a piece of cookie dough on her jeans and uses a napkin to wipe them clean. Her phone dings, and she reaches for her laptop, her eyes flicking as she reads. "We have another murder in town."

I finish my ice cream. "Murder?"

"Yeah. Look-alike to you. Brunette, yellow dress, aquamarine necklace. Face smashed in beyond recognition," she reads out loud.

Rosalie leans toward her. "That's not a coincidence I like."

I bite my lip. "Me either. You've set up a notification for similar murders?"

"Obviously," Ella says, still staring at her screen. "I didn't want to alarm you, but I did look into the murder of the young woman who the news hinted was you the other day. Her name was Lisa Alson, and she was a twenty-two-year-old waitress at the Crux Bar."

"No connection to me?" I ask.

"None." Ella shoves the spoon into the carton and sets it aside. "However, hers is the third death in two years with the same MO. Now there's a fourth victim. Young women, multiple injuries, raped, smashed-in face found outside of popular bars. Many we've visited, by the way."

Rosalie stiffens. "Same characteristics for the victims?"

Ella swipes at the stain on her jeans. "Not sure. They were young brunettes, but that's as far as it goes. The other two known vics were a doctor and a computer programmer. The police are looking at the cases separately and together, and so far, they don't have anything. There's nothing on this newest victim. Yet."

So the murders appear to be a coincidence. Except for the aquamarine necklace. That's my signature. Of course, with six million followers on our site, I'm often copied. Especially when it comes to clothing and accessories.

Rosalie stops with her spoon halfway to her mouth. "What if it's Thorn? I mean, he's obsessed, right? He can't have you so he's killing lookalikes?"

That doesn't sound like him. I don't think. Maybe. How well do I really know him? "I'm not sure," I say lamely.

"So there's no record of him obsessing about someone, and . . . I don't know, maybe authorities later finding her body in a moat somewhere?" Rosalie drawls, her eyes sparking.

"No," Ella says. "Of course there's no mention of him killing anybody, which . . ." She lets her voice trail off.

I nod and shove another spoonful in my mouth. There's no question in my mind that Thorn Beathach has killed more than once. My phone vibrates and pulls my gaze. Reading the text, my heart flutters in my chest, the rhythm frenetic.

THORN: It's good to know that you're behaving yourself. Good girl for not posting.

My head jerks up and irritation swims through my bloodstream. I pick the phone up and immediately text back.

ME: I haven't had time. I've been too busy reassembling my dress.

THORN: Get used to it.

"Is that him?" Rosalie asks.

"Oh yeah, it is." I walk over to the big screen. "Ella, give me a nondescript background, would you?"

She types and a lovely watercolor of a lake takes up the entire screen. "Are you sure you want to do this?"

"Absolutely." I know I'm making a mistake, but in my tired and sore state, I just don't care. He goaded me—calling me a good girl in that condescending tone. I'm nobody's good girl. He should know better. I flick on the video app of Aquarius

Social and apply a light filter because I'm sure I have huge bags under my eyes. The green light starts to flicker. I smile.

"Hi, friends. Sorry about the delay. I've been rather busy. However, as you know, I still have a story to tell. So Thorn Beathach is sexier than any of you can imagine. He's about six foot six, solid muscle, and I'm going to be truthful here, he kisses like a god. And his hands. Just wait until I tell you about those broad, sexy, talented hands." I then look away as if somebody's coming. "Oh, I have to go. Make sure you explode-star this and share it with your friends if you really want to hear more about Thorn's supernatural anatomy. If you do, I'll be back in several hours. Now, get some sleep, y'all." I click off.

Rosalie chuckles. "Are you sure you want to poke the beast?"

"It's too late," Ella murmurs. "I think she just did."

My phone buzzes.

THORN: That was a mistake and you know it.

ME: I'm feeling pretty safe with my rotating security guards in every direction.

THORN: I don't make idle threats. You will not enjoy your next punishment.

My stomach drops. Yeah. I definitely just poked the beast. My heart races and my abdomen rolls over. "I might need another set of bodyguards."

TWENTY-FIVE

❧

Thorn

A wave of ire surges within me, staining my thoughts red. I return to the man I have strapped in a chair who's bleeding from a cut in his eyebrow from a simple backhand. The blood drips into his eye and he keeps blinking to clear it. I removed all of his clothing before I bound him, and he's shivering from the cold.

I crunch on another hot mint, not wanting to taste even a hint of his words.

He sees me approach and stiffens, fighting the restraints securing his wrists to the arms of the chair and his feet to the bolts in the ground.

We're alone in my boathouse, and the scent of the waves crashing below adds to the smell of salt and blood. I reach for a different knife from the one I used on Alana the night before— it's sacred to me now. "Where were we, Nelson?" I ask calmly.

He twists against the restraints, bleeding from several areas. Oh, I haven't sliced anything important yet. "I've told you everything I know."

Actually, he hasn't told me shit. "What are you? About forty?" I ask, spinning the weapon around in the air.

His gaze tracks the blade. "Forty-four."

"You know jack about women?" I look at his bare feet.

"Sure. I'm happy to help." He's getting a bit of his spirit back.

I drop the knife directly on his big toe.

He shouts, his face turning purple. "No—" he starts when I reach down, yank the knife free, and his toe rolls away. "God. Why are you doing this?"

"God has nothing to do with this," I say thoughtfully, anger churning in my gut. How dare Alana emote another video about me. Wasn't I clear? "Women don't make sense. What is it with her that she doesn't believe I'll keep my word?"

"Maybe she's testing you," he groans, scrunching his other four toes on the rocky floor.

I look at him. Maybe she wants me to punish her. To prove that I will and I mean what I say. The woman certainly needs boundaries. "That's a thought, Nelson." I wipe the blade on his bare thigh. "Why did you target little Julie McDonald? The girl who fell out of the van?"

He somehow shrinks into himself. "I saw her and had a buyer for her. Right age." He sniffs. "Didn't mean to drop her from the van."

My fury goes ice cold. "Was she targeted because of her family? Because they work for me?"

He shakes his head wildly. "No. Didn't know who she was or that her dad works for you. I swear, it was a coincidence. I'm so sorry."

Not yet, but he will be. So at least nobody is targeting the kids of my men. One bright spot in this shitty situation. "Where did you get the kids you gave to the losers on the street?"

He flinches. "I told you about your girl. Why do you even care about other kids?"

It's a fair question. "My brother and I were taken as kids and tortured. Our mom was killed. The experience haunts me." Honesty is a rule with me, and I employ it unless circumstances are dire. "This helps keep the ghosts at bay."

"Torturing people?" Snot bubbles at his nose.

"Yeah." I crouch to better see the wound close to his right armpit. "People who hurt kids and women . . ." I shrug. "I figure if I can keep others from being hurt, then maybe I'm making it up to them somehow."

He blinks more blood from his eye. "Your mom and brother?"

I nod.

"That's fucked, man."

Yes, it is. I slide the knife into him above his protruding right hipbone, and something eases inside me. A pain dissipates. It's temporary, but I'll take it.

He sucks in air and bites through his bottom lip as if determined not to scream this time.

I admire that. Not a lot. "The kids, Nelson."

"There's a whole pipeline, man. Don't you get it? It's so easy these days."

It's always been easy to take advantage of the young and weak. I pull out the knife but his flesh tries to keep it in. He isn't as strong this time and cries out.

"I like symmetry." I plunge the knife into his other hip. "Keep talking."

He coughs, tears filling his eyes. "About eighty thousand kids have gone missing from the southern border. It's like shooting fish in a barrel, man. The government has no clue and frankly doesn't care where they are."

"But you do. At least some of them." I reclaim my knife.

The blood flows from his hips to his groin, pooling obscenely. "At least I make sure they get fed."

I punch him in the mouth for that one.

His head snaps back and he spits out a tooth.

"Do you use little kids, Nelson?" I ask, eyeing his fingers.

"No," he says loudly. Too loudly. "Never."

I stare at him, knowing he sees death. "I told you when we began that I wouldn't lie to you and you wouldn't lie to me. Remember?"

He sniffs the bloody snot back up his nose and nods.

"Yet you just lied to me."

He whimpers. "No, I didn't."

I sigh and walk behind him silently, letting his imagination take over. He's bleeding more than I expected, and he hasn't put up much of a fight. Even so, he's hurt kids, and he needs to pay. I lean over slightly and drop the knife onto his index finger. It slices right through.

He shrieks this time.

I walk around to face him, my head canted. There exist those who can experience the agony of others. I'm not one of them. All I feel is a slight lessening of my own pain. I punch him in the rib cage, shattering several bones. "Give me the list of where you get the kids." Even though they're not connected to my case, I figure somebody should try to help them.

Sobbing, he gives me five names. "That's all."

I slam my fist into the other side of his rib cage, about the same spot. "And a list of where you send them."

He's wheezing now, no doubt with a collapsed lung. Maybe two. Yet he gives me the names.

I look down at the blood covering my white shirt. He's a sprayer as well.

He gasps in a useless attempt to fill his lungs. "I've told you everything I know. Now you have to get me help."

"I will," I say, retrieving my knife.

He yells as his finger separates from his hand.

I do like a sharp knife.

"You'll let me go?" The hopeful light in his brown eyes is

visible. Surely he knows better. Yet most individuals harbor optimism, no matter how bleak the situation.

I don't. Never have. Not until I first glimpsed Alana. When honey first kissed my taste buds. "No. You don't seem to understand. I have to show my men that they're protected. Or at least avenged."

Tears slide down his bloodied face. "Can't you just tell them?"

"No. I need to show them your head on a spike by my moat and then post it downtown in San Francisco as a warning." Kind of gross, but effective. I walk behind him, and in a whisper of sound, lean over and cut his throat.

Then he's forgotten.

I tear off the clothes I'm wearing and stuff them in a black plastic bag. Wet wipes work to rid me of the blood before I open a gray bag by the door and change into another black suit, making sure to slide my garnet signet ring on my finger. Then I walk outside, where two of my men are waiting for me. "Small pieces of his body, take the boat out, and dump him in the middle of the ocean. Mount his head on a spike. One day on my property, out of view from air transport, and then downtown in the city." I keep walking up the trail, taking my bag with me.

I trust my men, but being paranoid is a good thing. About halfway up I stop and shove the bag into an open fireplace in the rocks—massive and already roaring. A brown screen in front of it keeps any stray pieces from flying out. My men know to bleach the frame when the fire goes out. Once at the top of the cliff, I climb into my vehicle and sit inside the driver's seat for a moment.

Returning home without Alana there feels wrong. Since her light has graced the stone fortress, it's a dark void without her.

I'm dark enough as it is. So I text her and wait.

Nothing.

The anger that had ebbed begins to boil again. Ignoring me

isn't wise. Starting the engine, I drive away from the ocean toward Silicon Valley, texting Justice on the way and giving him an update.

I appreciate that Alana and her friends have helped abused women in California. Not that I care about the women themselves, because honestly, I don't care about much. Alana and Justice are about the only people who matter to me. But the fact that Alana helps people because she wants to, or because it's the right thing to do, and not because she's banishing pain and ghosts, illuminates something inside me.

Sleep will elude me tonight as usual. Nelson broke too easily, so I call Justice.

"Hi. I have a line on the freezing curse that's killing you," he says without preamble. "I'm close. How much have you progressed?"

I pause to gauge the sensations in my body. "Fingers and toes are colder, as is the end of my nose. Curiously, it feels as if my kidneys are holding ice crystals as well." That would explain the dull throb in my lower back right now.

"What about emotions or thoughts?"

"Same as always." These feelings come from a cold place, so I doubt I'll ever experience a difference. Oddly enough, I'm utterly devoid of anxiety regarding my love for Alana. It's an inferno, scorching and indomitable, immune to any ailment. Of that, I am profoundly certain. "Give me a report on the teams covering Alana."

"It's a clusterfuck of multiple security teams, and I've ordered our men to stay under the radar. I do have two long-shooters with scopes on all four snipers, just in case you want to make a move."

I roll my neck until it pops. "Do you have a plan in place?"

"Not yet. Every scenario I run leaves us with multiple casualties, and not one strategy guarantees her safety, which I'm acutely aware is your primary concern."

Right now, she's very fortunate I can't get my hands on her. When I reflect on her audacity, my palms tingle. She's treading on thin ice, and retribution awaits her. Shortly. "Memorize their movements and send the pattern to me soon. If I can't get her out, I want in."

"I'm on it." With a slight rumble in his throat, Justice coughs. "Are you coming in to work the crystals? I could use some help." Like me, he doesn't sleep much.

"Yes, unless you've found anything interesting in town," I say, a rioting heat rolling through my chest. The beast inside me isn't appeased right now.

Quiet ticks across the line and then the sound of keystrokes. "I've got one," he says. "Thirty-year-old male named Mike Raptor. Beat the shit out of his pregnant young wife for the sixth time in San Francisco. Wife didn't press charges, and the DA didn't either. Wife will be in hospital for at least three months. She lost the baby, too."

The image of Charity's bruised and broken body flashes across my mind. They'd let us see her dead.

Justice still has nightmares, although he denies it. I let him get away with that lie because he needs it in order to survive.

I turn the vehicle toward San Francisco. "Give me his address."

TWENTY-SIX

❧

Alana

I receive orders from my father that I'll be joining Cal Sokolov for dinner the following night to discuss our merger as I ride the elevator up to Nico's penthouse, along with a rather smug note that Thorn is dining with the Rendales this evening. My father believes they're trying to consolidate power, and apparently his spies within TimeGem agree.

The idea makes my stomach feel like I've been gut punched. Hard.

My cousin lives only a few blocks from headquarters in a condominium tower that is a modern marvel of glass and steel.

I tap my foot, with Quinlan busily texting on one side of me and Ella reading her phone on the other. While I'm dressed in my customary yellow skirt and white top with both aquamarine and rose quartz jewelry, I'm not surprised to see Quinlan wearing an aquamarine-crested watch. "Scarlett couldn't make it?" I ask.

He pauses mid-text. "No. She's working."

Right. "She doesn't like me much, does she?" The girl-power statement at the bar notwithstanding.

He shrugs. "She likes you fine, but we've been excluded from Aquarius Social for years, and it's going to take some time for all of us, you know?"

Considering my father runs the business and not me, I guess. Sighing, I turn my phone back on since I'd left it off the night before. Stubbornly, to be honest. I'm not surprised to see texts from Thorn, and my breath quickens.

THORN: Meet me and take your punishment now.

THORN: For every text you ignore, I'm withholding an orgasm.

THORN: If your phone is off, you won't sit for a month.

THORN: You didn't learn your lesson the other night. See you soon.

I shiver and fight the very real urge to text an apology. But that's crazy. He doesn't deserve one, and my sense of self-preservation obviously isn't as strong as I thought.

The door opens and we walk into the vestibule of the penthouse where Nico is waiting. As usual, he's dressed in a three-piece suit.

He looks us over. "So, Nancy Drew and her posse have arrived."

Ella looks up from her phone, a light peach dusting her cheekbones. "Hi, Nico."

His grin is charming. "Hi, El. I have some of the kombucha you like in the fridge."

I look from one to the other. "How do you know what she likes?"

"I keep track," he says, and her blush deepens. "I'm glad you came. We need your computer skills."

At the mention, I lose any amusement. The idea that somebody possibly murdered my brother creates a palpable tension.

Nico gestures us into the heart of his condo, which is a wide

living area with floor-to-ceiling windows that grant a breath-
taking view of Silicon Valley. The dark hardwood floors emphasize the minimalist decor. Nico likes things contemporary,
from his plasma TV over the utilitarian fireplace to the plush
light gray furnishings.

"Do I still have my beer in your fridge?" Quinlan asks, his
gaze solidly on the TV.

"Yes. I don't drink that swill." Nico gestures us beyond the
living area to another room. "I'm set up in here."

Anticipation thrills through my veins. I like the idea of investigating a crime. If I hadn't been so entrenched in Aquarius
Social, I might have pursued a line of work as a private detective or maybe even a spy, though I'm not a very good liar, so
probably not. But this is personal, and nobody cares about
finding the truth more than family.

We stride into the adjoining room, which Nico has used as
an office from the day he moved in. A set of windows frame
Silicon Valley, opposite an oak and glass desk with matching
credenza. The wall across from us has been cleared, and Nico
has created one of those murder boards like I've seen on mystery television shows.

In the center, he has Greg's picture and then lines drawn on
the light gray paint to other people, including the coroner, a
police officer, and then a row of suspects. My heart jolts when I
see Thorn as one of the suspects, as well as the owners of the
other two social media companies. I reach for a file folder on
the desk and start flipping through it to see a timeline of Greg's
movements within the week preceding his death.

"What do you have?" Ella asks, claiming the only chair and
plopping onto it.

"Not a lot." Nico walks over to pictures depicting the lethal
car accident, including the crumpled-up BMW. Greg loved that
vehicle. I rub my chest because suddenly it hurts even worse.

"If you look at the accident report," Nico says, "there are no skid marks. So it appears as if he just drove right off Vulture Perch at about a hundred miles an hour. Greg was sober that night and he had excellent reflexes."

Quinlan moves close to the board. "I agree. Greg was drinking water that night, even before I left."

Ella finally looks up from her phone. "There has to be more."

Nico's gaze narrows on her. "Greg had been receiving threats for the last year or so. Never digital, which makes sense."

"Threats?" I ask. "I didn't know anything about those."

Nico's chest expands as he employs that deep breathing technique both he and Greg used all the time. "I know. I'm not sure he even told your old man. The threats annoyed Greg but he wasn't worried."

In the time we'd spent together, not once had I caught a whiff of concern from my brother. "What kind of threats?"

"The usual: You're a capitalistic pig, you need to die, you're going to burn in the bowels of hell," Nico says without much emotion. "He showed me a couple of them, but when we helped clean out his apartment after his death, I didn't see them."

Those two days still haunt me. "Neither did I." But I wasn't looking, either. "Have you searched his office?"

"Of course." Nico rubs his left eye. "Nothing. Seriously, it was Greg. He probably threw them away."

That's true. If the notes irritated him, he would've just tossed them.

Ella taps a finger against her red lips. "The directors and higher-up employees at all of the social media companies receive threats all the time. That's why we have security."

Good point.

"Tell us about the night he died," she murmurs. "I haven't heard the full story from you."

Nico's eyes are somber. "We went out to celebrate the new algorithms we created to speed up the servers. We were in a good mood. We went to the Green Train Tavern just down the street from work and were having a great time." He points at pictures of three women on the other side of the accident pictures on his wall. "Those are the three women I believe Greg was dating at the time of his death, but there could be more." All three are blonde with green eyes. Beneath their pictures are names and occupations.

"Anything there?" I ask.

"Not that I've found," Nico says. "I've spoken with all three and they're pretty cut up about Greg's death, but none of them thought he was exclusive with them. They all had hopes, though."

My brother was a charmer, a quality I loved about him. "Yeah, I remember that. Everybody had hopes with Greg. But he was never going to settle down," I say.

"Agreed," Nico says. "That night, however, we did run into Corinda Rendale."

My head jerks. "You did? I didn't know that."

"That's because nobody's talking about Greg's death," Nico shoots back. "I know your father is also investigating, but every source I have at the police department has said that this case is closed."

"The two aren't mutually exclusive," Ella says, pushing her glasses up on her nose. "It's quite possible there is no case with the authorities and Mr. Beaumont is pursuing his own leads. It is the way the four families have conducted business ever since we were living in caves and hitting mega beasts over the head for dinner."

I look again at the picture of my brother on the wall. If he were here, he would know exactly how to pursue this investigation. Instead, I really do feel like Nancy Drew. "So what do we do?"

Nico glances at me. "You need to get all of the details from your father. He has to know more than we do."

"Then why not let him figure it out?" Ella twirls on the chair. "Mathias has the best resources, and I'm sure if he finds out that somebody killed Greg, he'll take them down."

"Because I need to know," Nico says bleakly. "I was with Greg that night, and if I hadn't had so much to drink, I could have driven myself here and he would have made it home safely." The guilt on his face is heart-wrenching.

I reach out and pat his hand. "We'll help you." Plus, I won't admit this to anybody, but my father would probably just have the killer murdered. If somebody hurt my brother, I want them to pay and go to jail for the rest of their lives. I want them to suffer, not die. "I'll help you, Nico. I promise."

Relief slides across his face.

Ella claps her hands together. "All right, I'll start hacking into both Mathias's and the police computers, just in case there's anything that has been missed. I really need you to get me access, Alana."

I nod. "I understand. I'll need to go to headquarters to do so. In addition, I'll talk to Thorn and Cal and feel them both out to see if they know anything."

Nico shakes his head. "I don't want you anywhere near Thorn."

"I agree," Ella chirps up. "The guy's bad news and you know it."

"Yes, but I think he'll tell me the truth." Except, do I? I look at Nico. "Was Corinda hitting on you or Greg that night?"

Nico crosses his arms. "Mainly Greg, but she did smile at me. Maybe I'll call her and ask her to lunch."

"That's a good idea." I don't have any way of getting into the Rendale brain trust. They hate Ella, so she can't be helpful, either.

"So that takes care of the other social media companies as

well as the women who were dating Greg," Quinlan says thoughtfully, his brown eyes sizzling. "I'll scour records at work for any threats within Aquarius Social. Greg was an excellent computer programmer, and more than once he caught a foolish employee trying to siphon off funds. I'll go through all of his data and make sure there wasn't a threat from within."

"Excellent plan." My head's starting to pound. The idea that somebody took Greg's life infuriates me, and I wonder again why my father doesn't trust me. Does he see me as a simpleton? I don't think so because he put me on the board, or perhaps he just thinks he can control me that way. I am, however, going to dinner with Cal Sokolov, just as he asked.

I walk out of the office to the main room and move closer to the windows to study the chrome and glass and wealth of Silicon Valley. From a distance it looks sparkling. Up close, it's cold, desolate, and computerized. I shiver. No wonder Thorn moved a half hour away to the ocean where he can hear the waves and smell the salt.

"Are you okay?" Nico asks.

I look at him. "I am. It's just been a long week."

He chuckles. "Isn't that the truth?"

I grin. "Hey, tell you what, I need to emote a video. How about you and I do it together with this background behind us?" He's a handsome man with that whole sharp Italian look going on. "You're not in front of the camera nearly enough."

He rolls his eyes. "That is not my thing."

"Yeah, but it could be. I bet you video well. Let's do one together and see what kind of reach we get. I need to grow our user base. Come on, Nico. What do you say?"

He sighs heavily. "All right. If you think it'll help Aquarius, you know I'll do it."

"I do," I say, hopping. "Why don't you ask me about Thorn?"

His dark brows draw down. "I'm not one to talk about Thorn Beathach."

"Too bad, because we're getting a lot of play anytime I talk about him. So let's have a little discussion, you and me—I promise it'll be painless."

Nico looks like I'm asking him to give up a testicle, but I know he'll do it. And yeah, this'll piss Thorn off even more. Who cares? Wouldn't it be just terrible if he's in a horrid mood when he goes on his date with the Rendale sisters tonight?

TWENTY-SEVEN

❧

Thorn

I sit in my car outside the Rendale gates, waiting for the guard to open them. Of course it's a show of dominance by Sylveria because they should've already been open and waiting for me, but I don't really give a shit. I reach for my phone to quickly text.

ME: I'm displeased about your earlier emote video with Nico.

ALANA: Making you happy isn't one of my goals in life.

ME: It will be.

ALANA: Ha. Enjoy your date. Try the salmon.

Amusement tickles my lip. She's jealous but too stubborn to ask me about tonight's get-together.

ME: Every time you post about me increases your punishments.

ALANA: Bite me.

ME: I fully plan to. Also, fair warning. I'll give you this once with Nico because you didn't know better. If you involve any

other person in a video about me without my express permission, I'll cut out their tongue and staple the bloody mess to your front door—before inflicting your original punishment for posting about me at all.

She doesn't answer for several heartbeats.

ALANA: You're evil.

ME: Now you're getting it.

Truth be told, I want to give her permission to use Nico for her videos. The guy looked like he was swallowing golf balls out of a mountain-high pile of manure the entire time. I doubt anybody hates being videoed for social media more than I do, but Nico comes close. He actually owes me one for this. I'm surprised when my phone vibrates and I look down.

ALANA: I hope you get herpes tonight.

I laugh out loud and then pause as the sound reverberates around my vehicle. When was the last time I actually did that? I swallow the honey taste in my mouth and text with one hand, watching the guard staring at me.

ME: Since you're the only person I'm fucking, if I get herpes, I'll make your life hell.

ALANA: You already are.

ME: Yeah. Multiple orgasms must feel terrible. Stop goading me.

It's as if she wants me angry when I attend this dinner. I pause. She does. My heart, if I still have one, swells.

ME: You're fucking adorable when jealous.

ALANA: You are going to die a very slow and painful death, and you're going to cry like a baby the entire time.

ME: I'm with you on the probable slow and painful part, but I don't cry.

It's time I took her home. Her impromptu meeting at Nico's with her little band of do-gooders is concerning. They're up to something.

ALANA: I'll never meet you. In fact, I'm looking elsewhere for a future mate. You're out of the running, buddy.

I growl. Deep in my chest.

ME: You're racking up punishments faster than a demon collects debts.

ALANA: You're the damn demon keeping score.

ME: Yes, I am. And baby, the house always wins. Prepare yourself.

The gate rolls open and I shove the phone into my pocket, wishing I could banter with Alana all night instead of attending this dinner. But I need to know if Sylveria created the cursed virus that's slowly killing me. My jaw aches and my gums are chilly. If my teeth fall out, I'm killing somebody.

I drive down the long and twisty driveway that leads to the looming mansion at the pinnacle of a rolling hill. Roses are everywhere, even though it's the end of the season. Rain falls onto them. They're all white, slightly swaying in the breeze.

Statues of different goddesses are strategically placed throughout the grounds. Even though it's overcast, parts of them sparkle. I have no doubt actual diamonds are inlaid in the materials.

Not one citrine is visible. Interesting.

I park near a set of gilded white double doors and stride up the stairs to knock. Normally, I would've brought flowers to a dinner such as this. But considering I'm now bound to Alana, it doesn't seem right to bring another woman flowers, even if this is a business meeting.

The door opens, and I'm somewhat surprised to see Sylveria herself performing such a menial task. Her pale features are perfectly contoured and accentuated by bright red lipstick, and her dark hair is pulled back in a fierce bun. She stands regal and tall in a silk dress with sparkling accents. It is a flattering A-line that reaches her calves, and even her three-inch heels sparkle. A diamond pendant falls beneath her breasts, matching those at her ears.

"It must be nice to have diamonds as your talisman," I say. She smiles, revealing perfectly straight teeth. "It truly is. I don't suppose you brought me one as a gift."

"I don't suppose I did."

She gestures inside. "Hmm. We'll have to work on your manners."

I walk inside a five-story-high vestibule with a black marble floor polished to a high sheen. The chandelier above us is grand and sparkles with crystals, diamonds, and a few citrines. The citrine crystals surprise me, but I figure the chandelier needs them for balance, as it was obviously handcrafted years ago.

"Come in." She leads the way to a great room with a portrait of her deceased husband over the silent fireplace, and into an already-set formal dining room. The grandeur of the place makes my back teeth clench.

Already seated at the long mahogany table are her two daughters and a man named Horace Whimple, who, it's my understanding, is both the top programmer for TimeGem, and Sylveria's love interest. There are rumors, which I care little about, that she and Horace have been together since their childhood days back in London.

He stares at me. He's a stately man in his early sixties with a bald head and intelligent grayish-green eyes. His Armani suit fits him well. "Thorn."

I stare right back. "Horace."

Then I turn to the other two ladies at the table. "Stacia, Corinda, you both look lovely." They both smile and twitter slightly.

I'm already irritated. They couldn't look more different. Corinda is a tall blonde with short hair, and Stacia is a shorter brunette with hair a little past her shoulders. They both have their mother's blue eyes.

Their father, I know from my research, died when they were young, and then Sylveria married Brooks Rendale, who also soon died.

I scout the room. "I'm still surprised you don't bring your other daughter into the fold. Rumor has it she's quite the computer guru."

"Stepdaughter," Sylveria says smoothly. "She's estranged from the family."

"Do you even know where she is?" I ask, cocking my head.

Sylveria waves a graceful hand in the air. "No, and I don't care."

I know exactly where she is. She's an integral member of Alana's inner circle. I wonder if that means she's also now in my inner circle. The thought intrigues me.

"Please sit here." Sylveria pulls out a chair across from her girls. Horace sits at the foot of the table, while Sylveria takes her place at the head. I have no doubt it's the dynamic of the duo in the bedroom.

I sit, and almost instantly, five servers enter the room and place salads in front of us.

"I hope you like the menu tonight," Sylveria says politely. "It's steak with cheesecake for dessert. I understand that's your favorite."

My favorite dessert is Alana Beaumont. "All right."

Horace pours wine in all the glasses, and it's an excellent vintage. "To new friends," he says, his eyes diamond hard, lifting a glass. We all do so.

I have two security teams on Alana right now, and I know her father has at least three. Last time I checked, the Sokolovs are keeping one on her as well. It's amazing the woman can go anywhere without tripping over a bodyguard or two. According to my men, she's safely working away at Aquarius Social right now. Good. There's nothing wrong with working late. I smile at the thought of honey.

The Rendale women instantly smile back. "So we thought it'd be nice to get to know you tonight and discuss a merger," Sylveria says smoothly.

Stacia, the brunette, sighs. "I've studied you."

"Have you, now?" I dig into my salad.

"Yes. You could benefit from combining diamonds, and possibly obsidian, with your garnet servers."

She's correct about the obsidian, because it runs in my family. "Why the diamonds?" I ask, curious.

"It's the strongest stone," she says. "We have found that combining diamonds with other crystals increases the strength of both." She smiles, and her canine is slightly crooked, which makes her much more appealing and interesting. "However, you need somebody with an affinity and a connection to the diamonds to make it happen."

I like her approach. It's smart, and she doesn't play games.

Corinda, the blonde, elbows her. "However, let's be honest. Your social media influencers need help. They're good, but they're not nearly as good as somebody at the top would be." Her gaze lashes across me and she emits a low hum from the back of her throat. "You're obviously not interested in mind-melding with your followers."

"God, no." I sit back as our salad plates are quickly whisked away.

"I am." Corinda smiles. "I have nearly five million followers on TimeGem Moments."

Soup, some kind of pumpkin soup, is placed in front of me. "You don't have as many as Alana Beaumont," I say smoothly.

"No, but I'm close," Corinda says, her bony shoulders going back. "If you and I combined, I could leave her in the dust."

That is exactly the opposite of what I'm planning for Alana. I turn and look directly at Sylveria. "There are rumors going around about Malice Media. What have you heard?"

She delicately wipes the corners of her mouth, as if thinking. I know I've caught her off guard with a direct question.

"I've heard that you're in trouble," she says smoothly. "My sources tell me that Mathias Beaumont traded a garnet the size of an inflated puffer fish to you. You obviously required the garnet."

"Did I?" I ask.

Corinda snorts. "Most likely, you just wanted to get rid of Alana."

I cut a glance at her and she swallows, turning pale. "What do you know about the garnet?" I ask Sylveria. She's obviously the only person in the know here.

"Just what I've heard," she says. "Why? Did something happen to yours?"

Did she infect my servers, garnet, and thus me? I give her the full force of my attention. Her hand trembles slightly as she reaches for the wine. "What did you do, Sylveria?"

"Nothing," she says.

I've gone without a mint this time, so I'm forced to taste the words around me. Horace's are like moldy licorice. Stacia's, too thick mulberry wine. And Corinda, lemonade that needs sugar.

But Sylveria, she's all smooth chocolate, and I can't read her completely. It's a true gift she has. "Rumor has it you killed your husband. Did you?"

She gasps and leans back. Even then, all I can taste is chocolate. Slightly bitter, but now strong enough to prove a lie? "Of course not."

Fuck. I can't tell if she's lying. She's too good. "You *want* to tell me the truth." I allow the killer lurking inside me to show himself.

Her head snaps up. "How dare you call me a liar in my own house! We are here to discuss our alliance, perhaps by marriage."

I turn and look at her daughters. "Are you both willing to marry me?"

Corinda nods and licks her lips.

Stacia lifts an eyebrow. "One of us is willing to marry you. You can't have us both."

There's something about her that's likable, the dry sense of humor and the clear mind. I wonder if Justice would be interested. Of course, we have to figure out what their mother did to our servers—if she's the culprit.

The soup disappears and the steak shows up. I take a bite. It's delicious, but combined with the other tastes in my mouth from these people, it's too much. "You do know that I believe in payback." I speak directly to Sylveria this time.

She throws her napkin onto the table. "Fine. Hypothetically, I may have an idea of who attacked your garnets and thus your servers."

"I believe said attack tried to maim me, although it's not having any effect." My feet are freezing, damn it.

"No effect?" The glint in her eye makes the blue sparkle brighter. "I will devote all of my resources to discovering who has attacked Malice Media"—she takes another sip of her wine—"after we consolidate our holdings in marriage. You do want to live, don't you?"

TWENTY-EIGHT

Alana

It's well after midnight when I stumble into my apartment, where I'm instantly swallowed by the smell of the fragrant roses. My lungs heat and I wander to my bedroom. Shadows wisp through the closed blinds, and I rub my eyes, heading to the bath to change into a well-worn T-shirt. At the office all day, I spent hours charging the aquamarines before scouring through personnel reports and threats to the company and my family for the last year.

Many people don't like us, and today I'm aware of the many threats my family members have kept from me. No wonder my father is so vigilant when it comes to security details.

There are at least six outside.

I also managed to get Ella into the company servers, which is something I should feel guilty about. Maybe tomorrow after I've had rest. Then I'll also worry about the other two emotes I posted, describing Thorn's chest and his sexy growl. No doubt the Rendale sisters got to hear the latter during their dinner with him. Thorn didn't text me again once he went inside.

Jerk.

Yawning, I tie up my hair, brush my teeth, and apply moisturizer to my face before padding back into my bedroom.

Something is wrong.

I pause in the doorway, looking around. Nothing is out of place. But tension thickens the atmosphere, and my heart rate hits mach ten.

The rose quartz light on the other side of my bed flicks on.

I yelp and jump back, prepared to slam the bathroom door.

Thorn stands there, somehow part of the shadows. Only his crisp white shirt shows within his expertly cut black suit. "Evening, Alana."

I gulp. "How in the hell did you get inside?" My gaze flashes to the closed window. The security is intended to prevent another kidnapping. Yet it has to be good enough to keep folks out. Thorn must be fucking brilliant.

"Are you ready for your punishment?" His voice is velvet soft.

My eyes widen, and suddenly, I'm wide-awake. I backpedal and try to shut the door, but he's already there, forcing it open. It occurs to me, much too late, that feeling safe with all the security around me is foolish, considering I'm dealing with a man like Thorn. Is he even a man? "Um."

"'Um' doesn't do it." His callused fingers trail down my bare arm.

Fireflies ignite inside me, zipping around, landing everywhere they shouldn't. My breath catches and my thighs tremble. Fear and anticipation clash in my body, and I frantically search for an escape route. My shirt suddenly flies over my head and then I'm in his arms, headed toward the bed. "No." I punch him in the throat.

His growl isn't pleased or sexy. It's pissed.

I freeze.

He tosses me onto my back, and before I can scramble away,

he has one wrist wrapped tight and is dragging my arm up toward the bedpost.

"Hey." I look up and see the belt of my comfy cotton bathrobe tying me securely in place. I jerk against it, but the material holds. Then he's manacling my other arm with my sexy silk bathrobe belt to the other post. Flopping back, my head on the pillows, struggling against the bindings, I gape up at him.

His gaze is on my breasts. "What is up with you and the multiple bathrobes?" Without waiting for an answer, he ducks down and wraps another belt around my left ankle, this one a starchy white, then ties it to another post.

I can't believe this is happening. The man has gone through my closet? "For different moods. Comfy, sexy, sick, chilly, and luxurious." Are we really having this discussion?

He secures my other ankle with the belt of the extravagant purple robe. "It's a handy habit."

I'm spread-eagled on the bed, tied tight. Fear wanders through me along with a furious lust I try to hide. This should not turn me on. Not at all. In fact, I suck in as much air as I can to scream.

He's instantly on me, shoving his tie into my mouth. Tears spring to my eyes and I try to push the silky material out with my tongue, but he lodged it well. "I'd rather not have witnesses. At least not yet." His grin is wicked. "Now, I'd like to talk. If you promise to be a good girl and not scream, I'll take out the tie. If you lie to me, in the mood I'm in, I promise you'll never do it again. Understand?"

I hate having something in my mouth, so I nod, a tear sliding down my cheek.

He removes the tie and leans over to lick up the tear.

Deviant that I am, I feel his tongue throughout my entire body, sliding right down to my pounding clit. There's something wrong with me. I had to have been dropped on my head multiple times as a baby. That's the only explanation.

He slides one finger beneath my panties, finding me swollen and wet. "Aren't you perfect?"

I close my eyes in mortification.

He slips that finger inside me, almost too easily, and I moan. Delicious flames lick through me, and I press against his hand.

"Fucking perfect." He moves and snaps the sides of my panties, yanking them off and tossing them across the room. "Now. Let's chat."

"I don't like this," I breathe.

His hand descends, right on my clit, hitting it center mass.

I cry out and buck, lashes streaking to my nipples. He has me bound too perfectly, and there's nowhere to go.

"Did you just lie to me?" he asks, peril lurking beneath his calm gaze.

My mouth opens and closes as my brain decides to take a vacation. So I start to babble. "Intellectually, I don't like this. That's fair. You can understand that."

He tweaks one nipple. Hard.

I moan and more wetness spills from me.

"How about your body?" he asks.

I gasp. "It's crazy. Every molecule has been infected with mad cow disease. Or a new gene they're about to discover that leads to insanity."

His smile is quick but amused. Then he leans over and blows warm air on my pussy.

My abdomen rolls. It's a gift he has, being able to draw my focus to just him. Right now, there's nothing in the entire world that matters except the proximity of his mouth to where I need him. "Please," I beg.

He looks up. "You want to feel good?"

"Yes," I breathe.

"By the time I'm done with you, you'll want to feel bad." He stands and tosses his jacket on the light green chair by the door before rolling up his sleeves. Then he returns to the other side of the bed and lifts up my good wooden salad bowl, several towels from my bathroom, and what looks like a sharp-edged razor that I have thankfully never seen before.

I pull against the restraints, panicking.

He ignores me and returns to place the bowl next to my thigh. "Stop moving. If you spill my water, I'll shave you without it."

I freeze. He spreads shaving cream all over my pussy, and I try but fail to keep another moan from escaping. Then he picks up the razor and I hold my breath.

"So. What are you being punished for?" he asks, his voice a dark rumble as he uses the razor.

I can't think. Don't want to breathe. That thing looks sharp.

The smack to my clit with the back of his hand has me jumping and then babbling again. "There were a few things, right? I mean, let me think." Don't move. God, don't move. "Um, ignoring your texts?"

"Yes." He returns to using the razor, his movements economical and smooth. But he's so close to where I don't want to be cut. Ever. "What is the punishment for that?"

I try to think. What was it? "Um, withholding orgasm?"

"Good. I believe I owe you four of those." His approving voice has my body relaxing from solid rock to slightly mushy concrete. "What other infraction have you repeatedly committed?"

He has to be about done. I mean, I shave regularly to go to the gym and swim. "Um. Emoting videos about you?"

"Yep." He wipes the razor off on one of the towels and then goes to town, hitting all of my very tender parts. I mean, everywhere down there. "Punishment?"

I think back. Didn't he issue some sort of threat in the bar bathroom? My memory clicks in and I gasp. "Spanking my bare pussy to orgasm?" No way. It isn't possible.

"After making you beg for it." He finishes, wipes me off,

and stands to look down at his handiwork. His eyes flash, and pure lust fills them.

I blink, feeling vulnerable and rather bare. "Listen, I— "

He leans down and flicks my clit, my very bare clit, with his tongue.

The sound I make isn't one I'll ever be able to repeat. But electricity burns through me, and I push up against him, seeking his mouth.

He stands and takes the bowl, towels, and razor into the bathroom. While he's out of sight, I pull against the restraints, unable to move an inch. Figures. His punishments are polar opposites, and I don't know which one he's chosen. It'd be like him to shave me, have me think one thing, and then go the other direction.

He returns and stares at me for several long moments.

I can't move, and the look in his eyes, on his scarred face, thrills my body to the point I can't stay still. Then he releases one of my ankles. A shocking disappointment crashes through me. But this is okay. I mean, I'm turned on and would love an orgasm, but if this is him withholding one, then big whoop. I'll take care of business when he leaves.

He releases my other ankle.

I wrap my hands around the belts, waiting for freedom. "I think I get it." Might as well appease the beast. "This withholding is tough."

He then cocks his head and reaches to slowly unbuckle his belt.

Warning ticks through my head. "What are you doing?"

He pulls it through the loops, and the sound is deafening. Quick as a thought, he flicks it through the air and lashes my clit.

I scream and press my legs together, twisting my legs to one side as much as possible with my hands still bound. Pain echoes through my pussy and torso, quickly warming into an intense craving that nearly has me sobbing.

He sets a knee on the bed. "Spread your legs and I'll make it better."

I look at him, unsure. Then slowly, I roll fully onto my back and do so, my legs trembling.

He leans over and licks me, kissing my abused clit.

The feeling is too much. I shut my eyes and push toward him. He chuckles against me, the sound vibrating from my sex to my tits. As if he knows, he reaches up and tweaks both nipples. I arch my back.

He licks me again, sliding two fingers inside my wet and welcoming body. His rhythm is perfect and I ride his face, climbing to the pinnacle. He stops.

My eyes fly open.

He slaps me, open palm, on my clit. Hard. Then he watches me.

The connection between us is terrifying.

Whatever he sees has him slapping my clit again.

Hunger fills me.

He smiles, the sight dark. Then he slaps me several times, harder each time, watching my reactions. I'm anticipating each blow and he knows it.

I sob out a protest but still push against him, pleasure and pain clashing together until I can't tell them apart but want more. Crave more. He kisses my clit and then licks me again, going at me with his fingers, teeth, and tongue until my head is thrashing against the pillow. Then he stops and spanks me again, top to bottom of my pussy, forcing shocking vibrations to spark each nerve inside me. Then he licks me again. He goes on for an eternity, keeping me on the edge, finally getting me to the point where even the slaps are welcome.

I'm so close.

We're completely connected. It's as if he knows what I'm feeling. What he's forcing me to feel.

Then he stands and picks up the belt again. He looks like an avenging god with intent to punish. Starkly beautiful and perilously dangerous.

My breath is heated and my eyes wide. The blood rushes through my head so quickly, the sound is deafening.

He flicks his wrist and the end of the belt lashes across my already abused clit. I jolt and close my legs, rubbing my thighs together and trying to protect my tender parts from him. "You want to come?"

Desperately. Numbly, I nod.

"Then spread your legs."

Despite the numbing hunger, I catch his meaning. He released my legs on purpose, not to give me freedom but to force me to submit on my own. I watch him, my legs shaking, my body warring with my spirit.

He shoves the edge of the belt between my legs and rubs me. I moan, gyrating against the leather. It feels so good.

Then he lifts it and presses it close to my eyes. "See how wet you are? How much you want this?"

I'm sure humiliation will come later. Right now, there's only need.

He slides the wet leather over my breasts and back down between my legs, rubbing my clit while his mouth takes mine. Hard, demanding, and all Thorn, he kisses me until I can't think and am actively riding the belt, climbing toward the pinnacle.

Then he stops and lifts up, his face inches from mine. "Beg me."

A tear leaks from my eye and he licks it away. I'm there. It's impossible to need this much. My body might just explode and leave me a head with no body. "Please," I whisper.

"Please, what?" There's no mercy on his hard face.

"Make me come." That belt is still between my legs. If he just moves it a little faster, I'm there.

He kisses me again, keeping up the slow and torturous rubbing. "There's only one way. Ask for it."

Silence takes me. "You want to break me." It's almost a sob.

"I've already broken you." His eyes are burning coals with flecks of silver on fire. "Now I'll put you back together."

He's right. I can't think of anything else. "Please spank me to orgasm." It's unhealthy to need this badly. I'm dying.

Partially rising, he lets loose with the belt, harder than before. The lashes come one after another, dead center, shooting spirals of sharp pain through me that slash right to a pleasure so dark it has to come directly from Thorn. I climb the jagged cliff and then fall over the edge of pain, climaxing with a shocking rawness that has my mouth widening in a silent scream.

The punishing waves crash through me, head to toe, shattering me into pieces that he can do with as he likes. He spanks me through the entire orgasm until I come down, mumbling.

He tosses the belt aside, reaches up and releases my arms, before roughly flipping me onto my belly. Hard hands yank me onto all fours, he releases his zipper, and then he's inside me, driving hard and fast.

My head flips back as he holds my hips in a punishing grip and wildly pounds, hitting a spot inside me that has me crying out and pushing against him. This isn't possible. My nails dig into the pillows and my body stiffens as he forces me up again, too high, my body not prepared for this much fire. I explode again with a sob, another orgasm taking me, as he shudders against me, filling me.

Then, silence.

I flop back down and he allows it. There's the slight sensation of a warm washcloth between my legs, but I'm gone. I feel his hard body wrap around me and the softest of kisses pressed to my ear before I drop into a deep sleep.

TWENTY-NINE

Alana

I'm small again, rocking back and forth, the carpet soft against my knees. I can smell vanilla. Where am I? Mama said to be quiet, so I am, but I'm scared. I can hear her with a man. Their words are sharp. Scary. I can't understand them but I hear them. I look up and see those windows. The long ones with the weird shape. It looks mean, but I don't know why.

She falls on the carpet next to me, her eyes so green, and I reach out, but big hands pull her back up.

I cry and shut my eyes.

Then glass shatters loudly. Seconds later, I hear squealing brakes.

I jerk awake as thunder bellows across the sky.

"Easy." Thorn rubs a hand down my arm, his body solid and strong behind me. His hand is chilled.

The room is warm. So I take his hand and pull it under the covers with us. Wait a minute. What's wrong with me? The man spanked me to orgasm the night before. *With a belt.*

"Tell me." It's an order. Sleepy, but a command nonetheless. So I do, submitting again, remembering more as I speak. I think they're memories.

"How long did your mother live after this?" His breath stirs my hair, and even though my body is sore, part of me is glad he's here. He has the most intriguing way of making me feel safe from everything and everyone . . . but him.

I think back. "I don't remember. Not long. That whole time after my accident is a blur, and before, I don't remember anything." I stretch against him and note that his calves are cold as well. Perhaps he's coming down with something. "I'm not even sure it's a memory. Could just be a nightmare."

"The windows you heard shatter. Can you see them?"

Bile rises from my stomach. "No."

His arm tightens around my waist. "Nothing can hurt you. Tell that little girl in the dream that I'll slay any monster that comes at her for the rest of her life. And have her look at those windows."

I snuggle into him and close my eyes because he's right. I try to take myself back to the room, but I already know what I'll see. I huddle in the corner, my little arms around my legs, and look up to see the windows with the argyle crisscross pattern. My body shudders. "It's the windows. First they're put together with the pattern, and then they're broken, pieces of the design hanging in the wind."

Thorn rubs his whiskered chin on top of my head. "I'll look into your past."

"I can handle it." First, I need to speak with my father and then have Ella do a deep dive if I'm not satisfied with his answers. "If somebody hurt my mother or me, and they didn't pay, I'm going to kill them." The terror of the dream still chills my blood.

"No, you're not." His hand flattens over my abdomen and caresses up across both breasts to stretch across my upper chest, over my heart.

243

I stiffen. "You can't tell me you haven't killed people."

"I have and I do. You don't."

I stare into the darkened room, noting the brightening sky outside. "Why do you care about some killer?"

"I don't. But if you kill, you'll become somebody else—you'll lose a part of yourself, which means we both lose that part. If you're giving up pieces, it's only to me."

I think that's sweet? Or psychotic. "I'm not promising forever, but—"

"You already have. You gave yourself to me. There's no going back. Period." His tone is still lazy but now has a hint of a possessive edge.

I'm too tired to yank his ass into the current century. "I'm going to age. My boobs will drop, my skin wrinkle, and I could gain a hundred pounds. What then?"

He snorts. "You're still you, no matter what you look like. I'll still play with your boobs, pinch your skin, and love more of you. It's the essence of you, the very spirit, that I won't allow you to change. The rest is up to you." He stretches. "I'm tiring of waiting for you to come to your senses and return home."

"You had a date with the Rendale sisters," I burst out.

He chuckles. "I wondered if you would ever ask about that."

"Considering we're naked in my bed, you might want to explain." I sniff.

His hand feels like a brand across my skin, no longer cold. Maybe I imagined the chill. "They offered marriage to either of the women and didn't acknowledge Ella's existence."

Jealousy sears through me. "Marriage? Which one did you choose?"

"I choose you and you know it. Stop trying to start a fight. You won't win."

The morning takes over. I'm sore, overwhelmed, and confused. So I elbow him in the gut. "I just think—"

"That's it." He tosses the bedcovers out of the way, yanks

me from the bed, and plants me on my knees with him standing over me. He grabs my hair and tugs back my head. "Find something better to do with that mouth." His hardened dick presses against my lips.

My mouth partially opens out of shock, and he shoves farther inside.

Truth be told, I'm curious about this. Although, he could've asked nicely. I wonder if he has any idea of how vulnerable he is right now.

His hand tightens in my hair. "If you even think of biting me, I promise you, I bite back. I'm sure you're sore from the belt."

My clit jerks in denial. "I'm not going to bite you," I say around the tip. "But I have no idea what I'm doing."

"Create a crater with your tongue, take me down your throat, and breathe out of your nose." His thumb presses into the hinge of my jaw, forcing it open wider. "And have some fun with it."

It's the last order that has me pausing. Good advice. So I do as he says, seeing how far I can take him. I gag a couple of times, but soon learn to breathe through my nose, and when he groans, I feel like a queen.

So I plant my hands on his thighs and feel them tighten. Then I go at him the same way he did with me, using my tongue and mouth and finally my hand, circling his girth. This would be impossible to do with a cold. I chuckle at the thought, and he groans louder. Fascinating. To have even a small ounce of command over Thorn Beathach is heady. I cup his balls and take him deeper, noting his hand tightening in my hair. He twists his fingers and regains control, fucking my mouth.

All I can do is lift my chin and breathe through my nose.

So much for command over him. My nipples sharpen and my clit pounds. My thighs become wet again, so I reach down and rub my punished body.

"Don't even think of coming," he says, his voice strained. "And you drink every drop."

I feel his body tighten before he spurts down my throat. He's so far down nothing even touches my tongue, so I grow still and wait, curious. Then it's over. He pulls out and I flick him with my tongue.

He lifts me back to the bed and kisses me, his arms tight. Then he leans back, a smile in his eyes. "Did you have fun?"

"I did." I bet I could get pretty good at that. He seems pleased, like a lazy lion in the sun. I like this side of him. My hands go back down my body.

"No." He pulls my hands free and pushes me back on the bed, dropping to a crouch and licking my clit. I'm sore, but the rough touch of his tongue nearly sends me into orbit. "You're close." He slides two fingers inside me.

I close my eyes, waiting for heaven.

Instead, he turns his head and sinks his teeth into my inner thigh.

I yelp and slap the top of his head.

His chuckle vibrates through me before he soothes the wound, kissing and licking it. Then he returns to my sex, torturing me until I'm writhing on the bed, making incoherent noises.

Finally, he stops and reaches up for my arms, pulling me to a seated position. This is new. Liquid is seeping from me, and I'm one good nip from an excellent orgasm.

I push my unruly hair away from my face. "What are you doing?"

"Punishment number one for not responding to my text." His eyes are still lazy with a hint of deadly seriousness.

What an ass. I reach down, and he slaps my hand.

"Hey," I say, shifting my weight and trying not to punch him in the face.

His hands encircle my wrists and he places them on my

thighs. "I have rules, and when you break them, there are repercussions."

Oh, whatever. He can't stay all freaking day. It's almost morning, and I'm sure he needs to sneak out. The thought that one of the many snipers out there might shoot him brightens me for a moment. "You can't leave me tied to the bed all day, unable to touch myself. I have to go to work." When his chin lowers, I hasten to say, "That wasn't a challenge. Not at all. Only a statement."

"Smart girl," he says.

I bite back a sharp retort because I do have a brain.

He glances at the clock near the bed and then retrieves his slacks and shirt, buttoning it up. I have no idea how his entire ensemble looks unwrinkled. Must be an unnatural gift. When he draws on his jacket, he pulls out a phone and reads the face. "I have to leave in a couple of minutes."

"Okay." I'm still naked and he's fully dressed, and the weight of last night presses in.

As if he knows—because he seems to know everything—he palms the back of my head and leans over to kiss me as I sit on my bed. "Everything we do, everything we are, is perfect. Tell me you understand."

I look up at him, so tall and powerful, so dark and dangerous. "I understand." The temptation to fall into his universe is fierce, and I dig deep for a backbone. "You know we're not just in your world, right?"

Dark stubble covers his jaw, giving him the look of a wild rogue, despite the designer suit. "You entered my world the first time you opened your mouth and said *please*." He caresses my nape with sure and firm fingers. "What you don't seem to have figured out is that you're the absolute center of that world."

The words are sweet—I'll consider them later. Right now I need to get him out of my bedroom so I can get my little vibrator from the bedside table. Even his hand at the back of my neck is driving me crazy.

"When are you coming home?" he asks.

I wouldn't be human if that question didn't give me a little thrill. "I am home." I do have some pride.

"All right. Soon, then." He cups my jaw, his hold firm. "Do you believe me when I tell you something?"

"Yes." The word slips out before I can contemplate the answer. So far, he's always given me the truth, even while issuing rules and administering punishments.

"Good." His gaze rakes my nude body as I sit on the bed. "Your orgasms are mine, Alana. Get me?"

I force a smile. "Sure thing."

His smile is both mocking and a warning. "Rule number four: If you make yourself come without permission, I'm going to bend you over and fuck your ass, after you beg for it. And baby, you *will* beg for it. You're not ready for that."

I lean back, shock rushing through me.

He pauses. "I'd never hurt you, and I promise I'll make sure you want it someday. But you won't like it this early—especially afterward when you have time to think. Don't make me prove it to you." He holds my attention until I instinctively nod.

With a hard kiss to my lips, he turns and slips out of the bedroom. All of the tension dissipates.

Well, crap.

THIRTY

Thorn

My mind still on Alana and the wisp of honey remaining on my tongue, I sit in the back offices of Harvard Lewis & Sons, Inc. There's no Harvard Lewis and there are no sons, but it's a good enough front, and with a sign like that on the street, nobody ever comes in. There's no hint as to the type of business this might be in the lower end of Silicon Valley, and if someone looks inside the wide windows, all they see is a quiet reception area with an often-vacant reception desk. The real action is behind the wide wall, and it's a sparkling and mercilessly clean series of trauma rooms, as well as an examination room or two.

I lounge on a black leather chair, my head back as I try and fail to warm my feet. Doc has them in stupid boot warmers, and if I had my gun, I'd shoot him.

"Stop thinking about shooting me," he mutters, reading a tablet across the room.

I glare at him. He's not fazed. I guess when you hit around eighty years old and have operated on everything from wounded soldiers to the neighbor's cow, not much upsets you.

He flicks through the tablet. "I have your X-rays here, and they don't tell me everything I need." He turns it around so I can almost see. "As you can tell, the organs that have begun freezing appear slightly brighter because their density has increased. The edges of your kidneys look like shit."

I scrub both hands down my face. His words taste like over-salted popcorn and I guess that makes sense because Doc is as salty as they get.

"In addition," he says, "the margins of your liver, kidneys, and even your heart are more distinct on these X-rays."

I just look at him because I have no idea what he's talking about.

He sighs. "Normal soft tissues like organs have slightly blurred or feathered margins on X-rays, but if you're freezing from the inside out, everything gets sharper."

I guess that makes sense. "Anything else?"

"It looks like your rib cage is widening. That would make sense if your organs are starting to freeze."

"I'm glad it makes sense to you," I say.

He just stares at me. Despite his age, he still has a thick head of wiry whitish-gray hair and the bushiest eyebrows I've ever seen. His eyes are a faded blue and his body is in surprisingly good shape. "I'd like to perform a thermography on you, but I have to go borrow a machine or two."

"Tell the boys what you need and I'll make sure you get it," I say.

"Good. I also want an ultrasound and an MRI machine."

I look around. "We don't have room for an MRI machine."

"You're right," he says brightly. "If I arrange it, will you go to the hospital and get an MRI?"

No equipment the current medical establishment has is going to help me. "No," I say shortly.

"Why not? I want to see the pictures," he complains. He's wearing his usual white overcoat over gray slacks, a green shirt, and a perfectly knotted silk tie. Since he's our main doctor, he doesn't have regular hours, but somehow always shows up looking like the perfect country physician.

"What does an MRI matter?" I ask. "It doesn't change anything. We know what's happening."

One of those caterpillar-like eyebrows rises. "We have no idea what's happening. Yeah, we know you're freezing, but this is unprecedented, Thorn."

"I'm aware of that, but seeing my organs crystalize in real time just because you're interested isn't worth my going to the hospital. The last thing I need is for anybody to find out about this. Besides, are you still licensed to practice medicine?"

He's been our back office trauma surgeon for as long as I can remember. If anybody in my organization gets shot and doesn't need immediate hospitalization, we bring him to Doc. He's the best.

"Of course, I'm still licensed. Otherwise, how would I sign prescriptions for everybody?"

"Good point," I say.

My phone vibrates in my pocket, and I pull it out, seeing a 911 from Justice. I dial. "What's going on?"

"We're under attack," he says tersely, the sound of alarms beeping over the line.

I remove the feet warmers and reach to put on my socks and shoes. "What kind of attack? Do you have security?"

"Cyber," he mutters. "Need your help." He hangs up.

I stand, grab my coat from the rack, and head out of the office. "Go ahead and have the boys pick up the thermography thing and an ultrasound," I say as I stride toward the back door. "But no MRI."

"Come on, Thorn." Doc shuffles after me. "We could fit one in the basement."

I look over my shoulder as I open the door. "Could we really fit an MRI machine in the basement?"

"Absolutely," he says.

I sigh. "All right, go ahead. Figure it out with Justice and you can have it."

He hops. "Oh, you've made me so happy."

"Yeah, that was my goal today," I mutter as I head through the rain to my car. What is wrong with me? I've never let anybody in my organization speak to me like that. Almost joke with me.

Is Alana mellowing me? It's unthinkable, and it will stop, if so.

Against all the rules in my organization, I've driven myself today with no backup because I didn't want to deal with anybody. Plus, I enjoy driving. Whenever one of my men is in the car, they act like they need to take the lead and make sure I don't get shot. I'm a better driver than any of them.

I zip through the city in my Audi A8 L Security that I have tricked out with integrated safety features. This thing is resistant to bullets, explosions, and other types of attacks. I need to find another one and make even more modifications to it for Alana.

I'm slightly irritated she hasn't decided to return to my home, and soon will take her independent nature in hand. Harshly if necessary. My mind remains on her as I travel through Silicon Valley and drive into the underground parking garage of Malice Media. One of my men instantly opens my door and then I'm covered until I reach the elevator, although there's no way anybody could have gotten inside this garage.

I leave them and travel down the many stories into the earth, where the door opens and I walk into the server room to see Kaz and Justice at their respective terminals typing furiously. I shrug out of my jacket and drop it as I stalk to my computer and boot it up. "Status," I bark.

"Multiple attacks," Justice says grimly, squinting at his monitor. "I'm on the first wave, which was an influx of contradictory data aimed specifically at the quantum memory of the garnet."

I pause. "That's a decent attack. What's your plan?"

"I'm introducing a slight delay into the processing of every garnet core."

Kaz looks over his shoulder. "That should disrupt the attacker's data influx. If we can do that, we can slowly shut it down."

"What are you doing, Kaz?" I ask.

He keeps typing and looks back at his monitor. "Second wave of attack focuses specifically on our users in an attempt to release personal data."

"Shit," I mutter.

He pounds the enter key. "Yeah, I'm on this one. I'm creating what I call quantum bubbles to force the requests into along with any loosened data. Once we get it all in one place and stop the attack, I can burst the bubble and our users will be fine."

That sounds excellent. "Good." I boot up my computer and rapidly dive deep into the system. "I'm assuming there's a third wave?"

"Yes," Justice says. "It's . . ."

"I've got it," I say, immediately seeing the fractured data. It looks like somebody is attempting to inject malicious scripts into our servers aimed specifically at the resonance and molecular structure of the garnets.

Simultaneously, I see a distributed denial of service attack aimed to slow Malice Media's response times so users can't access their accounts. I start to type, hunting the malicious code through the servers, anticipation lighting my blood. Oh, I'm hell in a fight, but put me in front of my computer, and I'm a god.

I find the traffic patterns and instantly deploy network filters that will segregate genuine user requests from these attacks.

Quickly finding the bubble sector Kaz has set up, I send the fake bots right into the bubbles. Fighting in real time, I write an AI algorithm that uses advanced heuristics to do so.

"Excellent," Kaz says. "I see what you're doing."

"Keep it up," I answer, typing faster than he is.

Then I turn toward the DDoS attack and spread out an even use of traffic over every single one of our attached garnets and servers. If I can relieve the pressure in any one area, it'll render the DDoS ineffective.

"I've started system patching," Justice says, typing rapidly.

I track him in real time while also looking for additional threats. This enemy came at us right now because they know we're weak. "All right, I'm sending the malware back to its source." I've shut down both of my attacks and it looks like Kaz and Justice are battling as well. "Let's find out who this is, even though I already have a pretty good idea."

"Check the honeypots," Kaz grunts.

"I am."

We have many honeypots set up throughout our system to track attackers, but I already know without looking that this campaign is too complex to have been sucked into any of those.

Justice grunts. "Shit."

"What?" I ask, looking over my shoulder.

He shakes his head. "Several more breaches. They're overwhelming the server. Our garnets can't keep up."

"Our diseased garnets can't keep up," I mutter, fury igniting my blood. Fine. They want to play? I turn and type in a rapid set of commands.

Kaz spins in his chair, his eyes wild. "Wait a minute."

"Nope. It's the only way," I answer, immediately activating a system-wide protocol that collapses all of the quantum states in our garnets to their base. The entire system stops.

"Fuck," Kaz says, lifting his hands.

Justice looks over at me. "You think this'll work?"

"I have no idea." I type in a command to reboot and nothing happens. I pause and will the universe to do as I want. The entire system comes back online. As one, we all go for our keyboards, typing rapidly.

"Oh my God, it worked," Justice says.

I look through the entire system, but all malware has been pushed out. It's a fail-safe I inserted when I created the system. I had hoped never to use it.

"We won't be able to track the attack back to its origination point now," Justice says, looking over his shoulder again at me.

"I'm aware." I stand and key in my code by the door before walking into the chillier room, looking at the flickering lights on the servers and the large garnet in the middle of the hub. I walk toward it. It's full, red and sharp-edged . . . and I feel no connection. I reach out and touch it. The crystal hums beneath my hand, but it's almost as if the diseased garnet is a barrier between me and this one. I wonder if I should smash the other to bits, or if that would end in my death as well. We may get to the point where I won't have any choice but to try.

"Your best option is to somehow heal the diseased garnet and yourself," Justice says from behind me.

I turn to look at him standing in the doorway. "Come here."

He walks closer. My younger brother, the one person in the world I vowed to protect until I met Alana, and now I have the two of them. I jerk my head toward the garnet.

He reaches out and plants his hand over it. Nothing happens. "I'm not connecting with it either," he says. "Its glow isn't any stronger for me than for you."

That's because I'm still here. If death takes me, according to the history of our family, he and the garnet will connect. It's a good thing.

"What did the doctor say?" he asks.

"Doc?" I roll my eyes. "He wants an MRI machine."

"Where's he going to put that?"

I chuckle, finally relaxing for the first time all day. "He thinks he can put it in the basement."

Justice stills. "I'm not having an MRI done down in that creepy basement. We'd probably catch leprosy down there."

"I don't care. Might as well make Doc happy. He does keep us alive," I mutter.

"Well, that's true," Justice says. "Who do you think created this attack?"

We have so many enemies, it's hard to say. "The Rendales know we're weak." I'd read that in Sylveria's eyes the night before, but she might just have good sources. Which doesn't tell me who's behind the attacks.

He nods. "I've been listening in on the devices you planted in their home the other night."

I'm surprised they didn't conduct a search-and-scan the second I left. "And?"

"Nothing. They haven't admitted to anything. There's some minor squabbling between the sisters on who's going to marry you." His lips draw back as if he just ate glue.

"I'm not marrying either of them."

"You didn't tell them that, did you?"

Of course not. "Not while we're at war. I'm wondering if Sylveria Rendale is the one who infected our servers with the computer virus that is killing our garnet."

"And you."

"And me. She hinted that if I married one of her daughters, there'll be a cure."

He releases the garnet. "Then she's the one."

"Maybe," I say. "She could be bluffing."

He sighs. "You're not going to like this."

"I rarely do," I say wearily, letting myself relax for the briefest second since only my brother is present.

"I think you need to go to the Silicon Shadows and Secrets Ball tomorrow night."

My mouth drops open. That is the last thing on the entire earth I expected Justice to say. "Have you lost your mind? I don't attend functions. I don't even go out in public if I can help it."

He crosses his arms. "I know, but this attack, it hurt us and we were already struggling."

"So?"

He takes a step back, as if thinking I'm going to charge him. "We need to post a social media hologram event that people can join in and experience. One they dream about but can't afford."

"With me?" Has Justice been hit in the head lately?

"Yes, with you. You're an enigma, a mystery. Every time Alana emotes on Aquarius Social about you, she gains twice the user interaction that she would attract otherwise. We need to harness that same power."

I glare at the half-charged garnet. "Why don't you do it?" I ask.

"Because I'm not Thorn Beathach. I'm the brother nobody knows exists. I'll do my part, but if you want to bring our service fully online, we need user interactions, and we need energy. And with the garnet dying . . ."

"We're losing energy too fast," I murmur. "Well, at least I have a date. Since I'm going, put plans in place to take her tomorrow night at the ball."

I'm done waiting.

THIRTY-ONE

Alana

The lower part of my abdomen has ached all freaking day. Not like, hey, this is sexy, but more like, ugh, I want to throw up, but I don't have the energy. In fact, my entire lower half throbs and I try to ignore it as I sit once again in the quiet basement of my apartment complex, with Ella typing happily away.

It's just the two of us since she lives in this basement. It's too risky for either Merlin or Rosalie to try the hidden entrance with so much security watching the building. I miss seeing Merlin but would rather he stay safe.

I'm sitting in the middle of the room, flipping through data Ella printed out for me regarding Malice Media and garnets. There's nothing here that helps me decipher what is so important about those garnets he traded me for.

I'd love to get something on him. As much as I'd like to defy him, I took a cold shower and then came to work without bringing out my vibrator. Not that I'm afraid. No. Not at all.

My skull even aches. A withheld orgasm really sucks. Shaking my head, I bring myself into the present moment. "What's up between you and Nico?"

Ella looks up. "What?"

"That's a pretty blush," I murmur.

She rolls her eyes. "Fine. Nothing is up. I mean, we ran into each other a couple of weeks ago at a coffee shop and sat for a while. He's handsome and has that intense thing going on."

"Why didn't you tell me?"

She shrugs. "You've been pretty busy and also so sad about Greg. I doubt Nico is really interested, so why bring it up?"

"He'd be nuts not to be interested."

Her smile is cute, and I instantly start plotting how to get them in the same room.

She starts typing again. "I love gaining entry to the Aquarius Social servers. Love it."

Now that I'm on the board of directors, I have access in a way that I didn't before, and I've handed it all over to her. She is currently hunting through everybody's corporate records and private emails. "You find anything relating to Greg's death?" I ask.

"Your cousin Quinlan likes to talk dirty," she says, still typing.

I straighten. "What do you mean, he likes to talk dirty?"

"He's got at least three girlfriends and, believe me, he has some creative ideas."

I barely bite back a groan. "He shouldn't be typing that kind of thing in company emails. Lesson one in all business transactions is don't put it in writing. Everybody knows that."

"Yeah. Well, they don't seem to mind. Ooh," she whispers. "A couple of these women should write romances. Oh, hey, one does, Lexi somebody. Ooh, I have to make a mental note to buy some of her books."

"Ella," I say. "Get back on track."

"I can do three things at once," Ella says.

That's actually true. Multitasking is just an urban myth for most people; however, not for Ella. I've seen her do three things equally well at a time. It's impressive. I don't have that gift.

Her fingers slow on the keys. "You haven't posted and asked for stars today. Why? Are you having no emotions?"

I chuckle but the sound is pained. I'm having more emotions than I can decipher, and they all center on Thorn Beathach. I'm pretty sure the summation of the emotions is that I want to kill him. Well, I'm feeling pretty brave and angry right now, but I haven't disobeyed his order. When he issues a threat, he means it.

Heat flies into my face and I ignore it. "Ella, please tell me you found something on my brother's death."

"I have," she muses, slowing her typing even more. "Your father has hired three different private detectives to look into the so-called accident."

I knew it. If there is any question about Greg's death, my father would never let it lie.

"Why isn't he working with the authorities?" Ella asks.

"That's not how the four families operate. Laws and countries and people come and go," I murmur. "The four families are forever."

"You're right. We happen to live here now, but we make up our own laws," Ella says wearily. "I can't believe Thorn might marry one of my stupid stepsisters."

"He's not," I burst out before I can stop myself.

She chuckles. "I thought so. Are you going to fight for your man?"

"He's not mine," I retort quickly.

"Huh," she says, sounding utterly unconvinced. "Okay, so I've hacked into one of the detective agency's servers. The defenses on it are laughable."

I perk up.

She just pauses. Then she pushes away from the computer and turns to face me. "You sure you want to know all of this?"

"Of course I'm sure."

She winces. "All right. Your father didn't bury Greg at the funeral." She speaks slowly as if trying to find a better word each time one comes out of her mouth.

A dull roar echoes in my ears. "Excuse me?" The coffin was closed, but I figured that was just because Greg had been beaten up pretty badly in the accident.

"Yes. Mathias sent Greg's body to a specialized coroner in DC. I can't imagine the strings he had to pull to do that." She shakes her head. "Anyway, this coroner determined . . ." She turns back to read the monitor. "The cause of death was blunt force trauma to the temporal lobe." She squints and leans closer to the screen. "Okay, so the coroner found a contusion on Greg's right temple." She looks over at me as if to gauge my state of mind and I nod. "There's evidence of a depressed skull fracture at the impact site leading to intracranial injury."

I gulp. "What else?"

"Toxicology report shows a blood alcohol level of 1.5. It's not a lot, but it's some," she reads.

"What's the conclusion?" I ask, my chest compressing.

She tilts her head. "Cause of death attributed to complications from blunt force trauma to the temple leading to significant intracranial injury. Most likely not from a car rolling over a cliff."

I can't breathe. "Not?"

"The coroner doesn't say for sure." She scrolls to another screen. "But she does say that the impact is small and definite. It's defined in the skull."

"But she can't tell what caused the injury?" I ask.

"That's all there is," Ella says. "At the bottom of this sheet there's a note that a phone call will take place to discuss the findings." She sits back. "The phone call would've happened two weeks ago."

The ache in my stomach turns to strong cramps. I can't believe this. "What else do you have?"

"I'm still looking," she says. "I'll break into the records of the other two private detectives, but it looks like your father is careful to conduct most business either face-to-face or over, I'm sure, very secure phone lines. I don't know that we're going to find much in these servers."

I rub my left temple. Why hasn't my father told me any of this? "Is that it?" I ask, trying to sound in control of myself.

A small smile plays on her pink lips. "I did hack Nico pretty easily."

"You didn't hack him. I gave you the keys to the entire system."

"Well, I guess that's true."

Enough. "Find anything good?"

"Yeah. He has reached out to several private detectives as well, but I don't see anything interesting that he hasn't already told you."

I like that Nico is up front with me. My father could take lessons from him. "What about Quinlan?" I ask. "I mean besides the dirty talk."

"Nothing," she says. "He does have a lot of pictures on his terminal, of family, pictures that go way back."

"Really?" I ask, standing.

"Yeah." She brings them up.

I smile when I see all the people, many I recognize, at a lake cabin. "Wow, that must be some sort of family reunion."

"Is that you?" She points to a baby held in my mother's arms.

"It *is* me." My hair was a wild mess even then. I look around. "Wow. We really did get together a lot."

Quinlan has an arm over my mom's shoulders. He mentioned they were close. He and Nico appear muddy with a football on the ground between them.

I smile and wish I could remember the good times. "They look happy. If I was around two, then they would've been maybe twelve or so. Is that Scarlett?" I lean in. She's pretty in a white dress, and yet it's obvious she's about to go for the football.

Ella stares at the picture. "Is it weird having more people on the board of directors?"

"Yes," I say. "But it might be good, since we're family." I pause as I think through her family drama. I know she misses her deceased father every day, and since her stepmother has discarded her, *family* is a four-letter word for her. "Oh wait, I didn't mean . . ."

She waves a hand in the air. "Don't worry about it. I don't consider Sylveria or the sniping sisters family."

"I can't believe they stole all of the company from you," I mutter.

"Someday I'll own the whole thing," she says.

I nod. "I agree and I'm going to help you."

She flattens her hands on her jean-clad thighs. "For now, let's figure out who killed your brother. Do you want to order pizza? It's way past dinnertime."

I glance at my watch. "I can't. I have a late dinner date."

She turns around and stares at me, her eyes wide behind the thick glasses. "You're going out with Thorn?"

"No, I'm going out with Cal Sokolov. I think I can talk him into some sort of arrangement between the families that will benefit both companies." My father has insisted, and I did promise to try.

"Does Thorn know?" she asks.

I lift my chin. "No. He's not in charge of my life." My phone buzzes and I lift it to my ear. "Hello."

"Hi." Just the sound of Thorn's voice sends shards of recognition through my entire body. While it was slumbering before, now it's wide-awake.

"What do you want?" I ask, sounding like a churlish teenager.

"I want to know if you've been a good girl. Have you touched yourself?" His voice is the rasping of sandpaper across old wood.

My clit tingles. "None of your business."

"We both know that isn't true."

Tension grips my nipples and they sharpen. "I'm busy, Thorn."

"Watch it, baby. I owe you three more withholds, and you want some space between them."

I can't help but rub my thighs together. The man is killing me. Plus, I have to go home and get ready for my date with Cal—something I'm not going to share with Thorn. "Fine. Bless your heart. It's so nice to hear from you, Mr. Beathach. What can I possibly do to make your life easier?"

His chuckle nearly sends me into an orgasm. "You're attending that stupid charity tech ball with me. Get a dress, and I'll pay for it."

I can feel the blood rushing to my cheeks as I blush. "That is not how you ask a woman on a date."

"I'm not asking."

"You're actually going to a public event," I say slowly.

His sigh is loud enough that I almost feel the air against my skin. "According to my brother, it's necessary at this point."

"You need user interactions to gain more energy," I say smugly.

"Apparently." He doesn't sound amused.

The idea of seeing him at a masquerade ball is way too enticing. "Since you didn't ask, I don't have to give an answer. However, I am attending, so I might see you there."

"That will be fine. But remember whose date you are." He clicks off.

"Huh." I look at the phone.

Ella chuckles. "You were saying that Thorn is not in charge of your life."

"He's not." I shove the phone in my handbag. Of course, he's right. My orgasms, for the moment, seem to be controlled by him.

Jackass.

THIRTY-TWO

❧❀☙

Alana

Unease stirs through me, leading to that prickling sensation of impending conflict. Even though Cal is in front of me, dishing up two plates from paper takeout cartons for an incredibly late dinner, it's Thorn at the root of my disquiet. He won't take kindly to knowing I'm here with one of the Sokolov brothers. Yet who is he to judge?

Not that it matters. Everything I know about Thorn tells me that he would never respect a boundary that he himself hasn't set.

There are plenty of security personnel outside of Cal's high-tech, one-level home on the outskirts of Silicon Valley, but it would've been rude to insist that anybody come inside.

I promised my father I would try to help Aquarius Social, and I am doing just that.

Cal appears to be on his best behavior as well. For our casual date, he's wearing dark jeans and a green cable-knit sweater, making him look like a handsome Ryan Gosling at home in his own kitchen. Unsurprisingly, amethysts adorn his expensive looking wristwatch.

I'm wearing a simple aquamarine-colored top and skirt set with rose quartz earrings and a diamond pendant. I purposely left my phone in the car.

"This is nice," Cal says as he pulls out his chair and sits. "I ordered from the Sharp Palate—I hope you like beef." He frowns, as if realizing he should have checked whether I'm a vegetarian or vegan.

"I do," I say, looking at the Wagyu beef burger.

"Oh, good." He smiles. "I ordered them both with melted aged cheddar, truffle aioli, caramelized onions, and arugula. The brioche bun is supposed to be the best." He points to the rosemary garlic fries. "And these are legendary."

"Wonderful," I say, taking a knife and cutting my burger in half, feeling off-balance. The nice act from him puts my teeth on edge.

He takes a big bite of his and chews before setting it down. "I have tiramisu for dessert." Reaching over, he pours a thick red cabernet into our glasses.

I take a look at the bottle. It's a Screaming Eagle Cab. "It's one of my favorites." I lift my glass and let the wine's scent fill my head, and then I sip. This vintage truly is delicious. "The wine's excellent."

"Good. I'm glad." Cal stares at my breasts and then jerks his gaze up to my face again. "I don't know about you, but my family has been on me about this whole merger thing, and now Hendrix seems interested in you, too, so the sooner we reach an agreement, the better. You do not want to end up with that guy."

I sample the fries. They explode on my tongue, and I make a mental note to remember this restaurant; I haven't tried it before. "I've been thinking," I say. "What if we reach a con-tractual agreement to work together to enhance both of our servers? I know I could speed up your user interface time, and we'd love to add some sort of holographic element to our emotional-intelligence platform."

He takes another bite. "Yeah, I already talked about that with my brother, and he said he wants marriage on the table. There's nothing that binds two families together more strongly than marriage—and, of course, shared grandchildren."

He's being so nice. Why? What's up with him?

My stomach drops. I don't want to have kids with Cal, much less tie my life to his. Plus, I have this thing going on with Thorn. I can admit to myself that there's a lot there; and if it's possible to have fallen in love in one weekend, I did it. Yeah, he's a complete jackass, and my body is still sore from his last lesson. We'll probably end up killing each other, but being with any other man just doesn't seem right. I frown.

"What's wrong?" Cal asks.

"I was just thinking. You don't seem too angry that I spent a few days with Thorn."

Cal waves a hand. "No, I was kind of being a jerk about the whole hymen thing. It's a good thing Thorn broke you in. I mean, who really wants a virgin? Hopefully he taught you a few things."

I cough up wine and rapidly wipe my mouth. So much for his nice-guy routine.

He nods, either not knowing or not caring what an ass he's being. "I do like the idea of taking what Thorn thinks is his, and I love the idea of getting you so my brother can't. He has a thing for brunettes with a lot of hair. Don't know why."

"I'm not a possession." I no longer want the burger.

"Sure you are." Cal polishes his off and swigs down his wine before pouring himself another glass.

The more he speaks, the more I smell scotch. Did he start drinking before I arrived? I guess I don't really care, but I mean, come on.

"Would you like dessert now?" he asks.

"No thanks. Not yet. Let's revisit that crazy thought that I'm an object to be possessed." Yet isn't that what Thorn says? That I'm his? That he owns me? I still have bite marks across my flesh from his possession. Irritation climbs up my spine.

Cal reaches over to take my hand. "We're a done deal. You're the face of Aquarius as I am for Hologrid, and while other people don't realize how hard it is to influence, you and I do."

"I also work at the company." And charge the crystals, but that's a state secret. I figure his older brother charges their amethysts.

"Sure. For now, anyway. Come on, let's go sit in the living room, where it's more comfortable." He pulls me up.

I stand, allowing him to keep my hand. His is warm and bigger than mine, but not nearly as strong or firm as Thorn's. There has to be a way to merge professionally and not personally.

We walk inside, and I find his living room is anything but comfortable. It's all sharp angles, fierce glass, and what looks like incredibly hard black leather chairs and sofa. I nearly jump out of my skin when I look at the windows and see the argyle pattern made out of shiny silver metal. The crisscrosses make my stomach lurch and I look quickly away. He draws me over to the sofa. "Do you have a library?" I ask.

"No. Why in the hell would I have a library?" He settles us both on the sofa.

I really need to get out of here. "Listen. Marriage is off the table, but we can still work together."

"We're a done deal," he repeats, yanking me onto his lap.

I push against his chest, my legs falling on either side of his hips. He pulls me close and I yelp when my sore pussy hits his erection.

Ignoring my struggles, he yanks me closer and kisses me. Hard.

My mouth is apparently also sore. I push against him, trying to get free, panic climbing through me. I don't want to get close to him.

Cal moans into my mouth and reaches for the zipper at the back of my dress. Whoa. I finally shove him hard enough he releases my mouth. He's panting. His nostrils are flared, and deep crimson colors his hands and face.

"Let me go, you asshole." I push against Cal's chest and try to slide off his lap.

He clamps both hands on my hips. "No. Beathach might've gotten here first, but I'm here now. I'll make you forget him."

I let out a slightly hysterical chuckle before I can stop it. "That's impossible. Even if I don't see him for a hundred years, I will never forget him." Is it possible what Thorn said is accurate? That he broke me and put me back together so that I can only fit with him? Or maybe he's who I've always been searching for. I have to get off this guy's lap. "Cal, it's not going to happen between us romantically, so how about we come up with a better solution? We're prepared to sign a contract that will be mutually beneficial for both companies."

"No. It's marriage." He kisses me again, this time even harder. "You're suffering from Stockholm Syndrome. Forget Beathach."

I try to evade him, panic catching me as he squishes my lips and shoves his tongue back into my mouth. Left without a choice, I punch up and nail him beneath the jaw.

His jaw snaps and his head goes back. I scramble away, falling to the side and rolling off the sofa before coming up. He's there before me and strikes out, hitting me beneath the right eye. Pain explodes across my cheekbone and I fly over the coffee table to land on the hardwood floor, the breath knocked out of me.

I roll until I smash into the fireplace. Panicking, I push myself up on all fours.

Cal kicks me in the side and I fly up before plummeting back down.

"What are you doing?" I gasp, turning to sit, and then crab-walk back against the wall.

His face is an orange red and his eyes are bugging out. "You're turning me down? *Me?*"

I somehow missed this. "It isn't personal." Are my ribs broken? My entire right side feels like he's wearing steel-toed boots. A quick look confirms that they're regular tennis shoes. I look around for a weapon, trying to appear defenseless. Actually feeling rather defenseless. "People know I'm here, Cal."

His fists slowly relax.

I speak soothingly as if trying to calm a wild animal. Perhaps he's on something? But our conversation at dinner was just fine. "I think this is just a huge misunderstanding."

He blinks several times as if coming back into himself. "Oh, shit. You're right." He holds out a hand and I barely keep from wincing. Clutching my rib cage, I accept his hand and stand, half expecting him to punch again. He looks at my face. "You okay?"

"Sure. I'm fine." I smile and force my arm to my side before giving a fake chuckle. "This is a date for the record books." I snort as if we're sharing the best joke ever. "Things got out of hand, but I assume that's normal for those of us in the public eye." I have no idea what I'm saying at this point and really want to run for the door.

He leans down. "Oh. That's going to bruise." He frowns.

I wave a hand as if it's no big deal. "Dude. I bruise all the time. I've been taking this boxing class, and as you can tell, I'm not very good at it." I barely keep myself from looking at the door and try to appear relaxed.

He winces. "I don't want your dad to think I hit you."

What's the alternative? He shoots me and dumps my body in the backyard?

I slap his arm as playfully as I can, wondering how close my bodyguards are right now. They're probably in the damn car. "I don't know about you, Cal, but I don't tell my father anything. I'm a grown-ass woman, and he doesn't need to know my business."

His expression relaxes. "Good point. I don't tell my brother or mom anything, either. They're all into responsibility and have no idea what it takes to be the chief influencer."

"Totally agree." I wonder if his family knows about his temper problem.

He's taller than I thought as he towers over me. Odd that I think of the way Thorn is even taller, yet I feel safe in the shadow he casts. I'm nowhere near safe right now.

"What are we going to do about the wedding?" Cal asks.

I pause, not sure how to play him. "I don't know. What do you think?"

"I think we should get married." He's frowning again.

I purse my lips as if not sure what to do. "You really think the thing with Thorn is Stockholm syndrome?"

"Yes," Cal says instantly.

I look down at my feet and see a lump forming on my ankle. Did I hit the coffee table on my flight across the room? "Maybe I should see a shrink about the Thorn problem?"

"Yes." Cal pats my shoulder and nods wisely. "Why don't you make a few appointments, and in the meantime, we can attend the Silicon Shadows and Secrets Ball together? My brother will see us together and give up his campaign for you. Then we can plan the wedding?"

I believe I already have a date to that ball. Even so, I continue to look sad and confused. "I'll meet you there. It's a nice start, and the platform-user numbers will go through the roof for the two of us." Might as well appeal to his business side, if he has one. Trying to walk normally and not limp, I reach for my purse on the end of the sofa. "Thank you for dinner. That was truly delicious."

"Any time." He walks me to the door and opens it. "I'll see you again."

I nod and smile, turning to walk sedately toward my town car. The security guys step out, and I manage to wait until I'm safely inside before I burst into tears.

THIRTY-THREE

Alana

My face feels like it's twice the normal size when I walk into my darkened apartment and drop my purse before kicking off my shoes and limping into my bedroom.

The atmosphere is tense.

Sighing, I flick on the light to see Thorn lounging on his back on my bed, his feet bare and his arms beneath his head. His jacket is tossed over my chair and his sleeves are rolled up. He seems to be sleeping but opens his eyelids and turns his head to look at me.

I sigh. "I'm not up to you tonight."

His soft gaze hardens as he swings his legs over and stands, zeroing in on my blazing face. "What happened?"

Tears gather in my eyes. "Nothing. I don't want to talk about it."

"Sokolov hit you?" His voice is so low and controlled, it reduces the heat in the room.

I don't ask how he knows where I've been. He always knows. "We had a scuffle."

"Is he bruised?"

I shake my head and a tear falls. Angrily, I wipe it away. "I need some space, Thorn." From men. From all men.

Yet my shock as he walks past me out of the bedroom nearly knocks me to my knees. He's just leaving? I don't know him at all. Sniffling, I limp into the bathroom and take a look at my face. A bruise covers my cheekbone in angry purple and red, extending to my ear. Eesh. It *is* bad. Feeling abandoned and lost, I shuffle to the attached closet and remove my jewelry before grabbing a worn T-shirt and limping back into the bedroom.

Thorn's waiting, sitting on the bed with frozen bags of vegetables next to him.

I frown, my brain not working. "I'm not hungry."

"Come here."

My feet move before my brain registers the words, and then I'm standing in front of him. Still sitting, he grasps my white halter top at the hem and gently pulls it over my head. Then he whistles, looking at my rib cage.

I glance down to see furious purple streaks across my ribs.

"Hold your breath." He gingerly probes the injury.

I suck in air, unable to do anything else. I know he's gentle, but agony ripples through my torso.

Finally, he stops. "They're not broken or cracked, but you're going to be sore. Punch or kick?"

"Kick."

A growl rumbles from his chest. He gently turns me, scanning my body. "Where else?"

"Right ankle."

He stands and switches positions with me, drawing down my skirt as he does so. Then he crouches, lifting my ankle. "It's a bump. How?"

"Not sure." I'm not up to complete sentences as I pull the soft cotton shirt over my head, still sniffling. "Maybe I hit a table?"

He draws in air, expanding his chest. Then he stands. "Lie on your side, facing me."

I do so and draw up my knees.

"Good girl." He places a bag of frozen peas that I'll never eat on my ankle and secures it with a bathrobe belt. What's his deal with bathrobe belts, anyway? A frozen bag of carrots folds over my aching ribs, providing instant relief. Then he wraps a towel around a baggie of ice and places it over my pounding cheekbone.

"Thank you," I whisper, surprised he can be so gentle.

He removes his phone from his back pocket and presses it to his ear. "Doc? I need a prescription of hydro, seven-fifties, sent to this address. Now." He gives my address and ends the call. "You need to contact your men and tell them to expect a delivery." He hands over my phone.

I call the head of my security and ask him not to shoot the delivery guy.

Thorn replaces his phone and crouches, brushing hair away from my face. "Do you hurt anywhere else?"

"No."

"Tell me."

I want to close my eyes and forget the night. "I don't want to."

"Too bad. Beginning to end. Right now." He's caressing my head, and I just want to purr and go to sleep. The ice is helping, but my injuries ache in time with my heartbeat.

I sigh and then tell him every detail, including that I played along with Cal to get freedom. Not once does Thorn stop massaging my head.

A knock sounds on my outside door and Thorn stands, walking away, his shoulders wide and strong. He soon returns with a glass of water and a pill. "Take this."

"No." It's an automatic response.

He leans over, his face closer to mine. "Your medical records don't indicate you have a problem with painkillers. Do you?"

Why doesn't it surprise me that he's read my medical records? "No, but I don't want to be out of it."

He presses the pill between my lips. "I'll keep watch over you, princess." Then he holds the water to my lips.

I'm at an awkward angle on my side, but I obediently drink and swallow the pill. Maybe it'll help with the pain. He places the glass and pill bottle on my bedside table near the rose quartz lamp and then sits on the floor with his back to the small table, so tall we're eye to eye. I'm not sure what to say, and I'm becoming drowsy. "I don't want to press charges against Cal." It would create a media frenzy that I don't want. I'm embarrassed, but I haven't done anything wrong, and it's confusing.

"I understand." Thorn lifts the ice from my cheek, takes a look, and places it back down.

I stare at him with my good eye. "I don't want to be responsible for his death, either."

"You're not."

That's not what I want to hear. "I mean it, Thorn."

"I'm staying right here with you, Alana Beaumont," he says softly. "Not going anywhere, so stop worrying about it."

I'm glad he's here. Maybe too glad. My eyes fill with tears.

"Stop that," he whispers, catching a tear with his finger. He licks it clean. "Salty honey," he murmurs. Then he focuses on me, all intent. "You know it's different, right?"

I blink away more tears. "Huh?"

"Us and what happened with Cal."

Oh. That. It *is* different, and I can't explain why, but I feel it. Thorn would never punch me in the face. Does spanking me to orgasm make him a good guy? I don't think so. I'm also not entirely sure I want a good guy. But I do want Thorn. "Yes. It's different," I agree. "But the whole withholding orgasm thing really sucks."

Amusement lights his eyes, fascinating me with the silver streaks. "It's supposed to."

"It's a little extreme." I might be milking this situation, but I'm okay with that.

His gaze is knowing. "When I text you and you don't text back, I imagine the worst. You. Hurt. It kills me." He trails his fingers along my arm. "If you're going to kill me, you're going to pay for it."

That's both sweet and irritating. "Why did you trade me for a big-assed garnet?"

He sits back. "I can't tell you about that."

"Why don't you trust me?" I ask quietly.

He lifts his chin. "Tell me you're all in, that you're mine, and I'll trust you with everything."

I'm not ready to do that. He's too terrifying, and he's all encompassing. "I don't want to lose myself."

"Maybe you'll find yourself." His grin is charming, and the scar on his face intriguing.

I sigh. I'll never win an argument with him. "Tell me about your mom." I need an insight into him. Any insight.

"Don't remember her, but I do consider Charity my mom." He grins, looking almost boyish. Not quite. He'll never look like anything other than the predator he is, even when amused or indulgent. "She would cut the crusts off our sandwiches. That's what a mom does."

"That's true." I remember my mom doing the same thing. "Did Charity look like Justice?"

Thorn pulls his phone free again and flicks through it, finding a picture. "I think so."

I look at a smiling young woman who should've lived forever. She has Justice's deep brown eyes and slightly curly brown hair. "She was pretty."

"Yeah." Thorn puts his phone away.

The pills are pulling me into a feather-field oasis of comfort. "I think somebody killed my brother."

Thorn stiffens. "Excuse me?"

Rebecca Zanetti

"Yeah. I'm investigating the matter," I say, trying to sound tough but I'm pretty sure I'm slurring my words now.

"Why do you suspect homicide?"

I yawn widely and give him most of the details. "Maybe you could help?" I'm sure it's the drugs, but he looks invincible.

"Sure." He checks my ribs and ankle before sitting back down. The man looks so handsome through the haze.

"You're pretty," I mumble.

His smile dazzles me.

"Are we going to the ball?" I wonder if he can dance. He has good hands. My thoughts tumble around.

"Yes."

That's nice. I've attended that charity event every year, and I've never had a date. Sure, I've danced a lot, but it's more fun going with Ella and Rosalie. At least it was. I bet it'll be nice to be with Thorn. "Do you dance?"

"Yes."

Figures.

"This is complicated, Thorn," I mumble.

"It doesn't have to be."

Maybe not. "You owe me an orgasm."

"You're not up to it right now."

He's not wrong. "I need to learn how to fight better." It's sad, but I didn't leave one mark on Cal.

"All right. I'll teach you."

"Are you sure?" I snort. "I might beat you up."

He stretches his neck and it pops. "I'll take my chances."

That figures as well. My eyelids are getting heavy. "I need to charge the crystals tomorrow before the ball. Then I'm going to find the prettiest dress. You'll be tongue-tied." I've always wanted to make a man tongue-tied, and doing it to this man will be incredible.

"What did you say?" His voice sounds sharp.

Geez. "Tongue-tied," I repeat. Surely he's not cranky about that.

"No." His hand is on my shoulder, still gentle but firm. "Before that. What are you planning to do tomorrow?"

What was it? Oh yeah. "I have to charge the crystals at Aquarius Social before the event. They're due."

"You charge the aquamarines?" Is he growling again?

That's a secret. Darn it. I forgot. "Yes. I'm the one. Don't tell anybody."

"Fuck me." It sounds like a groan.

"I'm not up to it," I remind him and slide into a dreamless sleep.

THIRTY-FOUR

Thorn

I shower at Alana's as she continues to sleep, then dress myself in fresh clothing I brought with me the night before. Her closet is full of yellows, pinks, and aquamarine blue, and I enjoy poking through her jewelry stash. The woman truly does love sparkles.

When she's finally where she belongs, I'll make sure she has any trinket she could ever desire.

I glance at my watch. The security teams are on set schedules, so it's fairly easy to slide inside when nobody's looking. I could probably get Alana out, but I want her to come to me. Oh, it's pride and arrogance, but I can live with that. Plus, when she voluntarily knocks on my door, it will be her own choice. I don't want her to give me a hard time about it, since no doubt she'll want to leave more than once during our lives. Hopefully long lives if I can cure the curse.

I won't let her leave, which is actually an assurance my girl needs.

Of course, if she doesn't get it in gear, I will take matters into my own hands. For now, I've taken illegal and likely immoral steps to keep her safe and have no intention of letting her know about them.

My phone buzzes and I read a note from Renaldo that he's still working on finding the money behind the kidnapping attempt on Alana. He's turning into a decent mole.

Buttoning up my shirt, I watch her even breathing and take note of the bruise on her delicate face. The purple has darkened and a sliver of yellow shows along the hollow beneath her cheekbone.

Cal Sokolov's death is going to be painful. Horribly so.

She murmurs in her sleep and draws her legs up, frowning. Is this another nightmare? Then she whispers my name, and sweet honey flits across my tongue.

Ah. Apparently I'm not as frozen inside as I thought, because my heart thumps. Hard. "Alana." I crouch down and brush her jawline. "Wake up."

She awakens, her eyes more green than brown in the early light. Pink infuses her cheeks. "Um, hi."

I kneel in front of her. "Having a good dream?"

The pink deepens to rose and she winces, gingerly touching the bruise on her cheekbone. "Shut up."

"Be nice or I won't make you feel better." I snag her good ankle and pull her around, tossing her legs over my shoulders before enclosing her entire cunt with my mouth.

She arches and makes a sound deep in her throat.

"That's better." I snap the side threads of her panties and re-move the offending garment before I go at her, wanting to give her pleasure for a few moments. She's already there, coming hard against my mouth with a muffled shriek. It's not enough. I lick her again, taking my time, and drive her slowly back up.

Her lithe body stiffens.

"Stay relaxed," I mumble against her engorged clit.

She shudders. "*You* stay relaxed."

I smile, lean back, and lightly slap her clit. "You want to play?"

She frowns up at me. "Not really."

"Then behave." I lean back down and take my time with my mouth and fingers, forcing her over all too soon. She tightens and covers her mouth again to stifle the scream. Kind of. I let her come slowly down and then stand, scooping her from the bed and striding into the bathroom where I place her in a lavender oil-scented bubble bath I drew earlier.

Her moan is much like the one when she comes.

"Stay sitting," I order, reaching for a hair tie on the counter that I quickly use to clumsily secure the mass atop her head. "All right. Lie back."

She slides beneath the bubbles, her eyes closing, pleasure relaxing her face. The lavender should both soothe her and reduce inflammation. "This is lovely."

As is she.

I snag a towel and place it by the tub so she doesn't have to reach for it. Then I put a pill and a glass of water on the edge of the bath. "Take these."

Her eyelids open. "I have a dance tonight."

"It's early. It'll be out of your system by lunchtime." After hopefully reducing her pain as well as some inflammation.

She does so, her gaze remaining on me. It's contemplative. "Why are you being so nice to me?"

"Because you're mine."

"What if I wasn't?"

"There isn't a universe or reality where you're not."

She moves slightly and the water splashes. "You're so sure of everything."

I truly am. She looks fragile and defenseless in the bubbles; the bruise on her cheek appears painful. Fury nearly engulfs me, and only the fear in her eyes grounds me, forcing me to remain in control. So I sit on the damn bathroom floor to face her. "We need to talk."

Her chin lifts, and bubbles cover the bottom half. "Sounds serious."

"You can't charge the aquamarine crystals at Aquarius Social right now." I keep my voice gentle as I issue the order.

Life sparks into her eyes. "I'm not letting you take Aquarius under, Thorn. Period."

"If I wanted Aquarius under, I wouldn't require your assistance." I'm fairly certain the attacks against me originated with the Rendales and TimeGem and thus I have no reason to hurt her father or his company. At the moment, anyway. "This is about your safety."

"Are you threatening me?" She sounds more curious than frightened or even angry.

I sigh. "You'd know it if I were." Navigating this situation with her is taking more energy than I'd like, especially since my feet are freezing and it feels like a block of ice has settled at the base of my spine. If my spine freezes, I'm screwed. "Have you told anybody about my synesthesia?"

"No."

Fascinating. "Why not?"

She looks away, ruffling more bubbles.

"Alana." I put bite into my tone this time.

She sighs. "I don't know. I guess you trusted me with something and I didn't want to let you down. Plus, it's nobody's business, right?"

I like that. A lot. She's a sweet doe in a lion's world and has no clue about her vulnerability. Or perhaps her power. "I have several options open to me right now," I say.

She turns back to study my face. "Like what?"

"I could take you back to my house and lock you down. Or I could trust you to come to the right conclusion about where you belong and ask me to take you." The long game has never bothered me, but with my body starting to freeze, I don't have that kind of time. Even if the illness takes me and I die, she'll always belong to me.

She rolls her eyes. "It's good those self-esteem modules you've been streaming are starting to work."

Smartass. "You can't charge the crystals because there's an enemy out there who has learned how to infect systems, crystals, and their human connections."

She stills. A wrinkle settles between her brows. "Are you serious?"

"Yes." I run my index finger down the unharmed side of her face.

She gasps. "You're freezing."

"I am. From the inside out, and my organs are crystallizing."

Panic tightens her facial features and she sits up, splashing water over the edge onto my pants. "That's insane."

"The only time I'm remotely warm is when I'm with you." I'm not going to start lying to her now.

She looks at the far end of the tub, the gears visibly working in her brain. "That's why you needed the larger garnet."

"Yes. Mine is infected and it's freezing at the same rate as me. Or faster." I frown. The garnet's demise is nearer than mine—what does that mean? When its life is snuffed out, will mine follow? When I prove the hacker's identity, I'm going to make them suffer in newly invented ways.

"You must have an idea of the mastermind behind this," she says softly.

I like her brain. A lot. "I'm fairly certain it's Sylveria Rendale. If I marry one of her daughters, she's all but promised a cure." Although I don't know yet if she's the one with enough talent to have created this clusterfuck. Is it Horace?

Alana shuts her eyes and breathes out. "Do you believe her?"

"Maybe. She might be bluffing." The chess game of life and death isn't new to any of the families. "Gut instinct says she at

285

least knows something, but I need more than that to cure the garnet, or I'd just take her and force answers from her botoxed mouth." But if she isn't the evil alchemist, that person might slip away. "We're working on it."

The struggle in Alana is visible on her face and fucking fascinating to boot. "I've been reading some of your books that deal with the ancient wisdom of crystals and I'll keep going through them. Maybe there's something there." Finally, her shoulders go back and she opens her eyes, zeroing in on me. "I might be able to gain you backdoor access to Sylveriaa's servers."

I sit back. Not an inch of me expects this. "Ella might still have a claim to the company. If I blow it up, she's hurt."

"So don't blow it up," Alana says. "Find your answers, cure yourself, and protect my friend."

Her trust nearly knocks me over. Taking in a lungful, I taste the intoxicating melodies of honey and lavender. "This means you trust me. Come home with me willingly so I don't have to take you by force again. My patience has boundaries."

"Man, somebody needs to drag you into the current century."

"Consider yourself the one."

Her small fingers play with the bubbles. "We need to discuss the event tonight."

Interesting. "What about it?"

"Everyone will be there, and I don't want a scene." She looks up, vulnerability glimmering in her eyes. "I know I conduct much of my life in front of the camera, but I choose the topics. Even though you beating the tar out of Cal would get huge play, I don't want that."

I don't like the undertone of her voice and take a moment to read between the lines, which is not one of my gifts. "You didn't do anything wrong."

She pushes her hair out of her face. "I acted like I liked him."

I grasp her chin, my thumb sliding through the bubbles.

"Nothing that happened was your fault. Not one iota of it. Tell me you understand."

Her gaze searches my face. "Fine. I understand. You're not mad?"

"Not at you." I'm careful not to aggravate her bruise. The one Cal will pay dearly for.

Her cute mouth pouts. "Well, I guess Cal will be safe tonight at the ball, at least."

That's what she thinks. I lean over and press a kiss to her sweet mouth. "I have to go. If you can get me into the TimeGem servers, let me know. But if Ella refuses, don't worry about it. I have my best people on it." After making a few preparations for the stupid event tonight, I plan to use everything I have to infiltrate TimeGem today.

Her head lolls. "Okay."

The pill is obviously taking effect. I alter my plans and pluck her from the bath before setting her on her feet and drying her from head to toe. Then I tuck her sleepy butt back into bed, my suit soaking wet. "Call me when you awaken."

Right now, I have a date with Cal Sokolov, who should be just about finished with his tennis match for the morning.

With that, I leave her alone for most likely the last time, because I haven't lied to her.

My patience is gone.

THIRTY-FIVE

Alana

I'm *six years old again, rocking back and forth on soft carpet. It's raining outside and I can hear the thunder. The smell of vanilla wafts around me, and then my mother falls to the floor, looking at me, fear sizzling in her eyes.*

"Run," she whispers. I don't remember this part. I look up, not sure what to do. Those hard hands grab her again and lift her. I look up and I see the window, and then she's flying through it. The outline of a man comes into blurry focus. A car crashes and metal crunches. I smell blood.

Thunder bellows outside and jerks me awake. Glancing at the clock, I see it's around noon. My heart racing, I force myself from the bed to shower and dress in jeans and a light gray sweater and expertly cover my bruises before emoting a couple posts about the event tonight. I hint that I plan on dancing with at least one very eligible bachelor, but I'm careful not to mention Thorn's name.

I've learned my lesson on that one.

Ten bouquets of red roses arrive and I scatter them around

my apartment, bemused. One white rose in one thin silver vase arrives a few minutes later. There's no card this time, but I know who they're from.

When Thorn makes a statement, he does it well.

But how can I think about a life with him? We feel connected, but our first meeting, those precious beginning seconds, are stained with blood. That poor waiter. I still haven't found his name and contacted his family.

I'm a coward.

I have to get out of the building so the security details do the same, leaving Ella a chance for a little freedom. We're meeting at Nico's place to see what he's learned about Greg's death.

Glancing at my watch, I hustle out of my apartment and down into the drilling rain and a waiting car, sliding inside and shutting the door before looking across the seat.

"Hello," Mrs. Pendrake says.

I jerk away from her and then look up at the driver. "I thought this was my car," I say lamely.

She shrugs, today wearing a pastel yellow sweatshirt and torn jeans. With her numerous piercings and the scars down the side of her face, she looks dangerous. "Your car might've been, um, removed."

I'm irritated. Oddly so. "He sent you to kidnap me?" How insulting. Yeah, that doesn't make a lot of sense, but if he wants me kidnapped, he can damn well do it himself.

"Of course not." She looks at me like I've lost most of my brain cells. "Drive."

The man in front starts to drive.

I stiffen in case I need to jump from the car.

"I won't hurt you, and your security detail is following, completely unaware that you're with me." She waves a hand in the air before tugging a laptop out of a bag near her feet. "Where do you want to go?"

Watching her, I give her Nico's address.

The driver turns in that direction.

She nods. "There's something you need to see." Flipping it open, she types rapidly, her blunt fingers surprisingly smooth on the keyboard. "My husband worked for Thorn, and when he was murdered, burned to death, Thorn took me in. Paid all of my medical bills and then gave me a job. Gave me a life."

That's nice. "Isn't that what the mafia does? Takes care of its own?" I ask.

"Yes." She taps one more key and slides the laptop my way. "The night of the attack in the bar."

I look to see the interior of Martini Money's and me with my friends.

She reaches over and clicks another button.

The exterior comes up—a side alley. As I watch, the sweet waiter who'd tried to help me approaches the building, no doubt heading to work. My stomach rolls over. "He looks so young." He seems to be whistling as he walks. My eyes sting, but I don't give in to the tears. "Why are you showing me this?"

"Keep watching," she says.

Two men move out of the shadows, pulling along another man who appears unconscious. He's young and wearing a waiter's uniform.

My young friend takes off the guy's shirt and jacket with smooth movements. Then he casually takes a gun from his back pocket and shoots the unconscious man in the head. Three times.

I gag.

As if he didn't just commit cold-blooded murder, he then dons the waiter's clothing. "He wasn't a waiter," I say numbly.

For answer, Mrs. Pendrake types again, bringing up the interior of the bar. "Watch his hands."

He's at the bar, slipping a small vial of liquid into a martini, which he then brings to me.

I gulp. "That's why I fell asleep in the car after Thorn kidnapped me. I was drugged." It didn't make sense that I would've relaxed so easily with him. "But how did Thorn know the waiter was dangerous?"

Mrs. Pendrake widens the screen. "Tattoo on his neck. It's a gang tattoo—the one who tried to take you."

I look at her, my heart expanding. "Why are you showing me this?"

She reclaims the laptop. "He deserves love, and he deserves for somebody to see him. All of him." She closes it and shoves it into her bag. "Don't tell him I told you. Please."

"I won't." I push my hair over my shoulder. "That same night, Thorn's knuckles were bloody, and he said he'd killed other people."

Her sigh is heavy. "Yes. He killed two human traffickers before calling me to rescue many children scattered throughout a San Francisco alley in tents. They're all at a safe place now. Because of Thorn."

The car rolls to a stop in front of Nico's apartment. "Thank you for explaining," I say. "But he's still a killer." But he doesn't kill the innocent. I'm pretty sure. My shoulders relax for the first time since I met him.

Her expression softens. "He's what he needs to be. What we need him to be."

I slide from the vehicle onto the chilly street, ducking my head against the pelting rain. What do I need him to be? Would I feel so connected to him if he suddenly turned that darkness into pure light? Not likely. "Bye, Mrs. Pendrake."

"I'm sure I'll see you soon." The car drives away.

I hustle inside and up the elevator to Nico's place where Nico and Quinlan wait in his breakfast nook. I walk inside, where they're chomping on some pizza, before turning toward me in welcome. Dead silence immediately echoes through the place.

"What the hell happened to your face?" Quinlan asks, partially standing. Lightning zaps outside the window as if in tune with him.

My whole head aches. "I don't want to talk about it right now."

Nico's chin lowers, and he glowers from the head of the table. "What do you mean you don't want to talk about it? That's a hell of a shiner, Alana. Somebody definitely punched you."

I've thought about all the excuses I could give, mainly going back to my lie about taking a boxing class, but frankly, I'm just not up to it. My face pounds, my rib cage echoes the throbbing, and my ankle twinges, although it's much better than the other two injuries. "Fine. I went on a date with Cal Sokolov and it went horribly south."

Drawing out a chair at the glass table, I reach for a paper plate and pluck a slice of pepperoni free of the carton. After taking a couple bites, I give them the entire story. When I'm finished, Nico and Quinlan look ready to start gathering guns.

Nico looks at Quinlan. "We need to take care of this."

My jaw hurts slightly as I chew. "Nobody is doing anything. I can handle my own problems." I haven't quite figured out what to do since I don't want to press charges. Maybe I should revisit the idea. At least I would alert the public that Cal is a nut job.

Quinlan stares at me. "We should call the police."

"I know," I say, "but it's his word against mine and I didn't call them right away."

"You have the evidence on your face!" Nico explodes. Apparently he has taken the place of my older brother since Greg is no longer with us.

I chew thoughtfully. "I know, but just think of the media circus that would ensue."

Nico leans back. "We'll get a lot of social media play if one of us punches him in the face tonight at the ball."

"As well as satisfaction," Quinlan adds, his brown eyes sparking.

"It's too much," I admit. "Not only that, people will take his side and then it'll turn into a big old issue, and the last thing I want to do right now is help Hologrid. If we accuse him, he'll deny it, and they'll galvanize their influencers. This might even help him more than us."

"We sure don't want that," Nico mutters. "All right. I'll steer clear of him tonight." He emphasizes the last word.

A knock sounds on the door. "Come in," Nico calls out.

Ella bursts inside, her hands full of file folders and haphazardly organized papers. "Hey, sorry I'm late." Her glasses are perched halfway down her nose. "I've been doing a deep dive and I think I've found something." She stumbles inside and drops the papers on the table. "Ooh, pizza."

I reach for a plate and give her a piece of the veggie pie. It's her favorite.

"Thanks." She pulls out the final chair and drops into it.

"What did you find?" Nico asks, his gaze warm.

She takes a big bite and chews before talking. "I hacked into Malice Media."

"You did what?" My ears start to ring.

She flicks me a glance. "Whoa. What happened to your face?"

"Cal and I brawled. I'll tell you all about it. But you first." How in the world did she hack Thorn?

Concern darkens her eyes. "All right. I keep a running status on all the social media companies, even a couple of the up-and-coming ones, and someone attacked Malice the other night with malware, and while they were busy countering, I snuck in the back door."

It's a brilliant move, but I don't know that I would want Thorn for an enemy. "Ella," I say.

"I know. I know." She reaches for another slice. "I still haven't forgiven him for kidnapping you, but I can maneuver within other servers better than anybody else."

She isn't bragging. She's that good.

"What does that mean?" Quinlan sits back.

She flicks olives off the slice. "The alexandrite crystals they now own have the ability to cut through data faster than any other gem."

"Seriously?" I ask, my chin dropping.

Her eyes sparkle. "You remember those cameras along the way to Vultures Perch?"

"Yeah. They were erased and broken and destroyed," Nico says grimly. "We've tried to trace them all back to their source and there just isn't one."

Quinlan finishes his beer. "All of those cameras have onboard storage but the SD cards were all taken. You know that."

"Yes." Ella holds both hands up. "Listen. The interior memory in those cameras is just damaged, and so far, we haven't found a way to reassemble it. We can with these new crystals. I just needed one of the cameras, and now I have one."

"Where'd you get it?" I ask.

"I climbed a tree." She scrutinizes her pizza and finds another olive, gingerly picking it off. "It's a long story. Anyway, I secured one of the cameras and yes, the SD card was gone, but the internal memory should be accessible now. It's like reassembling data in a computer."

For the first time, hope lights in my breast. "Are you serious?"

"Yes. It takes time and I'm still writing the algorithm."

Nico holds up his beer. "Here's to finally figuring out what happened to Greg." We all clink. He winks. "At least now you don't have to worry about marrying that asshole Cal, especially after we show your father that bruise."

I smile. That's a true statement. I feel sure that nobody in my family will take out Cal at the ball, and Thorn has given me his promise that he won't cause a scene, and yet I can't dispel this hollow feeling in my stomach that something's about to go horribly wrong.

I lose the happiness for a moment and study the group. They've been in my life since I was a child. Somewhat separated because of our age differences, but still. I need to ask questions, and they're here right now. "Do you guys remember when I was hit by the car as a kid?"

Nico pales. "I do. You were in the hospital for over a month. You were so small and young. It was terrifying."

"Yeah," Quinlan says, "Scarlett and I had already lost our parents, and then to have your mom taken and you so injured . . . it was just a blow."

I had no idea they felt like that.

Nico places his beer on the table. "Greg and I were out of our minds with worry. We both grieved your mother, but we were afraid we'd lose you, too."

It's sad, really. The only parent still standing is my father. People think that the owners of these companies are infallible, but in truth we seem to be more vulnerable than anybody else.

Nico's parents died in a fire that was later determined to be arson, and my parents took him in. Of course, the culprits were caught. They were from a rival social media company that never really saw the light of day. I have no doubt my father made sure of it. Their parents died in a helicopter accident that appears to have been natural. Well, as natural as a helicopter crash can get. And Ella and I are still trying to figure out how her father died. She suspects that Sylveria had something to do with it, but we haven't found any proof.

"Is it the truth?" I ask. "Did my mother really die in a car accident, or was it more like Greg dying in a car accident that wasn't?"

Nico finishes his beer. "Oh, no. Your mom definitely died in a car accident. You jumped out and tried to run and got hit, remember an accident?"

"No!" I explode. "I don't remember anything!"

He sighs. "I promise you. You were only six years old, but Greg and I were teenagers. I remember every moment of that entire week. We slept on the floor in your hospital room."

I do vaguely remember that. They were a constant comfort in a time of pain.

"Why do you ask?" Ella asks.

"I've been having these dreams."

"About her death, the accident?" Quinlan stands and crosses into the kitchen to fetch two more beers as well as mimosas for Ella and me. He places the scrumptious drinks in front of us before retaking his seat.

I sip delicately, enjoying the subtle taste. "The nightmares focus more on my feeling terrified while somehow hearing my mom's voice."

"What's going on with Greg's accident is probably messing with your head," Nico says. "I promise you, there wasn't any sort of doubt or even investigation at the time. Your father was beside himself and he would've found anything suspicious."

That's true. I know without a doubt that my father would've avenged any slight, much less murder of family.

We finish lunch and I walk Ella out of the apartment, noting how her fingers trail across Nico's hand as she leaves the table. We wait for the elevator. "I need a favor," I say.

"Of course. Anything."

I chew on my lip. This is a tough one. "Thorn needs access to your servers. That Malice attack you talked about with the malware? He needs to trace it back, and he thinks it came from Sylveria and TimeGem."

Ella tries to soothe the stacks of papers into some semblance of order. "Um, no. Sorry. I don't let anybody into my servers. Tell him to go with his gut."

I'm not surprised but I am a little hurt. "Please?"

"No." Her lips firm in a look that isn't usual for her. "Sorry. I don't trust him. That guy is a killer, and I'm not entirely sure he hasn't murdered substitutes for you. It makes a sick kind of sense."

"That's not his style," I say, knowing that to be true.

Quinlan walks out. "Hey. I need to go find a tux that fits. Nico's extra doesn't."

The elevator door opens, and he nudges Ella inside.

For the first time in my life, duty and desire are clashing. Thorn draws me with an irresistible force, but I love having my friends in my life. Do I love him? If so, how am I going to broker peace with everyone?

Ella doesn't meet my gaze as the doors close.

THIRTY-SIX

Alana

My chest aching, I turn and walk back into Nico's place to help him clean up. Thunder sounds outside and I jump. How silly. A chill pierces down my spine. I gather the rest of the dishes and carry them into the kitchen.

Nico is sitting at the table typing rapidly on a laptop. "Damn, I wish I was as good as Ella is at this," he mutters.

I place the dishes in the sink and study him. "Speaking of Ella . . ."

He looks up. "No."

I grin. "Come on, tell me what's going on. She blushes every time you come near her."

He rolls his eyes. "I like her. She's brilliant, and she understands computers better than anybody else. In fact, if we could talk your father into it, I'd like to hire her at Aquarius Social."

I think it would be a lot of fun to work with my best friend, notwithstanding her dislike for my . . . what is Thorn? I can't exactly call him a boyfriend, because there's nothing boyish about him. "I don't know that she would work for a rival of TimeGem's," I muse.

He sits back. "Why not? They cast her out. She's not part of their family."

"No, but she has plans to retake her interest someday," I say. "Helping us build Aquarius Social isn't in her best interests, although I'm happy to talk to my father."

"Good," he says. "She can be quite handy."

"Do you like her?" I ask in a singsong voice.

He rolls his eyes again. "Yeah, I like her. She's funny and sweet, and she has that whole wounded-animal thing going on."

"Wounded animal?" I ask.

"You know. She's alone in this world. You can see it in her eyes."

I think that's one of the saddest things I've ever heard about Ella, even if it is true. "She's not alone. She has me."

"Yeah, but it's not the same as family, is it?" His gaze darkens.

I feel for him, having lost his parents young. I know what it's like to grow up without a mother. "No," I admit. "It's not the same." Although I can't exactly say that my father is touchy-feely.

The TV drones on quietly in the background, hung below the cupboard across the way, mostly about the ball tonight.

"I really do need you to behave at the event," I tell him. "No matter what Cal has done, I don't want a scene."

Nico gives one short nod. "That's fine. Cal and I can have a discussion tomorrow. I won't do anything to cause you a problem. You and I are family, Alana. You're all that really matters."

He misses Greg as much as I do. Probably more, considering they hung out a lot.

"I'm glad you found Ella," I say.

He shrugs. "I don't think there's any longevity with that, but I'm glad I found her, as well."

"Why not?" I ask, smiling. "She's perfect."

He snorts. "Nobody's perfect. Well, almost nobody." His gaze catches on the TV, and he stills, peering forward.

"What?" I say, looking.

A tall, redheaded reporter stands down from several other reporters, all speaking adamantly into microphones. I catch two words: murder and Cal. "What?" I move closer, looking at the rainy scene. "Turn it up," I say.

He grabs a remote and turns up the volume.

"Hi, this is Christine Salisbury with Channel Two News." The woman's green eyes light. "We're standing outside of a crime scene"—she moves slightly to show the yellow flapping tape— "where the body of Cal Sokolov was found an hour ago."

I fall into the seat next to Nico. "Oh, my God," I whisper.

Nico's mouth gapes open, and he just watches the TV.

The reporter tries to dampen her enthusiasm and almost manages a somber look. "My sources tell me that Mr. Sokolov was beaten severely before having his jugular cut." She leans toward the camera. "In a disturbing twist of events, all of his fingers are cut off."

The screen splits and shows an older man in a studio. "Christine, are his fingers anywhere near the body?" He actually sounds properly somber at this turn of events.

She shakes her hair wildly, standing under a lime-green umbrella. "No, his fingers are nowhere to be found, according to my source."

I gulp. Bile rises in my throat. The fingers weren't found because Thorn forced Cal to eat them. Isn't that what he said? Anybody who touched me would eat their own fingers? I gag.

Nico looks at me. "What?"

My stomach turns over. "I think it was Thorn."

"What? When?"

My body chills. "When he left me this morning."

"What else do you know?" the male reporter asks.

Christine moves slightly away from the crime scene tape, her hair blowing in the tempestuous wind. Even with her umbrella, the rain is coating her smooth skin. "Just that he was found on his front stoop. His own property."

"So was he killed there?" the reporter asks.

Her brightly painted pink lips turn down. "It doesn't look like it. My source believes he was dumped here, so maybe his fingers are wherever the crime took place."

His fingers are currently dissolving in his own stomach acid. I cover my mouth with my hand. How could Thorn? I mean, Mrs. Pendrake was pretty clear that he only killed the guilty, but to go this far, just because of me, I can't believe it.

I gag again and stand up, clapping both hands over my mouth to run to the nearest bathroom where I lose my breakfast. Chaotic thoughts keep whipping through my head. Thorn has never lied to me. He told me what would happen, and it's exactly what happened.

Standing, I rinse out my mouth and turn, looking into Nico's bedroom. I glance down at my shirt, which has vomit on it. Wincing, I walk into his room and tug open a drawer to find a T-shirt. Inside are several aquamarine necklaces, beautiful ones, just like mine. I pause. Wait a minute. My head is fuzzy, and I can't believe this. Why does he have all of these necklaces that look like mine? I take one along with a T-shirt and walk through the apartment to where he's standing next to the window.

Lightning flashes outside, illuminating him. He turns and looks at me. I've seen him like this before. Illuminated by lightning.

It all comes back so quickly, him in front of the window and with my mother crying. My jaw slackens and I drop the neck-lace. The stones shatter across the floor, a shard cutting my foot.

Thorn

The server room of Malice Media smells like hinge oil and stale coffee. I'm pacing while Justice and Kaz sit at their computers. Ice is chugging through my veins like chunks in a river when the snow melts. Every once in a while, a piece will catch and shoot pain through my entire system.

I had to use a cane to get to the car today. It's unthinkable. Tonight's ball with Alana might be my last night. The garnet is fading fast, as am I.

"Maybe there's a way to tie the garnet into the alexandrite crystals," Kaz says, scrubbing both hands through his hair. I idly wonder when he slept last. He looks like hell, not that I slept last night, either.

My phone buzzes and I lift it to my ear. "Beathach," I snarl.

"It's Sylveria. I'd like to announce your engagement to one of my daughters tonight at the ball. Which one do you want?"

Neither. "It's not going to happen." Alana is the only woman I'll ever want.

Sylveria scoffs. "If you want to fix your servers, you'll stop playing around."

I stiffen. My servers? "What do you mean?"

"Don't play stupid," she snaps. "If you want me to repair what ails Malice Media, you'll do as I say."

She doesn't know. It hits me then. She's fishing. "Fine. Tell me what kind of resonance disruptor you used to interfere with the functioning of my fucking garnets."

Her chuckle is throaty. "Those garnets can be sticky with their resonant frequencies, right? I'll give you the code to recalculate all of your frequencies the second you take your vows."

The bitch has no clue that I'm as ill as my garnet. I growl as my chest freezes and a rib cracks. Scrambling in my pocket, I pull out a chunk of aquamarine I filched from Alana's closet.

The pain ebbs slightly. I frown and look down at the glowing crystal. Is our connection such that her stone soothes mine?

Sylveria clears her throat.

I end the call. "It's not her," I say. So who the hell infected me?

Justice shakes his head. "Who else is that good? You think Mathias has somebody?"

I rub my aching rib cage. "I don't know."

Justice keeps typing and barely flashes a smile. "The alexandrites are working within our system. Fast. Are you seeing this?"

Kaz nods. "Yeah, I am, but the malware that infected the garnet is exhibiting polymorphism and it's doing a good job."

"It's changing its behavior to hide?" I ask.

That's impressive. Whoever came up with this is brilliant. Kaz and Justice will be able to fight the malware, and even counteract it, but probably not within the next few days.

Long after I'm gone.

Justice's computer dings and he types quickly. "Holy shit. Thorn, bring up the local news on your terminal."

I sit and connect to the local news stream to see a report about Sokolov's body being found, freshly dead. The sirens were already echoing over the hills after I dumped him on his porch around noon. We looked through traffic cams and destroyed what we could, but I still don't know how the police found out so quickly.

"There was another body at the scene besides Sokolov's," Justice hisses.

"What?" I type and bring up a different news station.

A young blonde reporter is speaking earnestly to the camera, the rain pummeling down on her red umbrella. "Yes, and apparently the female was beneath a rosebush, close to the front door. Her face is smashed in. She's a brunette and she was wearing a yellow dress, much like the four other victims found these last two years. What's notable is that she's wearing a lovely aquamarine necklace that looks like the one Alana Beaumont always wears."

Everything inside me that's already not frozen goes stonecold. I stand, kicking the chair back.

"Did you see another body today?" Justice asks, one hand yanking his hair straight up.

"Of course not." It can't be her. It absolutely can't be her. My hand trembles as I pull my phone from my pocket and dial. The call goes directly to Alana's voice mail. I left her in bed early this morning. "It can't be."

Justice is already on the phone, calling our men.

No, this makes no sense. I know that she left her place and went to her cousin's safely that morning. This is not her.

But as I look at the screen, I recognize that necklace.

It's Alana's.

Fire lights me from within. Then reality smacks me. I grab my phone and click to an app to see a pink blinking light. "She's at Nico's." Yeah, I chipped her when she was sleeping after going too many rounds with Sokolov.

Justice exhales loudly. "You didn't."

"Yeah, I did." Why in the world is he surprised?

My phone buzzes and everything settles inside me as I see that it's her. My shoulders relax. "Hey, baby," I answer. "I'm coming to get you." I hear muffled sounds. "Alana?" I ask. Her voice comes through tinny, as if far away.

"I don't understand, Nico," she's saying. "Where are we going?"

"Shut up or I'll shoot you." Nico's voice is higher than normal.

The words come through way too clearly. Heat roars down my torso, warming the freezing crystals inside me. I click mute.

Why would Nico be threatening her? "She's in trouble with Nico. Where are our men?"

Justice looks up. "We have two teams outside his place."

"Go in—take her now," I say, already running toward the elevator, not liking where my thoughts are going. Nico has always been in the background, and much of the time I spent watching her, he was right there. But he's family, so his constant presence made sense to me.

Justice and Kaz are on my heels. I turn and plant a hand on Kaz's shoulder. "I need you here on the computers."

"Got it." He returns to his console as Justice and I ride the elevator. I'm running for the door before it opens and barrel outside to my armored SUV. "Get out." I pull my driver out and jump inside. I don't need anybody else on this. Justice barely makes it around the front and inside before I punch the gas.

He slams his door. "Jesus, hold on a minute."

"No." I can't believe it. I've never felt fear like this. In fact, I'm not entirely sure I've felt fear since I was kidnapped as a kid. She has to be okay.

He reads the screen on his phone. "They've just breached the front door and they're headed up to the penthouse."

I lift my phone to my ear and try to listen. Everything's muffled. This isn't making any sense. Why would Nico want to hurt her? How is her necklace on the body of a dead girl? "Call Kaz. I want a deep dive, deeper than before, on Nico Beaumont."

"I'm on it," Justice says, barking orders to our team before giving instructions to Kazstone.

I listen. Her voice is muffled. "Nico, talk to me. Where are we going?"

Shit, does that mean they're not in the penthouse? I strain to hear better.

"Trust me, I'll get us out of here," he says. Then there's the sound of a running vehicle.

"He has her in a car," I mutter.

Justice listens to his phone. "Our team breached the penthouse. Nobody's there."

"He got her out of there somehow. They're in a vehicle. Look on the street," I bark, my ears ringing. I am going to tear that asshole apart molecule by molecule. She's in danger and I'm not there. I'm not entirely sure there's a God, but I think about praying anyway. If there's anybody who should be saved, it's Alana.

I hear her cry out and it's like fingernails shredding me from within.

"Damn it," Nico swears. Something shuffles loudly and then a large crack echoes.

I can track the woman, but time isn't on my side. Nico could hurt her, maybe even kill her, before I can get to them.

The phone goes dead.

THIRTY-SEVEN

Alana

"You have a hidden elevator in your penthouse?" I lean back against the seat, acutely aware that he's tied my hands and put the seatbelt over me. I can't move, and I'm still in shock that my cousin, my wonderful older cousin, has a gun pointed at me as he drives us rapidly away from safety.

"Of course I have a hidden elevator. Don't you?"

"No," I burst out. "I live a normal life." Well, except for the secret computer room in the basement. Turns out Nico has one in his basement as well with a door to a private garage. We're out in the street before anybody knows what's happening. Okay, I want to throw up, so I draw in several deep breaths and look over at the man I thought I knew. The last nightmare finally opened the cracks in my memory. "I remember you."

He glances at me. "I was worried about that when you said you were having nightmares again."

"Why?" I cry out, struggling against the restraints. I can see his face and his hands in my memory now. He's only fifteen years old, but he's tall, and he's gangly, and he's fighting with my mother.

"I didn't mean to throw her through the window." He grips the steering wheel tightly. "I told her I loved her and that age didn't matter. I tried to kiss her and she said no, and I don't know what happened. I saw red."

"You killed her." Pain lances through me. "Nico, she loved you. She took care of you."

He slams his hand against the steering wheel. "I loved her, too. She was the perfect woman—if she could have just seen me as an adult."

"You were fifteen years old." I try to remember the rest of it. "I ran, didn't I?"

His shoulders slump. "Yes. She yelled at you to run, right before she went through the window."

"Before you threw her through the window!" I shout, tears streaming down my face. I feel sick again and I'm not sure if it's from the mimosa or the shock of what's happening or both. "Nico, how could you?"

"*It was an accident!*" he shrieks.

I press back against my seat. No man should make that sound ever. I wish fleetingly for my phone, but he threw it out the window. I had pressed text, to hopefully contact my father, but maybe I'd gotten hold of Thorn. I look out the window at the rapidly gathering clouds that are already plopping fat raindrops onto Nico's windshield. There have to be cameras on this street.

He glances at me. "I took care of the cameras."

"Of course you did." I feel both ridiculous and vulnerable, wearing his shirt, with my feet bare.

"I have a jammer. I am the computer expert at Aquarius, even if I can't charge the crystals." Now he sounds bitter.

I try to think back, and I see him throwing my mother through that window inlaid with the horrible argyle design. I ran. "Where were we that day? I've never been able to figure it out."

"We were in an apartment that I bought myself."

"At fifteen?" I ask.

He jerks the wheel to the left, narrowly avoiding a downed tree. We're in the middle of nowhere already, headed up a mountain. "I have a trust fund. I told her it could be our special spot where we could sneak away together. When she met me that day, I didn't know you were going to be there."

"She probably had no idea why you wanted to meet."

"She didn't, but she loved me. I know she did."

He's crazy. There's no other explanation. How did I miss this? "She loved you like a son or a nephew," I blurt out.

"No, more than that." He almost casually reaches out and backhands me.

My head smacks the headrest, and tears well in my eyes. At least he hit the unbruised side of my face. I chuckle, the sound slightly hysterical.

"And then there's you."

"Me?" I ask.

He pounds the wheel now with both hands. "You're just like her. I've been trying to get your attention for years but you see me as . . ."

"My cousin?" I mutter.

"Several times removed. I told your father that you and I should marry. Any child we create will have an affinity with the aquamarines."

It's almost unthinkable. I gag. I can't help it. "I remember falling down a set of stairs after you killed her." I try to capture the rest of the day, but there are just blank spots and darkness and rain.

"You did. You ran out the front before I could stop you, right into traffic."

The scar on my belly is real. "So I did get hit by a car."

"Of course you got hit by a car." Tree branches scrape his

window. "The driver hit you, then swerved, smashing into a light post and dying. It was all so easy to fix from there."

I try to gauge how far we are from his home. We're heading up into the mountains. "What's your plan here, Nico?"

"I have a place," he says. "You like to be kidnapped, right?"

Only by Thorn. "What, you think you're going to take me away and I'm going to fall in love with you?"

"It worked for Beathach," Nico growls. "I just need to think. I have a cabin. It's not registered in my name, but it's a place we can hide out for a while."

I have to get away from him. "What does my father think happened to my mom?"

"That there was a car accident." Nico turns up what appears to be a long, winding dirt road. Trees loom on either side of us and I shiver. "Because there was," he says. "I put both of you out in the road near the smashed car. It was a quiet, exclusive street back then. It was pretty simple. I'm surprised you survived, to be honest."

I look at him agape. "Why did you stay with me in the hospital?"

"I had to make sure you didn't wake up and tell them what happened, but you didn't remember anything. Man, Greg was beside himself." Nico chuckles. "He was really a good guy, but clueless."

I can't breathe. For the briefest of seconds, it's like a hand encloses both of my lungs and squeezes. "Did you kill Greg?"

Nico shifts. "I don't want to talk about it."

"*Too bad!*" I shriek. "Why would you kill him?"

Nico casts me a look and then concentrates on the muddy road. "When your dad decided to merge with the Sokolovs, I told Greg I had a better idea, that you and I should get married."

Bile rises up my throat and I ruthlessly swallow it down. "I take it Greg said no?"

"Not only that, he told me it was crazy. And then he

looked at me, actually looked at me, and asked me how I felt about you. I told him how perfect you are and how much you remind me of your mother and how I would protect you." He rambles on. "That I want to protect you like I failed to do for your mom."

I swallow. "He guessed what happened."

Nico hunches his shoulders. "Yeah, he did."

"So you killed him," I explode.

"I hit him in the temple. We fought. I didn't mean to kill him."

I fight the restraints. Not for freedom but so I can attack him. Hurt him. "You pushed him over a cliff."

"I don't want to talk about it anymore," Nico says. "Don't make me hit you again."

He's too far gone. Has he always been a psychopathic bastard? He mimics emotions well. I think back through everything I know about him. "Did you kill Cal?"

"No, I didn't kill Cal."

Oh yeah, that's right. The fingers were gone. Thorn killed Cal. "What about the girl under the rosebush?"

Nico's chest puffs out. "Yeah, that was me." He sounds proud of himself.

I shake my head. "Why?"

"Every once in a while I need a release," he says, turning once again between thick trees on a barely there road. The potholes get worse and we hump and bump as he drives even higher up the mountain. "She was just a local woman—another stuck-up bitch. They all look like you."

"I noticed that," I say. "You gave her a necklace like the one I always wear?"

His smile is gruesome. "I like them to wear the crystal while I kill them."

This is unbelievable. "How many women have you killed?"

"I don't know. The only one that really matters is your mother."

He's a serial killer and I had no idea. "Why did you put that dead woman at Cal's house earlier today?"

"I wanted to frame him," Nico says easily. "I can't let you marry him. Not that I'm worried about it now." His smile is sly. "Who do you think killed him? Do you really think it was Thorn?"

I wish Thorn had seen Nico at their mutual crime scene. "Yes," I say. "I know it was Thorn."

"Huh, we probably just missed each other." Nico smiles brightly as if amazed by the wonders of the universe. "What a coincidence."

"I guess." I hope there's some way for Thorn to track me. Without my phone, it doesn't look good. My face aches, my hands hurt, and I really need to throw up again. The last few weeks spin through my head. "Wait a minute. Did you send that kill squad after me in the bar?"

He snorts. "Kill squad. Their orders were to kidnap you and bring you to me. But Thorn interfered."

Thank goodness. "What's your plan for me, Nico?"

He sighs. "Well, either you fall in love with me or I'm going to kill you."

I'm a dead woman.

He parks at a ramshackle cabin with a rotting front porch. "I meant to get it ready for you. For a rustic honeymoon." He tucks his gun at his waist and releases my seatbelt before hauling me over the center console. I land with my bare feet on the ground and cry out as a stick cuts into my heel. Pain rips up to my knee as the rain mercilessly pounds us.

"Sorry." He picks me up, and I feel his chest muscles play against my shoulder. Though he's not nearly as strong as Thorn, I'm still surprised by his strength.

The interior of the cabin is worse than the exterior, and he places me on a wooden chair, looking around. "It's not that bad. Be good, and soon we'll control all four of the social media companies. I have a plan, and it's coming to fruition."

Something scurries into the corner and out of sight. The place is one room with a bed, kitchenette, and living area with fireplace. It's the absolute last place in the world anybody will look for either of us. My wrists are securely bound together, but my feet are free.

"I'll start a fire." He strides across the uneven boards and starts stacking firewood.

I gauge the distance between my body and the door.

"You won't make it, and I have the car keys," he says congenially.

I look toward the kitchen and see red splotches on the floor. My stomach revolts. "Is that blood?"

He glances at the planks. "Yeah. Sorry. I haven't cleaned up after my last guest."

Oh God. He really is going to kill me.

"Nico," I say. "This is a bad idea. Let's go back home and talk to my father and see if we can work something out."

He looks at me as if I've lost my mind. "It's way too late for that and you know it. Our only way out of this is if we get married."

I'm not entirely sure that's a way out of anything. "Alrighty," I say brightly. "But I want a big society wedding."

He laughs, the sound strained. "Don't play me for a fool. I'm not stupid. It's going to take a while for you to fall in love with me."

Like never.

The fire starts to crackle and warm the chilly cabin. Rain continues to pummel the earth outside, giving the entire place a musty smell that's nearly overwhelming. I idly wonder what Nico's words taste like.

Where is Thorn right now? No doubt cleaning up after his murder, or maybe he's at Malice Media trying to save his life. I hope so. Even if I depart this world, I hope he survives the illness. I know we don't make sense to most people, but I feel him where it counts, and I want the best for him.

Love hurts. It's like a constant slicing of a blade through my insides when I'm not with him. Maybe we'll meet in death. The macabre thought cheers me, which is all sorts of fucked up.

Nico dusts his hands together. "Tell you what, I've got the place stocked with food. I'm going to make you a nice meal, because you didn't eat much earlier, and then we're going to talk and figure this out."

So long as I can keep him talking, at least I'm not being shot or stabbed. "All right." Curiosity gets the better of me. "Why did you smash those women's faces in?"

"Because they weren't you," he says, tossing me what could be considered a charming smile if he wasn't a psychopathic bastard.

"Oh," I say lamely. I'm going to have to run for it, but I really need my hands free in case I have to fight. "Nico, will you untie me?"

"Not quite yet. Let me cook for you first." Surprisingly, he grabs the back of my wooden chair and drags me closer to the kitchen. "Just in case you decide to run."

I'm not bound to the chair, but it's unlikely I can reach the door before he tackles me onto the blood-covered wooden floor. "What are you making?" I ask lamely. "More pizza?"

He shakes his head. "No, I can do better than that. Let me look through the fridge."

There's a small avocado green fridge at the end of a torn Formica counter that probably was orange at some point. He starts humming as he brings out fruit and berries, before reaching in a cupboard for pancake mix. "How about hotcakes? I'm pretty good at making those."

"Sounds great," I say, searching the kitchen. There have to be knives somewhere.

"Good." He's oddly cheerful. Maybe killing does that for him.

My feet are going numb, it's so chilly. "Why did you set up the whole murder board and have us play detectives?"

Pride fills his face. "I needed you to find out what your dad knew. Plus, it was fun."

What an ass. I look for a way to reach him. "Nico, I have to get back to charge the crystals. You know that."

"Oh yeah." He starts whipping the batter in a bowl. "You're right, but that's not going to happen for a while. Mathias should be able to handle things."

"He's not as good as I am."

"Nobody is," Nico says and winks.

Oh man, I might throw up again. I watch him carefully, looking for a way to get that gun from him. It's my only chance. Perhaps if we eat together, he'll relax and then I can go for it.

He dishes up two plates and moves me closer to the two-person table at the far end of the other counter. "Isn't this cozy?"

"Sure is," I say, looking down at my hands. "You're going to have to untie me. I can't eat like this." I'm trying really hard to ignore the bloodstains on the floor.

He sighs. "I'll feed you."

I gag. I can't help it. My legs are freezing and my cheek aches from where he hit me. "Nico," I start.

Just then the door bursts open and Thorn barrels inside with Justice on his heels. He lunges for me. Nico wails and backs away, grabbing his gun. Thorn jumps at him and Nico fires. Pain explodes in my shoulder and I fly back, my head thunking on the floor.

Then darkness takes me under, and I feel nothing.

THIRTY-EIGHT

Alana

I wake up in the hospital, everything hurting, and look up to see my father asleep in a chair, dressed in a golf shirt with tan slacks. His gray suit jacket is hanging over the arm of the chair.

"Dad." My voice cracks.

He bolts awake. "Alana."

I look at a bandage around my left arm. "What happened?"

"You were shot."

"Oh, by Nico." Tears gather my eyes. "He killed Mom."

My dad scrubs a hand down his worn face. "I know. Thorn filled me in."

"Thorn!" I look wildly around. "I'm surprised he's not here."

"He was, but . . ."

My heart stops. "But what?"

"He passed out and the doctors took him to another room."

I blink. Thorn's invincible, right? "He passed out? Was he shot?"

"No. I don't know what happened. It's like ice covered his lips and then he went down. The doctors took him away, and I believe his brother showed up. They're both gone."

I try to scramble out of the bed. "Where is he?"

"Whoa, whoa, whoa." My dad grabs the covers and pushes me back down.

The panic feels worse than my pounding arm. "He's freezing to death, Dad. I have to help him."

"Freezing to death? What are you talking about?"

I explain the entire situation as I swing my legs over and my bare feet touch the chilly floor. I pitch forward.

My dad grabs my good arm. "Knock it off. You need to get ready for the damn ball."

I jerk. Shocked. "Are you kidding? I've been shot."

His jaw firms. "I know, and the doctor says it was a through-and-through. You're fine, and we need you at the ball to post for Aquarius Social. Just one or two emotes, and then you can leave."

Betrayal and hurt rush through me. "Dad."

"We need you. It's imperative. The event is the biggest event of the year, and our reach has doubled after you've emoted each year. Your highest and strongest posts of the year are during that ball. You know it." He tosses scrubs at me.

He doesn't care about me. Not at all.

My phone buzzes and I fumble for it on the table. "Hello."

"Hey. It's Thorn. Sorry I left but I'll be back in about an hour. We're trying something new with the alexandrite crystals."

My chest aches. "I'm getting dressed right now, heading home, and then going to the ball."

"The fuck you are. Get your ass back in that hospital bed."

I smile but my lips tremble. "I'll post about you at the ball on both Aquarius and Malice Media. The extra energy you get from that, and it'll be substantial, will help." It's true. Perhaps it'll be enough to actually heal him.

"I don't give two fucks about extra energy. Get your butt back into that bed, or I swear on all that's holy, there's not an inch of you I won't spank when you're feeling better." He's not kidding. His tone is low and pissed.

My heart freaking soars. He loves me. Oh, he probably won't define it as that, but that's what it is. My health is more important than his to him. He's the direct opposite of my father. We're two halves of the same whole. Just like that coin he told me about. An idea strikes me. What if I can save him? "Meet me at the ball, Thorn." I end the call.

I hurriedly dress and storm out of the room, my arm feeling like it's on fire. But honestly, only a small white wrap is around my biceps. A through-and-through sounds weak but hurts like hell. "Let's go."

My father waves off a doctor trying to stop us in the hallway. "You are not posting on Malice Media tonight."

"Yes, I am." I jerk my head up, tears streaming down my face. "Either you help me with this or we're done, and I'm not kidding. I'll never charge a crystal for you again."

His face goes ashen. "Alana—" He looks at me. "You care about him that much?"

"Yes." I don't have time to examine my feelings or convince my father of anything. I try to button his jacket over me with my good hand as I charge toward the door and down the hallway.

Another doctor tries to stop us, but I ignore him and keep jogging through the hospital and outside to my father's car, my bare feet burning on the rough pavement. Soon we're speeding away. "Drive to Aquarius headquarters, Dad."

He looks at me from the driver's side. "You've lost your mind. Did you hit your head?"

"I think so," I say. "I hit everything else."

"Alana, this kind of love isn't healthy."

"I don't care. It's what I have." My brain still isn't connecting to reality. All I know is how I feel, and I love Thorn Beathach with everything I am. He's rough and lives by his own rules, rather dark ones, but he loves me. He'll always choose me in every situation, and I need that. I also want to choose him. "How did Thorn find me, anyway?"

My dad grimaces. "He wouldn't admit it, but he must've chipped you when you were kidnapped."

I chuckle, even though everything hurts and the world is disintegrating around me. That asshole.

"You have to see that he's not healthy."

No, but he's mine. He came to rescue me while he was freezing from the inside out. I can rescue him after a mere bullet wound. I've been scouring his books on crystals every chance I get, and I know the answer is in there. If somebody created a new virus, I can create a cure. Or is it a curse? It feels like it. If so, I'm the woman to banish it. "How bad is my shoulder?" I probably should've asked before rushing out of the hospital.

"Not bad, really. The bullet didn't hit anything important."

Now that my brain is returning to reality, I have so many questions. "What happened to Nico?" I believe I know, but I need confirmation.

"He's in the custody of the police right now."

My jaw drops, and I swing to face my father, pain plummeting down my arm. Good tip. Don't move suddenly. "Thorn didn't kill him?"

"No," my dad sighs. "I have no doubt Thorn plans to kill him in the future—Thorn told me so directly—but Justice convinced him to wait so the families of the women he killed have some closure. Also so they can trace any other murders to Nico once he starts confessing."

I think about how proud Nico was to have killed and have no doubt he'll spill all the details when he gets the chance. He wants to be famous and this will do it. We're going to have a mountain of bad press to deal with, but considering he kidnapped me, I'll be able to protect Aquarius Social. "I had no clue of the killer lurking in my cousin," I whisper.

"Me either. It's unthinkable, really." Pain laces my dad's words. "He killed Greg. My legacy. My son." A tear gathers at Dad's eye and he wipes it angrily away.

That's all my father cares about. Someday that might not hurt. "Have you talked to Scarlett and Quinlan?"

"Yes. They're at the company now beginning a crisis campaign. They're both shocked and angry." He grips the steering wheel until his knuckles turn white. "I've ordered them to attend the ball, so we can show a united front. We're walking in together."

I don't care. Not even a little bit.

My father clears his throat. "You can't save Thorn, from what you've said. Please don't make a fool of yourself tonight. Post about the great ball, show that you're a survivor and that Nico is the bad guy, and then leave. Make them want more of you. Forget Thorn Beathach right now."

Not in a million years. I know Thorn loves me. But if he nearly passed out, then he's close to death. Thorn is too damn stubborn to let anybody see him in a weakened state, and my entire body floods with adrenaline. He can't die. The idea is unthinkable. "Just hurry up. I have to get to him." My brain is running through all of the information I gleaned about the crystals. The key is in the stones, not the computer malware. I just know it.

Father mutters to himself but drives to Aquarius and parks underground. I'm out of the car in a flash, trying not to fall on my face. My feet hurt, but I don't care. I run to the elevator and he barely catches up to me.

"Where are we going?" he snaps.

"To the servers," I say. He presses the button and we plunge into the earth to the main hub, where I run to the center of the servers, feeling so cold that the skin on my legs prickles.

"You want to charge the crystals now?" he asks as we blast past three guards who look at me like my hair is on fire. Maybe it is. It's a snarled mess and I don't care. I have to look ridiculous in the hospital scrubs with my dad's jacket. The bruise on my face pounds as if I hit it again when I was shot. Did I land on my face?

I open the glass box holding the basketball-size aquamarine. "I can charge them later. Right now, I need help."

He looks at me as if I've lost my mind. "Help doing what?"

"Lift this for me. I need to take it." The stone glows the way it does every time I come near it.

He holds his hands up. "You're not taking that anywhere."

Scarlett and Quinlan burst through the door.

"We saw you arrive in the security feeds. Why the hell aren't you in the hospital?" Quinlan snaps, looking as if he hasn't slept in weeks.

"I need help," I say to him. "Please pick this up. I only have one good arm and the stone is too heavy."

Quinlan looks from my father to me. "What is going on?"

I frantically turn to Scarlett. "Scarlett, I have to help Thorn. I need this stone."

Scarlett shrugs and reaches for the crystal.

My father grabs her arm. "No, you're not taking this away. We'll be helpless."

My feet are freezing. "Either we take that stone, or I never charge it again. I mean never. I'll let the whole place go under."

My dad steps back. "You're bluffing."

"No, I'm not." I meet his stare directly.

He shakes his head. "The servers will cease to function."

"No, they won't," Scarlett says, running over to the supply cabinet. "We don't have anything that size in here, but we have enough crystals to put in the center for, what, a couple of hours?"

Quinlan lifts a shoulder. "Maybe. I wouldn't let it go any longer than that. We need the solid core in that one stone."

"I have to do this." I try to lift the stone out.

Quinlan swears and lifts it out for me. "Where are we going?"

"My apartment."

"So you can get dressed for the ball?" Scarlett says helpfully.

I gulp. "Yes. Also, I have one more stone to get."

THIRTY-NINE

Thorn

I'm freezing to death. There's no question about it. I can't feel my legs and my left arm is completely frozen over. My fingernails are blue and it feels as if my heart is slowing, the warm blood bouncing off frozen walls.

Though I wear a suit every day, for some reason a tuxedo feels restrictive. I fight the urge to tug on the stupid tie as I barely keep myself upright near the bar, my masquerade mask serving to hide my scar. The mint at the back of my tongue is doing its job, so at least there's that.

Justice stands at my side, an odd energy pouring off him. He wants to be back at the computers, trying to cure the garnet, and I don't blame him. So do I.

I see Sylveria and her daughters across the ballroom, walking along the rows of silent auction items that range from new computers to skydiving lessons.

The ball takes place at the Natural History Museum and Estates. With its vast property, there's plenty of room for security, and so far, the event has gone perfectly smoothly. The main ballroom opens out to a garden area and outdoor lounge where people have already gathered now that the rain has finally ebbed and it's a rather nice night.

I nod to Justice and ignore his angry look. We are going to post tonight and reach far and wide. If I'm going to die, I'm going to leave him a powerful company. "Now," I mouth.

Justice edges to my side, his phone up. "Hi, all! I'm hitting Thorn Beathach up right now. He's here, waiting for the lovely Alana Beaumont to arrive. She's been posting about him all week. Right?"

"She's not doing that any longer," I say, a growl in my voice.

Justice chuckles. "We'll just see." He ends the mind meld. "Good job. That should gain us a bunch of energy."

"Get away from me before I break your jaw," I grind out.

Justice, not being a moron, turns and heads toward the bar.

Alana and her entourage are fashionably late, which does not surprise me. However, I know from the men I have on her that she'll be walking in the door any minute. I'm curious whether she'll be wearing my offering.

Even though she's clearly disobeying me, I created a gift for her before tonight, and I'd left it at her place. If I survive this, when we're both feeling better, it'll be the only thing she's wearing when I teach her not to disobey me.

My entire body tightens in anticipation, even through the ice coating my veins.

Everybody who's anybody in Silicon Valley is either scouting the auction items, hitting the bars, or eating by the buffet table. The music is playing lightly in the background, but thus far the dance floor is vacant.

The Sokolovs are not present, no doubt because of Cal's death. I did make him eat his fingers.

The Rendales apparently decide they've waited long enough and make their move to approach me.

"Thorn, don't you look nice in a tux," Sylveria says. Both of her daughters nod. She is dressed in a champagne-colored gown that sweeps the floor and has more diamonds on her than is present in most mines. Corinda is in a black sequin number and Stacia a blue, both decked out with diamonds everywhere. It's a cold stone and it fits them.

"Do we have an announcement to make tonight?" Sylveria asks smoothly.

"I hardly think this is the place for announcements," Justice says, coming up by my side. His mask is slightly askew and he fixes it. The masks are stupid, but I do like camouflaging myself behind one. The last thing I need is a bunch of pictures, especially if I'm about to pass out and die. Most people don't know what I look like, or at least they don't know who I am, and I travel through the city's underbelly much more easily that way.

Corinda leans in, as if she has the best secret ever. "I heard that Aquarius Social is losing members by the second because of Nico. A serial killer! Can you believe it?"

Yes. I definitely can. "Sylveria, did you attack my servers yesterday?" I ask smoothly.

She presses a diamond-adorned hand to her chest. "Why, Thorn, how could you even ask such a thing? We're about to be family."

I don't like torturing women. It doesn't mean I won't do it. "If you did, I suggest you tell me now." I already know it's her. It has to be.

"I would never do such a thing. Now, the girls and I are going to fetch something to eat. Something small, of course, and when you've regained your manners, we will be back." With a swish of her skirts, she pivots and storms off rather gracefully.

Stacia sighs. "Seriously, can't we just all get along? Are we getting married or not?" She is eminently likable. I don't know why, because she shouldn't be.

"Have you met my brother, Justice?" I ask.

"No." She holds out a hand.

Justice shakes it. "It's very nice to meet you," he says smoothly.

"I'm sure it is." Winking, she turns and saunters toward the buffet.

Corinda lingers. "I'll make a much better wife than she will," she says, her voice several octaves too high. "Seriously, I have five million followers, Thorn. I could bring them all right over to Malice Media." She looks me over and I feel like a slab of meat. "You're hot. We could have a good life together. What do you think?"

I find her colder than the diamonds around her throat. "No."

She lightly trails her fingers down my arm. "You'll want to reconsider." With that, she turns and follows her mother and sister.

Justice gives a mock shudder. "That's a shark."

"Yeah, no kidding," I mutter, and then the doors open, and I taste honey.

The entire world grinds to a halt and warmth roars through my chilled body. Alana is absolutely exquisite. Her gown is a canary yellow silk embellished with what have to be pure diamonds and aquamarine crystals that make the dress shimmer with every movement. On her, the diamonds look warm and inviting.

I don't like the white bandage around her arm, but the color in her face is good.

A deep heart-shaped neckline plunges to the tops of her breasts before the bodice narrows to her slim waist. The skirt descends perfectly to the floor, but as she walks, I can see hints of aquamarine-and-diamond shoes that match the jewels on the dress.

I look at her neck and see the gift I had created for her. An eighty-karat diamond serves as the centerpiece with folds of aquamarine crystals bracketing the stone on each side. The main collar is aquamarine and curves around her neck, changing to diamonds as it coils to the end. It is stunning and yet nowhere near as beautiful as the woman herself. I'm pleased that she decided to wear it.

As if she knows my thoughts, she gingerly touches the timeless piece. It's the first of many I plan to give her.

I like how Quinlan and Mathias scout the ballroom before they all walk inside. Oh, they're not as good a protector as I am, but at least they're on alert. Quinlan has a backpack over his shoulders.

How odd.

The mask over the top half of Alana's sculpted face hides her bruise. Next to her, Ella is in a deep blue gown, Rosalie in a surprising pink, and Scarlett in a deep red that matches her name.

The entire place stills and turns to look at my woman.

She's royalty. Her chin is up, and she looks like the survivor she is. A rumbling starts throughout the crowd and then several people clap.

It's not every day the Silicon Valley princess survives a serial killer.

I've waited long enough. I place my drink on the bar and stride toward her with Justice at my side. I reach them and bow slightly, my gait slower than usual and my vocal cords chilled. "Alana."

She smiles and appears delightfully nervous, as if she isn't sure what I'm about to do. Her eyes sparkle behind the mask, and I believe she's happy to see me. "Hello."

I like that she doesn't use my name. "I've been waiting for you. Would you like to dance?"

Mathias puffs up as if ready to object.

"I would love to." She slips her hand in mine.

I turn and draw her to the middle of the dance floor, noting

Justice and Scarlett next to us. Oh, he's flanking me as he always does, but the woman's enticing, so maybe he'll have a good time for a few minutes.

We really have become brothers, probably thanks to Alana.

I shoot a pointed look at the orchestra and the conductor stiffens, turns, and immediately starts a waltz. I move easily into the dance, pressing Alana close.

"What in the world are you doing?" she whispers.

"Dancing with you while I can."

The woman warms me. As we move, my legs loosen up.

"It took a while to get this necklace fastened." She leans back to look up at me, feeling right in my arms, exactly where she should be. "Thank you for the flowers, and for this exquisite piece. I don't even know what to say. It's the most beautiful thing I've ever seen."

"It suits you," I say.

"It's made of lovely stones," she murmurs. "It must have taken a long time to create."

Six months, to be exact. I've been hunting her that long, at least. "I knew someday you'd wear it."

She rolls her eyes but moves easily within my arms to the music. "There's that ego again." Then her nails dig into my neck. "Did you chip me?"

"I did."

She stumbles but quickly regains her balance, and I hold her tighter. "Where?" she hisses.

Between two of her toes. "That's irrelevant. How are you feeling?" I ask.

"Just fine. A through-and-through is no biggie." Her smile does look a little off, but she's dancing gracefully, so her motor skills haven't diminished. "I am not happy about the chip, and we are having it removed, but thank you for rushing to my rescue."

"I protect what's mine." I lean down and brush her mouth in

a firm kiss, well aware of the many phones and cameras focused on us right now. Several people crowd the dance floor, taking advantage of the music. I steer her toward the middle so we stay out of view of as many of those cameras as possible.

"What are you doing?" she hisses quietly after I release her delectable mouth.

"Making a claim," I say calmly.

She stumbles and I quickly right her. "I thought you were going to behave tonight."

"I don't know what that means," I say honestly, tucking her closer. "Now be nice and dance with me, or I'll make a claim nobody will forget."

Her irritated groan coincides with a half laugh. "How frozen are you?"

"Better now that you're here." True statement.

She nods. "It's my stones. I've been reading all of your books, the ones I borrowed, and certain crystals interact with each other in ways we've forgotten." Pink filters across her high cheekbones. "Or you and I interact and our stones follow."

Now that, I believe.

I clamp my hand against her waist and move us into a slower song. Finally giving in, she melts against me, and for the moment, everything's right in my world. We dance three more sets before I see Kazstone rush inside, a backpack over his shoulders, his eyes wild. "What the fuck?"

She pauses. "It's about damn time he got here."

I pause. "What?"

For answer, she grabs my hand. "Come on, Thorn. Trust me."

FORTY

Thorn

I allow her to lead me outside with Kaz and Justice flanking us. She looks over at her friends and motions for them to follow. I stumble but right myself as she hurries all of us into an outbuilding that houses potted plants.

"What the hell?" I mutter.

Kaz tugs off his backpack and draws out the two garnets to plop on a worn wooden table. The healthy garnet sits next to the diseased one, and now it looks like they're both freezing over.

"Well, shit," Justice says, shaking his head. "That didn't go as planned."

I chuckle. It's not funny, but his tone is.

My nostrils are freezing. Soon I won't be able to breathe. "I think it's too late. You'll make sure she's all right."

"Of course, always."

We glare at the two garnets as ice tunnels into them from the outside.

Alana motions for Quinlan, who yanks an aquamarine the size of a beach ball out of his pack. "What do you want me to do with this?"

"Put it next to the two garnets. In fact, put it between the two garnets," she says rapidly. "Kaz. Computers. Now."

Kaz draws two laptops out of his bag, quickly attaching leads to the garnets.

"Keep them touching the aquamarine," she orders.

She's a bossy little thing. I wish I had an eternity to absolve her of that bad habit. Or even just a few decades. My breath puffs out white in the evening.

Kaz looks at me, looks at her, and then shrugs.

Quinlan pulls a rose quartz out of his bag.

Alana points. "Put my quartz on top of the other crystals."

Quinlan does as he's told while his sister watches along with Mathias in the doorway.

"Okay," she says. "All right, everybody here has some charging ability. Kaz," she calls out.

"What?"

I like his snappishness.

She doesn't because she hisses. "Do you have any ability to charge?"

"Not in the slightest," Justice answers for him.

"Okay, you start rapidly typing code," she says and then frowns. "You're almost the best, right?"

He puffs up. "I *am* the best."

Her gaze swivels to Ella and thoughts scatter across her face. She blinks and a frown settles between her eyes. "Wait a minute. No, you're not. Ella is."

Ella turns beet red.

Fury lances through Alana's eyes. "Ella? You and Nico seemed rather close. Right?"

Oh, shit. I stare at the little blonde.

Now she pales. "Yes, but I didn't know he was a serial killer."

Alana's chin lifts. "But you did know he wanted to control all four social media companies. He said that to me, but I was so busy trying to survive that I didn't catch it. What was his plan, Ella?"

Ella stares at the aquamarine. "You know I've studied crystals as well as coding. So did Nico. He actually came up with the idea of infecting the servers, the crystals, and finally Thorn. I just implemented the plan." She blanches and looks at me. "Sorry?"

"*Sorry?*" Alana explodes. "You infected the man that I love!"

The little Rendale girl has killed me? I breathe out. Impressive.

Ella winces. "You didn't love him when I first infected his garnet and then him with the freeze curse. Didn't even know him yet." She kicks a small pebble. "We all thought you were a cold-blooded killer."

"I am," I say softly.

Ella's shoulders slump. "I knew about the interview with Jackie for Malice Media, and Nico paid her the money to upload the virus."

Truth be told, I like Ella even more now.

Her gaze meets mine. "I'm sorry."

"You're forgiven," I say, knowing Alana will need her friends once I die. "Did you make Jackie overdose?"

"No," Ella says. "She did that on her own. Shouldn't have given her the money, I guess. Didn't know she was going to buy drugs with it."

Alana whirls on me. "We'll discuss this issue later. For now, everybody here is going to help fix this mess. Right, Ella?"

Ella nods and moves to the second laptop. "I want to assist, but the virus has progressed too far for me to reverse the damage. I can slow the bug down, though."

"I'll follow your code," Kaz says, fingers already flying over his keyboard.

Alana nods. "Everybody should touch two stones and one of them needs to be a garnet."

I'm barely standing. Have my knees frozen solid? "What are you doing?"

"Trust me." Her eyes are blazing.

"All right." If it's the last thing I do, I guess I'll trust her. I touch the diseased garnet and instinctively reach for the aquamarine. Justice does the same, as does Alana.

Nobody else moves.

Alana jerks her head. "Listen, assholes. Either you help, or I'll move into Thorn's castle, all by myself, and let Aquarius Social die. Hell. I'll post first about all of you and how you were working with Nico. I'll destroy you."

Mathias growls and then motions the other two forward. Quinlan grins and Scarlett shrugs. I kind of like them, to be honest. Not Mathias. I still want to kill him but probably won't because it'd upset Alana.

Her cousins both touch a rose quartz and a garnet, and Mathias, grumbling, reaches for his aquamarine and seems to take forever to decide to plant his hand on the healthiest garnet.

"Would somebody please explain to me what we're doing?" he asks.

"Alchemy," Alana says, her voice sharp. Her face is bruised. Her body looks beaten and the white bandage on her arm glares beneath the meager lights. "Okay, I need everybody to charge as if these are regular crystals."

Mathias purses his lips. The sounds of the ball echo in the distance. "They are regular crystals."

"Oh, that's right." She looks around. "Kaz, did you bring the alexandrite pyramids? The ones you guys stole from my dad?"

Kaz reaches into his pack. "Of course. Your orders were clear."

"Put them in a triangle around the diseased crystal but make sure they're touching at least one other crystal." He does so.

"Excellent," she says. "You're sure that these can contain more data and transmit faster than anything else?"

"They're supposed to," I say.

She swallows, her face pinched. "All right, good. So each of us will charge different crystals, and they'll amplify each other. As you know, garnets are warm gems, which is why they're being killed by the frost. Aquamarine is a cold stone and rose quartz is thick."

"Thick?" Scarlett asks.

"Yeah, it's dense."

Fascinating. "How do you know this?" I ask.

"Your library," she bursts out. "Do you think I took all those books for fun?"

"Yes."

"Okay," she admits. "I did borrow them for entertainment, but I chose the ones all about crystals because that's what I'm interested in, and then when you told me about your illness . . ."

Oh, the little sweetheart. "You dove deep," I murmur.

"Yeah," she says. "I dove deep. I need everybody to concentrate and charge, but I want you to think heat and healing instead of fire and power. Okay?"

"All right." I don't think I could heat a battery at the moment, but the idea is intriguing.

"Kaz and Ella," she calls out.

"Yeah," Kaz growls.

She sucks in air. "I want you to run an anti-malware program, starting right now. In fact, run every one you got."

"I have about twenty of them," he mutters. "A couple you've never heard of."

"So do I," Ella says. "I'm really sorry, Thorn."

I try to smile at her, but my lips are frozen. "I've already forgiven you, but you seem to require penance. So you will work for Malice Media for a bit."

She pales but nods.

"Good. Hit us *now!*" Alana yells.

Kaz and Ella start rapidly typing, sending code and energy through the leads to the stones. The garnet beneath my hand vibrates.

"Charge the crystals now," she orders.

I concentrate and try to charge the crystal just as I normally would. Energy violently bursts around us and I feel the tension. I look up and lock gazes with Justice. He then looks down at the aquamarine. The crystal is humming and glowing a bright blue.

"Harder, concentrate," Alana orders.

I'm going to have to do something about that bossy nature of hers if I survive this. Nonetheless, I do as she says, and force every ounce of energy I have into the garnet. Red sparks fly from the stone.

Scarlett cries out and flies back to hit a rough wall. Quinlan releases the stones and goes after her. The alexandrite crystals start to glow and ebb as if they have a life of their own.

"What the hell?" Mathias hisses.

"It's the different crystals and their unique energies," Alana says excitedly. "As well as Kaz and Ella getting rid of malware."

I shake my head. "It's just malware."

She looks up at me, her eyes wide. "Don't you see? It's a computer virus."

I do. The woman's brilliant. It took special stones and the right energy. A potted plant explodes behind me and I pivot to make sure pieces from the clay pot don't hit her.

Mathias backs away from the crystals.

Justice looks at me. "What do you want me to do?"

I try to control the energy in the garnets. Mathias, Scarlett, and Quinlan return and put their hands on the crystals, succumbing to blackmail. I like that. I feel the ice disintegrating inside me but then the melting stops. I'm still half frozen. It's not enough. I look at Alana and I try to show her how I feel. "You tried. You did everything you could."

"No," she says, her brows drawing down, fury lighting her gaze. "It's not enough. We can do this."

I can feel my feet freezing again. We were close, but the disease has progressed too much in the garnet. There's no way to save it.

"Try harder," she says, tears streaming down her face.

"It's okay," I say.

"It's not." She lifts her hand and I feel the energy draining from me into the stone. She grabs her dad's phone out of his pocket.

"What are you doing?" he asks.

Her eyes widen. She instantly starts typing on the screen. "I've got it," she says, backing away and holding the phone up to her face.

Justice looks at me. "She's emoting a video now?"

I stare at her.

"Hi, there," she says earnestly into the camera. "This is Alana Beaumont. Many of you don't know me because I'm usually on Aquarius Social. This is my first time mind-melding on Malice and I have to say it's because I think Thorn Beathach is the hottest guy on the planet, and I'm so ready to dish all about him to you. We're at the ball right now, having snuck off to a cute little potting barn. He's such a mystery, right? I need you to get all your friends and come back to this post ASAP."

I feel a hum in the healthy garnet. The sound of ice breaking resounds through my head.

She lifts the camera higher, sucking energy from her users and pushing it into the stones. "Hi, y'all. I'm back on Aquarius Social. Yes, I survived a serial killer, and I'll tell you all about it later. Thank you for all the kind wishes; however, I need a favor. Would everybody watching me now hop on over to my account at Malice Media? Some of you may not have an account there, but I want you to go ahead and create one. We're going to try something really cool, and if it works out, I'm going to give away a Porsche."

"A Porsche," her father mutters.

She looks at me. "You doing all right, Thorn?"

If anything, I'm bemused. "If this is my last day standing, I'm enjoying it."

"Just keep charging." She takes a deep breath and then flicks the button again. "Hi there. I'm back on Malice Media. Look at all you new users! Thank you to those of you who are coming over from Aquarius, and thank you to those who are new." She pauses and leans around the corner. "Hey, Kaz. I need you to get me all the users I can."

"Already on it," he retorts. "I've been following you."

"Isn't that sweet?" she says, and she brings up the video again. "All right. I need everybody to explode-star on Aquarius and mind-meld here. Jump into the hologram with me and enjoy attending the ball from afar."

She scans the room and shows her friends in their ball-gowns. "Everybody right now, interact and feel what I'm feeling."

A pot on the other side of Justice shatters and he partially turns to shield Scarlett. I can feel the ice receding from my legs.

"That's it!" Alana cheers all of her followers. "Everybody, keep interacting. It's like you're all here—and don't forget, you're entering to win not only a Porsche but a Bentley."

The woman is giving away every car I own. I can't help laughing. My arms warm as social media users send energy to us through the two platforms. Ice cracks away in my chest, and finally I can breathe again. As I watch, the diseased garnet slowly warms and the ice falls away. It takes at least thirty minutes, and she keeps posting the entire time. The crystals all start to glow with a healthy hum.

She looks over the phone at me. "You good?"

I smile. "I'm better than good. Hey, Kaz!" I call out.

"Yep."

Might as well take advantage of the moment. "We have enough juice right now. Send a spike directly into TimeGem and the Rendales. We'll see just how they like that." While they didn't poison me, they still tried to attack my servers when they knew I was down.

Alana chuckles. "I like how you think."

"It's a good thing," I murmur. "Because you're coming home with me."

EPILOGUE

Alana

We're back at Thorn's place, just the two of us. I'm not entirely sure how he made it happen, but within seconds, seriously seconds of curing him, he had me out the door and in the elevator headed to the parking garage—leaving my family and his at the ball. I'm sure my father secured our aquamarine and rushed it back to Aquarius Social.

Thorn leads me into the library, which is, quite frankly, my favorite place on the entire planet. "There's something for you in here."

I look around. "Another necklace?"

"No, and you can put that one upstairs in your jewelry box."

"I have a jewelry box?"

He looks strong and vital. No one would guess he was nearly dead an hour ago. "You have a whole fucking jewelry room, sweetheart."

I like that. I like it a lot. "What am I looking for?"

"The first thing you should notice is the empty places where my books need to be returned."

"They're in my apartment. I'll get them later today."

His eyes glitter like a lion's about to pounce. "Actually, your entire apartment is being moved here within the hour." He glances at his watch.

"I don't believe I agreed to that," I say calmly, looking over my shoulder at him.

"I don't believe I asked." He's already changed into fresh slacks and a white shirt.

I've changed into a simple yellow-and-aquamarine sundress that was conveniently hanging in my closet. "So you think I'm going to take up residence in my old room, huh?"

"Absolutely not. We're moving everything into my room." He looks around. "Aren't you curious?"

Of course, I'm curious. It's one of my default settings. "What am I looking for?"

"It has to do with the moors of Scotland and the Battle of Thistlewind. Such a sad tale."

"Ooh," I say, clapping my hands together. "The poetry of Enoch Fife." I'm impressed Thorn not only has heard of the obscure poet but actually owns Fife's only compilation. I move unerringly toward the Scottish poetry section of his library and climb the ladder to a section where the tomes are ancient and probably priceless. I rifle through them, finding the correct book.

"You did spend a lot of time in here," he murmurs.

I'm halfway up the ladder, leaning to the right. "I love it in here."

"If you fall, you're in trouble."

"Maybe you should secure me. I only have one good arm."

He's already there, bracketing me so I don't fall, his warmth heating my entire backside.

"How is your arm?" he asks quietly.

"It's fine." I shrug my good shoulder as if it's no big deal, even though my entire body is pretty damn sore. "How are you feeling?" I ask him, looking through the books.

"Hot. All the ice is gone from my body."

The relief that floods me will concern me at a later date. Right now, I'm looking for a present. I love gifts. "That's good."

"You're brilliant, you know," he says from behind me.

"Your books did help," I admit. Though, in the end, the idea of putting all the gems together was mine. I was desperate to save him. "I'm glad you're not dead."

"I appreciate that," he says dryly.

I pull out two of the books and note a little black velvet box behind them. My heart drops. I reach in, my hand trembling, and pull out the box.

"Off the ladder," he orders.

It's a good idea because I have a feeling I may just fall when I open it, unless it's a toe ring. If it's something like a toe ring, I'm going to kill him. I move down the ladder and then turn to face Thorn. I look down at the box in my hand.

"Open it," he says.

I'm not quite ready to open it. The box is beautiful, simple, tasteful. Swallowing, I slowly flip open the lid and then gasp, as it's the only thing I can do. A striking square garnet sits in the middle between a halo of brilliant cut aquamarines reflecting the purity of a clear sky. The band is a harmonious line of white gold, studded with alternating diamonds and rose quartz. It is the perfect ring made specifically for me.

"Marry me," he says.

I can't stop looking at the sparkles. "I think you're supposed to ask."

He takes the ring out of the box and slips it on my left ring finger. "If I ask, you'll think 'no' is an option. It isn't."

I roll my eyes. "There's no way I'll say no."

He reaches down and kisses me. "Say yes."

The ring is heavy and feels right on my finger. Knowing Thorn, it has magical properties and can never be removed. "Yes."

He kisses me again, going deep in a way that is all Thorn.

"So let's talk about the future." Thorn leads me back into the library, turns and kisses me until my ears ring.

I open my eyes to find my dress drifting to the floor and his hands on me. I can't wait for the future. "I love you."

"I know." He glances at the ring on my hand. "I've loved you since the first time I saw you and will do so for eternity. You're mine, Alana."

Yeah. I can live with that.

One Cursed Rose Playlist

Grimm Bargains #1
Rebecca Zanetti

Link on Spotify: https://spoti.fi/48MJevu

1. "What If I Was Nothing," All That Remains
2. "Fiend," Talia Shay
3. "Beauty and the Beast," JAE
4. "Where It Ends," Bailey Zimmerman
5. "Star Walkin'," Lil Nas X
6. "Wicked as They Come," CRMNL
7. "Cool for the Summer," Demi Lovato
8. "One Last Breath," Creed
9. "Don't Cry (Original) 2022 remake," Guns N'Roses
10. "Being Evil Has a Price," Heavy Young Heathens
11. "Kings Never Die," Eminem, Gwen Stefani
12. "Bad Guy," Billie Eilish
13. "Angeles," Elliott Smith
14. "Wildfire," Demi Lovato

Acknowledgments

The idea of writing a dark retelling of Beauty and the Beast was a challenge I just loved, and I hope readers enjoy Thorn and Alana's romance as much as I did. There are many folks to thank in getting this book to readers, and I sincerely apologize to anybody I've forgotten.

A heartfelt thanks to Big Tone for your understanding and support as I wrote at the lake during the summer and edited between football games in the fall. Even though the kids are in college, it seems like we're busier than ever these days, and I love that you make sure we take some time for the two of us. I promise I don't use anything you say in my books. Honest. You can trust me. For sure.

Huge hugs and love to the kids, Gabe and Karlina, who are patient and put up with my odd questions, like what's a better way to describe the color green? It is a lot of fun to watch you in college, and even more fun to visit and take you out. You're both doing so well, and I can't tell you how very proud we are of you, and I work with words. A lot. I love you both so much.

Thank you to my intuitive agent, Caitlin Blasdell, who always comes up with the best twists, turns, and plots. I really enjoy bouncing ideas off you, and I hope we're still doing so

Acknowledgments

when we're old, which is a long, long, long time from now. I appreciate your insights and great assistance in navigating this career.

I know I dedicated the book to my editor, Alicia Condon, but I also need to send a big thank you right here. You not only have great ideas for fascinating plots but you edit with a fine eye for every detail. I also appreciate your rare ability to handle stressed-out creative people . . . like me. When I was a lawyer, I just fired irritating clients. I appreciate you being so kind and understanding when I feel like my head is about to explode sometimes.

A heartfelt thank you to everyone at Kensington Publishing: Alexandra Nicolajsen, Steven Zacharius, Adam Zacharius, Lynn Cully, Vida Engstrand, Jane Nutter, Lauren Jernigan, Barbara Bennett, Elizabeth May, Steven Roman, and Carly Sommerstein.

I want to thank Liz Berry for helping me plot this one while we sat by a pool and relaxed as much as either of us is capable of doing. I love our time together—you're a wonderful friend.

A thank you to my amazing assistant, Anissa Beatty, for your hard work with Rebecca's Rebels, my FB street team, and for handling all of my social media. Also, a huge thank you to my Beta readers: Rebels Madison Fairbanks, Kimberly Frost, Heather Frost, Leanna Feazel, Asmaa Qayyum, Suzi Zuber, Jessica Mobbs, and Joan Lai.

Also, thank you to my constant support system. Special thanks to Gail and Jim English, Kathy and Herb Zanetti, Debbie and Travis Smith, Stephanie and Don West, Jessica and Jonah Namson, Chelli and Jason Younker, Liz and Steve Berry, and Jillian and Benji Stein.

Finally, a heartfelt thanks to you, the reader, for coming on this new journey with me. I hope you liked my first dark romance. (Yes, I know that the Dark Protectors and the Scorpius Syndrome were dark . . . but this is darker. Right?)

Keep reading for a special excerpt of the next
Grimm Bargains novel,

One Dark Kiss.

Rosalie

Alone, I cross my legs again beneath the intimidating metal table secured to the floor, feeling as out of place as a raven in a nursery rhyme. The heat clunks and whispers from a grate in the ceiling but fails to warm the interview room, and when the door finally opens, the heavy frame scrapes against the grimy cement floor.

My spine naturally straightens and my chin lifts as my client stalks inside, his hands cuffed to a chain secured around his narrow waist. He doesn't shuffle. Or walk. Or saunter.

No. This man . . . stalks.

His gaze rakes me, and I mean *rakes* me. Black eyes—deep and dark—glint with more than one threat of violence in their depths. He kicks back the lone metal chair opposite me and sits in one fluid motion. The scent of woodsy male wafts toward me.

I swallow.

The guard, a burly man with gray hair, stares at me, concern in his eyes.

"Please remove his cuffs," I say, my focus not leaving my client.

My client. I don't practice criminal law. Never have and don't want to.

The guard hesitates. "Miss, I—"

"I appreciate it." I make my voice as authoritative as possible, considering I'm about to crap my pants. Or rather, my best navy-blue pencil skirt bought on clearance at the Women's Center thrift store. I don't live there, but I'm happy to shop there. Rich people give away good items.

In a jangle of metal, the guard hitches toward us, releases the cuffs, and turns on his scuffed boot toward the door. "Want me to stay inside?"

"No, thank you." I wait until he shrugs, exits, and shuts the door. "Mr. Sokolov? I'm Rosalie Mooncrest, your new attorney from Telecom Summit Law Group."

"What happened to my old attorney?" His voice is the rasp of a blade on a sharpening stone.

I clear my throat and focus only on his eyes and not the tattoo of a panther prowling across the side of his neck, amethyst eyes glittering. "Mr. Molasses died in a car accident three months ago." Molasses was a partner in the firm, and he'd represented Alexei in the criminal trial that had led to a guilty verdict. "I take it he wasn't in touch with you often?"

"No." Alexei leans back and finishes removing the cuffs from his wrists to slap onto the table. "Don't call me that name again."

I frown. "Sokolov?"

"Yes. It's Alexei. No mister."

Fair enough. I can't help but study him. Unruly black hair, unfathomable dark eyes, golden-brown skin, and bone structure chipped out of a mountain with a finely sharpened tool. Brutally rugged, the angles of his face reveal a primal strength that's ominously beautiful. The deadliest predators in life usually are.

Awareness filters through me. I don't like it.

Worse yet, he's studying me right back, as if he has Superman's X-ray vision and has no problem using it. He lingers inappropriately on my breasts beneath my crisp white blouse before sliding to my face, his gaze a rough scrape I can feel. "You fuck your way through law school?"

My mouth drops open for the smallest of seconds. "Are you insane?"

"Insanity is relative. It depends on who has who locked in what cage," he drawls.

Did he just quote Ray Bradbury? "You might want to remember that I'm here to help you."

"Hence my question. Not that I'm judging. If you want to do the entire parole board to get me out, then don't hold back. If that isn't your plan, then I'd like to know that you understand the law."

It's official. Alexei Sokolov is an asshole. "Listen, Mr. Sokolov—"

"That name. You don't want me to tell you again." His threat is softly spoken.

A shiver tries to take me, so I shift my weight, hiding my reaction. I stare him directly in the eyes, as one does with any bully. "Why? What are you going to do?" I jerk my head toward the door, where no doubt the guard awaits on the other side.

Alexei leans toward me and metal clangs. "Peaflower? I can have you over this table, your skirt hiked up, and spank your ass raw before the dumbass guard can find his keys, much less gather the backup he'd need to get you free. You won't sit for a week. Maybe two." His gaze warms. "Now that's a very pretty blush."

"That's my planning a murder expression," I retort instantly, my cheeks flaming hot.

His lip curls for the briefest of moments in almost a smile. "So do you know the law? Usually women who look like you aren't expected to use their brain. Fuck, you're a contradiction." He flattens a hand on the table. A large, tattooed, dangerous looking hand. "As a rule, a beautiful woman is a terrible disappointment."

Now he's quoting freakin' Carl Jung? "You must've had a lot of time to read here in prison . . . the last seven years," I say.

"I have." A hardness invades his eyes. "You any good at your job?"

The most inappropriate humor takes me and I look around the room. "Does it matter? I don't see a plenitude of counsellors in here trying to help you."

"Big word. Plenitude. I would've gone with cornucopia. Has a better sound to it."

I need to regain control of this situation. "Listen, Mr.—"

He stiffens and I stop. Cold.

We look at each other, and I swear, the room itself has a heartbeat that rebounds around us. I don't want to back down. But also, I know in every cell of my being, he isn't issuing idle threats. A man like him never bluffs.

Surprisingly, triumph that I refrain from using his last name doesn't light his eyes. Instead, contemplation and approval?

I don't like that.

My legs tremble like I've run ten miles, and my lungs are failing to catch up. I suppose anybody would feel like this if trapped with a hell beast in a small cage. There's more than fear to my reaction. Adrenaline has that effect on people. That must be it. I reach into my briefcase on the floor and retrieve several pieces of paper. "If you want me as your attorney, you need to sign this retainer agreement so I can file a notice of appearance with the court."

"And if I don't?"

I place the papers on the cold table. "Then have a nice life." I meet his stare evenly.

"My funds are low. I don't suppose you'd take cigarettes or sex in trade?"

Is that amusement in his eyes? That had better not be amusement. I examine his broad shoulders and no doubt impressive chest beneath the orange jumpsuit. How can he look sexy in orange? Plus, the man hasn't been with a woman in seven years—he'd be on fire. A little part of me, one I'll never admit to, considers the offer just for the no doubt multiple and wild orgasms. "I don't smoke and you're not my type. But no worries. My firm is taking your case pro bono."

He latches onto the wrong part of the statement. "What's your type?"

I inhale through my nose, trying to keep a handle on my temper, which doesn't exist.

"Don't tell me," he continues, his gaze probing deep. "Three piece suit, Armani, luxury vehicles?"

"Actually, that's my best friend's type," I drawl. Well, if you add in guns, the Irish mafia, and a frightening willingness to kill.

Alexei scratches the whiskers across his cut jaw. "Right. When was the last time you were with an actual man? You know, somebody who doesn't ask for guidance every step of the way?"

The fact that I don't remember is not one I'll share. My thighs heat, and my temper sparks. "Was this approach charming seven years ago?"

"Not really. Though I didn't need to be charming back then."

True. He was the heir to one of the four most powerful social media companies in the world before he'd gone to prison.

Apparently his family had deserted him immediately. "You might want to give it a try now."

His eyes warm to dark embers, rendering me temporarily speechless. "You don't think I can charm the panties off you?"

"All right. You need to dial it down." I hold out a hand and press down on imaginary air. "A lot."

"Dial what down?"

"You," I hiss. "All of this. The obnoxious, rudely sexist, prowling panther routine. Use your brain, if you have one. It's our first meeting, and you're driving me crazy. You want me on your side."

"I'd rather have you under me."

I shut my eyes and slam both index fingers to the corners, pressing in. This is unbelievable.

"Getting a headache? I know a remedy for that."

I make the sound of a strangled cat.

His laugh is warm. Rich. Deep.

Jolting, I open my eyes. The laugh doesn't fit with the criminal vibe. It's enthralling.

He stops.

I miss the sound immediately. Maybe I *am* going insane.

Using one finger, he draws the paper across the table. "Pen."

I fumble in my bag for a blue pen and hand it over.

He signs the retainer quickly and shoves it back at me. "What's the plan?"

The switch in topics gives me whiplash. Even so, I step on firm ground again. "The prosecuting attorney in your case was just arrested for blackmail, peddling influence, and extortion . . . along with the judge, his co-conspirator, who presided over your trial and sentenced you."

His expression doesn't alter. "So you can me get free?"

"I don't know. Best guess is that I can get you a new trial."

"Will I be free for the duration?"

"I'll make a motion but can't guarantee it." I tilt my head. "Your family's influence would be helpful."

His chin lowers in an intimidating move. "I don't have a family. Don't mention them again."

I blink. "One more comment."

"Go ahead."

"I'm sorry about your brother's death." His younger brother, rather his half-brother, was killed a month ago, probably by my friend's boyfriend, if one could call Thorn Beathach a boyfriend.

Alexei just stares at me.

I feel like a puzzle being solved. "There's a chance his death was part of some sort of social media turf war against Thorn Beathach, who owns Malice Media."

"So?"

"Thorn is currently dating my best friend, so if there's a conflict of interest, I want you to know about it." Not that anybody would ever catch Thorn, if he had killed Alexei's brother after the man had injured Alana. I'm still not sure he was the killer, anyway.

"Are you finished mentioning my family?" Alexei's tone strongly suggests that I am.

"Yes," I whisper.

He cocks his head. "How many criminal trials have you won?"

"None," I say instantly. It's crucial to be honest with clients. "I haven't lost any, either."

His head tips up and he watches me from half-closed lids. "You're in charge of the pro bono arm of the firm?"

"No."

"Why you, then?"

It's a fair question as well as a smart one. "I've never lost in trial, and the partners assigned me your case."

"Why?"

"Because I'm good and they want you free." I shrug. "This is positive exposure for the firm." Which is what my boss, Kay Ramstead, told me when assigning me to the docket. We have several verdicts being overturned because of the judge's corruption, and yours came up, being the most high profile. The loss of your case hurt the firm seven years ago."

His nostrils flare. "The firm? The loss harmed *the firm?*"

"Yes." Damn, he's intimidating. Do I want him free to roam the streets? "This is a chance to fix the damage caused."

"And promote you to partner?" he guesses.

My life is none of his business. "I'm good at my job, Alexei." Yeah, I don't use his last name. "You can go with outside counsel. I'll rip up your retainer agreement if you want."

"I want you."

I hear the double entendre and ignore it. "Then it's my way and you'll follow my directives."

Now he smiles. Full on, straight teeth, shocking dimple in his right cheek.

Everything inside me short circuits and flashes electricity into places sparks don't belong.

He taps his fingers on the table. "I signed the agreement, and this means you work for me. Correct?"

"Yes." But I call the shots.

He moves so suddenly to plant his hand over mine that I freeze. "You need to learn now that I'm in charge of every situation. Do you understand?"

I try to free myself and fail. His palm is warm, heavy, and scarred over my skin with the hard metal table beneath it a shocking contrast. My lungs stutter and hot air fills them. "Whatever game you're playing, stop it right now."

His hand easily covers mine and his fingers keep me trapped in sizzling heat. "I don't play games, Peaflower. Learn that now."

"Peaflower?" I choke out, leaving my hand beneath his because I have no choice.

"Your eyes," he murmurs. "The blue dissolves into violet like the Butterfly pea flower. A man could find solace from everlasting torment just staring into those velvety depths."

I have no words for him. Are there words? Scarred, barely uncuffed, and intense, he'd just whispered the most romantic words imaginable. And he's a killer. Just because the judge was corrupt doesn't mean Alexei hadn't committed cold-blooded murder. Two things can be true at once. "We need to keep this professional, if you want me to help you."

He releases me and stands. "Guard," he calls out.

My hand feels chilled and lonely.

Keys jangle on the other side of the door.

"Rosalie, this is your out. If you tear up the retainer, I'll find another lawyer. If you stay, if you continue to represent me, this is gonna become a lot more personal. Tell me you get me." Fire burns in his eyes now.

I stand, even though my knees are knocking together. "I'm doing my job."

"Just so we understand each other."

The door opens and the same guard from before moves inside, pauses, and visibly finds his balls before securing the cuffs on Alexei, who watches me the entire time. He allows the guard to lead him to the door.

Once there, he looks over his shoulder. "I hope you stick with me in this. Also, you might want to conduct a background check on Miles Molasses from your firm. He was a co-conspirator to the judge and prosecutor." His teeth flash. "How convenient that he had an accident. Right?"

Look for One Dark Kiss, *on sale soon.*

Visit our website at
KensingtonBooks.com
to sign up for our newsletters, read
more from your favorite authors, see
books by series, view reading group
guides, and more!

Become a Part of Our
Between the Chapters Book Club
Community and Join the Conversation

Submit your book review for a chance to win exclusive
Between the Chapters swag you can't get anywhere else!
https://www.kensingtonbooks.com/pages/review/